YOU'VE GOT MAIL
The PERILS
of
PIGEON
POST

4

❧YOU'VE GOT MAIL❧
The PERILS
of
PIGEN
POST

❀ 4 ❀

WRITTEN BY
Blackegg

COVER ILLUSTRATION BY
Leila

INTERIOR ILLUSTRATIONS BY
Ninemoon

TRANSLATED BY
alexsh

Seven Seas Entertainment

You've Got Mail: The Perils of Pigeon Post - Fei Ge Jiao You Xu Jin Shen (Novel) Vol. 4

Published originally under the title of 《飛鴿交友須謹慎》
Author©黑蛋白 (Blackegg)
Illustrations granted under license granted by I Yao Co. Ltd.
English edition rights under license granted by 愛呦文創有限公司 (I Yao Co. Ltd.)
English edition copyright © 2025 Seven Seas Entertainment, Inc.
Arranged through JS Agency Co., Ltd.
All rights reserved

Cover Illustrations by Leila
Interior illustrations by Ninemoon

Seven Seas press and purchase enquiries can be sent
to Marketing Manager Lauren Hill at press@gomanga.com.
Information regarding the distribution and purchase of digital editions is available
from Digital Operations Manager CK Russell at digital@gomanga.com.

Seven Seas and the Seven Seas logo are trademarks of
Seven Seas Entertainment. All rights reserved.

Follow Seven Seas Entertainment online at
sevenseasentertainment.com.

TRANSLATION: Tywon Wynne, Liting Xiao
ADAPTATION: Abigail Clark
COVER DESIGN: G. A. Slight
INTERIOR DESIGN: Clay Gardner
INTERIOR LAYOUT: Karis Page
COPY EDITOR: Ami Leh
PROOFREADER: Imogen Vale, Nino Cipri
EDITOR: Hardleigh Hewmann
PREPRESS TECHNICIAN: Salvador Chan Jr., April Malig, Jules Valera
MANAGING EDITOR: Alyssa Scavetta
EDITOR-IN-CHIEF: Julie Davis
PUBLISHER: Lianne Sentar
VICE PRESIDENT: Adam Arnold
PRESIDENT: Jason DeAngelis

ISBN: 979-8-89160-591-6
Printed in Canada
First Printing: September 2025
10 9 8 7 6 5 4 3 2 1

CONTENTS

5	A Story of a Perfume Sachet	9
6	In Times of Adversity, One's True Face is Revealed	35
7	If You Strike at a Goose Every Day, One Day It Will Bite Back	63
8	Together, Forever, Just the Two of Us	95
•	Wedding	127
•	The Origins of Yan Wenxin's Love– A Blessing or a Curse?	153
•	Raising a Child	209
•	AU: Stepfather and Stepson	243
•	Secret Room	281
•	May All Lovers Be Past Lovers	303
•	Absolute Lovers (Omegaverse)	393
•	Repaying Favors is Pledging Oneself in Marriage (Beastman AU)	447
•	Author Afterword	499
•	Character & Name Guide	507

CHAPTER FIVE

A STORY OF A PERFUME SACHET

"I don't believe it..." Bai Shaochang still remembered Yan Wenxin's kindness, the way they spoke and laughed together, as well as the day he had come swooping in to save him from Du Fei.

"H-he said that in this life, he would never let me down..."

Wu Xingzi paused for a moment, but in the end he still replied, "He has already let you down."

Bai Shaochang stared blankly at Wu Xingzi, at the look of sympathy on his face, and let out a bitter, self-deprecating laugh.

MEETING BAI SHAOCHANG again after a few months had passed, Wu Xingzi had the inexplicable feeling that there were truly many variables in life.

The place where Bai Shaochang was being confined was right within the Protector General's estate. The interrogation was conducted in secret, and the ministers presiding over Guan Shanjin's case weren't aware this interrogation had occurred at all. It was a trap Guan Shanjin and the emperor had worked together to lay for Yan Wenxin, attempting to see if they could garner any useful evidence from Bai Shaochang's lips.

As Guan Shanjin's right-hand man, this important responsibility naturally fell upon Man Yue's shoulders. He had done a fairly decent job; he had at least managed to force Bai Shaochang to admit that the evidence he planted was all fabricated.

Although Bai Shaochang was refined and elegant, he was unfortunately a very stubborn man. He turned pale from fright a number of times during the interrogation, but even when he was trembling in fear, he still refused to change his testimony. Man Yue truly had no more tricks up his sleeve.

And so he'd been left with no choice but to turn to Wu Xingzi. Unlike his boss, Guan Shanjin, Man Yue did not see the need to shelter and protect Mr. Wu. The way Man Yue saw it, if he'd survived twenty years working at the magistrate's office, Wu Xingzi had to possess an extraordinary temperament and finesse.

It would be foolish to see a path available and choose not to take it. Man Yue didn't want to waste too much time in case more difficulties cropped up later. If everything were to fail at the very last minute, what were they going to do? If Guan Shanjin didn't approve, Man Yue could always just run straight off to hide in Horse-Face City when he got out of jail.

The two of them entered the Protector General's estate through a secret passageway. The people Yan Wenxin had assigned to spy on Wu Xingzi didn't notice anything was wrong at all; they believed Wu Xingzi was quietly hiding at Rancui's place as usual.

Bai Shaochang was staying at Changyou Yard, on the west side of the Protector General's estate. After the incident occurred, he'd carried on living there. Although his movements were being watched and he was not allowed to leave the estate, everything else seemed to stay the same.

Yan Wenxin didn't seem to be in the least bit concerned that Bai Shaochang would let anything slip. Man Yue and Guan Shanjin's personal guards had secretly looked into all the people living in the compound a number of times, but they never found any of Yan Wenxin's spies. The secret guards reported the same thing.

Man Yue sneered in anger. How confident and careless of Yan Wenxin.

He understood that this meant Yan Wenxin was confident in his firm grip on Bai Shaochang, and that he had no fear of anything escalating beyond his expectations. However, it was also Yan Wenxin's arrogance that allowed Man Yue to dig out his weakest link.

"It's safe in the Protector General's estate. You can just hide outside the window and sneak a few looks inside. If you notice anything wrong, just go ahead and let me know." Man Yue led Wu Xingzi to a spot outside the bedroom where Bai Shaochang was confined. At this time of day, Young Master Bai was normally seated in front of the qin in a dazed sort of state. It had been many days since he played it.

"All right." Wu Xingzi nodded vigorously, wiping his sweaty palm on his leg. He touched a fingertip to his tongue and carefully tore a hole in the paper-covered window to peep inside.

Just as Man Yue had expected, Bai Shaochang was seated in front of the qin. He stared at his beloved qin in a stupor, his complexion ashen.

He was still as ethereal as before in his white robes; with his thin figure, he seemed even more delicate in his loose clothing. Looking at him, Wu Xingzi couldn't help wondering why he was never dressed in any color other than white. Did he have some sort of fixation on it?

Embroidery the color of moonlight adorned the edges of his sleeves, impossible to notice without paying close attention. His hairpin was made entirely of snow-white jade, and the thin belt around his waist was also as white as snow. Rather than saying that the young man looked as fair as jade, "terrifyingly pale" was probably a more apt description. What could be seen of Bai Shaochang's skin seemed to hold no color at all. When he pressed his lips tightly together, though, some color could finally be seen around his mouth.

Only his eyes and hair were a bright, shiny black—so black that it was enchanting.

Wu Xingzi liked to look at beautiful men. He was worried for Guan Shanjin, but nonetheless, he was still attracted to Bai Shaochang's ethereal, unworldly appearance.

"Mr. Wu?" Man Yue called out when Wu Xingzi didn't respond for a while.

"Ahh..." Wu Xingzi was jerked back to reality. Quickly, he turned to glance at Man Yue, shame and self-reproach appearing on his face. "I'm sorry, I-I..." He rubbed his nose and told himself to get a grip.

Again, Wu Xingzi peeped through the hole in the window. This time, he realized that Bai Shaochang seemed to be tightly holding something in his hand. It turned out he was not staring at his qin in a daze, but at the item in his hand instead. The expression on his face showed both sadness and joy.

Whatever it was, it was small, so Wu Xingzi couldn't see much. Bai Shaochang held it protectively in his hand, so from this distance he could only vaguely make out that the object was colorful, though not bright; it even looked a little old.

Wu Xingzi frowned, pondering over it for a moment. He then stepped away from the window, signaling for Man Yue to step back a little. "Man Yue, I have a presumptuous request," he said. "I must trouble you to get someone to make a trip."

Man Yue's spirits lifted a little. It seemed like there was hope! "Please don't hesitate, Mr. Wu. The only thing the Protector General's estate never lacks is manpower."

Wu Xingzi's instructions were meticulous. "Five miles north of Goose City is a little place called Tongkou Town. There's a merchant on the south side of town named Xia Dagen who sells sundries there. Please send someone to bring him and his wife here, as well as all the perfume sachets he has in stock. Just tell him that Adviser Wu of Qingcheng County would like to seek his help—he'll definitely come with you."

A hint of confusion appeared on Man Yue's face, but he did not probe further. With a wave of his hand, he summoned an attendant and gave him some instructions. The attendant cupped his hands toward Wu Xingzi in gratitude before sprinting away.

"Don't worry," said Man Yue. "He'll be back in a week or so, and I'm sure he'll bring the man with him."

But his guarantee didn't put Wu Xingzi at ease. When he thought about how many days Guan Shanjin still had to spend in jail, Wu Xingzi's heart felt troubled.

Noticing his anxiety, Man Yue brought him to his own room, where he poured a cup of tea and passed it to him. "Have something to drink and put yourself at ease."

Wu Xingzi made a sound of agreement. He started sipping at the tea distractedly, then heaved out a gusty sigh like he was trying to exhale both his lungs out of his mouth.

"Mr. Wu, may I ask a question?" said Man Yue.

"Ah, go ahead, go ahead." Wu Xingzi straightened up in his seat, blushing.

Since his boss was not in any sort of danger in prison at the moment, Man Yue had the time for a leisurely chat. "What sort of relationship do you have with this Xia Dagen?" he asked. The name, meaning "big root," really did make one wonder, especially if you were dealing with Mr. Wu, who liked to collect pictures of penises.

Wu Xingzi pressed his lips together in a smile, but he looked a little embarrassed. "He owes me a favor."

"A favor?" Man Yue was even more curious now. He leaned forward slightly, his eyes shining so brightly that Wu Xingzi unconsciously averted his gaze.

"Oh, it's only a small matter. It's nothing worth mentioning. Y-you could say I did something a little underhanded and helped him entrap another person."

Wu Xingzi couldn't keep from blushing as he talked about this. It wasn't because he felt that he did something bad back then, only that it was a little shameful to mention such scheming little tricks in front of Man Yue. Tricks like that only worked on uncultured villagers who knew nothing of the world. However, in the face of Man Yue's keen questioning—and having just been served a freshly steamed osmanthus cake to boot—Wu Xingzi's mouth was finally pried open.

Embarrassed, Wu Xingzi bit into a piece of the osmanthus cake before he recounted the story. It was only a small conflict among villagers.

About twenty years ago, despite being such a tiny place, Qingcheng County had met with some fortune. People were on the fence about whether it was a negative or a positive thing. A rich man from Sun City, one of the most prosperous cities in the south of Great Xia, had taken a fancy to a piece of land in the east of Qingcheng County near the water. He brought seven or eight feng shui experts with him along the entire span of the south of the country before finding this plot of land with truly superlative feng shui.

Wu Xingzi felt that most laymen like himself couldn't tell if a piece of land had good feng shui or not. But it was close to the river, and when the rains were a little heavy, the area would flood. Due to his innate kindness, Wu Xingzi tried to persuade the magistrate not to sell that piece of land to an outsider who didn't understand the conditions of the local environment. However, the magistrate himself was an outsider too, so he didn't know how serious the flooding could be either; he ended up selling the land anyway.

In the end, everyone was happy. The county received some money, while the rich man received a plot of land he thought was perfect for him. The rich man started construction at once on a landscape of buildings and pavilions so beautiful it might as well have been the immortal realm.

Perhaps the heavens pitied Qingcheng County for having endured so many years of hardship. In all the seven months of construction and the two years when the rich man lived there with his beautiful concubines, not a single flood occurred.

However, while he lived there, not only did the rich man fail to bring any benefits to Qingcheng County, he even stirred up quite a bit of trouble.

Most people in the county thought that the vegetables they grew were of decent quality considering the conditions and how far away the county was from everything else. The farmers were even able to get quite a good price for their crops in Goose City. The only issue was how little they could produce: It wasn't really enough to make any money.

Things were looking up for the farmers now. With a rich man moving here, there would be at least seven or eight people living in that household, and they all needed to eat, right? Perhaps they might even be able to raise the price of their produce!

However, these dreams were only that—dreams. The rich man had absolutely no intention of eating cheap local produce.

He transported cart after cart of goods from faraway places. There were cabbages that cost five silver taels each, beans that cost seven silver taels per handful, chickens with colorful plumage that cost five gold taels each, and many other ingredients that the villagers had never seen before. It was said that even their rice cost one gold tael for fifteen pounds. Every day, the rich man's household discarded the unused food in the river.

Although this river was not the main body of water that Qingcheng County residents used for their daily needs, there were still families who relied on it to survive. When they saw food waste and grease floating past them every day, they weren't sure how they could keep using the river's water. Their suffering was indescribable.

Even more infuriating was the behavior of the rich man's servants. Although they were mere servants, they acted as though they were above the villagers. On their occasional outings to the county market, they always stirred up all sorts of trouble. One day, they would destroy a stall in the east; the next, they would harass a girl who lived in the west; the day after that, they would push a granny who lived in the south, and her grandson would get so angry that he would fight them, only for them to beat him up instead. These servants threw the entire county into chaos.

The magistrate clamped his ears shut and pretended that none of this was happening. He had an ordinary education and an ordinary family, and had just reached twenty years of age. After getting assigned to such a remote, faraway place, all he wanted to do was quickly muddle through this six-year assignment and leave—being assigned literally anywhere other than Qingcheng County would be an improvement.

Xia Dagen, a merchant, came to Qingcheng County for a month every year to sell his goods. It just so happened that he came across the rich man strolling about with his nineteen concubines. His stall was destroyed, and the rich man beat him up.

Xia Dagen, however, had quite the backbone. Despite receiving injuries all over his body, he did not make a single sound. This made the rich man angry—he felt his power and dominance had been threatened. This little merchant was belittling him. Rage rushed to his head, and he immediately decided to report this to the magistrate's office and stamp out this tiny little ant. Now *that* would be a way to show off his might!

"So he sought you out to write a report for him?" Man Yue asked, listening with so much pleasure that he'd forgotten about his osmanthus cake.

Wu Xingzi nodded. "The rich man looked for me in particular," he said in a soft voice, "because there were not many in Qingcheng County who could read or write. In fact, the rich man himself didn't know how to read or write. Later on I learned that he hadn't come to Qingcheng County because of the feng shui, but because he was no longer welcome in Sun City. He had only become wealthy recently, and he was crude and uncultured. Soon after he became rich, he lost his sensibilities. He terrorized others, and many people took legal action against him. His wife, however, was a very impressive woman who helped him brush off all his problems. In the end, she chased her husband away and became the proper head of the household. So this was actually not his first time coming to the local authorities."

Man Yue clapped his hands, laughing. "What an interesting fellow! So, how did you deal with him?"

Wu Xingzi scratched his nose, embarrassed over being asked about his past, and bowed his head. "I told him that I had many duties to attend to, and I was afraid that I wouldn't be able to take on the matter right away. If the tasks that the magistrate had assigned were not completed, everyone would be punished. He felt stifled with anger about the situation, and he wanted to quickly deal with it. He insisted that I help him find a capable person to replace me. I tried to put him off a few times, telling him not many people in town knew how to write, but in the end, I told him Auntie Li's second son was apparently quite educated, and many of the neighbors could attest to that."

Auntie Li's second son? As Man Yue searched his memories, his eyes widened. He looked at Wu Xingzi in disbelief. Auntie Li was Qingcheng County's most gossipy woman, and she often aimed her vicious tongue at Wu Xingzi, daring to say all sorts of disgusting things about him. She had never gotten along with Auntie Liu; they were like oil and water. She had a son who had gone to school, and she always wanted him to replace Wu Xingzi as the county adviser and bring honor to her family.

It turned out that the second Li son *did* know how to read, but he wasn't a good student. Even by the age of thirty, he still had not achieved the basic qualifications to become a child student, never mind becoming a scholar.

Wu Xingzi had laid a trap for the rich man!

Things played out as Wu Xingzi expected. The rich man was no fool, so he naturally went around asking about the second Li son's education. But you could count the number of people who could read and write in Qingcheng County on both hands. To the county's residents, the ability to read alone was already very impressive. Auntie Li was always both overtly and subtly insulting Wu Xingzi while praising her son, and so there were quite a number of people who thought the second Li son was well-educated and feared by Adviser Wu.

Delighted, the rich man took his money to the Li family and asked the second Li son to write a report for him.

As for Wu Xingzi, after he'd sent the rich man away, he turned and sought out Xia Dagen. He explained that he would write a report for him seeking legal action against the rich man, and that he would help him fight back and get the money to cover the cost of treating his injuries.

Although Xia Dagen was a little doubtful, Wu Xingzi looked too earnest for him to say no. Caught up in Wu Xingzi's enthusiasm, he ended up agreeing.

The next day, the rich man happily took the report the second Li son had written for him, dragging along with him his newly hired lawyer—who was also the second Li son—to the magistrate's office. He complained that Xia Dagen was cheating people out of their money by selling shoddy items, and that after he was exposed, he became violent with his customers. The rich man believed that the second Li son was second to none in Qingcheng County, and that even Adviser Wu was jealous of him. With the second Li son on his side and his own money and power, he'd be able to make things so difficult for Xia Dagen that he'd rather die than go on living!

Unexpectedly, though, when the magistrate read the report written by the second Li son, he hesitated, instinctively glancing at Wu Xingzi. As county adviser, Wu Xingzi immediately leaned over and exchanged some words with the magistrate.

Then, the rich man and the second Li son were both promptly given ten smacks on their buttocks. They wailed and cried like pigs being slaughtered until their mouths were stuffed shut by the magistrate and they were promptly chased out of his office.

"The laws of Great Xia state that official documents, reports, progress records, and other court papers must meet certain specifications.

No mistakes are allowed. If there are any errors, a light punishment is ten strikes of the rod, and a harsh punishment is the imprisonment of all three generations of their family." Wu Xingzi picked up another piece of the osmanthus cake, nibbling away at it with his two front teeth. Feeling utterly embarrassed, he mumbled, "I went a little bit overboard."

As for what happened between the rich man and the second Li son afterward, Wu Xingzi did not concern himself with it. He handed his report to Xia Dagen and introduced him to a very capable retired lawyer in Goose City. They won their case against the rich man and received dozens of taels in compensation.

Wu Xingzi then found a way to ensure the news would reach the rich man's wife. Soon, the rich man packed up and left Qingcheng County; no one knew exactly how his wife ended up dealing with him.

Xia Dagen was naturally very thankful to Wu Xingzi for both the sudden windfall and the opportunity to vent his grievance. He patted his chest and declared he would be willing to do anything for him. If Wu Xingzi requested anything from him, he would never refuse it.

Smiling, Wu Xingzi accepted Xia Dagen's gracious offer, but he never thought once of getting anything out of him. He believed that as the adviser of Qingcheng County, it was his duty to settle any of the citizens' troubles. After all, he'd spent many days relying on their kindness. Xia Dagen was very grateful, but Wu Xingzi was just using the opportunity he'd provided, so he felt there was no need for the merchant to be so grateful to him.

He never expected that twenty years later, he'd be cashing in on this favor that was owed to him.

Man Yue reassured him by saying that since Xia Dagen could not have forgotten his kindness from twenty years ago, this was something of an opportunity for the man to pay back the favor he owed.

They finished the tea and the story—as well as the plate of osmanthus cakes.

Man Yue then stealthily sent Wu Xingzi back to Rancui's residence, telling him that when Xia Dagen arrived, they would return to the Protector General's estate and settle the issue of this troublesome Bai Shaochang.

The people of the Protector General's estate dared not be lax about anything concerning the safety of their master. They expected that Xia Dagen would need at least four or five days to reach the capital. Who would have thought that early in the morning on the fourth day, before Wu Xingzi had even woken up, Man Yue would come knocking on his door?

Hearing the rapping at his door, Wu Xingzi startled awake and nearly rolled off the bed. In a daze, he stared at Man Yue's gleaming teeth and bright eyes—those were the only things visible in the dark.

"Mr. Wu, Xia Dagen has arrived. Shall I take you to the Protector General's estate?"

"He's here already?" Wu Xingzi rubbed his eyes. The burden weighing on him finally settled, and he hurriedly grabbed and put the robe next to his bed on over his pajamas. Without stopping to wash his face, he urged Man Yue, "Quick, quick, bring me there. Who knows how much hardship Haiwang has been through the past few days? We need to hurry up and get him out of there."

Man Yue agreed completely. However, it wasn't because he was worried about Guan Shanjin experiencing hardship, but because he didn't want to carry on watching Yan Wenxin living in such carefree confidence.

Leaving a note asking the two serving girls not to worry, Wu Xingzi followed Man Yue and crept out of Rancui's residence.

Whenever Xia Dagen and his wife went to Qingcheng County to sell their goods, they always dropped by to visit Wu Xingzi. They knew Wu Xingzi quite well, so they knew all about him being whisked away by the godlike Guan Shanjin. Xia Dagen wasn't the gossipy sort, and he had no interest in the rumors Auntie Li was spreading; he thought that Wu Xingzi was a very good person, and it was heaven's blessing for him to have such good fortune.

Two days ago, in the middle of the night, there came a fierce pounding on Xia Dagen's door, so loud that even his neighbors woke up at the commotion. When he opened the door, he learned that Wu Xingzi needed his help.

There was no reason for him to refuse. If Wu Xingzi had never helped him that year, he would not be enjoying his current life, with a wife, children, and a warm bed. Straight away, he packed up all the perfume sachets he had on hand, woke his wife, and handed their children over to his mother. Then, they left with the people who'd knocked on their door.

The journey was rushed; there was no time to properly eat or sleep. In the blink of an eye, they arrived at the capital, and Xia Dagen and his wife were brought to a luxurious manor the likes of which they'd neither seen nor dreamed of. When they saw Wu Xingzi, they finally exhaled in relief.

After exchanging some pleasantries, Wu Xingzi thanked them profusely as he took the perfume sachets. Xia Dagen didn't know how to react to his gratitude. He didn't feel worthy of such appreciation from Wu Xingzi, as he was merely returning the adviser's previous kindness.

No matter what Xia Dagen thought, though, to Wu Xingzi this favor was much greater in importance than the past kindness Xia Dagen was repaying. He asked Man Yue to help the couple settle down, as they were surely exhausted from hurrying here. Once they were well-rested and well-fed, they could stay a few more days in the capital if they wished.

Man Yue instructed the steward of the Protector General's estate to handle the matter, then turned and brought Wu Xingzi to Changyou Yard.

"Mr. Wu, do you really want to confront Bai Shaochang directly?" Man Yue was a little worried. He wasn't afraid that Wu Xingzi would make a mistake; rather, he wasn't sure how quickly he would need to flee the capital to escape Guan Shanjin's wrath.

Wu Xingzi nodded. "Yes. If you're worried, you can watch from the side." He had interrogated quite a number of criminals before. Although Qingcheng County was a small place and no major crimes had ever been committed there, there were still occasional conflicts that needed to be tried.

Man Yue considered it. He didn't have many qualms about Wu Xingzi, but he was curious about how this gentle and kindly old advisor would interrogate Bai Shaochang—who was wholly devoted to Yan Wenxin—into defecting.

"If you don't mind, Mr. Wu, I'll watch from the sidelines."

"Ah, what's there to mind?" Wu Xingzi smiled. As Man Yue prepared to push open the doors to Bai Shaochang's room, Wu Xingzi clenched his fists and took a deep breath. Managing to calm his rapidly beating heart a little, he gave Man Yue a firm nod.

Man Yue had already sent people to wake Bai Shaochang up. Perhaps he had not gotten a good night's rest for a few days now—he looked even more haggard than before. Dark circles

sat under his soft, gentle eyes, which looked quite stark on his ashen face. When he heard people come in, he did not panic. He simply looked up quietly and glanced at Man Yue and Wu Xingzi, seeming a little puzzled. It was evident he didn't remember that he had met Wu Xingzi before. After a quick glance, he lowered his head again.

When Wu Xingzi saw that Bai Shaochang didn't remember him, he felt very relieved. Pulling out a chair, he sat down across from Bai Shaochang. Man Yue remained standing at a distance, his arms folded as he gave Bai Shaochang a mocking, disgusted glare. Seeming to sense the vice general's unconcealed loathing, Bai Shaochang hunched his shoulders slightly and creased his brow.

The unyielding yet fragile image Bai Shaochang presented could really make one's heart ache. Although Wu Xingzi liked beautiful men, his heart ached even more for his Haiwang, so Bai Shaochang's wretched state didn't sway him.

Wu Xingzi was an amicable person with a placid temperament, and was never in a rush. He was in no hurry to speak with Bai Shaochang; instead, he poured out two cups of tea, handing one to Bai Shaochang before picking up the other and sipping from it.

By now, Bai Shaochang was used to being interrogated. Even though the stranger in front of him looked sincere and did not give off even the slightest air of authority, Bai Shaochang still remained on guard. However, he'd been waiting for a while now, and the middle-aged man in front of him was preoccupied with drinking tea and eating snacks at the table. He held a piece of walnut pastry like a mouse, nibbling away at it with his front teeth. He looked so cautious and humble that Bai Shaochang quickly let down his guard—he even felt a bit of scorn toward this man.

"Ah, I'm sorry. It's so early, and I haven't eaten breakfast. I'm no good at enduring hunger, so..." A look from Bai Shaochang made Wu Xingzi blush brightly. "Are you hungry? Do you want something to eat?"

"There's no need." Bai Shaochang shook his head. His brows knitted sternly as he watched Wu Xingzi endlessly eat. "Who are you? Are you here to interrogate me?" The Protector General's estate must be at the end of their rope if they were sending someone like this to interrogate him. Bai Shaochang exhaled in relief, but at the same time, he felt belittled.

"Interrogate?" Wu Xingzi hurriedly brushed away a few crumbs of walnut pastry from his mouth. He first shook his head, then nodded forcefully. "I'm Wu Xingzi, and I was fortunate enough to listen to you play the qin before."

"Oh." Bai Shaochang's expression did not change. He lowered his eyes in indifference, staring at his empty palms. He was not curious about where Wu Xingzi had heard him, as he often played in teahouses and restaurants. Even servants and small-time tradesmen had heard him play.

"You are very skilled at the qin, Bai-gongzi, and your music lingers even after the song ends. After hearing it once, I never forgot it." Wu Xingzi looked at Bai Shaochang with wide, earnest eyes. Not a trace of deceit could be detected in his admiring gaze.

Bai Shaochang couldn't resist smiling a little. After all, who could remain aloof in front of a person who admired their talents? "You flatter me," he said. "I'm still lacking in some areas, but many thanks for your recognition."

"I'm only a commoner. I can't speak eloquently, nor am I as clever as Bai-gongzi. Please, Bai-gongzi, I hope you're not offended." Wu Xingzi finally finished the plate of walnut pastries. A little nervous, he dusted the crumbs off his hands, then drank a mouthful of tea to wet his throat.

Bai Shaochang gave a self-deprecating smile. "To be able to meet me here, one can't exactly be considered a commoner." This was the Protector General's estate, after all!

This response put Wu Xingzi ill at ease. He scratched his cheek in embarrassment and lowered his head. Both the back of his neck and the tips of his ears went red; he had noticed the discrepancies in his words as well.

"Wu-gongzi, an honest man doesn't beat around the bush," said Bai Shaochang. "I know that it will be very difficult for me to leave the Protector General's estate, but I still hope this will be quick for me. If there's something you'd like to say, say it." Bai Shaochang sat very straight, his back as tall and upright as a stalk of proud bamboo. He could not say he was not a little frightened, but he was willing to give his all for the person in his heart.

Wu Xingzi looked at the young man in front of him, sighing internally. Outwardly, however, he still looked a little discomfited. He opened his mouth, seeming as though he wanted to say something, but he quickly closed it again. Finally, he clenched his jaw and took out a small item from inside his robe's lapel, shyly pushing it toward Bai Shaochang.

"Th-this perfume sachet... I-it's a little gift from me! I hope that Bai-gongzi won't look down on it!"

A perfume sachet? Man Yue, who was lazily leaning against the wall, finally opened his eyes and glanced at the small item on the table. It truly was a perfume sachet. This was getting interesting. Gifting a perfume sachet, something one wore close to their person, implied someone was declaring their affections toward the recipient. It was usually a token to pledge one's love. Was Wu Xingzi seeking a new lover right under his nose? Oh, his poor general—he had yet to leave jail and he was already about to be cuckolded!

Bai Shaochang was stunned as well. He'd never expected to hear something like this. A frown quickly appeared on his face. Just as he opened his mouth to sternly refuse, though, his eyes fell on the perfume sachet, and his voice was stuck in his throat.

The perfume sachet was not made of a high-quality material, and it looked rather old. It featured quite ordinary images of birds and flowers. There were loose threads here and there; rather than saying it looked plain, it might be more apt to call it rough-hewn. However, its shape was rather unique, as most sachets tended to be circles, squares, or shaped like gourds. This perfume sachet was instead shaped like a plum blossom, round and plump, and it was pleasing to the eye.

"This perfume sachet..." Bai Shaochang's voice was hoarse. His fingers trembled, wanting to touch the item on the table. However, he jerked his hand back as though he had been burned. His eyes, flaming with rage, fixated on that sachet.

"This perfume sachet?" There was no sign of the timid attitude Wu Xingzi had displayed before. Instead, he repeated Bai Shaochang's words in a placid manner.

"Wh-why do you have this perfume sachet?" Panicking, Bai Shaochang reached into his sleeve. He found the familiar item within, but he still trembled, his teeth chattering. His complexion went from red to a deathly pale, and he looked like he might faint.

"This was something I bought from a traveling merchant," Wu Xingzi said.

Wu Xingzi looked at Bai Shaochang with sympathy in his eyes, but he said what needed to be said. "Bai-gongzi, may I ask if you have the exact same perfume sachet on you?"

Bai Shaochang jerked violently, nearly falling right off his seat. Faltering, he took out the object inside his sleeve, his fist tightly clenched around it. He stared at Wu Xingzi with bloodshot eyes. His mouth opened and closed, but not a single word came out.

"Did he tell you that his mother left it to him before she died? That the plum blossom represents the integrity of a scholar, and that the bird is the love of a mother? That even if his mother wasn't around, she would always be by his side?" Wu Xingzi sighed. "That this was the only keepsake his mother left behind...?"

Bai Shaochang shuddered and nearly fainted. Every word, every sentence—it was all so acutely familiar. The pleasant-sounding words stabbed at him like a thousand knives. His mind blanked out and his throat gurgled, blood dripping from the corner of his lips.

Wu Xingzi sat stunned for a moment before leaping up in shock. He hadn't expected such an intense reaction from Bai Shaochang. He was about to walk over to see how he was doing, but Man Yue was faster. A black shadow flashed past, and Man Yue appeared right next to Bai Shaochang. He took out a pill and shoved it past his lips, then poured a cup of tea into his mouth to help him swallow it down.

Although the medicine was administered in time and color returned to Bai Shaochang's ashen face quite quickly, Man Yue had been very rough with him. After recovering a little, Young Master Bai nearly lost his breath again from choking on the tea; he went through a long coughing fit before he finally settled down.

Wu Xingzi patted himself on the chest. He knew it would be difficult for Bai Shaochang to accept the information he'd shared with him, but he hadn't expected the young man to cough up blood. Wasn't he too weak? He should remind Man Yue later to take care of

him a little better, maybe by preparing something like a tonic soup so that Young Master Bai could improve the condition of his body.

As the old fellow lost himself in his thoughts, Bai Shaochang recovered. He gritted his teeth. The taste of blood still lingered in his mouth, along with the bitterness of the pill and the fragrance of the tea. It was truly a dissonance of flavors. For some reason, his emotions settled, and he started to question Wu Xingzi.

"How did you know what he said?"

There was no need to clarify who *he* was.

"Zaizong-xiong hails from the same hometown as me," sighed Wu Xingzi, his fingers unknowingly digging into his palms.

"The same hometown?" Bai Shaochang was astonished. He studied this ordinary middle-aged man in front of him with even more doubt. "It's been twenty years since he came to the capital, and he has never mentioned his hometown or any close friends."

Wu Xingzi smiled wryly. "If I were him, I wouldn't mention anything either." He sighed again, picking up his cup and gulping down a few mouthfuls of tea. Wu Xingzi seemed rather shaken, leaving Bai Shaochang feeling even more anxious and doubtful.

"You mean, the two of you were once..." *A couple?* Even though Bai Shaochang grew up sheltered, he was raised among aristocrats in the capital. He knew all about scandals, secrets, and schemes; he was quite a clever man, and he quickly caught on to what Wu Xingzi was implying.

Bai Shaochang didn't judge people by their appearances, but it had to be said that Yan Wenxin was very handsome, and most of the people close to him were very good-looking as well. He thought this would be the case back in Yan Wenxin's hometown too; Yan Wenxin could have his pick of the litter. Why would he pair up with someone with such an ordinary, easily forgotten face?

Wu Xingzi did not know how to react to the questioning look directed at him. He hung his head and scratched his cheek. His original bashfulness was back, and he'd completely lost the earlier sharpness that shook Bai Shaochang so badly that he vomited blood.

The next question was a lot more painful. "If you were truly a couple, why didn't he return to see you?" Bai Shaochang asked.

What he was really asking was if Wu Xingzi was only flattering himself about having a relationship with Yan Wenxin. Yan Wenxin probably hadn't done anything that could be considered intimate with him, and the two of them were at most only well-acquainted. However, it was clear that Wu Xingzi had fallen for Yan Wenxin; perhaps he'd continuously badgered him, refusing to listen to his advice to stop. As such, Yan Wenxin ended up not returning to his hometown after becoming the top scholar, all because he wanted to hide from a friend's misguided warmth. And somehow, the people from the Protector General's estate discovered this matter. They found Wu Xingzi to deliberately frame Yan Wenxin, and now they were trying to trick Bai Shaochang into spilling his secrets. The more he thought about it, the more he believed it was the truth, and he started to feel a sense of contempt.

With just one glance, Man Yue saw right through him. He burst into laughter.

Wu Xingzi also understood what Bai Shaochang was implying, but he looked back at him with a normal expression. "If we weren't a couple, how would I know about the perfume sachet and those words of affection?" he said gently. "My tongue is clumsy, and I'm not highly educated. How could my words compare to Lord Yan's talent and wit?"

Man Yue laughed again. Wu Xingzi was usually so bashful, cautious, and reserved. He always behaved like a helpless little quail in front of Guan Shanjin. Man Yue was surprised his tongue was so sharp!

Bai Shaochang was surprised as well. He had never met anyone like Wu Xingzi. He seemed so discomfited and cautious on the surface; his tone was agreeable, but as sharp as a knife, leaving Bai Shaochang speechless and unable to argue. Many expressions moved across the young man's face.

His convictions, he realized, had been unwittingly shaken. Even if Yan Wenxin truly held affection toward him, a number of hidden motives lay beneath. That affection clearly was not as intense as Bai Shaochang had believed.

"I don't believe that this perfume sachet is fake." Bai Shaochang tightened his grip on the perfume sachet in his hand, forcing himself to speak. He laid extra emphasis on *fake*—it was unclear if he was trying to convince Wu Xingzi and Man Yue, or trying to convince himself.

"You can study it more closely, or..." Wu Xingzi again nudged the perfume sachet toward him with the calmness of a professional mediator. "I have someone who can embroider one right in front of you, if that's all right with you."

Bai Shaochang jerked violently, only now realizing he had stepped into a trap of his own making. He could no longer avoid it. During Man Yue's interrogation a few days ago, he had still been able to stand his ground, and he never had a shred of doubt about Yan Wenxin. But he had no defense against Wu Xingzi's quiet, gentle approach.

"I don't believe it..." Bai Shaochang still remembered Yan Wenxin's kindness, the way they spoke and laughed together, as well as the day he had come swooping in to save him from Du Fei. All these memories were still fresh in his mind! "H-he said that in this life, he would never let me down..."

Wu Xingzi paused for a moment, but in the end he still replied, "He has already let you down."

Bai Shaochang stared blankly at Wu Xingzi, at the look of sympathy on his face, before letting out a bitter, self-deprecating laugh. He laughed and laughed, tears dripping down his face and splashing onto the table, into his cup, and onto the identical perfume sachet in his hand. There was nothing he could say.

Wu Xingzi finally looked at Man Yue. Man Yue gave him a nod of gratitude, aware that the obstacle Bai Shaochang posed had now been torn down. Love was a double-edged sword—it could make a person unafraid of anything, but it could equally crush one's soul. Bai Shaochang's resolve had all been because of his love toward Yan Wenxin. Now, his tears could be considered a memorial of that love.

Seeing Bai Shaochang crying pitifully, Wu Xingzi could not help but console him. "Bai-gongzi, think about Lord Bai, your father. Please don't shroud yourself in regret and hate for the rest of your life—it's not too late."

"How...how did he betray you?" Bai Shaochang's eyes and the tip of his nose were red from crying, but he had already wiped his tears away. He tried his best to maintain his usual elegance.

Wu Xingzi looked a little flustered in the face of this question. He looked down and fell into silence for a while. Just when Man Yue was about to help him answer, Wu Xingzi hoarsely spoke up.

"It was twenty years ago. He was a poor scholar, planning on going to the capital to take the imperial exams. However, he did not have enough money, so I gave him everything I had. I borrowed around a dozen silver taels for him on top of my own money."

When it came down to it, his grievances only came down to a few simple sentences. With a freedom he had never felt before, he looked up at the handsome young man in front of him.

"I don't blame him for his change of heart. At the end of the day, our feelings were mutual, and neither of us were forced into it. There is nothing wrong with wishing to reach new heights. However, Bai-gongzi, think about the citizens living at the southern borders. Yan Wenxin is not asking you for twenty-three silver taels this time, but the peace and lives of Great Xia's citizens. Will you be able to settle such a debt for him?"

With one blow, this question destroyed Bai Shaochang's infatuation, along with the satisfaction he felt over sacrificing himself for Yan Wenxin. It was as if the fog in his head had finally cleared. Now, fear sent chills running down his back.

That was right—Man Yue had mentioned it while he was interrogating him a few days ago. When it came to those letters Bai Shaochang claimed to have fabricated himself, original copies did exist. Most of them were integral to events that had already occurred. Living in the capital, and without any government position, how did he know about such confidential intelligence? Furthermore, even if he somehow really knew all those military secrets, how did he manage to falsify the stamp of the Nanman king so well that it was indistinguishable from the real one?

Before now, Bai Shaochang had been unwilling to think too much about it. The correspondence had been prepared for him by Yan Wenxin, and Bai Shaochang figured it was natural for Yan Wenxin to know these secrets—after all, he was Minister of Personnel and had a good relationship with the other court officials. As for the stamp, surely it was a forgery, and it was Man Yue who could not see the scheme for what it was.

Now that Bai Shaochang thought about it...if he insisted on his original testimony and refused to change it, then the only explanation would be that he, the oldest son of the Bai family, was inextricably linked to Nanman. But how could it be possible for a man with the kind of simple life he led to come in contact with the enemy like that? Ultimately, the blame still fell on Guan Shanjin—but now, it looked like Bai Shaochang had lied on Guan Shanjin's behalf in order to save him. In that case, he would never be able to absolve himself from involvement in this matter. Even if his father could help him out, it would be impossible for him to be with Yan Wenxin... But this must have been Yan Wenxin's plan from the very beginning.

And how had Yan Wenxin fabricated the correspondence Man Yue had talked about?

"Zaizong, he..." Bai Shaochang turned pale in fright at this speculation. He looked toward Man Yue in disbelief.

Man Yue's eyes curved into a broad, honest smile. "Bai-gongzi, I have always told you that Lord Yan's intentions are sinister."

Sinister? In a daze, Bai Shaochang looked at Man Yue, his lips quirking up into a bitter smile. He wasn't a fool, and he had always kept out of trouble. He'd never thought he would fall so low for love.

Bai Shaochang's usually straight back hunched over. His easy grace had completely vanished. "I-I'll tell you everything..."

Right until this very moment, his life had been smooth sailing. Even the harassment from the Defender Duke's son was usually quite mild, as he was normally very careful in trying to placate him. He feared how the emperor might react, and he did have some affection for the man. When the Defender Duke's son had suddenly acted so rudely to him on the streets last time, it had probably only been a moment of frustration and overwhelming emotion. Although Bai Shaochang had been shocked, he had never felt humiliated—only somewhat disgusted and irritated.

That was when Yan Wenxin had appeared before him, as charming and handsome as an immortal. He was too beautiful to put into words. Bai Shaochang willingly offered up his heart, despite knowing that he would never be able to officially stand at his side. Once the matter was exposed, he might even be subjected to curses and names, but he would take the hardship with a smile.

But it turned out that it was all a lie. He had loved and believed in the wrong man. What exactly did Yan Wenxin think of him?

CHAPTER SIX

IN TIMES OF ADVERSITY, ONE'S TRUE FACE IS REVEALED

"Why did you come, hmm?" Guan Shanjin looked down at the person in his arms.

"I missed you..." Wu Xingzi murmured, placing his hand on top of Guan Shanjin's and nuzzling into that hand with great affection. "How did you become so badly injured?"

"It's not that bad—they're only superficial injuries."

Wu Xingzi harrumphed, clearly not believing him. However, he was unwilling to waste the precious time they had arguing over this.

BAI SHAOCHANG looked very lost; it seemed he might faint at any moment. Still, with a trembling voice, he answered all of Man Yue's questions, and finally put his signature and thumbprint on a copy of his testimony.

Yan Wenxin truly lived up to his reputation as a sly old fox. After he started his love affair with Bai Shaochang, he casually mentioned the situation at the southern border. At the southern border, Guan Shanjin was a god of war respected by all. The citizens revered his decisiveness and ferocity on the battlefield. Despite a few terrifying rumors, they sincerely idolized and loved this general who protected the peace.

However, things were different in the capital. The capital was a long way from the northwestern border, and even further from the southern border. The young Guan Shanjin was talented, willful, and arrogant, and there would always be people trying to tear such a promising young man down. However, his reputation was strong, and there was no way for those people to defeat him. Every attempt they made was thrown back in their faces; they were the ones who ended up suffering instead.

On the surface, the officials in the capital all flattered and praised him. Underneath, they never let a chance to insult Guan Shanjin slip from their grasp.

Bai Shaochang had heard Guan Shanjin play the qin before. The rumor that he covered his ears and ran away in fear because of the violent undertones in the general's music was not false. Right from the start, Bai Shaochang had felt both fear and disgust toward Guan Shanjin, and it was easy for Yan Wenxin to convince him that Guan Shanjin had traitorous intentions toward Yan Wenxin and Great Xia. Bai Shaochang cared for Yan Wenxin; naturally, he was willing to follow the man's instructions.

Yan Wenxin told Bai Shaochang that he cared for him, too, and that he did not wish for his beloved to take such a risk. However, the more Yan Wenxin insisted, the more reluctant Bai Shaochang was for him to face Guan Shanjin alone. Determined, he convinced Yan Wenxin to let him help, then found an opportunity to get close to Guan Shanjin. He did everything according to Yan Wenxin's instructions.

He foolishly walked into the trap under his own initiative.

"Many thanks for your honesty and integrity, Bai-gongzi," Man Yue said. "You're welcome to remain as a guest at the Lord Protector's estate for a few more days. Once our young master is back, he will escort you home. If you do have any needs, please feel free to inform the staff. Don't feel too upset over people like Yan Wenxin—the general will surely seek justice for you."

As he took the written testimony, the smile on Man Yue's round face became a little more sincere. He turned around and started to lead Wu Xingzi away when he was called to a halt by Bai Shaochang.

"H-how are you all planning to deal with him?"

"Hmm..." Man Yue smiled apologetically. "Like a family has its rules, our nation has its laws. If it is confirmed that Lord Yan colluded with Nanman and endangered our Great Xia, the emperor will make the final decision. I ask that you not worry too much over it, Bai-gongzi."

Man Yue looked gentle, but his words warned Bai Shaochang to not even think about pleading for mercy for Yan Wenxin—it was pointless.

It was true that people were innately selfish; if this had been a simple fight for power in the courts, Yan Wenxin's actions couldn't exactly be deemed unforgivable. However, to offer up the lives of Great Xia's citizens for his own benefit? Even a saint couldn't make any allowance for that!

Bai Shaochang shuddered, his face paling a little more. His lips moved, but in the end, he said nothing more, only bowed his head in hopelessness.

After instructing the servant standing guard outside the door to take good care of Bai Shaochang, Man Yue led Wu Xingzi away. Once they were in the parlor, he bowed deeply toward Wu Xingzi. "Mr. Wu, the Lord Protector's estate and the Guan family's army owe you a great debt. In the future, if there's anything that we can do for you, please let us know."

Wu Xingzi was shocked, and he hurried to move away from the bowing Man Yue. "No, no, there's no need for that. I did this for Haiwang." Panic turned his face red, and his palms dripped with sweat.

"I am certain the general will be grateful as well." This time, Man Yue truly was relieved. He hadn't expected that Wu Xingzi would be able to go so far, using his own painful past to help Guan Shanjin. He really was someone who could be ruthless as well.

Wu Xingzi again shook his head. He looked at Man Yue, wanting to speak but faltering. But Man Yue could see his unspoken request, and he wasn't at all surprised.

"Is Mr. Wu hoping to visit the general in jail?"

"Ah, I was just wondering how Haiwang is doing, and I keep worrying about him... However, Yan Wenxin will undoubtedly have eyes on the jail. I'd only be making things difficult for you." Wu Xingzi truly missed Guan Shanjin with all his heart. Because he feared Guan Shanjin was suffering in prison, he hadn't been able to enjoy his food at all in recent days.

Man Yue considered it for a moment, then made his decision. "It shouldn't be impossible for you to see him just once. In any case, you're already in the Protector General's estate, and Yan Wenxin hasn't found out yet. Why not take advantage of this opportunity and take you there? That piece of shit won't ever guess you'd be so daring!"

"We can do that?" Wu Xingzi's face shone, and he bowed to Man Yue right there and then. "Ah, I'm so very grateful to you, Vice General Man!"

Man Yue avoided Wu Xingzi's bow. He held Wu Xingzi's arm and took a large stride forward. "In an hour's time, there will be a change of guards at the jail," Man Yue said, stroking his chin. "It'll be our men, so why don't we take advantage of that timing and sneak inside? It's just that your face... Well, it's better if we disguise it a little."

He did not say much more. Man Yue opened the door to summon a secret guard. The two conversed for a moment, and the guard gave Wu Xingzi an ingratiating smile.

It was dark and damp in the prison, but it was still clean enough, and there were not many prisoners in custody, so they were all locked up a distance away from each other. Gusts of eerie wind blew from places unknown, accompanied by occasional wails and moans. Dim oil lamps dotted the long and winding corridor, flickering in the dark; it was enough to send chills down anyone's spine.

The guards had just changed shifts, and it was a little noisier than usual, so the head jailer went out to ask a few questions. Not too long later, he returned with two people, one fat and one thin, and an impatient look on his face.

The fat one was Man Yue of the Lord Protector's estate; the head jailer knew him.

As for the thin one, he looked like a lackey. He had a face no one would want to look twice at, and his cheek sported an ugly, black birthmark. His head was lowered subserviently.

"Vice General Man, I'm paid by the government. This time, I've helped you out, so I hope you can take care of me." With a superficial smile, the head jailer cupped his hands toward the plump vice general.

Man Yue hurriedly returned the gesture, offering up a basket of wine and food. "Many thanks, Sir Wang! I promise not to make things difficult for you!"

Now that he'd gained something from this exchange, the head jailer's expression softened. He jerked his chin up. "There, you can go ahead by yourself. You'll have to leave in an hour's time, understood?"

"Of course, of course. Thank you, Sir Wang." After giving his thanks again, Man Yue led the thin, ugly lackey further into the jail.

Guan Shanjin was locked up in the deepest part of the jail. Due to his prowess in martial arts—and his insolence—he was chained to the wall by his neck. The chain was not long, just enough for him to walk to the gate and speak to a person standing there. However, it was impossible for him to reach out between the bars to try anything.

"Haiwang!" Wu Xingzi, disguised as a servant, could not help lunging over the moment he saw Guan Shanjin. He tried his best to reach through the bars and touch his beloved, whom he had not seen in a long time.

"Wu Xingzi!" Guan Shanjin was astonished. Although Wu Xingzi's face was disguised to look ugly and strange, he still recognized him at a single glance.

With no care for the piercing screech of the chain tightening around his neck or the choking pain it caused, he appeared by the gate in a flash, tightly grasping Wu Xingzi's outstretched hands.

Guan Shanjin's imprisonment was a ploy to deceive Yan Wenxin and his cronies, but the show had to be convincing. After he was thrown into jail, Guan Shanjin had suffered a number of hardships. Every few days, he would be dragged out and interrogated; if the emperor hadn't hinted that his life was to be spared and he was not to be excessively tortured, Wu Xingzi might not have seen Guan Shanjin as whole and complete as he was now.

The cell was dimly lit, and the stains on Guan Shanjin's prison uniform looked ghastly. Blood stained his clothes in dark splashes, and there were even a few places where his clothes stuck to his wounds.

Wu Xingzi clenched his jaw, not daring to cry aloud. He'd long suspected that Guan Shanjin had made light of the risk he would be taking. If it was not as dangerous as he said it was, why did he have to come in himself to suffer this torture? The emperor really was too harsh toward the Protector General's son.

After a moment of excitement, Guan Shanjin frowned. He directed a fierce glare at Man Yue, who was doing his best to try to shrink behind Wu Xingzi. "Why are you here?"

Man Yue decided to pretend that he hadn't noticed how ready Guan Shanjin looked to flay him alive. "Mr. Wu," he said quietly, "would you like me to let you into the cell so that you can talk to the general?"

Wu Xingzi was still holding onto Guan Shanjin's hands, unwilling to let go. When he heard this good news, his face brightened. "Can we do that?"

"Stop fooling around. What sort of place is this? It's so dirty in this cell—why do you want to come in?" Guan Shanjin rebuked him harshly, trying to pull his hands back, but Wu Xingzi grasped them even more tightly, as if pleading with him to reconsider.

Afraid of hurting Wu Xingzi, Guan Shanjin was forced to stop what he was doing. He glared at Man Yue darkly.

"General, don't worry," Man Yue said. "You're Great Xia's number one criminal, and there are no other prisoners nearby. The ones standing guard right now are our own men, so there's nothing holding you back from having a short heart-to-heart with the missus here." Man Yue really hoped that Wu Xingzi would be able to calm his boss down so that he would have time to run away once Guan Shanjin got out of jail.

At Man Yue's guarantee of safety, Wu Xingzi could no longer endure the wait. He squeezed Guan Shanjin's hands again and immediately shifted away to make space in front of the door for Man Yue.

Man Yue quickly and deftly picked the lock with his plump fingers. He left the lock completely undamaged, so when it was put it back later there would be no trace of it having been picked at all.

"General, I'll be waiting just around that corner," he said. "Whatever you plan on doing with him, I won't be able to hear."

Man Yue shot a shameless smile at the chained-up Guan Shanjin, who was helpless to do anything but glare daggers at him. In a flash, Man Yue's plump body disappeared from view.

Wu Xingzi turned to look at the corner Man Yue had mentioned. Noticing that it was about six cells away, he no longer felt as bashful. He hurried into the cell. He looked at Guan Shanjin for quite a while before he asked him falteringly, "C-can I hug you?"

He wished for nothing but to throw himself into Guan Shanjin's broad and warm embrace, but the blood on that prison garb made him afraid to do anything rash. Wu Xingzi's heart ached so much that both his eyes and his nose reddened.

Guan Shanjin looked back at Wu Xingzi for a moment before finally sighing and opening his arms. "Come here."

Wu Xingzi immediately moved forward, carefully tucking himself into Guan Shanjin's embrace. When he felt a pair of solid arms encircling him tightly, he released a breath of relief and satisfaction.

As Wu Xingzi breathed, he noticed Guan Shanjin's usual delicate fragrance was so faint that it could barely be detected. In its place was the scent of fresh blood and sweat mixed with dirt and a trace of something burnt. It was nothing pleasant to smell, but Wu Xingzi took in a few deep breaths nonetheless. His heart still hurt, but his anxiety lessened significantly.

The cell was not that dirty, and the dried straw on the ground that served as a mattress could be considered clean. As they embraced, the two men lay against the pile of straw so as to prevent the chain around Guan Shanjin's neck from making him too uncomfortable.

"Why did you come, hmm?" Guan Shanjin looked down at the person in his arms. The old fellow's face was disguised to look very ugly. He poked at the marks with his fingers, and when he discovered that it was a mask, he simply removed it, caressing the face underneath with an aching heart.

"I missed you..." Wu Xingzi murmured, placing his hand on top of Guan Shanjin's and nuzzling into that hand with great affection. "How did you become so badly injured?"

Through the thin prison garments, Wu Xingzi could vaguely feel the crisscross pattern of whip marks. Worried that leaning against Guan Shanjin would hurt him, he tried to shift away a little. However, the arms around him only tightened further, as if afraid he would disappear in the blink of an eye.

"It's not that bad—they're only superficial injuries." Guan Shanjin kissed Wu Xingzi's fleshy nose in consolation. This was not bravado. Although he did have quite a number of welts from the whip on his chest and back, compared to the injuries he had suffered on the battlefield in the past, these wounds felt barely any worse than scratching an itch.

"The ones who enforced the punishment were all the emperor's men. There was a lot of superficial bleeding, and the wounds look savage, but the whips did not injure my muscles or tendons at all. Once medication is applied, there'll barely be any scars left."

Wu Xingzi harrumphed—he clearly didn't believe him. However, he was unwilling to waste the precious time they had arguing over this.

Guan Shanjin looked at the old quail in his arms. Wu Xingzi's red-rimmed eyes brimmed with tears, and the tip of his nose was still flushed. The general's heart almost completely melted into a puddle.

"Did that asshole Man Yue seek your help?" He pinched the tip of Wu Xingzi's nose, then tugged lightly at his short eyelashes, suppressing the heat that he felt rising at a very inopportune moment.

"Ah, Man Yue is just worried about you." Wu Xingzi allowed Guan Shanjin to carry on, his cheek resting on his shoulder. Quietly, he said, "Bai Shaochang confessed that he was acting on Yan Wenxin's instructions when he placed those items and letters in your study."

Guan Shanjin's ear burned as he felt the air from Wu Xingzi's mouth brush over it; he nearly missed what Wu Xingzi told him. Once he understood, his sharp brow creased deeply.

"Man Yue let you meet Bai Shaochang?" His vice general was getting more and more emboldened, just because of their childhood friendship! Before he went into jail, worried about Wu Xingzi's safety, he'd deliberately left Man Yue with instructions not to let the old quail become involved. But just look at that little bastard, completely ignoring his orders!

Wu Xingzi felt Guan Shanjin tense up and knew that he was getting angry over Man Yue's actions. Hurriedly, he cupped Guan Shanjin's face, shyly leaning forward and soothing him with a kiss. "Don't be angry with Man Yue. I was the one who insisted he take me to see Bai Shaochang. You asked him to tell me to wait a little while more—but how could I just keep waiting? Prison is such a dangerous place, and Yan Wenxin wishes nothing more than for you to die in here." Wu Xingzi shuddered a few times, clearly recalling the fear and helplessness of a few days ago. "I've been so afraid that I haven't been able to eat or sleep well at all. I finally had a chance to help you, so how could I let it go?"

All of Guan Shanjin's rage dissipated. He no longer cared that this place was unsuitable; holding Wu Xingzi tightly, he kissed him. It was as though a flame blazed through them, and once their lips touched, neither could part from the other. They were as close as they could possibly be, their tongues entangled, each wanting to swallow up the other and keep him forever. Never again did they wish to part in this life.

Guan Shanjin's kisses were always passionate and intense. Nibbling and sucking on Wu Xingzi's tender tongue, he licked at the sweet flavor of his mouth and brushed the sensitive spots within. The kiss was so demanding, it felt like the general was reaching into Wu Xingzi's throat. The old fellow in his arms could barely catch his breath, yet Guan Shanjin still refused to let go.

The sounds of lips smacking gradually echoed down the long and dim corridor to where Man Yue was hiding. He blushed and quietly moved further away.

Guan Shanjin only reluctantly pulled away from the kiss when he saw Wu Xingzi was about to faint, allowing him a moment to gasp for air.

A pair of charming, wolflike eyes stared at Wu Xingzi's red, kiss-swollen lips. He'd barely caught his breath before Guan Shanjin kissed him again. This tender, intimate cycle repeated again and again until Guan Shanjin finally managed to just barely settle his longing. He buried his face in the crook of Wu Xingzi's neck and deeply inhaled his clean scent before sucking a mark on the skin behind his ear.

All they'd done was kiss, but it was enough to send shivers through Wu Xingzi's body. A flush spread across his entire face as he sagged in Guan Shanjin's arms, unable to move. A moment later, when he finally recovered, he felt something hard against his belly.

His blush intensified. Quietly, he reached out, wanting to caress it. But Guan Shanjin was faster, gently yet firmly blocking his hand.

"Y-you... Shall I help you with my hand?" Wu Xingzi tilted his head back, looking up at Guan Shanjin. A big, weighty, burning-hot pengornis pressed right against his belly. They were basically an old married couple—what was there to feel shy over anymore? He couldn't bear the thought of Guan Shanjin having to endure his desire alone.

"You're only concerned about me? What about your little pengornis, hmm?" With a twist of his arm, Guan Shanjin deftly captured both of Wu Xingzi's wrists with one hand. With his other hand, he slid into Wu Xingzi's trousers with great familiarity, rubbing the prick that had perked up when they kissed.

"Mmmm..." Unable to hold himself back, Wu Xingzi moaned sweetly at Guan Shanjin's touch, and his eyes became very unfocused. His red, swollen lips parted a little as he panted lightly.

Guan Shanjin's palm was hot and broad, and his years of martial arts training had left it covered in calluses. Just a couple of casual strokes had tingles shooting through Wu Xingzi from head to toe and his mind whiting out in pleasure. His hips jerked along with Guan Shanjin's hand, and the sight ignited Guan Shanjin's desire. His mouth went dry, and his movements gradually became more rough.

He rubbed his thumb right at the slit of Wu Xingzi's cock, spreading out the fluid that beaded at the tip; then, he tightened his grip, jerking the little thing that felt like iron encased in velvet. Sometimes, he lightly scraped right at the little slit, smearing his palm with the leaking precum before wiping it across the shaft and stroking wildly.

Wu Xingzi's soft, lewd moans echoed in the cramped jail cell along with the wet slide of skin and heavy, urgent pants, thrilling and sensual—how could this be a cold, freezing jail meant to hold criminals? It sounded much more like the warmth and life one could find at a brothel.

Wu Xingzi was not a man with a lot of stamina. It didn't take long for Guan Shanjin's skilled hand to bring him close to his peak. Wu Xingzi's legs jerked and kicked in the dried straw as he twisted his hips; tears welled up in his eyes as he softly cried out his lover's name. "Haiwang... Haiwang..."

"Be good." Guan Shanjin withstood the burning desire below and bent his neck to press a kiss to Wu Xingzi's forehead. He kissed the tip of his nose before finally capturing the lips that called out his name. Slipping his tongue inside, he twirled and teased as he brought the old fellow to an intense orgasm with his hand; Wu Xingzi almost fainted dead away.

"You've been holding yourself back these days." The fluids collected on his palm quickly lost their warmth. Guan Shanjin released his grip around Wu Xingzi's wrists, caressing the older man's red nose with a finger as he teased, "Just look. See how thick it is, how much come there is. Why didn't you use Mr. D to soothe yourself, hmm?"

Wu Xingzi had yet to recover from his climax. At the mention of Mr. D, the dildo Guan Shanjin had gifted him, he became bashful.

Mr. D had originally been left behind in Horse-Face City. A while ago, after the two of them properly confessed their feelings for each other, Guan Shanjin had returned the item to Wu Xingzi. Inside the box was also a lewd, seductive poem meant to tease and taunt Wu Xingzi. It delighted and embarrassed him; he did not know what he should do with Mr. D. It was well made, and it looked so appealing! However, if he were to actually use it, it was highly likely that Guan Shanjin would become jealous of an inanimate object and need to settle this matter with Wu Xingzi.

Seeing the vague complaint in Wu Xingzi's eyes, Guan Shanjin chuckled brightly. He deliberately opened up his palm, showing Wu Xingzi the white, viscous fluid trapped there. Then, he stuck out his bright red tongue to lick up the cooling substance bit by bit as Wu Xingzi watched.

Guan Shanjin's appearance had always been seductive and captivating; now, thanks to his injuries, he seemed a little delicate. Under the sun, he looked like an ethereal being, but in the dim light of the prison cell, he looked like an incubus set to suck out everyone's souls. One glance at him was enough to make one entranced, obsessed, and willing to offer up their heart to him with both hands.

Wu Xingzi couldn't drag his eyes away. No matter how many beauties there were in the world, none could compare to the one in front of him.

Because of the extreme pleasure still coursing through him, Wu Xingzi's body trembled slightly. Still, he reached out, caressing Guan Shanjin's face.

"Haiwang... I really do care for you..."

"But of course." Guan Shanjin laughed. "My ancestors accumulated a wealth of good luck, giving me both a fantastic face and a prized pengornis just to your liking." His seductively red tongue licked up the rest of Wu Xingzi's cum from his palm, his actions seeming both deliberate and nonchalant at the same time.

Wu Xingzi's breath caught. He finally understood what *The Song of Everlasting Regret* meant by the words "From then on, the emperor never attended the morning court."[1] However, his Haiwang was even better than any imperial consort.

---

1   The Song of Everlasting Regret, or *Chang Hen Ge* (長恨歌), is a *Tang Dynasty poem about Emperor Xuanzong's romance with his concubine, Yang Guifei. This line describes the emperor declining to attend court because he is preoccupied with his beloved.*

"Do you want me to help you as well?" Wu Xingzi asked. He had been pleasured, but Guan Shanjin's cock still throbbed and twitched! It'd only gotten harder, poking rigidly at him, almost scalding the skin on his belly.

However, before Wu Xingzi could wrap his hand around it, Guan Shanjin stopped him again. If not for the intense desire in his eyes, Wu Xingzi would have thought he was completely unaffected.

Guan Shanjin shook his head. "You've been here for too long. Get Man Yue to take you back to Rancui's place as quickly as possible. Wu Xingzi...Xingzi, don't worry. Just wait for me. If Bai Shaochang has confessed, it won't take long for us to deal with Yan Wenxin. News will come from the southern border soon as well. Don't worry, or else my heart will ache."

"But..." Wu Xingzi glanced at Guan Shanjin's crotch. His trousers were almost bursting at the seams; the general's cock looked savage, even through the fabric.

"You dirty darling, always looking down there." Unable to help himself, Guan Shanjin pinched Wu Xingzi's nose. "Once I'm out of here, you'll be able to have your fill. Be good."

Wu Xingzi grudgingly accepted that he couldn't convince Guan Shanjin. Guan Shanjin hugged him, sharing a few more kisses, before finally letting him go and leading him to the cell door. After a couple of knocks on the door to get his attention, Man Yue's plump figure soon appeared.

"Mr. Wu, I'll let you out now." Man Yue darted his eyes toward his boss obediently, making no attempt to poke at the tiger. He deftly unlocked the door, letting Wu Xingzi out.

"Xingzi, wait to the side for a moment," said Guan Shanjin. "I have some things to say to Man Yue."

"All right." Wu Xingzi turned his head back, clasping Guan Shanjin's hands one last time before taking a few steps away to wait, reluctantly but dutifully.

"General." Man Yue could not resist glancing at Guan Shanjin's conspicuously bulging trousers. "Have you lost interest in your wife?" He'd been prepared to wait for around four hours—to his shock, Guan Shanjin took less than two! His boss could really hold himself back.

Guan Shanjin snorted. "Do you want me to skin you alive?"

He was only barely suppressing his desire, and he wished for nothing more than to strip Wu Xingzi naked and feast to his delight. However, this was prison, and although he had been wiping himself clean, there was still quite a stink that clung to him. How could he bear to lose his dignity and let Wu Xingzi suffer the stench? He had no other choice but to endure his desire. And Man Yue still had the audacity to tease him. How did the heavens grant him such courage?

Since Man Yue had already poked the tiger once, it wouldn't make much of a difference if he poked him twice. He was going to have to start running as soon as his boss was out of jail regardless, so he wasn't worried about adding to the score Guan Shanjin needed to settle with him once he was freed.

He shrugged, shooting Guan Shanjin a mischievous grin. "General, you're the son of the Lord Protector. Yan Wenxin isn't just planning to take you down, he wants to root out the entirety of the Lord Protector's estate. There's not much time left, and your safety is my top priority. Furthermore, Mr. Wu is not Lu Zezhi—he can bear quite a heavy burden on his shoulders. It would be quite a pity for you to clip his wings."

Guan Shanjin frowned, but he did not speak. He understood that no matter how unpleasant Man Yue's words were to his ears, he only spoke the truth. It was simply difficult to calm the anger in his heart; once he was out of this place, he needed to discipline Man Yue properly.

"Just get out of my sight," he said. "If you dare to make Wu Xingzi do anything like this again without my explicit permission, don't blame me for my viciousness."

Although the words were harsh, Man Yue was relieved. His smile became more earnest. "If I need his help in the future, I'll definitely not let you find out about it!"

He didn't dare stay any longer. He fled with Wu Xingzi in tow.

Yan Wenxin was feeling a persistent a sense of unease.

During the morning court session, he felt like the emperor kept staring at him suspiciously, but he didn't seem to have any questions about anything Yan Wenxin said. Just like usual, the emperor only asked after his well-being, then moved on to the next official. However, fifteen minutes later, the emperor glanced over at him again.

Yan Wenxin felt as though he could hear the puzzlement of the entire court. Some of the other officials couldn't stop sneaking looks at him; this happened so often that Yan Wenxin felt like he was sitting on pins and needles. On the surface, though, he still looked completely unbothered. He kept his face looking down at the ground, as if he hadn't noticed anything unusual.

He managed to ignore it until the end of the session. After answering a few inquiries from some members of his faction, Yan Wenxin prepared to return to his residence. He needed to deliberate over the emperor's attitude. Unexpectedly, though, someone called him to a halt.

"Lord Yan, His Majesty wishes to see you."

The man calling out to him was a close attendant of the emperor, a eunuch who'd attended to the previous emperor too. He had a grin on his old, wrinkled face. Yan Wenxin was good at reading people, but he had never been able to see through this old man.

"Eunuch Chun." Yan Wenxin cupped his hands toward him. He wanted to probe the old man, but when he thought about it, the emperor's actions this morning did mean something. If he were to probe too deeply, it would make him look guilty. He elected to quietly follow Eunuch Chun.

Yan Wenxin thought he'd be meeting the emperor in the royal study, but to his surprise, Eunuch Chun led him to the gardens.

It was autumn, and by now the lotuses in the pond had wilted and been cleaned up by the servants. Without them, the pond looked a little bleak. The curtains around the white jade pavilion in the center of the pond were pulled down halfway, allowing only a portion of the light to shine in. An indistinct bright yellow figure could be made out within, leaning lazily against the seat and sipping tea.

The emperor was no longer a young man. In another three months, it would be the Imperial Birthday, and he would turn fifty-five years old. His appearance, however, did not reflect his age. His long, thin eyes were always lazily half lidded, his nose was handsome, and his brows were sharp and defined. The only wrinkle that ever showed on his snow-white skin was the crinkling of his eyes when he smiled.

The emperor spotted Yan Wenxin from afar and lifted his arm to wave him over. Eunuch Chun immediately hastened his steps. As a scholarly man, Yan Wenxin had a bit of a hard time catching up with him, and after he finished bowing and showing his courtesies, he was panting a little.

"Beloved Minister, have a seat. Here's some tea." The emperor's long seat was covered with two soft cushions, and he half reclined on it in contentment without putting on any airs whatsoever.

Yan Wenxin was long used to how casual the emperor was in private. He sat upright on the stool beside him and voiced his gratitude. When Eunuch Chun handed him a cup of tea, he raised it and took a sip, heaping praise on the tea thereafter.

"If you like it, I shall ask Chun Si to prepare some leaves for you to take home with you," said the emperor, supporting his chin in one hand. He was smiling, but for some reason, Yan Wenxin felt an inexplicable clench in his heart, and the hair on the back of his neck stood on end.

"Many thanks to Your Majesty for the gift."

He wanted to stand up and show his thanks, but the emperor acted first, waving his formality away, and instructed Eunuch Chun to serve some snacks.

Yan Wenxin ate a piece of phoenix-eye cake, but he tasted nothing as he chewed. Contemplating what exactly the emperor might have in mind, he did not dare to relax for a second. He was sure he hadn't made any mistakes recently. He had schemed against Guan Shanjin about half a month ago, but he had covered his tracks flawlessly. As long as Bai Shaochang kept his mouth shut, the blame would never fall on him, no matter how things dragged on. And considering how deep Bai Shaochang's affections for him ran, Yan Wenxin was confident he would never betray him, even if his life were on the line.

It was difficult to determine the emperor's attitude, so Yan Wenxin held back for now.

And so they ate and drank, chatting about various romantic affairs that had become fairly infamous in the capital. Inadvertently, the topic turned to their own families. Having been an official for decades, Yan Wenxin naturally knew how to hold a delicate balance when he spoke of his personal affairs in front of the emperor, to express his loyalty but to protect himself at the same time.

When Yan Wenxin spoke about planning to let his foster son, Huaixiu, marry his youngest daughter, the emperor did not respond. He fell silent for a moment, frowning, and Yan Wenxin's heart jolted. Speculation began to surface in his mind.

"Does Your Majesty think that it's unsuitable?" he probed.

"Zaizong, you've helped shoulder my burdens for about twenty years now, haven't you?" The emperor signaled at Eunuch Chun to help him up. Looking at Yan Wenxin, he sighed. "I've always trusted you deeply, and you've helped me deal with quite a number of issues. I've always remembered them well. I am thoroughly aware of the sort of person you are."

"Your Majesty speaks too highly of me." Yan Wenxin drew his brows together and bowed his head. Overwhelmed with fear, he fell to his knees. "It is my duty to share Your Majesty's burdens, and I dare not have any other thoughts than that. Please, Your Majesty, you need not worry."

"Stand up, stand up. I know that you care about Great Xia, and I know you are loyal to me. I have no need to worry." The emperor waved a hand for Yan Wenxin to stand. Without waiting for Yan Wenxin to steady himself, he sighed again. "Now that I think about it, you know, I've been troubled by that son of the Guan family. I watched Haiwang grow up, and although he has always been a little arrogant, he's hardly a child who cannot tell right from wrong. It's even harder to imagine him colluding with Nanman. Ah, I've lost sleep over it recently."

"Your Majesty, the Lord Protector and his family have always been loyal ministers of the court. His heir has put his life on the line for Great Xia for over a dozen years; it is impossible for him to collude with Nanman and betray the country like this. Perhaps someone is framing him?" Yan Wenxin decided to make a tactical retreat. He was a clever man; he could tell that the emperor had gotten hold of evidence that could allow Guan Shanjin to be freed from jail.

The emperor seemed to have been waiting for this very sentence from Yan Wenxin. "Then, Zaizong, who do you think is framing Haiwang?" he asked. His tone had turned sharp; there was no trace of the casual, languid attitude from before.

"Ahh... In my opinion, the one who has the most enmity with the Protector General's estate is probably me." Although Yan Wenxin was on high alert on the inside, he let none of it show on his face. Right now, rather than proclaim his innocence, his strategy was not to protest too much.

"Ha ha ha, you are very honest, Zaizong!" The emperor clapped his hands, laughing. "You've only met the young general a few times—why are the two of you as incompatible as oil and water?"

Giving a couple of wry laughs himself, Yan Wenxin said nothing further.

The emperor soon stopped laughing. "Zaizong, you're a very sensible person," he said heavily. "Although you have a contentious relationship with the Protector General, I know you've never hindered or harmed him over the years. However, there are some people by your side who have other thoughts. It's hard to say if they might have done anything behind your back. That youngest daughter of yours is the apple of your eye—don't let her marry the wrong person."

"Your Majesty means..." The expression on Yan Wenxin's face became alarmed, then quickly changed to shame and anger. "I understand! I'll give you an answer tomorrow about this matter."

"It's good that you understand. You're my right-hand man, and Haiwang is Great Xia's blade. I do not wish for either of you to be harmed. Those unnecessary people around you... It's best that you get rid of them if you can. The responsibility for failing to watch your people closely of course falls on you, but I won't punish you for that—I'll only withhold half a year's salary. In the future, you must be cautious." The emperor's meaning was clear: He wanted to minimize this incident, as well as let it serve as a reminder to Yan Wenxin.

Outwardly, Yan Wenxin was bursting with gratitude. He vowed solemnly that once he was home, he would tie up his foster son, and send him to the Court of Judicial Review. The emperor seemed very satisfied with this promise. After some words of reassurance, he let Eunuch Chun lead Yan Wenxin out of the palace.

Once he'd left the palace, Yan Wenxin rushed home immediately. Just as he entered his residence, his youngest daughter lunged over and grabbed his hand.

"Father, something has happened!" she exclaimed. "Some imperial guards have captured Huaixiu-ge!"

"Imperial guards?" Yan Wenxin immediately knew that something was wrong; a deep frown appeared on his face. He patted his daughter's arm to soothe her. "Don't panic. Go back to your room and wait there. I'll deal with this."

"But Father, why would the imperial guards want to capture Huaixiu-ge?" Yan Caijun was extremely anxious. She tightened her grip on her father's hand like a drowning man clutching at a piece of straw.

She was close to Huaixiu, and she did have some feelings for this foster brother of hers. Seeing him dragged away by the fierce, savage-looking imperial guards frightened her out of her wits. Now that her father had returned, her heart could finally settle back down from her throat to where it was supposed to be.

"You don't need to worry about this. Go back to your room." Yan Wenxin was not in the mood to comfort his daughter right now. Freeing himself from the girl's grip, he had an attendant lead her away before hurrying to his study.

The doors to his study were wide open. Outside stood two imperial guards dressed in the dark attire of officials, swords hanging at their waists. Yan Wenxin indistinctly heard a voice speaking from inside; he couldn't determine if it was Huaixiu.

Seeing him walk over, the two imperial guards by the door both cupped their hands toward him. They then held their hands out toward the doors, gesturing for him to enter. The guards were expressionless, and Yan Wenxin could not glean anything from their faces. He hesitated for a moment, but the two men did not urge him on. In fact, they did not even look at him. Yan Wenxin sneered internally—they were already so sure of his guilt. Straightening his robes, he entered his study, looking as unbothered as usual.

There were a total of four people in the study. One of them held Yan Huaixiu down to the ground as he bled from a wound on his forehead. He appeared to be in quite the predicament, yet he still stubbornly glared at the other two men rummaging through the study.

"Lord Yan." When they saw Yan Wenxin enter, the three imperial guards cupped their hands at him.

"Dare I ask the vice commander what the meaning of this is?" Yan Wenxin suppressed his anger. In all the days since he had become an official, he'd never experienced such humiliation. Even though he understood that the imperial guards were only following the emperor's orders, he still felt as though he had received a series of slaps to the face; his cheeks burned in pain.

"This was the emperor's order," the vice commander of the imperial guards said. The vice commander of the imperial guards was an old friend of Yan Wenxin's, and the emperor deeply trusted him. The guard smiled, ripping apart the binding of a book to investigate it page by page.

Yan Wenxin choked. Gathering anger finally began to break through his unconcerned facade. "Did the emperor also order the vice commander to destroy every single one of my books?"

"Of course not." The eyes of the vice commander crinkled as he smiled. "It's just that everything has to be taken apart and investigated—even paper, so as to bear witness to Lord Yan's innocence. After all, your foster son was captured here—we're only afraid that you'll be implicated as well."

"I thought that the emperor wanted me to settle this matter myself." He glanced at Huaixiu's bowed head. Yan Wenxin had already made his decision.

It seemed that Guan Shanjin's men had already gotten their hands on evidence proving that Huaixiu was conspiring with Nanman. It was a good thing that Ping Yifan had long left the capital and had returned to the southern border—Yan Wenxin did not believe that Guan Shanjin would be able to capture Ping Yifan as well. Otherwise, why would the emperor have summoned him to tell him those things? There were countless ties between Ping Yifan and Huaixiu, and if he had been caught, there'd be no need for them to be destroying his study for evidence.

It looked likely that Huaixiu would need to be sacrificed for the cause. Although this would essentially be cutting off his right hand, it was his only choice; he had to grit his teeth and bear the blow.

Huaixiu had followed Yan Wenxin for so many years, and he was his close confidant. Naturally, the young man understood what the subtle changes in Yan Wenxin's expressions meant. When he caught sight of Yan Wenxin's dark eyes, his heart ached slightly, but Huaixiu's expression soon hardened again. He knew his foster father was planning on sacrificing him to survive.

Huaixiu no longer struggled. He understood that this was the last bit of use he could be to his foster father, so he could not make a single mistake.

Huaixiu was an orphan. His earliest memories were of roaming about the streets, homeless. Until he reached the age of five, an old beggar woman took care of him. Every day, he managed to receive a piece of a not quite spoiled bun to fill his tummy. All he'd wanted was to hurry and grow up so that he would be able to find things to eat himself—and have the chance to take care of his granny instead of the other way around.

But unfortunately, he did not have a chance to fulfill that wish.

When he was five, tensions were high at the borders of Great Xia. They faced countless losses both in the northwest as well as in the south. A silent, unsettling fear permeated even the capital, spreading through the streets.

That year, the Protector General's son stepped onto the battle-field, and the emperor took the lead in conserving food and clothes. As such, it was very difficult for the beggars in the capital to get any food. Although welfare organizations would regularly offer porridge, children like Huaixiu and his thin, weak granny couldn't fight for their share of the food.

At the start of winter, his beggar granny froze to death. All alone, Huaixiu huddled in a corner, his little body almost entirely concealed by snow.

It was then that Yan Wenxin walked past. He picked him up and brought him home. From then on, Huaixiu had a roof over his head, a soft and warm jacket, and tasty food to fill his tummy until it bulged out. He went from a little beggar boy on the brink of death to the foster son of Yan Wenxin.

Yan Wenxin was very good to him. Not only did he foster him, he even taught him how to read. Lady Yan was graceful and kind-hearted, and she never doubted her husband's actions, so she treated this foster child extra kindly. Even though she later gave birth to her own children, Lady Yan's warm, familial attitude toward Huaixiu never changed, and neither did her husband's. There had never once been conflict.

At that time, Huaixiu had thought that this happened because his old beggar granny specially brought him to pray to Buddha before winter. They had asked for Buddha to ensure his safety, and he believed that was why such a good thing had happened to him.

He held great respect and admiration for Yan Wenxin. The man was everything to him. No matter how dirty or awful the tasks were, Huaixiu was more than willing to do anything for his adoptive father. All he wished for was to become the man's shadow and his last defense. He wanted to guarantee everlasting peace and prosperity came to the Yan family. And now, it was time for him to sacrifice himself for that cause.

The imperial guards searched for a while, but they didn't manage to find anything suspicious in the study. After a few insincere apologies, they started to drag Huaixiu along with them.

"Wait a moment," said Yan Wenxin. "May I speak with Huaixiu?"

"Please, go ahead." The vice commander did not mind at all, generously letting his subordinates remove the ribbon of cloth wrapped around Huaixiu's mouth.

"Yifu..." Because his mouth had been obstructed for a long period of time, Huaixiu's voice sounded hoarse and unpleasant. However, it carried with it a heavy sense of filial piety and respect, as well as a sentiment that was hard to define.

"Huaixiu, I have treated you very well over the years, showing you even more care than I had toward my own biological children. You should be well aware of that." Yan Wenxin stooped down, tenderly brushing away the dirt on Huaixiu's face. There were tears in his eyes, as if he could not bear to see this happening. It was as though he could not understand why this child, on whom he had spent so much effort raising and teaching, had ended up taking this path of no return; he seemed genuinely heartbroken.

"I understand..." In a daze, Huaixiu stared at the tears in Yan Wenxin's eyes. He struggled a little, wanting to free his hands to wipe away the wetness in his foster father's eyes. Who was he to let his foster father feel such sorrow for him? "I've let you down, Yifu..."

"Ah, one should not continue walking down the wrong path. I hope that you can understand that." Yan Wenxin sighed in disappointment. As if he could no longer bear to look at Huaixiu, he stood up and turned around. "I'll visit you."

Huaixiu stared at Yan Wenxin, fixated upon the man's desolate back. He even seemed to wipe at his eyes. Huaixiu's heart ached terribly, and he became even more certain of his decision. No matter how cruel the interrogation or punishment he would face, Huaixiu would endure it all for his foster father. He would uphold the glory of the Yan family!

Not too long after, the news spread like wildfire in the capital: Huaixiu was hauled off to prison, while Guan Shanjin had been cleared of his crimes and thus released from jail.

CHAPTER SEVEN

ꟾF YOU STRIKE AT A GOOSE EVERY DAY, ONE DAY IT WILL BITE BACK

Yan Wenxin kept staring at Wu Xingzi. This honest man, who had once looked at him, utterly unable to conceal the love in his eyes, was standing in front of him once again. However, this time, his dark eyes were filled with emotions that Yan Wenxin could not understand.

"Zaizong-xiong," Wu Xingzi called out to him.

"Chang'an," Yan Wenxin responded, but the smile on his face had completely vanished. Instantly, he understood. Wu Xingzi had sent him stumbling all on his own.

NOT TOO LONG after Huaixiu was sent to jail, Yan Wenxin offered his resignation, stating that his virtue was lacking and that he wished to retire and return to his hometown. He did everything he was supposed to say and do, and he expressed a very remorseful attitude.

The officials of the court made their own moves. Some pleaded with the emperor to investigate whether Yan Wenxin was involved, while others urged the emperor to keep him. The court was filled with the scent of gunpowder, yet the emperor never said a word. He even rejected Yan Wenxin's resignation; he just put him on house arrest for a month.

As for Huaixiu's crime of treason, the evidence was irrefutable. After being cross-examined, he was sentenced to death by dismemberment. For now, he would remain in jail, waiting to be executed after the new year.

At home, Yan Caijun's face was awash with tears every day. She had no idea how Huaixiu had ended up conspiring with Nanman. How had he managed to conceal it from her father? She was even more bewildered that her father wasn't giving him any aid at all!

She wanted to visit Huaixiu in jail. However, prisoners awaiting execution were not allowed visitors. Even items sent in to them needed to be unpacked and examined. Seeing that the weather was getting colder, Yan Caijun worried that Huaixiu would be freezing. She brought two jackets to the prison, only for them to be torn apart and examined thoroughly in front of her. It made her so angry that she cried all the way home.

Yan Wenxin, meanwhile, was keeping quiet and biding his time. He made no use of any of his power or skills to claim his own innocence. As the court officials all made their own moves, he didn't interfere with that either, instead trying to feel out what the emperor was planning.

Everyone knew that betraying the country was a great crime; the execution of all nine generations of the traitor's family was not a harsh punishment for this crime. But the emperor was clearly biased in this instance. The emperor had no intention of executing other members of the Yan family, only Huaixiu, and the house arrest didn't hurt Yan Wenxin at all. The Protector General called for a strict investigation again and again, but the emperor only gave a few words of sympathy, glossing over the matter entirely. This made the Protector General so furious he called in sick from his duties, and he did not attend court for a week.

Guan Shanjin had suffered great hardship in jail. Some were saying it took him two entire weeks to recover. Now, he followed in his father's footsteps and called in sick too. It was evident that both father and son were extremely disappointed in the emperor.

Yan Wenxin leafed through the information his spies had brought him. He looked at the porcelain cups placed on the table and smelled the fragrance of tea wafting from them. The emperor had commanded Eunuch Chun to deliver the tea leaves to him along with a few light refreshments. These gifts were clearly meant to pacify him.

Yan Wenxin smiled. He had come out of this crisis completely unscathed. Yes, he'd lost Huaixiu and had no one to replace him, so he'd have no choice but to deal with Nanman by himself for the time being. But the road they'd built together was not obstructed in the least. He could still carry on his merry way.

Losing Huaixiu in exchange for the emperor's care and a path to Nanman... It wasn't exactly a loss.

Once Huaixiu was executed and the matter blew over, Yan Wenxin would be able to completely eradicate Guan Shanjin and his lackeys from the southern border and replace them with his own people. Although he had not yet succeeded in taking out the Protector General's estate, he'd still managed to deal a severe blow.

Now, Yan Wenxin was able to put away the tension he had been feeling over the past few days. He was finally willing to make time for his daughter, who was still crying her eyes out.

"Father!" Yan Caijun exclaimed. Her eyes, swollen to the size of walnuts, started tearing up again. She looked nothing like her cheerful and bright self.

Yan Wenxin consoled her gently. "Why have you cried yourself into such a state?" He was, after all, her father.

"Father, please visit Huaixiu-ge, all right?" she begged, her voice hoarse from crying. "The weather is getting colder, and I wanted to send him some warm clothing, but the prison guards stopped me!" She seemed even more pitiful than before, having cried so much that she suffered from a headache and blurred vision; her words were incoherent. Over and over again, she implored her father to visit Huaixiu.

"Nonsense!" Yan Wenxin said. He slapped the table forcefully, scaring Yan Caijun into trembling. "Huaixiu is a traitor to the country! If not for the benevolence of the emperor, our entire family would be in dire straits. Why are you still thinking about that traitorous, ungrateful wretch? Your father is still under house arrest—if someone were to find out that I went to visit Huaixiu, do you know how much danger our family would face?" He was rarely ever so stern toward his daughter. Her mouth opened, but she could not speak.

"Dear child, I know that you've been close to Huaixiu since you were young. I had plans to betroth you to Huaixiu once you were of age, so as to bring your relationship to fruition. Now, however, Huaixiu has brought great danger to the family. Even if you don't care about my career, if we take a single wrong step now, the ones facing execution next year will be our entire family!" Half in consolation and half in reproach, Yan Wenxin held his daughter's hand and patted it. "You're the daughter of the Yan family. Think things through."

Yan Caijun looked at her father in a daze. Inexplicably, she felt chills run down her spine. Still, her tears dried up. Scared out of her wits, she gave a few confused nods. She understood that there was no way she could save Huaixiu.

Days passed. Yan Wenxin's house arrest ended, and he returned to court. He enjoyed the emperor's trust just as he always had, and if it hadn't been for his spies telling him that the Protector General had taken a trip to the jail, he would have long forgotten about Huaixiu.

Why would the Protector General visit the prison? Yan Wenxin felt a trace of unease. After a moment of contemplation, he called his daughter over.

"It's the coldest days of the year now, and I've been worried about Huaixiu. Prepare two jackets and I'll...visit him."

Hearing this, Yan Caijun brightened. She knew that her father's power in the court had not been affected by Huaixiu's traitorous acts at all. The emperor had showered them with even more attention, and she had been wondering herself if she should try again to beg her father to visit Huaixiu. Now, things were happening just as she wished they would. Yan Caijun hurriedly packed up the two jackets she had prepared along with a box of food three tiers high, and handed it all to her father.

On Yan Wenxin's face was a look of surrender, but he did not dampen his daughter's excitement. He had men positioned in the jail, so it was hardly difficult to bring whatever he wanted inside. Yan Wenxin only felt conflicted about his daughter's persistent concern for the son he had abandoned.

It had been nearly two months since Huaixiu had been arrested. Although the name of the capital city meant "long summer," winter had come early. The weather turned cold before autumn had even ended. Accompanied by the autumn rain that came on and off, the days only grew colder.

On a rainy night, once Yan Wenxin confirmed that no one would be alerted by him visiting his foster son, he went to the jail and successfully brought the items in with him.

The head warden was someone Yan Wenxin had placed himself. Once they reached Huaixiu's cell, the man withdrew respectfully.

"Huaixiu," Yan Wenxin called out gently upon seeing the young man inside.

Dressed in thin prisoner's garb and huddling from the cold in the pile of dried straw, the youth jerked violently as he turned his head in disbelief toward Yan Wenxin.

"Y-Yifu!" Huaixiu called out, bursting into tears.

His features were handsome yet delicate. There was something about his face that made people feel for him—perhaps because he'd lived on the streets as a young child. Right now, with how haggard he looked, his appearance kindled more pity than ever. His dingy prison cell and stained attire only made him look even more delicate and fragile; just one glance at him was enough to induce a heavy dose of heartache.

If not for being charged with such a serious crime that required him to be kept in solitary confinement, and for some of the prison guards—the Yan family's pawns—taking care of him, something awful would have happened to him already.

"Yes, I have come to see you." Yan Wenxin gave him a hint of a smile, then sighed deeply. Lowering his voice, he said, "Huaixiu, I've done you wrong."

Huaixiu stumbled to the door, disregarding the cold, and shook his head forcefully. "No, Yifu, it's my fault. It's me who could not repay your kindness and affection. I even...caused trouble for the Yan family."

Huaixiu's words sounded very earnest, without revealing anything. Yan Wenxin then understood that no matter how much the Protector General and his son threatened or tempted Huaixiu, they would never be able to gain any information detrimental to Yan Wenxin or his operations.

"Ah... Don't blame me for not saving you. Working with the enemy is a grievous crime, and I have to consider the safety of the dozens of people at home." As Yan Wenxin spoke, he reached into the cell, stroking his foster son's sunken cheeks with an aching heart. "You've lost weight. Seeing it hurts me."

Huaixiu's skin was cold when he touched him, but a faint wash of red followed his caress.

"Yifu... Yifu..." It seemed Huaixiu had a thousand things to say, but what left his lips were only quiet calls of respect and longing.

"Come, have something to eat. Caijun prepared this for you. Come, put on these jackets." Yan Wenxin pulled his hand away, shoving the jackets into the cell for Huaixiu to wear them. Smiling, he praised, "You look good."

Huaixiu's face reddened even more. Just as he reached for the chopsticks, Yan Wenxin pushed his hand away, his expression suffused with gentleness. "Let me feed you."

The young man was unable to refuse him. To him, this person was his savior, the one he'd admired and respected since his youth. Even now, Yan Wenxin had not forgotten him, gently protecting him as he always had. His adoptive father's care felt like the warm waters of spring pouring over him, as sweet as honey.

Yan Wenxin fed his foster son at a steady pace, mouthful by mouthful. Huaixiu eagerly enjoyed the food, his face aglow with happiness. The entire time, he stared at Yan Wenxin as though he desperately wished to permanently carve this scene into his mind. Even if he were reborn in the next life, he would never forget it.

Seeing that the food was half finished and Huaixiu was full, Yan Wenxin put the chopsticks down and took out a container of water, giving the young man a drink. After that, he helped him wipe his mouth clean.

"When you first came to us, I fed you like this a few times. Back then, you were small and thin, but your eyes were as bright as the stars in the sky. I thought to myself, 'In the future, this child will do great things and bring honor to the Yan family.'" Yan Wenxin sighed with great emotion, patting Huaixiu's shoulder warmly. "I know you're a sentimental, grateful child, and that you would never deliberately harm my family."

"Yifu..." Huaixiu stared at Yan Wenxin, his lips still warm from the touch of his foster father's hand. "Even if Guan Shanjin were to rip my lips from my face, he could never make me betray the Yan family."

A few days ago, Guan Shanjin's right-hand man, Man Yue—who was as round as a ball—had come to see Huaixiu. Subtly and overtly, he kept trying to hint that Yan Wenxin was a cruel, vicious, and ungrateful man—that even if Huaixiu offered up his life, that Yan fellow would not feel grateful. He would have already forgotten about him.

How could Huaixiu believe Man Yue? Was his foster father not visiting him right now?

"I believe you, of course. But..." Yan Wenxin patted on his foster son's hand in comfort, murmuring, "This time, the Yan family has escaped unscathed. It has angered Guan Shanjin and his group of filthy compatriots. I'm afraid that they will not give up on any opportunity to obstruct me in court from now on. Your two younger brothers have yet to find their proper footing in court, and Guan Shanjin will not let them off easy... Ah, what's the point in saying all of this to you? You don't have to worry about it."

The moment Huaixiu heard this, he became anxious. "Yifu, don't say that," he urged, keeping his voice down. "As long as I can do something for the Yan family, I will do it—no matter what!"

"Even if you're in jail, even if..." Yan Wenxin paused, then spoke softly, as though he could not bear it. "Even if you're abandoned?"

Huaixiu shuddered. Unable to conceal his pain, he looked at his adoptive father with sad, glimmering eyes, but he never let the tears fall. He gritted his teeth and nodded. "Yes."

Yan Wenxin gave a long sigh. "Good child."

"Yifu, what would you have me do?" The tears in Huaixiu's eyes now fell, splattering on the back of Yan Wenxin's hand where it covered his.

"When Guan Shanjin comes looking for you again, help me figure out his next move, hmm?" Yan Wenxin looked at the teardrops on the back of his hand, wiping them away gently. "Don't cry. My heart hurts."

"Mm..." Huaixiu obediently suppressed his tears, even giving Yan Wenxin a smile. "Yifu, don't worry, I'm serious. I promise I will not cause any more trouble for the Yan family."

Yan Wenxin glanced at his adopted son. He opened his mouth to speak, but no words came; finally, he sighed. He patted Huaixiu's hand, stood up, and left.

Huaixiu gripped the bars of the cell door, watching emotionally as Yan Wenxin departed. Even when the man's figure vanished completely, he was still lost in thought...

Perhaps the Protector General's estate had recognized that Huaixiu would never switch sides, or perhaps they had some other plan in mind. Either way, over the next few days, they stopped sending people to the jail.

This did not worry Yan Wenxin. He doubted Guan Shanjin would seek Huaixiu out again so soon. Furthermore, he had already cut Huaixiu off from the family. Yan Wenxin's words that day had been mainly to secure Huaixiu's loyalty. If he did really end up being able to sniff out any information, that was only a side dish to the main course.

The conflict between the emperor and the Protector General's estate could no longer be resolved. After Guan Shanjin was removed from his position, he was not reinstated. The emperor wished to seek someone else to carry the enormous responsibility of protecting the southern border, and the only people who could replace Guan Shanjin in court were the Defender Duke's men.

As expected, when the capital had its first snowfall of the year—which was also the third month after Guan Shanjin left prison—the responsibility of being the general of the southern garrison stationed in Horse-Face City fell upon the shoulders of the Defender Duke's previous subordinate. This man's achievements on the battlefield could not compare to Guan Shanjin's, but he was obedient. Throughout his career, he had spent more time in the capital than at the border, and he had commanded military forces for around a dozen years. The emperor trusted him.

Yan Wenxin was completely at ease now.

It was then that he received an invitation from Bai Shaochang.

Nothing much was said in the invitation. Written in Bai Shaochang's elegant script was a simple invitation to listen to him play, mentioning that it was a repayment for last time, when the performance had been cut short.

The last time? It took a moment for Yan Wenxin to remember. Guan Shanjin had brought Lu Zezhi along to that performance, while Ping Yifan had brought Wu Xingzi. Due to his deliberate incitement, the session had been stopped, but no one was concerned over that matter any longer. A few months had already passed; why would Bai Shaochang suddenly mention it again?

In the past, rumors about Guan Shanjin and Bai Shaochang getting married had spread widely through the capital. After Guan Shanjin went to jail, though, the subject of Bai Shaochang fell out of discussion altogether; it was as if he'd quietly vanished.

A few days ago, the emperor had summoned Yan Wenxin to dine with him, making a casual mention of the master qin player and his son. The emperor couldn't stop sighing, saying he felt he had held up the young man's marriage. In the past, Guan Shanjin had been so prominent and had attracted a lot of attention, but now, he was gloomy and silent—certainly not a suitable spouse for Bai Shaochang.

"We've let the qin master take his child home," the emperor said, his tone filled with pity. "Once the rumors have subsided, another suitable partner will be sought for him."

The Protector General's estate must have given up on using the Bai family to get back into the emperor's good graces. The Guan family truly had stiff spines; they would rather break than bend. Yan Wenxin wanted to see how much longer they could remain this stubborn.

Putting the invitation down, Yan Wenxin decided to accept this appointment. It was time to meet with Bai Shaochang.

The date of his appointment with Bai Shaochang quickly arrived. There had been a heavy snowfall the night before, and everything gleamed white and silver. Even as Yan Wenxin left his house, the snow had yet to stop; feathery snowflakes gathered in a thick layer on his umbrella.

Yan Wenxin's shoes got a little wet as he walked from the entrance of the alley to the Bai residence. With an unhappy expression, he stood under the eaves and closed his umbrella, straightening his clothes out before knocking on the door.

Silence reigned for a moment before the woven bamboo door slowly opened. Bai Shaochang appeared behind the door, wrapped in a cloak, his face pale. When he saw Yan Wenxin, he revealed a small smile. He took half a step back to let Yan Wenxin in.

"Lord Yan."

"Bai-gongzi." Yan Wenxin cupped his hands together in greeting. Peering into the courtyard, he could only see Bai Shaochang's footprints alone in the snow. "I'm disturbing you."

"It's no disturbance." Bai Shaochang shook his head. He, too, peered behind Yan Wenxin. Noticing that Yan Wenxin had not brought any servants along with him, he seemed a little puzzled.

"Since I'm here to listen to you play the qin, there's no need to bring unnecessary people to disturb your peace," Yan Wenxin explained considerately, and walked through the doorway.

"Lord Yan is very thoughtful." Bai Shaochang smiled shyly. When the door closed, he turned around abruptly and threw himself into Yan Wenxin's arms, his pale face nuzzling into the older man's chest with great emotion.

Yan Wenxin reached out, hurriedly wrapping his arms around him. Gently, he patted the young man's slender back. "Ah, I've missed you too."

Bai Shaochang did not reply. He hugged Yan Wenxin tightly with his thin arms like a fledgling swallow flying back to its nest.

"I let you down, making you endure such hardship for so many days in the Protector General's estate," Yan Wenxin said.

Snow still drifted through the air. In the blink of an eye, a thin layer of snowflakes had gathered on their shoulders. Yan Wenxin seemed completely unbothered, gently soothing the man in his arms.

"I was willing," answered Bai Shaochang, his voice muffled. Yan Wenxin's scent filled his senses, light and elegant with traces of paper and ink. Although he was a little cold from the snow, every breath he took felt warm.

"I've made you suffer," Yan Wenxin sighed, tightening his embrace a little. He considerately brushed away the snow in the young man's hair to prevent it from melting and refreezing. "The snow is too heavy—let's go inside first."

"Mm..." Bai Shaochang seemed a little unwilling. He nuzzled into Yan Wenxin's chest again before reluctantly pulling himself away, taking the initiative to hold Yan Wenxin's hand affectionately.

Bai Shaochang's open affection left Yan Wenxin a little startled. This young man, who was as gentle as jade, had always been very reserved. Although the two of them had already exchanged love tokens, he never expressed any overt passion. Even when it came to the occasional act of hand-holding, Bai Shaochang had only dared do it in his own courtyard.

Still, in spite of this confusion, Yan Wenxin thought perhaps it had been too long since he last saw Bai Shaochang; maybe the young man had simply missed him. At the end of the day, no matter how reserved Bai Shaochang might be, he was still a young man in the early stage of his life. It made sense that he would show such affection when they hadn't seen each other for many months.

Allowing Bai Shaochang to take his hand and lead him further into the residence, Yan Wenxin held up his umbrella to shelter them both. He made sure to say some honeyed words of fondness to comfort the younger man. Every now and then, Bai Shaochang looked up to glance at him. His pale face now held a slight trace of red, and his actions became a little flustered. Yan Wenxin laughed secretly in his heart—Bai Shaochang had always been easy to sweet-talk.

Old Master Bai did not appear to be home. On snowy days, the emperor liked to admire the snow accompanied by the qin; it was likely he had already sent people over to bring Old Master Bai into the palace to play his qin. The Bai residence retained only a few servants, and their training was strict. Right now, it was as if they had vanished into the snow—it felt like there was no one around but them.

Bai Shaochang did not lead Yan Wenxin toward the place where he normally played the qin, but to his own little courtyard. Other than his own footprints, the snowy ground was completely unmarked. However, Yan Wenxin swiftly came to a stop. He stared at the footprints as a thin layer of new snow covered them, an inexplicable hesitancy rising within him. This hesitancy was mixed with caution and a sense of unease. This little picturesque yard somehow exuded a piercing chill—and not just from the snow.

"Zaizong-gege?" Seeing him stop, Bai Shaochang looked at him in confusion, tightening his hold on Yan Wenxin's hand.

"Hmm?" Yan Wenxin managed to drag his attention back. He smiled gently, imperceptibly observing Bai Shaochang's expression.

Bai Shaochang's face paled by a few more degrees. His eyes darted away, unable to hold Yan Wenxin's gaze for too long. His shoulders trembled underneath his cloak, as if chilled by the cold.

Being such a clever old fox, Yan Wenxin saw right through him. Bai Shaochang was not trembling from the cold, but from fear. What was he afraid of?

Yan Wenxin suddenly understood why he felt so uneasy.

Those footsteps in the snow had clearly been made by Bai Shaochang not too long ago, which was why they were still very distinct. They had yet to be completely concealed by the large, fluffy snowflakes. That meant that after Yan Wenxin knocked on the door of the Bai residence, Bai Shaochang had left his room and walked out to open the door for him.

Although the Bai residence was not big, it wasn't exactly small. It would be difficult for Bai Shaochang to hear the knocking from his room. If he instructed his servants to not open the door, but to inform him when there was a knock, there should at least be one or two more sets of footprints in the snow. But other than this lonely set of footprints, there was no sign of anyone's presence.

If Bai Shaochang could not wait to see him, and had already been waiting near the door, this set of footprints should have been barely visible.

"You have other guests?" Yan Wenxin lowered his eyelids, his tone extremely gentle, but Bai Shaochang shuddered. He turned his head away and refused to look at him. Yan Wenxin laughed. "Someone from the Protector General's estate?"

"No..." Bai Shaochang gave him a swift glance, his eyes reddening. "You... You said, that perfume sachet... Your mother really wouldn't have minded that I'm a man?"

The perfume sachet? Yan Wenxin pulled his hand away, and Bai Shaochang hurriedly tried to grab it back. However, he'd already cupped his cheek, caressing it gently as though he held the world's greatest treasure.

"Why would she mind?" Yan Wenxin said, brushing away the snowflakes on Bai Shaochang's eyelashes. "That was the only keepsake my mother left me, and I only wanted to give it to you."

The snowflakes melted into water, blurring the young man's vision. "You said that the plum blossom represents scholarly integrity," Bai Shaochang murmured, as if in a dream, "and that the bird represented your mother..."

"Yes."

"You said that your mother used the last of her strength to embroider it for you before she passed away. That even if she wasn't around, she would forever be by your side..." Bai Shaochang's voice trembled slightly. His eyes clouded over, close to tears.

Yan Wenxin kept smiling, stroking the corners of Bai Shaochang's eyes tenderly. "Yes."

"I believe you, I believe you..." As Bai Shaochang blinked, tears rolled down his face. They were ice-cold, painful, and itchy, but he could not control them. "You said that once your youngest child is married, you'll be able to accompany me for the rest of my life. That you hold no love for your wife, only respect. You said that in the past, your in-laws had guided and supported you, and even if you're the Minister of Personnel now, you cannot break your bonds so easily—otherwise, your reputation would be ruined... I'm willing to wait for you, wait for your youngest child to get married, wait for you to leave the court..."

"I understand. You're so lovely, of course I truly have great affection for you..." Yan Wenxin's thumb brushed Bai Shaochang's lips, and the young man shut his eyes in despair.

"Then why is there a second perfume sachet?" Bai Shaochang had thought he would not be able to ask this question—he had never expected it to slip so easily out of his mouth. His nose was red from crying, and the tear tracks on his face stung from the wind and snow, yet he could not hold back his tears.

Even Yan Wenxin, as cruel and heartless as he was, felt a flicker of true pain. "Was it Wu Xingzi who told you?" he asked.

To be able to stand at the top of the court, to become a greatly trusted adviser to the throne, Yan Wenxin had never relied on the power of his in-laws, but on his own intelligence. Considering the evidence, what other conclusion was there to draw? He only needed to consider it a little to understand the situation.

He gave a low chuckle, a swirl of feelings rising within him. If you struck at a goose every day, one day it would bite back. Bai Shaochang looked at him, astonished. He clearly had not expected Yan Wenxin to make such an accurate guess.

Just then the door to the room in front of them opened.

A large, tall man led a thin, middle-aged man outside. The two of them had their hands clasped tightly together, and the tall one looked worried, bowing his head and tugging the collar of the middle-aged man closed. When he'd made sure that the older man would not be cold, he finally turned his icy gaze on Yan Wenxin.

"Heir to the Protector General. It's been a while." Yan Wenxin gave Guan Shanjin a polite smile, acting as though no tension existed between the two of them, as if they'd simply happened to pass each other on the street.

"Lord Yan." Guan Shanjin curved his lips in a faint smile, not surprised by how calm the other man was. "I do like talking to clever people. Let's go. The snow is getting heavier, and the emperor has warmed up the palace for our visit. We shouldn't keep him waiting."

"The emperor... I see." Yan Wenxin laughed and shook his head, then sighed. "I'm truly getting on in age. Thinking on it now, the emperor's every action was a warning, but I've been careless."

Yes, the emperor had always held great trust in the Protector General's estate. After all, he'd watched Guan Shanjin grow up. He had the Protector General's absolute loyalty—it was exceedingly strange for him to shield Yan Wenxin like this. Having raised the Yan estate up so high, the emperor had completely shut off Yan Wenxin's cautiousness.

And Yan Wenxin himself had neglected to think about the threat of an old friend.

He turned his eyes toward Wu Xingzi, who stood next to Guan Shanjin. He was dressed in a wrap edged with silver fox fur, and he seemed just as fragile as before. His ordinary face bore the marks of time; the wrinkles at the corners of his eyes were obvious. With his placid facial features, they looked like laugh lines. He appeared warm and gentle, and he even seemed to be cowering a little. Perhaps he was feeling cold—he looked a little comical hiding his chin in his furs.

"Chang'an," Yan Wenxin called out to him.

Wu Xingzi gave Yan Wenxin a bewildered look, but did not respond.

"I thought that you were in a relationship with Ping Yifan," said Yan Wenxin deliberately, just to see Guan Shanjin's darkening expression and the pent-up fire in those dark eyes.

Now that it had come to this, Yan Wenxin would not be so naïve as to think that Ping Yifan, who had been working with him, was on the side of Nanman. He was certainly a pawn put in place by Guan Shanjin and the emperor. Yan Wenxin had been lured into this trap step by step, and he was no longer able to extricate himself from it. However, he was still able to unsettle Guan Shanjin.

Wu Xingzi began to speak, only to start sneezing from the fur around his face. Guan Shanjin quietly scolded him for being a foolish darling, taking out a handkerchief and wiping his face. The devoted affection and tenderness on Guan Shanjin's face really was nauseating. Yan Wenxin's smile faded away.

"Ah, I'll just do it myself." Blushing, Wu Xingzi quickly reached out for the handkerchief, but Guan Shanjin caught his wrist and held it down before carefully wiping his face clean for him.

"I asked you to wait inside, but you insisted on coming out." Guan Shanjin kept his handkerchief, putting on a fierce expression as he pinched Wu Xingzi's nose and made the old fellow feel very embarrassed.

"Ah, isn't this...isn't this...just because..." Wu Xingzi scratched his cheek, looking just as shy as he did twenty years ago. He looked at Yan Wenxin. "...I'm meeting an old friend?"

It was as though an eon had passed.

The last time they had met, Yan Wenxin had stood proudly at the top, showing contempt for the ordinary man in front of him. He mocked him for his daft behavior. He judged him for being unable to clearly see either his own status or the heart of the person in his bed. Even if they'd once shared an entanglement, it wasn't enough for Yan Wenxin to remember.

Now, Yan Wenxin kept staring at Wu Xingzi. This honest man, who had once looked at him foolishly, completely unable to conceal the love in his eyes, was standing in front of him once again. However, this time, his dark eyes were filled with emotions that Yan Wenxin could not understand. There was pity, there was wistfulness, there was loss, there was disappointment... There was everything but anger.

"Zaizong-xiong," Wu Xingzi called out to him. With his southern accent, he sounded both soft and demure, exactly the same as he had twenty years ago.

"Chang'an," Yan Wenxin responded, but the smile on his face had completely vanished. Instantly, he understood. Wu Xingzi's actions had not been orchestrated by Guan Shanjin. Instead, he'd managed to make Yan Wenxin stumble all on his own.

"It's been twenty years, and there's something I've always wanted to say to you," Wu Xingzi told him.

"What is it?"

"Congratulations for your success in the imperial examinations." Wu Xingzi smiled, bowing properly to Yan Wenxin. "You've brought glory to your family."

Yan Wenxin looked at Wu Xingzi. For the first time in his life, he realized that he had underestimated the person in front of him.

The case of Yan Wenxin conspiring to betray the country caused a storm in court. At first, he'd still had allies who wanted to speak up for him, to exonerate him. However, none of them had anticipated that the emperor held such irrefutable proof in his hands. The evidence was concrete. There were even letters Yan Wenxin had personally written to the confidants of the Nanman king. In an instant, all voices in the court fell silent.

Yan Wenxin had been a court official for twenty years, and his power in court was like the roots of a towering tree, deep and intricate. However, this tree still couldn't escape a lightning bolt; in one strike, it was split in two, all the way from crown to root.

His allies cautiously shrank into themselves. Afraid to be dragged forward to face the might of the emperor, around a dozen people called in sick at the same time, and another dozen sent up appeals for their own retirement. Their replacements were all people with no strong family backgrounds, a group of young talents who were mindful of the country's rules and regulations.

A man had to be clever to make it in court. The emperor had held great trust in Yan Wenxin, favoring him in particular, and rumors spread both in court and on the streets about the emperor and his official sharing a bed. After all, when that stir with Yan Wenxin's adopted son had occurred not too long ago, the Yan family escaped from it completely unscathed. The emperor had even comforted Yan Wenxin specifically.

Now, looking back at it, the emperor had actually been leading him to destruction by lauding him to the heavens! Not only had the emperor been swift and resolute, the trap had clearly been in place for a long time. Just look at how quickly the Protector General recovered from his illness, and how his son was reinstated as the Great General of the Southern Garrison. None of those who should have been rewarded and favored were left out, and there was no need to name who was truly trusted by the emperor.

In less than seven days, all the voices that had been ready to start trouble and planned to probe into the matter fell silent. It was truly over for Yan Wenxin now; more than half of his allies had been eradicated without a single drop of blood being spilled. Despite the whirlwind at court, though, things were otherwise completely tranquil, and the storm silently subsided.

Yan Wenxin relied on his in-laws as the foundation of his power, and he did not have any other relatives. Before Yan Wenxin was even sentenced, Madam Yan notarized her divorce papers. Then she brought her daughter along with her to the Guanyin Temple, a day's journey away by carriage. There, she and her daughter devoted themselves to Buddhism, becoming nuns but still keeping their hair; in this way she was able to shield the two of them from the consequences of Yan Wenxin's actions.

Madam Yan was unable to protect her sons so effectively. She could only watch as they were stripped of their titles and locked in jail. She didn't know if they would even be able to keep their lives in the end. But the emperor did show the Yan family one last shred of benevolence. The two Yan sons would live, but they would be sent to the northwestern border as slaves. They were to leave the capital once winter ended. As for what exactly would happen to Yan Wenxin, the emperor did not utter a word, and no one dared to ask.

Half a month later, it was as if the entire court had forgotten that there once existed a powerful minister named Yan Wenxin.

When Guan Shanjin was released from jail, he took Wu Xingzi home with him, and the two enjoyed their days of honeyed affection.

Today, after Wu Xingzi had finished planting his vegetables in the morning, he hugged a hot water bottle and chatted away with the Protector General's wife about day-to-day affairs.

Wu Xingzi had worried at first that the Protector General and his wife would look down on him for his age. Although he had met the Protector General's wife before, and she seemed to be quite satisfied with him, Wu Xingzi still felt uneasy.

When he thought about the Protector General himself, more shivers ran through him. But he'd worried for nothing; it turned out the Lord Protector was entirely unbothered about his son's choice of partner. It was Guan Shanjin's lover, not his, so what did it have to do with him? Guan Shanjin was hardly a man his father could easily manage, anyway—it was a moot point.

As for the Protector General's wife, she and Wu Xingzi became very close. No disagreements cropped up between the in-laws at all, and whenever the two of them had nothing to do, they would meet up for tea and a chat. Wu Xingzi heard quite a number of anecdotes from the Protector General's wife about his father's days in the capital.

A steward came over at that moment, cupping his hands together and addressing Wu Xingzi. "Young Madam, Bai Shaochang-gongzi has requested an audience. Would you like to see him?"

Being called "Young Madam" made Wu Xingzi shrink into himself and shiver, a blush flourishing on both his nose and cheeks.

"The child from the Bai family?" The Protector General's wife was surprised.

"Yes."

"Why is he looking for Xingzi?" The Protector General's wife knew there had been a romantic entanglement between Bai Shaochang and Yan Wenxin. Furthermore, the Protector General's estate had made use of the young man—shouldn't he want to stay as far away from the estate as possible? Why would he come to their door?

"Bai-gongzi did not mention anything." The steward also looked a little puzzled. "Would Young Madam like to meet him?"

"Yes, yes, yes." Wu Xingzi nodded firmly, worried as he looked out into the snow-covered courtyard. "It's so cold. Quickly, let Bai-gongzi inside to warm himself up."

The steward left at his instruction, and the Protector General's wife contemplated the situation. The young master of the Bai family was prideful and sensitive, and she was not sure what he wanted to speak to Wu Xingzi about. However, since she was an outsider to this matter, he wouldn't be able to say anything, even if he were to choke on his words. Seeing how pitiful this young man was, the Protector General's wife thoughtfully bade farewell and left.

Man Yue led Bai Shaochang inside. Although the young master was still dressed in his usual pure white outfit, he no longer shone with elegance and ethereality. He was like a snowflake that had finally fallen into the dust, losing its clarity in the grayness.

Without thinking, Wu Xingzi stood up to welcome him, but Bai Shaochang cupped his hands together in a respectful, aloof greeting.

Wu Xingzi returned the greeting a little awkwardly. Feeling ill at ease, he invited him to take a seat.

When Bai Shaochang sat down, the two men found themselves at a loss for words. Man Yue did not leave; instead, he lazily stood to the side and watched Bai Shaochang until the young man was so uneasy that his face alternated between blushing and paling.

"What is the reason for your visit, Bai-gongzi?" Wu Xingzi hurriedly spoke up in order to him help out. He knew that Man Yue disliked Bai Shaochang, and Bai Shaochang, for his part, held Man Yue in fear and disgust. He looked ready to flee at any moment.

"Uhh... Umm..." Bai Shaochang straightened up, nervous. He shot a swift glance at Wu Xingzi as his white teeth nibbled on his red lip, exuding a stubborn yet fragile air.

Wu Xingzi loved admiring beautiful men; it was his favorite pastime. Naturally, he didn't want to see such an expression on this beauty. He looked toward Man Yue, panicking slightly. Of course, Man Yue would never slack in his duties, smiling as he took a couple of steps forward.

"Bai-gongzi, Madam is kindhearted and cannot bear to see people cry in front of him. Why don't I take you somewhere else so you can cry to your heart's content before returning?" Man Yue clearly had no consideration for Bai Shaochang's dignity. After all, this man had framed his boss. The only reason Man Yue didn't throw him out was out of respect for the emperor.

Bai Shaochang choked, glaring at Man Yue in embarrassed indignation. He gritted his teeth. "I would like to speak to Mr. Wu alone," he said quietly. "May I ask if Vice General Man can step away for a bit?"

"Of course not," replied Man Yue, smiling mischievously. With his round and honest appearance, he looked like the prophesied future Buddha; only those who had fallen victim to his schemes knew the malice behind his smile. "I have absolutely no interest in what you're about to say, but the general has commanded me to take good care of Madam and not give anyone the chance to get between them. As such, I have no choice. If you don't wish to say what you need to say in front of me, then I'll have to send you out."

Bai Shaochang's face reddened in anger and he bit his lip almost until it bled, but there was nothing he could do about Man Yue. Wu Xingzi only looked easy to manipulate—he certainly couldn't be counted on to send Man Yue away in consideration for Bai Shaochang's dignity.

As expected, Wu Xingzi looked apologetic but did not say anything. Bai Shaochang had no other options.

"Mr. Wu, why...why were you so sure that Zaizong-gege would use the perfume sachet again?" he asked.

After he separated from Yan Wenxin that day, Bai Shaochang had been continuously plagued by this thought. Despite his mortification, he pleaded for an audience with the emperor. After finding out that Wu Xingzi had helped the merchant who sold the perfume sachets and gained a favor in return, he'd been astonished.

This shy, ordinary middle-aged man in front of him had laid this trap years ago, and he'd stepped into it so foolishly. Had he been exploited when he testified against Yan Wenxin? He thought it over and over, but never managed to reach a conclusion. After all, he'd wholeheartedly loved Yan Wenxin. He couldn't bear to see him fall so far.

Bai Shaochang could not explain the pain and trepidation in his heart. He thought that perhaps Yan Wenxin had not lied to him at all—was he instead too big a fool to see the truth and became nothing more than a tool others utilized for their own gain?

All sorts of thoughts formed one after another in his mind; he couldn't get them to stop. He'd worried so much he'd become skin and bones. After a bout of illness, it took him about a month to recover and get some life back in him. No longer able to just sit around, he insisted on seeking Wu Xingzi out to clear up his doubts.

Hearing this, Wu Xingzi was stunned. A little troubled, he came to a sudden realization. "Does Bai-gongzi think that I framed Zaizong-xiong?"

At such a direct counterquestion, Bai Shaochang turned red, then green, nearly losing his breath. He'd lived among the nobility of the capital since he was young. All the nobles constantly talked in circles, speaking cautiously and ambiguously. Even if they were insulting someone, they would always leave them a path out of the situation. What kind of person spoke like this?

"No, I..." Bai Shaochang clenched his teeth. He paused for a moment, thinking about how miserable Yan Wenxin was right now. His heart aching, he came to a decision and nodded. "Yes. After all, it's been twenty years. How could such a coincidence happen—how could th-that perfume sachet still be available for sale?"

Wu Xingzi gazed at Bai Shaochang with sympathy. Beads of sweat formed on the young man's forehead, and he tightly clenched his fists. He was as taut as a bow, ready to break at any moment.

Wu Xingzi sighed. "I did hold some resentment at first. Twenty years ago, Zaizong-xiong asked me for twenty-three taels to cover traveling expenses to the capital. That was more than all my savings. I had to borrow money from the magistrate's office. This was something I gave willingly, and I could not resent Zaizong-xiong for it... Bai-gongzi, do you know how much ten taels is?"

The unexpected question jolted Bai Shaochang. Blankly, he shook his head. Behind him, Man Yue burst into mocking laughter.

Bai Shaochang's cheeks reddened in color, and he nodded in shame and resentment. "I know, it's not a lot." What did it have to do with all this?

Wu Xingzi tightened his hold around the hot water bottle in his arms. "I've worked as an adviser my entire life in the magistrate's office of my hometown, and my monthly salary is four hundred coins," he said placidly. "I'm also allocated some rice and cloth, and living alone, it's enough to survive. Still, I'm quite inadequate—at this age, I've only amassed a fortune of ten taels."

Bai Shaochang looked at him in astonishment. He didn't understand why they were talking about this.

Wu Xingzi clearly did not expect the young master to understand, so he continued with his usual imperturbable air. "When I received the news that Zaizong-xiong had gained the Top Scholar rank, and that he would take a wife and become an official in the capital with no intention to return to his hometown, I could not help but feel resentful. You're right—when I discovered the source of the perfume sachets, I was a little upset over it. However, at the end of the day, it was me who failed to understand Zaizong-xiong well enough, and I had to find a way to continue living. I helped Xia Dagen fight his case without any personal motives, and I never once thought that I would ever make use of the favor he promised me."

When Wu Xingzi spoke, his accent was soft and flowing, as gentle as cool water. Some of his syllables drawled together, further emphasizing his agreeable, noncompetitive nature. However, Bai Shaochang inexplicably shrank into himself, shivering, and his face stung vaguely in pain.

He finally understood. Right now, Wu Xingzi was telling him that Yan Wenxin was an ungrateful person. During the most impoverished time of his life, he still took everything he could from someone he was close to without any intention of repaying him. Meanwhile, Wu Xingzi gave up his entire fortune and half his life just because Yan Wenxin had spoken a few sweet words. He truly had no energy to hate Yan Wenxin for it; he could only do his best to move on with his life.

"But..." Bai Shaochang was still struggling. A few days ago, after pleading with his father, he'd finally managed to visit Yan Wenxin in jail. The once gentle and warm man, whose elegance inspired devotion, had been like a pearl encased in dust in the dim, cramped cell. He still looked unyielding and unbreakable, but the image still made Bai Shaochang's heart ache.

Yan Wenxin hadn't said a word as he silently stared through the slatted cell door at Bai Shaochang. As though the young man was a world away from him, Yan Wenxin gave a faint smile. Bai Shaochang fled the jail in misery and returned home in a daze, then broke down in tears in his room.

He'd thought he might be able to find something out from Wu Xingzi that would help Yan Wenxin.

"Bai-gongzi, I only have one question for you. If you can answer it, I'm willing to go to Haiwang and say a few things to protect Zaizong-xiong."

This was as good news as any. Bai Shaochang gathered his spirits and fixed his stare at Wu Xingzi, silently urging him to continue.

Wu Xingzi lowered his head slightly and gently asked, "All those years ago, the things that Zaizong-xiong said to me... Why would he tell you the exact same thing, without changing a single word?"

Bai Shaochang's eyes widened. His pink lips parted, but he was unable to utter a single sound.

It was Man Yue who broke the silence, bursting into laughter again behind them.

It was some time before Bai Shaochang finally managed to force out a response. "I-I don't know..." It seemed as though his soul had left him. Certainly, no matter how much he wanted to help exonerate Yan Wenxin, no matter how much he wanted to blame Wu Xingzi for taking advantage of him, he was not able to answer this simple question.

Yan Wenxin gave him that same perfume sachet. Yan Wenxin spoke those same words of affection.

"Bai-gongzi, please go home," Wu Xingzi said, sighing inwardly. It was not his place to say anything more. Bai Shaochang's shoulders

sank deeply, and his shaky, unsteady appearance was truly too pitiful to witness.

Bai Shaochang refused to leave. His eyes had become bloodshot, and he looked a little crazed. "Then you tell me, Mr. Wu—why would he say the exact same thing?"

That stare made Wu Xingzi shiver, and he shot a pleading glance toward Man Yue. Wu Xingzi was softhearted, and when he knew that someone was just one piece of straw away from breaking, he was really unwilling to state things so plainly. Bai Shaochang was still young. Once he had a few more years' experience, he would be able to see how treacherous Yan Wenxin truly was and slowly recover from this pain.

Man Yue pretended not to see anything. He looked out of the window, paying great attention to the snowy landscape, as though looking for a blooming flower amid the snow.

In the end, Wu Xingzi had to send the young master off by himself. There was no way he could bring himself to tell Bai Shaochang that the reason why Yan Wenxin said the exact same thing was that Bai Shaochang and the young Wu Xingzi were the same to him. They had been worth something to Yan Wenxin at one point, but once he got what he needed, it was easy for him to turn away and leave them behind forever.

Bao Shaochang was extremely lucky that, after it was discovered he'd hidden the letters proving collusion with Nanman, he was not facing the same fate as Yan Huaixiu: dying without knowing the full truth. If the emperor hadn't needed Bai Shaochang to expose Yan Wenxin—if the emperor had genuinely been fooled by Yan Wenxin, if he truly trusted and relied on him—there was no way Bai Shaochang would be able to survive the combined fury of the Protector General and the emperor himself. To Yan Wenxin,

Bai Shaochang was a dead man walking. Why would he spend the extra effort to come up with new words of affection? The lines he used twenty years ago to enchant Wu Xingzi had proved rather useful. Bai Shaochang had been sheltered to the point of naivety, so it was easy to manipulate his feelings. A perfume sachet was all it took for Yan Wenxin to sink his claws into Bai Shaochang's heart.

Despite how badly it had ended, Bai Shaochang still held onto a shred of hope that Yan Wenxin felt true affection for him.

"Y-you really can't..." Gritting his teeth, Bai Shaochang's eyes shone with tears as he made one final, futile effort.

"Bai-gongzi, I understand your intentions. It's only human for you to seek a way out for Zaizong-xiong, but..." Wu Xingzi tightly furrowed his brow. "Why not plead with the emperor directly? Why seek help from Haiwang instead? Colluding with the enemy is a great crime. No one in the entire court, with all their wit and talent, dares to say a word in support of Zaizong-xiong. The emperor might even be waiting for someone stupid to make a move so that he can sweep the court clean. What you're doing is asking Haiwang to be disloyal to the country."

Bai Shaochang jerked violently. His face first turned pale before a flush rushed to his cheeks. He opened his mouth, stammering away, but he was unable to form any words.

"You wish to protect Zaizong-xiong," said Wu Xingzi, "while I only wish to protect Haiwang... You...you should head back." He stood up to send off his guest. He was rarely ever this uncompromising. Even Man Yue looked startled by his behavior.

"I'm not... Help him! He shared a relationship with you in the past—do you not think about him, for old times' sake? Being an official in the capital, he needed to marry a woman and have children; why can't you understand him? If he didn't go back to find you, it was only because he didn't want to make you sad! Why do you have to hate him? Even hate him to the point where you dragged me in to harm him as well? You..." Bai Shaochang wailed like a madman, completely losing his usual elegant demeanor; he looked wretched and pitiful.

Wu Xingzi gazed sympathetically at Bai Shaochang, who had tears and snot smeared all over his face, but he turned a deaf ear to his wails. Instead, it was Man Yue who could no longer look on. He deftly tapped at an acupoint that rendered Bai Shaochang temporarily mute. As gently as if he was carrying a baby bird, he carried the man away so he wouldn't disturb the peace around them.

CHAPTER EIGHT

TOGETHER, FOREVER, JUST THE TWO OF US

Wu Xingzi shrank into Guan Shanjin's arms and nuzzled against him. "This is our second New Year together."

"Yes..." Guan Shanjin chuckled softly as he thought back to last year. "I have something for you. Would you like to see it?"

"For me?" Wu Xingzi's eyes were full of curiosity.

"I'm sure you'll like it." Guan Shanjin lips quirked up slightly. Although he was smiling, Wu Xingzi could see some gloominess in his eyes.

WHEN GUAN SHANJIN returned, he saw Wu Xingzi sitting alone in a chair, hugging his already-cooled hot water bottle and staring into space.

"What happened?" Guan Shanjin hurriedly made his way forward and took the hot water bottle away. Holding onto Wu Xingzi's frozen, reddened hands, he carefully warmed them up with his inner qi.

"Ah, it's nothing..." Wu Xingzi shook his head. Wrinkling his nose, he sneezed abruptly. Although he was dressed warmly, and there was a fire burning in the furnace to heat up the room, it was too cold in the north for Wu Xingzi. His hands were always so icy that he needed to warm them with a hot water bottle, and if he breathed just a little bit harder than usual, his nose started itching. He kept sneezing pitifully for a while; he looked like a wilting flower.

"Hmm?" Guan Shanjin snorted a laugh, tugging the older man into his arms. They both nestled into the chair as he kneaded Wu Xingzi's fingers in his hands. "I've heard all about it from Man Yue. Bai Shaochang came to look for you, wanting you to plead to me for mercy on Yan Wenxin's behalf."

Ever since they'd confessed their feelings for each other, Guan Shanjin rarely kept any secrets from Wu Xingzi, and he spoke a lot more candidly as well.

"Mm." Wu Xingzi nodded, unconsciously shrinking into Guan Shanjin's embrace. "He's young, so it's understandable he can't see things clearly right now. I was just thinking about returning to Horse-Face City, and there's the matter of making offerings to my ancestors during the New Year..."

"I know that you want to return. It's cold and boring in the capital, and who knows the state of that garden in your courtyard in Horse-Face City. When you left, you made sure to harvest everything that you could eat." Guan Shanjin couldn't help making fun of him. "You're the only one who'd think about something like that, you silly old fellow."

"Ah, those crops grew so well," Wu Xingzi sighed. "It would have been such a pity not to eat them. And besides, you must have been furious when you found out I left back then. If you'd noticed that the plants were still there, wouldn't you have stomped them all flat in a rage?" Wu Xingzi licked his lips, grazing his fingers along Guan Shanjin's palm intimately.

Guan Shanjin snorted. "It's good that you know that." It had been only about half a year now, but it felt as though a lifetime had passed since then. Guan Shanjin could still remember the pain and confusion he had felt at the sight of Wu Xingzi's empty room. He'd been so angry that his head hurt, and he had clenched his jaw so hard that his teeth creaked. He'd wished he could catch Wu Xingzi at once and drag him back, but he was also worried he would end up scaring him.

Guan Shanjin bowed his head and kissed Wu Xingzi, their bodies intertwining closely. His tongue nimbly twisted and teased its way into Wu Xingzi's mouth, and Wu Xingzi lost his breath before their mouths parted. He barely had time to gasp in some air before he was kissed again, and the relentless affection left his limbs weak and his vision hazy. Guan Shanjin's hand even slipped into his clothes; with only the barrier of his inner robe, he rubbed and caressed the older man to his delight. Wu Xingzi completely melted at his touch, falling limply into the younger man's arms as he panted for air.

"Come, touch it. This huge treasure has really missed you." Guan Shanjin pulled Wu Xingzi's now warmed-up hand toward his crotch. The tent there had been present for some time already. When Wu Xingzi's hand touched it, it jerked in excitement.

Wu Xingzi cried out quietly but could not bear to pull his hand away. Too many things had happened these last few days, and he'd missed Guan Shanjin's pengornis so much. The huge cock under his palm had clearly missed him as well—it twitched violently several times before he could even start stroking it. Its girth and heft knocked against his palm, leaving a trail of scorching heat in its wake.

"You don't want to look at it?" Guan Shanjin chuckled, sucking on Wu Xingzi's earlobe. His heated breath surrounded Wu Xingzi's ear, and the warmth sent a tingle running through Wu Xingzi's entire body. His breath caught in his throat.

"I do..." How could Wu Xingzi resist such blatant temptation? He gulped, but his throat still felt dry. He undid Guan Shanjin's belt with trembling hands. Just as he was about to reach his target, a wave of shyness suddenly crashed over him. Instead of slipping his hand inside, he carefully wrapped his hand around the huge pengornis through the fabric. Another hand bashfully pressed against Guan Shanjin's muscular abdomen and caressed it. His face flushed red, and he gazed at Guan Shanjin with teary eyes, stammering and stuttering, not daring to slide his hands inside his pants.

"My dirty darling, are you feeling shy, or are you deliberately teasing your husband?" Guan Shanjin asked.

Wu Xingzi glared at him tamely. He slid the hand he had against Guan Shanjin's abdomen down by half an inch, only to stop right at the edge of the hairs surrounding the shaft. Guan Shanjin panted heavily, his hungry eyes fixed on this man who seemed shy but was actually rather daring.

"You've certainly got some audacity." The ominous statement was filled with affection. At this moment, even the tips of Wu Xingzi's ears were blushing, but he still continued to trail the tips of his fingers through Guan Shanjin's pubic hair, scratching lightly. As Wu Xingzi stoked the flames of his desire, Guan Shanjin wanted nothing more than to push the older man down and be done with the teasing.

However, just as he was about to make his move, a knock came at their door.

"General, Madam," came Man Yue's voice. "Don't shoot the messenger, all right? It's not that I couldn't tell that I shouldn't be interrupting, but I have no choice... Mr. Lu wishes to see the general, and he's kicking up quite a fuss."

After he returned to the capital, Lu Zezhi spent his days in discontent. No matter what rumors were drifting around outside, ever since he returned to the Protector General's estate, he almost never saw Guan Shanjin around.

The Protector General's wife came from the same hometown as him, and it was on her recommendation that he'd become Guan Shanjin's teacher. Still, years passed, and the two men parted ways. After they came back together, the Protector General's wife had never concealed her dislike of him.

Before Wu Xingzi appeared, the Protector General's wife doted on her son, so she turned a blind eye to Lu Zezhi. Once the old fellow Wu Xingzi appeared, however, she could no longer be bothered to keep up any perfunctory courtesy toward Lu Zezhi.

Although Lu Zezhi had been pampered by Guan Shanjin to the point where he had become useless—his brain didn't work very well, and his personality had become parasitic—he was still not a complete fool. How could he not sense the awkwardness of his own position?

He waited and waited for Guan Shanjin to return to him, refusing to believe that the feelings Guan Shanjin had held for over a decade would lose to this one-year affair with a newcomer. Guan Shanjin was attached to him—at least, this was what Lu Zezhi told himself. However, what was the conclusion of all this waiting?

He hadn't been the slightest bit concerned when Bai Shaochang moved into the Lord Protector's estate, as he understood that that was part of a scheme. He even prodded it along.

Lu Zezhi had never intended to harm Guan Shanjin at all. After all, the doting and pampering he hoped to receive in the next half of his life relied completely on this man. He was wholly unwilling to return to his hometown and become a teacher there. Lu Zezhi only wanted to pull Guan Shanjin back to his side. Although his methods were rather underhanded, he felt the ends justified the means.

As expected, Bai Shaochang managed to get Guan Shanjin locked up in jail, and the Protector General's estate was thrown into a flurry of chaos. Wu Xingzi had pretty much vanished into thin air, too, and Lu Zezhi wondered if he had fled back to Qingcheng County.

Finally, Lu Zezhi had managed to clear away all the people hanging around Guan Shanjin. Haiwang had grown up under his watchful eye, so Lu Zezhi knew what sort of man he was: ruthless, extremely clear about the things he loved and hated, and utterly decisive. If anyone dared to cross him, they'd be paid back a thousandfold. Once he decided he hated something, that was it; he'd never change his mind .

Wu Xingzi had clearly aroused Guan Shanjin's hatred toward him the first time he'd run away. This time around, Wu Xingzi had even chosen to cling onto another man. To top it all off, when the Protector General's estate was facing such danger, Wu Xingzi didn't do or say anything about it. Would Guan Shanjin still dote on him after this? Still love him?

So Lu Zezhi hid within the Protector General's estate, waiting, feeling completely at ease. Man Yue forbade him from visiting Guan Shanjin in jail, saying it was the general's request—that sort of place was filthy and gruesome, and he did not want to defile Mr. Lu's eyes.

Lu Zezhi knew that Haiwang would always dote on him.

However, months passed, and he was still waiting. Snow was falling in the capital, Bai Shaochang had already been kicked out of the Protector General's estate, Guan Shanjin had been freed and given back his original titles, and news of Yan Wenxin's betrayal was spreading throughout the country. Even tucked away in that little yard of his, Lu Zezhi knew all about these goings-on, and yet, no matter how long he waited, he still saw no sign of the man who was always on his mind.

Today, when Lu Zezhi woke up, the ground was blanketed in white. It had snowed last night, and a thick layer of it covered his yard. The furnace was burning, though, so the room felt as warm as a spring day in March. He pulled on a robe and walked to the window, pushing it open and looking outside. The snow on the ground was untouched and pristine, not a single footprint to be seen.

Lu Zezhi lived in the capital city at the estate of the Protector General, who was one of the most noble families in Great Xia. Only the emperor stood above the Protector General's family; their status was unmatched. However, Lu Zezhi discovered he had been practically forgotten by everyone; he was like an island surrounded by nothingness. No one was concerned about him, no one asked after him...

"Someone, come here!" Lu Zezhi called out, gripping his own hands. It was so warm that a layer of sweat formed on the back of his neck, but a chill still permeated his body down to the bone.

After a pause, he heard no response. He raised his voice, shouting again, "Quick, someone get in here!"

This time, someone finally came running from afar. Lu Zezhi came to the alarming realization that he no longer had any so-called personal attendants nearby!

The person coming over was a maidservant, panting slightly, her expression aloof. It seemed like she had needed to hurry over from quite a distance, and even though it was winter, her temples shone with beads of sweat.

The maidservant wiped her sweat away and bowed respectfully. "Mr. Lu, do you have any instructions for me?"

"Ask Haiwang to come see me." Lu Zezhi could no longer put on his usual haughty, distant air. He was panicking so much that he could no longer speak carefully.

The maidservant frowned slightly, but her tone remained detached. "Mr. Lu, it's not that I am refusing to pass the message on for you, but the general is not someone any random person can easily see."

"Am I just any random person? Go, go bring Haiwang here. As they say, a teacher for a day is a father for life. What excuse does he have for not seeing me?" Lu Zezhi had done so much and waited so long—how could he tolerate Guan Shanjin distancing himself from him?

The maidservant hadn't expected Lu Zezhi to say something like this. She raised her head in astonishment and glanced at him askance. "All right, I will pass on the message to the steward on your behalf."

"There's no need to go through the steward. Why do I need to go through the steward if I want to see Haiwang? Just go and bring him here!" Back in Horse-Face City, any of his servants would have been able to pass a message directly to Guan Shanjin, and no one would dare stop them. Lu Zezhi did not believe things were any different from before. Haiwang had personally taken him away from the wedding hall; obviously he must still love him.

The maidservant didn't waste any more time talking. She, too, was an experienced person. There was no point talking to someone who had fallen out of favor and was unwilling to face reality. She would just do what she had to do. There was no need to waste any effort persuading Lu Zezhi or explaining things to him, and this would prevent her from attracting any trouble to herself.

Seeing the maidservant leave with his instructions, Lu Zezhi still felt uneasy. He wrung his hands, vaguely understanding that the servant was not actually going to see Guan Shanjin, and she was going to pass his message on to the steward.

He didn't know if he would be able to see Guan Shanjin today. But what more could he do?

Lu Zezhi closed the window wearily. He sat by the table for a long time, his emotions unusually chaotic, but he had no other ideas.

It was only when his back ached from sitting too long that he jerked back to the present, gazing out of the window in despair. He gritted his teeth. He dressed himself up, wearing the same clothes as when he'd reunited with Guan Shanjin during the lantern festival. Without bothering to pull a jacket on, he walked outside in thin layers, leaving his footprints in the snow.

The snow quickly melted and seeped into his shoes and socks. Within a few steps, Lu Zezhi was so cold that his face went pale and his lips turned slightly blue. His thin figure looked like a ghost in the snow, the hazy winter sun casting golden light upon him.

This time, no one dared ignore him. As a matter of fact, there were two guards standing right outside his yard, and when they heard the sounds coming from within and they turned to look, his appearance shocked them so much that their expressions changed. They hurried forward, wanting to persuade Lu Zezhi to return indoors.

"I want to see Haiwang. I'm not going back until I see him." Lu Zezhi was so cold that his limbs were stiff, but he still stubbornly stood in the snow, his words slow yet clear. He knew that there was no turning back. If he did not see Guan Shanjin today, he would be trapped in this yard for the rest of his life.

"Uhh... Mr. Lu, I'll send a message to the general on your behalf right away. But it's far too cold outside. You should head back indoors and wait," the guard persuaded him gently. He turned around and gestured at his fellow guard. It seemed like they really were going to call Haiwang over.

However, Lu Zezhi's mind had never been this clear. He would not be so easily dissuaded. The matters of the Guan family army always went through Man Yue first, and Man Yue would then decide if there was a need to report it to Guan Shanjin. For a small matter like this, Man Yue would certainly prevent it from going any further.

Lu Zezhi was perfectly aware that Man Yue disliked him. If he went back to his room to wait, he would not get another chance. After all, Man Yue had all sorts of methods to allow him to live in comfort here—but he would no longer be able to take a step out of this yard.

Even if Lu Zezhi already found it painful to breathe, he refused to give in. "If I don't see Haiwang, I'm not going back," he insisted.

Mr. Lu was standing his ground for once. With no other choice, the guards hailed a servant to bring over some hot water bottles as well as to convey Lu Zezhi's insistence to Man Yue.

When he received the message, Man Yue was very annoyed. Why wasn't Mr. Lu just living his life quietly? Every now and then, he kicked up a fuss like this—what exactly did he want? Had he not reflected on his past actions at all? However, no matter how annoyed Man Yue was at Mr. Lu, he could not let the man freeze. He braced himself and went looking for Guan Shanjin.

As expected, Guan Shanjin had almost completely forgotten that any such person lived at his residence. If Wu Xingzi hadn't been right next to him at the time, it was hard to say if Guan Shanjin's heart would have softened at all.

In the end, Lu Zezhi had finally managed to get his long-awaited visit from Guan Shanjin. He was dressed in dark-colored fox fur, looking even more majestic and handsome than usual. But he did not come alone—he'd brought along a person who hadn't so much as crossed Lu Zezhi's mind in some time.

Although Lu Zezhi was holding onto a hot water bottle, he was frozen stiff. Unable to free himself from the support of the guards to go up and welcome the man, it took him some time before he noticed the man next to Guan Shanjin.

"Y-you... Why are you..." Lu Zezhi's teeth chattered, his blood running colder than snow.

Next to Guan Shanjin stood Wu Xingzi.

Lu Zezhi had forgotten this man's name a long time ago, but he could never forget that old, ordinary face, those small eyes, and those thick lips. The man had a friendly yet obsequious appearance. He looked comically cumbersome wrapped up in a robe of pure silver fox fur. He stumbled about in the snow as though he might fall at any moment. However, Guan Shanjin was very patient and gentle, walking with him slowly and considerately and supporting him with his arms. Guan Shanjin could not hide the affection and delight in his eyes. As he looked at the person in front of him, it was as if Guan Shanjin held the entire world in his hands.

No matter how foolish Lu Zezhi was, he knew what was going on. The man Guan Shanjin had been spending his time with this entire time was the old fellow in front of him!

"H-Haiwang..." Lu Zezhi could barely make a sound. A wave of dizziness washed over him, and a sense of panic he had never felt before rose in his breast.

"Teacher, why aren't you waiting inside?" Guan Shanjin finally deigned to direct a glance at Lu Zezhi, and then immediately turned back to Wu Xingzi. "You're getting cold, right?" he asked gently. "Shall I carry you the rest of the way?"

With Lu Zezhi's courtyard being deliberately ignored, no one had remembered to sweep away the snow in the yard. As a southerner, Wu Xingzi had great difficulty making his way through snow, and Guan Shanjin couldn't bear it.

Blushing, Wu Xingzi hurriedly waved his hands and refused the offer. "No, no, no, it's only a few more steps. I can do it." There were outsiders watching them, and he was not a child. How could he let Guan Shanjin carry him?

"Your shoes and socks are soaking wet already—you'll get sick." Guan Shanjin frowned. Ignoring Wu Xingzi's cries of alarm, Guan Shanjin lifted the older man up in a bridal carry.

"It's only a few steps, and carrying you is no trouble... By the way, did you lose weight again?" Guan Shanjin tested the weight of the man in his arms. "Why do you feel lighter?"

Wu Xingzi stiffened in embarrassment. "How could I lose weight?" he reasoned softly. "You, Mint, and Osmanthus have all been feeding me nonstop. And it's been so cold lately that I haven't gone anywhere, either. I've even gotten plumper around my waist."

"Why haven't I felt that at all?" Guan Shanjin lowered his head, nuzzling Wu Xingzi's nose with his. In his eyes, Wu Xingzi was very thin and weak. No matter how hard he tried, he could never fatten him up. He had to get some food into him now, while they were still in the capital. When they returned to Horse-Face City, he was going to get skinnier again.

"You hadn't made your way there yet," Wu Xingzi answered honestly, then realized what he had just said and quickly covered his mouth. In his embarrassment and alarm, he dared not look in Lu Zezhi's direction. *Ah! There's still outsiders around us!*

Red-eyed, Lu Zezhi could only watch the two men behaving affectionately, unable to do anything about it.

Guan Shanjin seemed to have just recalled that there was someone waiting for his attention, and he finally looked back at Lu Zezhi again. "You must be very cold, Teacher. Lao-Hu, why aren't you quickly helping Mr. Lu back to his room?"

The guard dared not move slowly at all now he'd been given a command. Half tugging and half carrying him, he dragged Lu Zezhi back indoors. Seeing the way this man foolishly gazed at the general, the guard sighed. "Mr. Lu, if it's not meant to be, don't force it," he said softly. "The general will protect your dignity."

Lu Zezhi could not accept the guard's words at all. Feebly, he pushed him away. "Who said you could speak?!"

The guard couldn't be bothered to talk anymore if he was going to get a reaction like that. He, too, had observed how the general had doted on Lu Zezhi in the past, and how Mr. Lu had put on airs. Not only did he play hard to get with the general, he even tried to cozy up to the Yue family. He was too greedy. How could he toy with a man like the general? Lu Zezhi deserved to be left with nothing. It was doubtful he'd get out of this with his dignity intact.

Guan Shanjin hurried inside, carrying Wu Xingzi. He did not care at all that his shoes, socks, and even the legs of his pants were all soaking wet. He carefully placed Wu Xingzi on a chair, then channeled his inner qi through his palms and warmed up Wu Xingzi's slightly frozen face. Once Wu Xingzi's face reddened with heat, Guan Shanjin instructed the guards to fetch people to send over new pairs of shoes and socks and to clear up the piles of snow in the yard.

Having given his orders, Guan Shanjin sat down and cuddled close to Wu Xingzi, almost plastering himself against him. He smiled at Lu Zezhi. "Teacher, is there any reason you are looking for your student today?"

"Haiwang..." Lu Zezhi's wet, thin clothes clung to him. Although he looked pitiful, with his lips purple from the cold and his eyes sparking with grief and anticipation, he was still an ethereal beauty. If he'd seen this sight a year ago, it would certainly have made Guan Shanjin's heart ache. But the past was in the past, and Lu Zezhi was unable to garner even the slightest trace of sympathy from the general.

Guan Shanjin sighed. "Teacher, your clothes are all wet. Why are you treating yourself so harshly in such cold weather? Why don't you change your clothes before we chat?"

Lu Zezhi gritted his teeth at the general's words. Stubbornly, he neither replied nor moved.

It was very warm in the room. Wu Xingzi had already removed his fox fur robe, and he noticed that the snow on Lu Zezhi's hair was melting and dripping down. The man looked both miserable and weak. Wu Xingzi wanted to help persuade him, but it occurred to him that Lu Zezhi probably disliked him, and so he closed his mouth awkwardly. He tugged on Guan Shanjin's sleeve, wanting him to persuade Lu Zezhi instead.

To his surprise, Guan Shanjin pretended to not notice anything. He had always been a ruthlessly cold person. There were only a few people he kept close to his heart, and he did not feel anything sincere toward anyone else. He only felt a great sense of disgust at this act Lu Zezhi was putting on—he was not in the mood to talk to him gently.

Lu Zezhi was much more familiar with Guan Shanjin's coldness than Wu Xingzi was. He stared in disbelief at the man who had once doted on him, who had once been so infatuated with him. He desperately searched for a trace of that past affection in the general's cold, even mocking eyes. Unfortunately, Lu Zezhi was fated to fail.

Guan Shanjin clearly had no patience to deal with him. "If you have nothing to say, Teacher, then I will take my leave. 'A teacher for a day is a father for life.' The Protector General's estate is still able to provide for the rest of your life. You don't have to stand on ceremony; you can just live here from now on. Once spring begins,

I will return to my duties in Horse-Face City. If you find it awkward to remain in the Protector General's estate during these days, just choose a place—I'll purchase a property for you. Rest assured that you will lack for nothing for the rest of your life."

Hearing this, Lu Zezhi felt as though his brain was exploding. He couldn't stop trembling. He had not expected this would be the conclusion to half a year's wait! Guan Shanjin was drawing a clear line between the two of them! How could he let this happen?!

"Haiwang! Did you forget who snatched me away from the Yue family's wedding hall? Who bound me to his side for so many years? Who was it who promised me we would spend the rest of our lives together?" Shaking, his eyes bloodshot, Lu Zezhi stood up, and approached Guan Shanjin step by step.

"It was me. I snatched you from the Yue family's wedding hall. I bound you to my side for over a decade. I was the one who did it all." Guan Shanjin laughed, the allure in his eyes so charming it could steal one's soul, but there was also a terrifying sharpness in them. "So you remember it all, Teacher."

How could he forget it? Lu Zezhi understood his scholarly skills weren't the best, and even if he tried his hardest, he could only amount to a private tutor in some unremarkable county. Before he met Guan Shanjin and experienced such a luxurious and extravagant lifestyle, he would have been content to while away his days quietly and peacefully. Why did life have to let him experience such sweetness? Why did Guan Shanjin have to entangle himself in his life? He was unable to leave! He could not let go of Guan Shanjin's gentleness or the riches and power the Protector General's estate could provide! If they wanted him to return to being a private tutor, they might as well...might as well...

"Are you angry with me?" Lu Zezhi choked out.

"For what?" Guan Shanjin could no longer bother to maintain a perfunctory respect for this ex-teacher of his. He knew that Lu Zezhi could not bear to let go of the riches he'd once enjoyed, but he did not expect the man to be so foolish.

"For refusing to give in to you..." Lu Zezhi turned away, averting his eyes, revealing a long and slender neck. He was like a stalk of green bamboo that could not withstand the storm, but kept proudly standing straight through it with great effort. One could not help but want to embrace him, to help shelter him from the wind and rain.

"Oh? Is that what you think?" Guan Shanjin smiled. Watching the man in front of him acting weak and meek disgusted him.

In the past, he did not mind favoring and doting on Lu Zezhi, despite knowing that Lu Zezhi only lusted after the luxurious and extravagant lifestyle he could provide. Lu Zezhi did feel something for him, but at the end of the day, his feelings couldn't hold a candle to his greed. And right now, although Lu Zezhi clearly knew his motives had been exposed, he still wanted to continue playing his act of unworldliness, trying in vain to regain the general's affections. As the Great General of the Southern Garrison, Guan Shanjin felt he was being taken for a fool.

"Haiwang, it's not that I'm not willing to accept you. It's just that relationships between men are still not viewed positively by society. I'm the only descendant left in the Lu family, and I cannot let my bloodline die off. I can't forget where I came from and show such disrespect to my ancestors!"

"What a coincidence—I'm also the only descendant of the Guan family." Guan Shanjin clapped his hands in laughter, but no amusement reached his eyes as he glared at the helpless and sorrowful Lu Zezhi.

Lu Zezhi was shocked to hear Guan Shanjin rebut him so impolitely. Panicking, he lifted his head to look at Guan Shanjin. The scorching gaze burning in those sharp, alluring eyes made his entire body tremble.

"Haiwang... You truly...do not miss our past affections?" Lu Zezhi asked, feeling sad and anxious.

Mr. Lu's pitiful image did not affect Guan Shanjin, but sympathy did swell within Wu Xingzi. "Mr. Lu, Haiwang..."

As soon as Wu Xingzi opened his mouth, Lu Zezhi shot him a harsh glare. He strode forward and slapped Wu Xingzi right in the face.

Lu Zezhi had clearly put all his strength into that one slap, and the power behind it sent Wu Xingzi tumbling from his chair. Wu Xingzi's cheek swelled. He was entirely stunned.

Guan Shanjin had never expected Lu Zezhi would have the gall to behave violently right under his eyes—and he had actually succeeded, too. The slap took the general by surprise, and he had no time to react and steady Wu Xingzi before he fell. His face darkened instantly, twisting into an expression so savage that he looked like a warrior of hell about to strip the man of his flesh and bones. Guan Shanjin grasped Lu Zezhi's throat and hurled him down to the ground.

Lu Zezhi's entire body shivered. He had yet to regain his vigor—that slap had taken nearly all his energy—and Guan Shanjin threw him to the ground without holding back. His vision turned black, and he nearly fainted. However, grasping onto his last shred of dignity, he managed to force himself to remain conscious. Still, he was so dizzy that he could not climb back up. He could only watch as Guan Shanjin helped up Wu Xingzi, who had yet to recover from the slap. Guan Shanjin treated him like a precious gem, daring not to even touch the handprint on Wu Xingzi's cheek.

Wu Xingzi had never been struck so harshly. He reached up, wanting to touch his face. However, the moment he touched that burning handprint, he jolted in pain. It was no wonder that one of the magistrates he'd worked under had liked to punish people by slapping their faces. Other than the embarrassment, it was also painful—a lot more painful than hitting any other parts of the body. His head spun, his ears buzzed, and his vision was a little blurry—Wu Xingzi had yet to process that the one who'd hit him was Lu Zezhi.

Guan Shanjin deftly helped him up from the ground, looking even more pained than Wu Xingzi, and lightly covered the swelling with his palm, clearly at a loss for what to do.

"I-I'm fine..." Wu Xingzi opened his mouth to speak, but the action of talking made him hiss in pain. The pain spread to his shoulder, and his eyes teared up.

"Shh, don't speak. I'm sure it hurts." Guan Shanjin's heart ached. At the same time, he was furious. He wrapped his arms tightly around Wu Xingzi, carefully avoiding putting any pressure on the injury. He wanted nothing more than to make mincemeat out of Lu Zezhi, but he was even more angry at himself for being so negligent. He had forgotten that even a trapped rabbit would bite when it had nowhere else to go. Lu Zezhi wouldn't dare behave so brazenly toward him, but he did have the audacity to vent his anger on Wu Xingzi.

"Lu Zezhi, because you have accompanied me for a few years, I wanted to leave you with your dignity, to assure you that all your life's needs will be fulfilled. And this is how you repay me?" Guan Shanjin carefully settled Wu Xingzi back into his chair. He did not look at Lu Zezhi at all as he spoke. His voice sounded so soft and gentle, almost as if he was speaking words of affection, but it made Lu Zezhi quake in terror.

The skin around Lu Zezhi's throat was so red and swollen, it looked like a rope had been tied around it. Guan Shanjin's murderous intent toward him was palpable, and it was likely he only held back for fear of scaring Wu Xingzi. Right now, every bone in Lu Zezhi's body ached, and his throat swelled so badly that he struggled to breathe. The croaking and wheezing of his every inhalation sounded like a pair of broken bellows. If he hadn't been supporting himself against the table, he would not have been able to stand at all.

Despite the current situation, Lu Zezhi was still unwilling to give up, and still unwilling to believe Guan Shanjin didn't want him anymore. Aggrieved, he cried as he stared at Guan Shanjin, tears slipping down his ashen face and pattering onto the ground.

They had been together for over a decade! The best years of his life were spent by Guan Shanjin's side. How could he just throw him away like this?!

"How can you be this heartless? I've never done you any wrong. And during your hardest times, I was the one who stood next to you! I was the one who helped you leave behind the harsh northwest! It was I who helped you live like a person again! And this is how *you* repay *me*?!" Lu Zezhi ignored the pain in his throat and finally gave up on his usual ethereal, haughty facade. Pointing at Guan Shanjin, he wept miserably. How could he *not* cry?

And oh, how he wished to give Wu Xingzi a few more slaps! Just look at how the old fellow was behaving right now, flinching and looking so pitiful—he was like an unwanted stray chicken, hiding under the eaves from the rain. What did he do to make Guan Shanjin fall for him? This old fellow had even been involved with other men!

"You didn't wrong me?" Guan Shanjin raised a brow. He burst out laughing, like he'd just heard the world's greatest joke. The laughter frightened Lu Zezhi. He bit his lip and braced himself, but he could not conceal his shivering.

Guan Shanjin's laughter came to a sudden stop. "Mr. Lu, my good teacher. Tell me again, you've never wronged me?" he asked gently.

Lu Zezhi hunched over reflexively, feeling guilty. He knew that Guan Shanjin was furious. The younger man was only waiting for him to give the wrong answer so he could deal with him. However... Lu Zezhi clenched his jaw. That one matter had been executed flawlessly—Guan Shanjin definitely knew nothing about it.

So Lu Zezhi shook his head. "The only time it could be said that I let you down was when I almost married the third young miss of the Yue family," he choked out. "However, you know that the person in my heart was always you, and I only wanted to marry Miss Yue to have a child. You can be willful and decide not to continue your family line, but I can't! Do you really still refuse to understand my struggles? Haiwang, can you blame me for not being able to trust the deep affection you speak about?"

These helpless, bitter, emotional words were truly moving. However, a faint smile curled around Guan Shanjin's lips; he still could not be bothered to even look in Lu Zezhi's direction.

The handprint on Wu Xingzi's cheek was severely swollen, but Guan Shanjin was applying a thin layer of ointment to it—the general had spent most of his life in the military and habitually carried such medicines on him in case of injury. The ointment carried a refreshing scent to it, and it was perfect for soothing the swelling and pain. Wu Xingzi's mental state also recovered a fair amount.

Guan Shanjin cupped the old fellow's face, examining it carefully. There was a tiny cut at the corner of his lips, so Guan Shanjin applied the ointment there as well. Thankfully, Wu Xingzi hadn't caused any further injury by biting his tongue or cheek. His inspection complete, Guan Shanjin exhaled in relief and pressed a few soothing kisses to Wu Xingzi's lips.

Lu Zezhi was so angry that his stomach hurt; he wanted to rush forward and tear the two of them apart.

"Haiwang!"

"Teacher, there's no hurry. I haven't forgotten about you." Guan Shanjin gave his teacher an indifferent glance before caressing Wu Xingzi all over again. Finally satisfied, he moved Wu Xingzi to a chair further away from Lu Zezhi and stood between the two men. It seemed like he planned on properly dealing with this situation right now. "Lao-Hu, get someone to bring in some tea and snacks."

"Yes, General." The guards had clearly heard the commotion within the building, but without explicit orders from the general, they dared not enter. They could only stand guard outside the doors, waiting. Lao-Hu deftly brought in the tea and snacks. Without looking at anyone, he placed the items down and ran out.

Before Old Hu closed the doors, he privately surveyed the situation inside. *Tsk, tsk, tsk. It seems Mr. Lu is really in for it this time! The general looks furious! Should I inform Vice General Man?* He decided to let Man Yue know; it would be prudent to prevent the situation from escalating to a point where it'd be hard to clean up.

A bizarre atmosphere filled the room.

When he saw the tea and snacks, Wu Xingzi's eyes immediately brightened. He had been utterly shocked from the slap just now, and he did need something sweet to recover. Although his face still hurt, the pain couldn't stop him from picking up a piece of jujube cake and nibbling at it with his front teeth.

Guan Shanjin picked up a teacup and drank from it, wetting his throat. "Teacher, I did things for you in the past because I wanted to. When it comes to who is in debt to whom, let's just let bygones be bygones. You yourself are aware that you used my affections to take advantage of my power and status. I can only blame myself for being blind." He did not plan on leaving Lu Zezhi with any semblance of dignity. In their relationship, things had been unclear on both sides—it was difficult to properly settle their debts.

Lu Zezhi opened his mouth, wanting to explain himself, but Guan Shanjin could not be bothered to listen; he decisively raised his hand to stop him from speaking.

His charming, keen eyes stared icily at his teacher. "However, since returning to the capital... Surely you're aware of what you've done?"

Lu Zezhi jerked violently. His eyes widened in disbelief, looking at Guan Shanjin as though he had seen a ghost. His lips trembled, and he let out an indistinct gurgle. The injury around his throat was too severe for him to speak. He had managed to shout a little just before, but right now, he was unable to say a word.

"I've been thinking... How did Bai Shaochang know the location of my secret study, and how to enter? He had only just moved into the estate, so when would I have ever let him into that room?" Guan Shanjin picked up his cup, skimming away the tea scum on the surface before sipping from it self-assuredly. "Say, during those years in Horse-Face City, did you ever enter my study?"

As for Lu Zezhi, he shuddered like a leaf in the wind, stumbling a couple of steps backward. He staggered and nearly fell over. Unable to make a sound, he could only shake his head. At first, it was a slow shake of disbelief; then, he shook his head so intensely that his hair was in disarray and his face went deathly pale.

"Don't shake anymore. Even if you shook your head off your neck, the things you've done will not vanish into thin air." Guan Shanjin's expression filled with loathing, and he tapped his long fingers against the table for a moment. "I never let you into my study in Horse-Face City, so why would I leave such a big hole in the capital and allow you to squirrel through? Lu Zezhi, if you want wealth and luxury, I can give it to you. The Protector General's estate can afford to support a useless person, out of consideration for the decade-long relationship we used to have. But why did you have to betray me and help Yan Wenxin harm us?"

It had been a test of Lu Zezhi's loyalty. Guan Shanjin wanted to know exactly how far Lu Zezhi, in his selfishness, would go, and so he'd deliberately worked with his mother to let Bai Shaochang agitate Lu Zezhi. Guan Shanjin wanted to see if Lu Zezhi would betray him if his position was threatened. What had happened next was terribly disappointing: Lu Zezhi actually took Yan Wenxin's bait and revealed the location of the secret study.

Tears rolled down Lu Zezhi's pretty face. He opened his mouth, wanting to explain, wanting to tell Guan Shanjin that he'd only been afraid of losing to Bai Shaochang. He was afraid that Guan Shanjin would not want him anymore, and he never had any intention of harming the Protector General's estate at all! He just didn't want to lose Guan Shanjin!

However, he couldn't say anything at all. With great difficulty, he finally managed to sound out a hoarse "Haiwang…"

At the sight of Mr. Lu's pitiful appearance, Guan Shanjin's heart softened a little. He sighed, standing up to support him. Lu Zezhi gripped his arms tightly and refused to let go, like a drowning man grabbing at driftwood.

"Teacher, I know that you only wanted to frame Bai Shaochang so he would be kicked out of the Protector General's estate, leaving only you by my side," Guan Shanjin said gently. Pityingly, he reached out and tucked Lu Zezhi's loose hair back. This was just the way he'd treated Lu Zezhi in the past, and it was like a thick glass of honey. It was so sweet that he was willing to drown in it, unwilling to leave.

Lu Zezhi nodded, hoarsely calling out Haiwang's name repeatedly.

"Lu Zezhi, I knew you weren't very smart, but I never realized you were this stupid." The general's tone was affectionate, but the words were icy and poisonous. Lu Zezhi instantly froze.

Guan Shanjin did not wait for him to recover. He shoved him to the ground. "You used the Protector General's estate in exchange for your future," he said, smiling, "but in the end, wasn't it all for nothing? As a weapon, you're easy to use, without any troublesome inconveniences. It's no wonder Yan Wenxin was willing to use you! If the Protector General's estate were to have fallen, who would help you continue your luxurious and indolent life, hmm?"

Lu Zezhi's mouth fell open, but he could not make a sound. He finally understood what a stupid decision he had made.

"Lu Zezhi, you'd better look out for yourself. Man Yue will arrange a place for you to stay. Don't ever show yourself in front of me again." Guan Shanjin took out a handkerchief and wiped his hands, as if he had touched something dirty; then he threw the used handkerchief into a brazier in disgust and let it burn into ashes.

Lu Zezhi stayed on the ground with a blank look on his face. He watched lifelessly as Guan Shanjin picked up Wu Xingzi, pushed the door open, and left.

"Haiwang—"

Lu Zezhi left the Protector General's residence without fanfare. He did not have another chance to see Guan Shanjin; Man Yue took care of everything.

Man Yue did not treat him harshly. He gave him a sum of money and bought him a property and a plot of fertile land back in his hometown. Even if he never taught again, he would be able to continue living off the rent from the farmland.

It was Wu Xingzi who happened to see Lu Zezhi depart. Guan Shanjin had been summoned to the palace by the emperor that day, and Wu Xingzi wanted to sneak out to buy some freshly made plum cakes. Just like that, they happened to bump into each other.

Lu Zezhi was no longer dressed in pure white. He wore a coat that was either gray or cream in color, and his face looked pale and his cheeks were sunken. The ethereal air he'd once carried was nowhere to be seen, and tiny wrinkles had appeared at the corners of his eyes. They were not obvious, but still visible. He looked so haggard that it was difficult to look at him directly.

He, too, saw Wu Xingzi, and his eyes fell straight to the place where he had slapped him a few days ago. The corners of his lips curled up in a twisted expression. Resentment and jealousy flickered in his eyes, as well as a thick layer of regret and resistance to his current situation.

Behind Lu Zezhi stood a pair of servants, a man and a woman, and there was an ox cart standing not too far away. The servants urged Lu Zezhi to get on quickly, saying that if they were to depart too late, they would not be able to reach the village to rest by evening. This winter was too excruciating to stay out so late.

Wu Xingzi opened his mouth, wanting to ask how Lu Zezhi was. He knew how much the other man resented him, but he personally did not feel much distaste for Lu Zezhi. No matter what, Lu Zezhi was the one who had helped Guan Shanjin emerge from the gloom left by the battles in the northwest.

Before he could ask, though, Lu Zezhi turned away, quickly getting into the cart. After greeting Wu Xingzi, the servants hurriedly drove the cart away.

Wu Xingzi watched the cart leave, lost in a daze for a while.

"Master?" Mint tugged at his sleeve. "Master, the plum cakes will already be out of the oven at Dainty Delights by now. If you don't go now, you won't be able to buy any. Shall we leave?"

"Ah... Yes, yes, we're going." Sighing, Wu Xingzi finally came back to himself, as if waking up from a dream. He looked at Mint and smiled. "Mint, say, am I too softhearted? I wonder what Mr. Lu's life will be like in the future."

"Don't worry about his future. He has nothing to do with you anymore, Master." Mint was not as softhearted as Wu Xingzi. In her eyes, Lu Zezhi was only reaping what he had sown. The general had doted on him so much, and yet Mr. Lu squandered all that affection away—as far as Mint was concerned, he completely deserved the consequences of his actions.

"That's true..." Although Wu Xingzi was softhearted, he was not illogical. After a few more sighs, he regained his spirits. He rushed excitedly toward Dainty Delights with Mint in tow, determined not to be even a second late—after all, he didn't want to miss out on the plum cakes.

Winter went by sweetly and peacefully. Taking advantage of his free time, Guan Shanjin twined himself with Wu Xingzi every day. Sometimes, after waking up and having breakfast, Guan Shanjin would nestle in the warm, toasty study with Wu Xingzi in his arms. Each of them would have a book in their hands, and on the tables next to them were tea and snacks. Reading and eating, they lazily passed the time together.

Guan Shanjin had ample time to prepare all three meals they ate each day. No matter how he looked at Wu Xingzi's figure, though, he was still unsatisfied. He worked hard making all sorts of supplements and food, until he'd fattened the old fellow up by two sizes. Wu Xingzi's cheeks finally rounded, and when tucked in Guan Shanjin's arms, he was soft and plump to touch. Guan Shanjin was finally satisfied.

The Protector General and his wife did not care that their son acted like his spouse's servant. Guan family traits were strong—no matter how frivolous and unrestrained they might be before settling down, once they truly fell in love, they wanted nothing more than to hang themselves from the other person's belt like a perfume sachet and follow them wherever they went.

Wu Xingzi spent his days comfortably. There was only one thing that worried him. He wanted to have a heart-to-heart conversation with Guan Shanjin many times, but whenever he found an opportunity to do it, he ended up flinching away.

As time dragged on, the new year came. This year, he was unable to return home to make offerings to his ancestors, but Guan Shanjin had already arranged everything. He sent people to Qingcheng County to make offerings on Wu Xingzi's behalf. Once spring began, they would head south and make their offerings again properly, and when they did, they would report their intentions to become life partners.

New Year celebrations in the capital were especially lively. On the last day of the year, nearing midnight, the sky was filled with brilliant, colorful fireworks. The glorious display featured images such as hundreds of children playing, springtime scenery, the four gods of good fortune, and butterflies flitting through flowers. It was a dazzling sight, beautiful and overwhelming.

Wu Xingzi's head tilted further and further back, his mouth hanging open; he couldn't manage to shut it. He even nearly stumbled, but thankfully Guan Shanjin reacted quickly and wrapped an arm around him before he could fall. Fortunately, when they admired the fireworks, both of them were seated on the ground, half reclined.

"Haiwang, I've never seen such pretty fireworks before," said Wu Xingzi.

The fireworks display lasted for an hour, and the smell of gunpowder hung indistinctly in the air. At midnight the sounds of firecrackers filled the streets, deafening yet delightful. Two strings of firecrackers were hung up outside the doors of the Protector General's estate as well, and they, too, were lit up. But Guan Shanjin and Wu Xingzi didn't walk outside to take a look. Instead, the two of them hugged each other, sitting in their yard as they looked up at the sky that was now dark again. It took some time before the stars slowly regained their light.

"Do you like it?" Guan Shanjin leaned down to place a kiss on the top of Wu Xingzi's head, and covered the two of them firmly with a big cloak. From afar, they looked like one person.

"I do." Wu Xingzi nodded. Reluctantly, he pulled his gaze away, shrinking into Guan Shanjin's arms and nuzzling against him. "This is our second New Year together."

"Yes..." Guan Shanjin chuckled softly as he thought back to the previous year. At that time, he and Wu Xingzi had not laid their hearts bare to each other, and he'd had yet to realize the depth of his feelings for Wu Xingzi. Why else would he have been so jealous that he tore up the pengornis pictures?

Holding the yawning, drowsy Wu Xingzi in his embrace, he swayed him a little. "I have something for you. Would you like to see it?" he asked gently.

"For me?" Wu Xingzi nuzzled his cheek against Guan Shanjin's chest, eyes full of curiosity.

Guan Shanjin had never been stingy with his presents, but he also would not seek approval deliberately. After all, to Guan Shanjin, it was no effort for him to gift such presents, so there was nothing much to say about it.

"I'm sure you'll like it." Guan Shanjin's lips quirked up slightly. Although he was smiling, Wu Xingzi could see some gloominess in his eyes. This piqued his curiosity even more, and his drowsiness vanished in an instant.

Lifting the older man up in his arms, Guan Shanjin stood up and carried Wu Xingzi back to their room. He tucked a hot water bottle into his hands to warm him up, then instructed him to sit properly on the chair and not run around. Then, he went to another room and rummaged about.

Guan Shanjin emerged carrying a red-lacquered wooden box. The box was exquisite, the red lacquer shiny and smooth. Gold threads were inlaid on the sides of the box, creating patterns of the flowers known as the Four Gentlemen—the plum blossom, the orchid, the bamboo, and the chrysanthemum. The images were tiny and delicate; the tiny blossoms on the plum tree were only the size of rice grains, yet even the hearts of each blossom could be clearly seen. It was as though real flowers had shrunk and been pressed directly onto the sides of the box.

The box was very pretty, but after exclaiming over it, Wu Xingzi grew puzzled. This sort of item was not something Guan Shanjin would deliberately mention to seek approval from him.

Guan Shanjin noticed the confusion in his eyes. "What I want to give you is not the box, but the things inside it." He laughed indulgently and pinched Wu Xingzi's fleshy nose, then opened the box, pressing it into Wu Xingzi's hands.

Within it was a pile of papers.

Wu Xingzi again looked at Guan Shanjin, bewildered. A note on top of the pile seemed to say something about drawings. Hesitating for a moment, he finally reached into the box and took out the pile of papers.

"This is..." Wu Xingzi gasped, his eyes filling with tears. Feeling both moved and grateful, he looked toward Guan Shanjin. "Haiwang, these are all...pengornis drawings?"

"Yes. There's a total of three hundred and sixty of them, and I've selected them from every region of Great Xia." Guan Shanjin was pleased yet frustrated. Seeing that Wu Xingzi was so touched that he'd started crying, he hurriedly stood up and wiped away his tears. "Why are you crying? Don't you like them?"

"I like them very much..." Wu Xingzi bobbed his head continuously. Afraid that his tears would stain the precious dick pictures, he quickly placed the three hundred and sixty drawings back into the box and closed the lid.

"Ah, Haiwang...Haiwang..." Wu Xingzi's interest in phallic illustrations had waned recently—he could not even remember the last time he'd looked through that treasured rattan case of his. He'd never thought that Guan Shanjin would still remember this embarrassing little hobby of his.

Wu Xingzi felt like his chest was bursting, but he could not say a thing. He had always been clumsy with words; all he could manage to do was softly call out Guan Shanjin's name again and again. There was nothing else in his mind but the man in front of him.

"I know that you like to look at these drawings. In the future, we can look at them together." Guan Shanjin cupped Wu Xingzi's face with his hands and kissed him, pulling the older man into an embrace. "We'll be together like this year after year, hmm?"

"Yes." Wu Xingzi nodded firmly, pledging his commitment. His heart was already full, so he no longer needed these pengornis drawings... But he was still a little partial to them anyway.

The sounds of the firecrackers outside ceased. All they could hear now was the sound of each other's breathing—of their hearts beating together, forever and always.

WEDDING

"WHAT HAVE YOU and General Guan decided on?" Rancui asked suddenly, pouring both himself and Wu Xingzi a cup of tea.

Wu Xingzi, who was in the middle of grabbing a plum from the plate Rancui had brought out, trembled. The plum rolled back onto the plate.

"Uh... What do you mean, decided on?" He blinked, his face flushing red, and his gaze started to drift.

"You've been together for two years now, right?" Rancui glanced at him, then huffed, pursing his lips. "I didn't want to mention it, but you can't just drag this on forever. As far as the capital's aristocracy are concerned, the Protector General's family is like a fatty piece of meat—it might be a little hard to chew, but everyone wants to take a bite. Despite Guan Shanjin's fickle and wicked nature, it's not impossible that someone might plot against him..."

Wu Xingzi sucked in a worried breath. "Does someone want to harm him?"

Rancui took a sip of his tea, then gave him an impatient glare. "Right now, the only person who could harm him doesn't have any such plans. Don't worry."

Wu Xingzi believed him. He patted his chest in relief. "That's good..."

After all, he knew Guan Shanjin had shown too much of his hand. Although the emperor had a part in all of this, in the end, it had all been down to Guan Shanjin's nature. He was too clever and too talented; he rarely took other people seriously. As far as Wu Xingzi knew, there wasn't anyone capable of successfully scheming against Guan Shanjin.

Seeing him so relieved pissed Rancui off. The fury in him kept growing, like a mother worrying about her disappointing son. He put down his cup, startling Wu Xingzi into shrinking in on himself a little.

Under Rancui's reproachful glare, Wu Xingzi silently put down his half-eaten plum and asked carefully, "Wh-what's...wrong?"

"I'm angry." Rancui pressed a hand against his chest. He glared at Wu Xingzi, who was looking down at his feet, with his beautiful eyes. "You and Guan Shanjin still aren't officially a couple yet. What will you do if someone tries to plot against him in the future? At that point, if you needed to bury him, you still wouldn't have a proper title!"

"Bury him?" Wu Xingzi suddenly gasped, then said hurriedly, "Didn't you say no one was out to hurt Haiwang? Why are we suddenly burying him?!"

"I was just saying." Rancui waved his hand, pushing the plums toward Wu Xingzi. "You must've thought about it at some point— but you don't want to think about it too hard. Guan Shanjin is still standing guard at the southern border. Although the Nanman aren't as fierce as the northwestern tribes, they're very stubborn. If they find any opportunity at all, they'll invade Great Xia. Guan Shanjin's position is not an easy one. He might be summoned to the battle- field at any moment. Aren't you worried?"

"I..." Wu Xingzi's shoulders slumped as he let out a long sigh. "Of course I'm worried." Which was why he didn't want to think about it too much. When Rancui had mentioned harm, he only thought of those people scheming in the capital, just so it would be easier on his heart.

"Think about it: If Guan Shanjin were to go into battle one day, wouldn't his family be completely exposed? With no one at home, what will stop someone from taking his place while he's gone?" Rancui coughed lightly, the subtext in his words obvious. Wu Xingzi froze, forgetting to chew on the plum in his mouth.

"But..." Wu Xingzi swallowed the plum, hesitating. "Haiwang has such complete control over his own estate as well as the Protector General's. And Man Yue and Steward Yuan are there to help. Who could possibly..." It was likely that if anyone even thought of attempting anything, Man Yue would chop their head in half.

Rancui had nothing to say to that. He glared at Wu Xingzi, angry but unable to do anything about it. Wu Xingzi truly was clever, but he could be slow on the uptake.

Rancui decided to stop talking circles around the subject. He should've known earlier that the best way to avoid rendering Wu Xingzi speechless was to be as straightforward as possible.

"I'm asking you... Don't you want to get married to Guan Shanjin? Do you want to go back to Qingcheng County to be buried all by yourself?" Rancui knew how much Wu Xingzi treasured his prize grave in Qingcheng County. He'd definitely be buried there in the future—no one could talk him out of it.

"Huh? Marriage..." Wu Xingzi froze, his mouth half-open. Then, he promptly choked on the plum in his mouth. He coughed alarmingly loudly, and it took him a while to recover. His face turned red, and his eyes shone with tears.

"Yes, marriage. Hasn't Guan Shanjin ever brought it up?" Rancui didn't believe it. Guan Shanjin was a cold man, but once he did care for something, he would stop at nothing to have it. Although Rancui really disliked the general, he couldn't deny that Guan Shanjin did genuinely love Wu Xingzi. He would follow through with his oath of only loving one person for a lifetime.

If that was the case, Guan Shanjin must want Wu Xingzi to have a proper title. He wouldn't want his beloved to suffer any injustice.

Wu Xingzi scrunched up his face with a sigh, then stammered, "I-it's not that he's never said anything... It's just...um..."

Seeing how Wu Xingzi kept stopping himself, Rancui grew curious. As a bystander, he knew the two of them were inseparable. They should've started wedding preparations long ago. It was odd that they'd dragged it out for so long that even Rancui was getting impatient.

Seeing Wu Xingzi's reaction made Rancui wonder if something else was going on. He hadn't wanted to meddle, but now he was interested. "Tell me and I can give you my opinion."

"Your opinion..." Wu Xingzi finished nibbling on his plum. He took a sip of tea before finally deciding to speak. "You should know that when it comes to marriage between two men," he said a little awkwardly, "it's usually the older one who prepares a betrothal gift and asks for the younger one's hand after observing all the proper rites and rituals..."

"So you want to..." Rancui, being as smart as he was, immediately understood. He paused for a moment, then laughed. "You want to ask Guan Shanjin for his hand in marriage!"

"N-not exactly. We're both men, so it's not exactly the same... Wait, that's not it, either... But I..." Wu Xingzi sighed. "When it comes to marriage, shouldn't I be doing my part too?" After all, he was going to be part of the Guan family in the future. Guan Shanjin wasn't just the Great General of the Southern Garrison, he was also the Protector General's sole heir. Even if Guan Shanjin had been a girl, Wu Xingzi would probably still be marrying into the Guan family and not the other way around.

He didn't have any problems with that, but he was worried this was a downgrade for Guan Shanjin. After all, no matter how you looked at it, Wu Xingzi was the one getting all the benefits here— Guan Shanjin was giving him everything.

"You want to be the one to bring it up?" Rancui immediately understood. He smiled at Wu Xingzi until the older man's ears turned red. "You're so thoughtful. What did Guan Shanjin do in his past life to be lucky enough to meet you?"

"Don't say that! We're both lucky to have met each other." Wu Xingzi smiled shyly, his mouth closed.

Rancui waved a hand, picking up a plum and crunching down on it. "Then why don't you just propose? I doubt he'll say no."

Guan Shanjin wouldn't dislike anything Wu Xingzi did. If Wu Xingzi had the courage to ask, Rancui was certain Guan Shanjin would happily accept.

"But...I..." Wu Xingzi sighed. "I only have fifty silver taels and a nice plot of burial land. Isn't that too little to propose to the Great General of the Southern Garrison, heir to the Protector General?"

"You were about to propose to Ping Yifan with your burial land," Rancui teased, laughing.

"Ah, that's not the same..." Wu Xingzi's face reddened. He truly had been far too bold with Ping Yifan. He was embarrassed just thinking about it now.

"Why don't you just ask? You can't keep delaying this forever. Guan Shanjin really cares for you. If you don't at least give him a hint, he'll never ask for fear that you don't want it." Then, Rancui pursed his lips. "Besides, it's not like you don't want to. You've already started saving for a betrothal gift."

Of course he had started saving! Wu Xingzi didn't have much money to begin with. Although Guan Shanjin gave him a monthly allowance, Wu Xingzi never wanted to take too much money from him. He kept meaning to return to Qingcheng County to be an adviser again so he could make some money for himself. He tried really hard to save these taels.

Not surprised that Rancui had seen through him, Wu Xingzi bashfully scratched at his face. "I wanted to wait until I had a hundred taels before I asked…"

"You sure plan ahead," Rancui sighed, begrudgingly respecting his stubbornness. "But I think it's better to hammer these things down earlier. Guan Shanjin attracts everyone everywhere he goes. There's bound to be some brainless idiot trying to hang around him."

"Really?" Wu Xingzi nodded, finally listening to Rancui.

He ate a few more plums and chatted with Rancui for a little while longer before he left.

As soon as Guan Shanjin entered the room, he could tell something was off.

The room smelled like both him and Wu Xingzi. Because Wu Xingzi spent a bit more time in here, his scent was slightly more prominent. It was gentle and subtle, with a hint of sweetness, and immediately calmed him down.

But today, while Wu Xingzi's scent was still very obvious, there was something else mixed with it. Guan Shanjin furrowed his brows and sniffed at the air, trying to figure out what it was.

At this hour, Wu Xingzi should be asleep. In the past, when he came home late, Wu Xingzi had tried to wait up for him, but he often couldn't stave off his sleepiness. Nine out of ten times, by the time the general returned home, Wu Xingzi was already off in dreamland.

Guan Shanjin didn't mind, of course. He loved watching Wu Xingzi while he was asleep. The old thing had a very ordinary appearance, but his fleshy nose was very cute. While he slept, his cheeks would flush, giving him a delicate, innocent look. In truth, neither of those adjectives suited Wu Xingzi, but still, Guan Shanjin's heart softened whenever he laid his eyes on him. This was the person he cared for the most—of course everything about him was pleasing.

He walked further into the room, still sniffing, and quickly realized what it was. But the answer did not provide him with any clarity; instead, he was even more confused.

It was the smell of alcohol—clear, sweet, and mellow in the throat. It was the wine he sometimes indulged in, Nine Pools of Spring. It tasted pure and sweet, but had a high alcohol content. He only dared to drink a little of it at a time so he would not suffer a hangover.

Right now, the smell of the wine hung heavy in the air, and it only grew stronger as he walked further in. Mixing with Wu Xingzi's scent, it smelled intoxicating... Guan Shanjin took a small breath in anticipation of what he would find.

As expected, in the inner room, several empty wine jars were scattered across the table. Some were crooked, and some had fallen over. There were also a few delicate dishes on the table, but shockingly, none of them had been touched. Even the prepared chopsticks and bowl were still clean. It was like Wu Xingzi had prepared all of this just to wait for him.

Guan Shanjin knew he'd told Wu Xingzi this morning that he had to attend the Left Administrator's banquet, and that there was no need to wait up for him.

Setting aside why Wu Xingzi would prepare wine and food to wait for him...where was he?

Guan Shanjin quickly surveyed the room. Neither of them liked extravagance, so the décor was quite simple. With a single glance, one could see everything inside. And yet there was no sign of Wu Xingzi. The old fellow had run off somewhere and left behind a room smelling of alcohol.

He must be drunk. The old quail was surprisingly unruly when inebriated. Guan Shanjin sighed in defeat, suddenly remembering that New Year he'd spent with Wu Xingzi in Qingcheng County. Wu Xingzi had gotten completely smashed, yet he still had Guan Shanjin utterly captivated. As for ripping all of Wu Xingzi's pengornis pictures in a fit of jealousy... Guan Shanjin would rather just pretend that never happened. After all, he'd suffered the consequences of his actions: He'd been forced to set aside his pride and go back to the owner of each cock to ask for a replacement drawing.

"Wu Xingzi?" There was no one next to the table or the window, nor was there anyone in the bed. Guan Shanjin walked over to the bed anyway and pulled open the blankets. He patted down the bedframe itself, too, to make sure no one was underneath.

"Wu Xingzi?" he called out again, but still no one answered.

Where could he have gone? Guan Shanjin grew worried. The Protector General's estate was very safe under his watch, but what if Wu Xingzi had fallen into a pond in a drunken stupor? As soon as the thought came to him, Guan Shanjin became so anxious that he could not stay put for a moment longer. He wanted to rush outside to look for him.

He'd only just turned around when he heard rustling from outside the window. Guan Shanjin darted to the window at once and looked outside. As expected, he saw Wu Xingzi on the ground under the window, completely sloshed. There was still a jar of wine in his hand as he stared up at the silver moon, lost.

This old thing... Guan Shanjin's heart settled back down into his chest, and now he had the peace of mind to tease him. "What are you looking at?" He sat down on the edge of the window, and his fingers were at just the right height to caress the hair at Wu Xingzi's forehead.

"I'm looking at...the moon," he said, hiccupping drunkenly. Regardless of how drunk he was right now, his voice sounded earnest.

"Why the moon?" Guan Shanjin asked.

"I'm thinking...did Haiwang go to the moon?" Wu Xingzi responded, staring straight ahead in a daze. He really looked quite intoxicated.

Guan Shanjin couldn't help but laugh. "Why would I go to the moon?"

"You have no idea... Haiwang... Haiwang... He's so beautiful, he looks like an immortal from the heavens..." Wu Xingzi raised the jar and took another gulp of wine—or at least, he tried to. Guan Shanjin could tell there was nothing left in there, but he still took a serious gulp.

"Oh?" Guan Shanjin covered his mouth with his fist in case he laughed out loud again. He could tell Wu Xingzi was feeling a little lonely, but more than that, there was a determination behind his eyes. Guan Shanjin couldn't tell what had stirred these emotions, so he just went along with it.

"Hey, hey... How should I go about asking an immortal for his hand in marriage? He's so good...so good..." Wu Xingzi sighed, then took another gulp of imaginary wine.

Marriage? Guan Shanjin wasn't expecting to hear that, and he didn't know how to respond. Sudden delight flooded into his heart, nearly washing out all rational thought. He stared at the old quail on the ground in disbelief with his beautiful eyes.

"Y-you want to ask Guan Shanjin to marry you?" Guan Shanjin's voice shook. He asked the question very carefully, as if afraid he was in a beautiful dream and any loud noise would shatter the illusion.

"I guess I'm not really asking him to marry me..." Wu Xingzi blinked. His brows were furrowed, and he looked somewhat distressed.

These words were like a splash of cold water. Guan Shanjin's face, flushed from delight, suddenly went cold.

"Wu Xingzi, you'd fucking better!" Guan Shanjin gritted his teeth. He wanted to haul the old man through the window and onto the bed and force him to say things he'd actually like to hear!

Wu Xingzi sighed. "We're both men, so it wouldn't really be asking anyone for their hand in marriage... We're just partnering up to have someone to spend the rest of our lives with... I have no talents, and the only thing I can do is be an adviser. If we do get married, I'll have to rely on Haiwang to provide..." He sighed again. "I feel indebted to him..."

Wu Xingzi never thought too highly of himself, nor was he needlessly prideful. Guan Shanjin was the Great General of the Southern Garrison, and in the future, he would inherit the title of Protector General. It was not an exaggeration to call him nobility. How could Wu Xingzi, a lowly advisor, provide for Guan Shanjin? If he were to compare their relationship to that of a heterosexual couple, he was definitely the housewife, and Guan Shanjin was the working husband.

The working husband…

Guan Shanjin understood Wu Xingzi's intentions, and his heart melted into a puddle. "Can't I be the one to take care of you?" He leapt out of the window and sat down next to Wu Xingzi. Reaching out to pull the older man into his arms, he said, "We're both men. You're the one sacrificing yourself for this relationship."

"No…" Wu Xingzi hiccupped again, then stared at the man next to him with narrowed eyes before asking, "You…Why do you look so much like Haiwang?"

"Who am I supposed to look like?" Guan Shanjin chuckled, tapping Wu Xingzi on the nose affectionately.

"You like to tap my nose like he does…" Wu Xingzi mumbled. He still hadn't figured it out, but his body recognized Guan Shanjin's; he pressed his cheek into Guan Shanjin's shoulder and nuzzled into him longingly. "I must've imagined you. That's why you're so similar to the real thing."

Guan Shanjin kissed his forehead and coaxed him in a deep, gentle voice. "If I came from your imagination, why don't you just take me for the real Haiwang and ask for my hand? You can pretend you're practicing for the real thing."

"You're right…" Wu Xingzi nodded in agreement. He had never been able to resist Guan Shanjin's tenderness.

"So what were you thinking?" Guan Shanjin asked impatiently, shaking Wu Xingzi lightly.

"I've already decided…" Wu Xingzi closed his eyes slightly. He put down his wine jar and started digging in his robes. "I'll tell you a secret: I'm actually saving up for a betrothal gift."

"A betrothal gift?"

"Yes…" Wu Xingzi nodded, finally finding his little wallet. It was different from the one he normally used. The fabric on this one wasn't very new, but it wasn't old or worn. It was clear he took good care of it, and it gave off the scent of camphor.

Wu Xingzi stroked the wallet gently, then brought it up to Guan Shanjin's face and shook it. His expression was smug. "There's fifty taels in here!"

"Fifty taels?" Guan Shanjin looked at the full wallet, his heart somehow melting even further.

"Yes... I wanted to save up a hundred teals, but Rancui said we shouldn't continue like this anymore. It was best to settle things so you could rest easy..." Wu Xingzi's expression was serious, and he even looked a little guilty. "It's my fault for only focusing on saving up for the betrothal gift and not thinking about you, Haiwang. Please don't blame me..." Wu Xingzi couldn't resist rubbing his face on Guan Shanjin's shoulder again.

"I won't blame you. I'm young. I can wait..." Guan Shanjin kissed Wu Xingzi on the forehead again. It felt like his heart was leaking honey; even his breath tasted sweet.

"No..." Wu Xingzi shook his head and held Guan Shanjin's hand earnestly. He put the little wallet into his palm, then closed each finger over it slowly. Then he wrapped his hands around Guan Shanjin's.

"Haiwang... Although I only have fifty taels, I still have that excellent burial ground. Would you be willing...to stay together, in life and in death?"

Guan Shanjin gripped that palm-sized wallet and stared directly into Wu Xingzi's anticipating gaze. "I'm willing... Of course I'm willing."

They'd already agreed to get married a year ago. But for some reason, Wu Xingzi had refused to talk about it again since then. Guan Shanjin always went with whatever Wu Xingzi wanted, so he'd never asked. As long as Wu Xingzi stayed by his side, that was enough for him. Whether or not they actually got married wasn't important.

It wasn't until now that he realized that he actually did care—he had just been too afraid to ask. He'd worried that if he sought it out, the answer would be the two of them parting ways.

So this was what Wu Xingzi had been planning all along. Guan Shanjin broke out into a bright smile. A gorgeous man smiling was already a beautiful sight, never mind grinning so radiantly. He was practically bewitching, and Wu Xingzi immediately lost himself in his eyes.

"Why are you looking at me like that?" Guan Shanjin asked, chuckling.

"Haiwang..." Wu Xingzi sighed, then reached for Guan Shanjin's shoulders to kiss him on the lips. Having been with him for years now, Guan Shanjin quickly picked up on Wu Xingzi's signals. The old fellow looked shy and bashful, but he was secretly salacious. Even if he was so drunk he didn't know left from right, he still knew how to set the mood.

"You old thing..." Guan Shanjin chuckled, then picked Wu Xingzi up. Climbing back into the room, he quickly stripped them both and got into bed.

"Haiwang... Haiwang..." Because Wu Xingzi was drunk, he was even less inhibited than normal. He kissed Guan Shanjin's lips, cheeks, and even his neck; his pale, delicate legs rubbed against Guan Shanjin as they wrapped around his torso. His delicate pink prick was already hard.

Guan Shanjin chuckled and reached down to rub Wu Xingzi's leaking erection. The roughness of his palm made Wu Xingzi's sensitive cock tremble, and he let out a soft cry. Twitching a few times, he came just like that.

"So fast..." Guan Shanjin laughed. He knew Wu Xingzi wouldn't be able to hold himself back much. The general himself was also quite eager, and he didn't want to stretch the foreplay out for too long. He held Wu Xingzi in his arms and kissed him thoroughly. Using Wu Xingzi's own cum, he started to poke and prod at the bud between the older man's buttocks.

"Ah!" Wu Xingzi cried out and tried to hide, but Guan Shanjin firmly held him by the waist. He quickly spread the fluid on his hand over his hole, making it wet and soft. When he slid two fingers inside, there was no resistance at all.

As his hand moved in and out, Wu Xingzi let out pitiful moans, then tightened his grip around Guan Shanjin's arms. His entire body began to shake.

Soon, the smell of sex filled the room. Together with the wet sounds and Wu Xingzi's moans, it truly set an erotic atmosphere.

"Haiwang... Haiwang..."

"Yes?" Guan Shanjin smiled and looked at Wu Xingzi gently. Pulling his fingers out, he lined up his hard cock at his entrance. "Good boy."

"Mm!" Wu Xingzi's hole was suddenly pierced through. His well-trained passage immediately swallowed down the thick, hot length as it entered him, but even so, Wu Xingzi could barely breathe. He threw his head back, his mouth open wide, but he could not make a sound.

Before he could catch his breath, Guan Shanjin clamped down on Wu Xingzi's hips and started to move, harshly, using a little too much force. He held Wu Xingzi down as he drove his strong hips forward in a series of savage thrusts. He rammed his entire length inside every time, making sure to brush against all the deepest parts of Wu Xingzi before he pulled back out again, leaving only the tip of his cock inside and then fully sheathing himself back in. His full, swollen balls slapped against Wu Xingzi's ass as he drove into him. In the blink of an eye, he had already thrust nearly a hundred times, fucking Wu Xingzi until tears dripped down his face. Wu Xingzi still couldn't catch his breath as he cried out in ecstasy. Once again, he came.

Guan Shanjin panted and leaned into Wu Xingzi's ear. "Does it feel good?" he asked with a laugh. But there was no answer— Wu Xingzi had long since lost his mind. His eyes were wide open but unseeing. Drool dripped from the corners of his mouth, but Guan Shanjin licked it back in, tangling their tongues together.

Wu Xingzi didn't even have the energy to struggle; his brain was like mush. He lay there limply and let Guan Shanjin have his way with him. With a shaking hand, he reached to touch his own belly. Guan Shanjin's dick was extremely long and thick; every time he reached that spot deep inside, a bump would appear on Wu Xingzi's stomach and his hole would leak fluid. But even so, the tears he cried were ones of pleasure. At first, he tried to match Guan Shanjin's thrusts, but after coming three times, he could no longer withstand it.

"Haiwang... Slow down... Hold on." He managed to beg for mercy, his voice hoarse.

Guan Shanjin lay on top of him, still thrusting. Although they weren't doing anything out of the ordinary tonight, somehow, he was fucking into him even deeper than usual. Wu Xingzi's flat belly soon protruded with the shape of the general's cock, even rubbing into Guan Shanjin's well-defined abs.

The bed nearly fell apart from their movements, but Guan Shanjin didn't seem to care. Holding Wu Xingzi, he sat up. With one hand on his waist and the other behind his head, he kissed the older man deeply, his tongue nearly reaching the back of Wu Xingzi's throat.

Meanwhile, his hips never stopped moving; his balls continued to slap against Wu Xingzi's soft buttocks, turning them red from the impact. The sound of Wu Xingzi's wet hole on his cock could not have been any filthier.

Wu Xingzi felt like he was about to be fucked to death. His eyes rolled into the back of his head as his entire body convulsed. His small cock had long since gone soft; he was no longer coming in spurts. Instead, fluid leaked out in a small, steady stream.

In his daze, Wu Xingzi vaguely heard a low chuckle from Guan Shanjin. His tongue hurt from being sucked on so much. Despite his inability to breathe properly, though, he still wouldn't let go of Guan Shanjin's tongue. His hole tightly held onto the large cock as it drilled into him.

"You greedy old thing..." Guan Shanjin laughed. The sound of his voice mixed together with Wu Xingzi's sobs and his own heavy breathing.

Since the old fellow was still capable of acting so salaciously, Guan Shanjin decided not to go easy on him. Gripping Wu Xingzi's waist even tighter, he pumped his hips harder, aiming for that spot inside.

"Ahhhh!" Wu Xingzi lost his mind, gasping like a fish out of water. He jolted and trembled as Guan Shanjin pounded the most sensitive parts inside of him. He put a hand on Guan Shanjin's shoulder, wanting to get away, but his strength was like that of a fly to the general. Guan Shanjin only pressed more firmly into his pelvis, fucking him so hard it felt like his prostate was swollen.

Crying and begging were no use; the man was determined to break him. His passage was just a sleeve for Guan Shanjin's cock. Wu Xingzi kept leaking fluids, and his ass was covered in bright red handprints, the sight nearly blinding. Guan Shanjin would soon render him useless.

His huge cock continued to grind deeply into Wu Xingzi's soft and malleable insides. Every twitching inch of flesh had been thoroughly fucked, and the bump of his prostate had swelled to the size of a soybean. Even so, Guan Shanjin's cockhead continued to press into it. Wu Xingzi couldn't even scream. His tongue hung out of his half-open mouth, drooling. Guan Shanjin fucked him so hard he could no longer think straight.

Wu Xingzi's twitching flesh tightly squeezed Guan Shanjin's cock. His body convulsed, and with a pitiful scream, he shook so hard Guan Shanjin nearly couldn't hold him. His little cock, caught between their stomachs, was only half hard. The slit opened and closed a few times as though something was coming out, but in the end, there wasn't even a drop of piss. Wu Xingzi's entire body tensed up one last time before he passed out completely.

Guan Shanjin held the unconscious old quail, panting heavily. He was almost at his limit as well. No longer willing to wait, he drove his cock into Wu Xingzi a few more times, thrusting so harshly it felt like even his balls would be squeezed inside. Wu Xingzi unconsciously struggled a bit, then tensed up again, twitching in the onslaught of Guan Shanjin's passion.

In the end, a stream of hot cum finally made its way into Wu Xingzi's belly.

The biggest news sweeping the capital in recent days was that the Protector General's heir, the Great General of the Southern Garrison, was soon to be married.

Homosexuality was not forbidden in Great Xia, and plenty of common men married each other. A marriage between two men was not any different from that between a man and a woman; they could even take concubines. However, the aristocracy did not follow such practices. After all, one of the greatest unfilial errors one could commit was failing to produce an heir.

Usually, a homosexual marriage was not a grand affair, as it wasn't something the nobility wanted to show off. That was what other people did, though. Guan Shanjin was different.

Everyone knew that this beautiful, handsome, powerful war god of Great Xia preferred men, and the Protector General's family line always produced faithful men who only took one life partner. Although the Guan family line had always only produced one heir, none of them had ever taken a second wife—or even another bed partner.

There was a saying that had been passed through the capital for years: "If you have to get married, you should marry the young Lord Guan." He was incredibly talented and tremendously beautiful. Plus, the emperor valued him. Many young ladies from noble families had their sights set on him.

So who was the lucky person who'd managed to climb on board the large, glorious ship that was the Protector General's family?

Regardless of how many rumors floated around the capital, this was the Protector General's private affair. No one had any plans to leak anything to the outside. After all, there were too many things to do when it came to a wedding.

Generally speaking, one could choose to either make it a grand affair or a smaller one. If each man planned on having a wife and family in the future, at least for the future of their family, they'd go the simpler route—performing the rites and rituals with just their families and choosing to live together. The older man of the two would even spend money for the younger one to get a wife, and he would also take a wife of his own to bear a son for his husband. These women were only there for the sake of having a child—the real couple was the two men.

It was different if it was made into a lavish affair. They would be written on each other's official family records, and they would never take wives. Instead, they would spend the rest of their lives together, just like a heterosexual couple would.

Guan Shanjin and Wu Xingzi chose the grander route, of course, and got ready to go through all the formalities. Since Wu Xingzi only had fifty taels and an excellent burial spot to his name, the Protector General's wife added another fifty taels, saying a full hundred would bring good fortune. Either way, they were going to be one family—the money would belong to both of them.

Guan Shanjin was delighted. Together with four of his personal guards and Man Yue, he started taking account of all his assets to calculate his dowry.

When Man Yue first heard of this, his eyes nearly rolled into the back of his head. *Dowry, my ass!* But Guan Shanjin was both his boss and his childhood friend. Who would he help if not Guan Shanjin?

"Would you like to embroider your own wedding robes, scroll, bedding, and veil, too?" Man Yue couldn't help asking as he counted out a trunk of little golden pigs.

"As if I need you to remind me," Guan Shanjin snorted. He didn't sound offended at all; instead, he sounded smug. "Xingzi said he'd prepare all that."

"Oh? The general's wife knows how to embroider?" Man Yue remarked, truly shocked. He knew Wu Xingzi lived by himself for many years, so he probably mended his own clothes. They did that often in the army, too. But embroidery was a whole other beast. Never mind his skill—where did he even find an embroidery teacher?

"He doesn't, but he wants to learn. He probably won't be able to make the robes, bedding, or the scroll, but he could at least attempt our handkerchiefs. My mother will handle the rest. Xingzi can just observe." Guan Shanjin chuckled; he was in a great mood. No matter whom he saw or what he heard, he could face it all with a bright smile.

Man Yue shuddered, his face scrunching up. He stopped talking to Guan Shanjin. Who wanted to hear his smug tone? But as he counted the little pigs, Man Yue couldn't help but smile. He truly was very happy for his boss.

The wedding plans continued without a hitch. Plenty of court officials tried to visit to get some clues, wanting to know who exactly had caught Guan Shanjin's eye. He was announcing his wedding to the world so loudly, he even let the emperor know. He was basically rejecting the possibility of any future children.

But obviously, these people failed to find out anything. Instead, they were invited to the wedding, then politely shown the way out.

As the days passed, all sorts of treasures were sent to the Protector General's estate. Silk, gold, jade, gems, tables, chairs, other furniture—the list was endless. Apparently, the Protector General even commissioned the most famous artisan in the capital to carve a table and chairs from fragrant rosewood, saying it would bring good fortune to the couple. It was clear how happy the Protector General was with this future son-in-law.

The storytellers in the tea houses stopped spinning their tales of legends and myths. Instead, they started telling stories about the general's wife. Honestly, they were quite entertaining, and they were so confident that their tales were true. Rancui thought that if he weren't involved, he might even have believed them. But this didn't stop him from bringing Wu Xingzi to the restaurant to have tea and listen to the storytellers.

"There was a clang! The general followed the sound. It was now midnight, and clouds covered the moon. If it weren't for the general's excellent martial arts skills, he might not even have been able to see where he was going. But the Great General of the Southern Garrison had once walked alone to the main tent of the Nanman, bringing back the enemy captain's head to hang outside Horse-Face City. So of course he could see who was making that sound."

"Did Haiwang really do that?" Wu Xingzi asked as he snacked on melon seeds, eyes bright.

This storyteller was quite talented. He made the listeners feel like they really were right there in the action. Wu Xingzi held his breath, wanting desperately to know who exactly the general had found.

"You can go ask him," Rancui lazily responded. He didn't like melon seeds, so when he listened to stories, he always snacked on pine nut candies. He stuffed two in his mouth, his cheeks puffing out.

"I have to." Wu Xingzi nodded repeatedly, looking like a little chick pecking at food.

On the other side of the room, the storyteller struck his mallet, grabbing everyone's attention. Wu Xingzi turned toward him too, forgetting all about his melon seeds as he stared at the storyteller with shining eyes.

"The moonlight suddenly shone through the clouds, landing on a thin figure. That person was like a white rabbit amidst snow. They had a pair of bright eyes, a delicate nose, and cherry-red lips. They stared shyly at the general... Stay tuned until next time!"

That was it? The customers of the restaurant were all lost in the story now; it felt like a cat scratched at their hearts. Wu Xingzi was no different. The general met his beloved—what was that person's background? Plus, this person was so beautiful! Clearly, they were a great match!

"You sure are carefree." Rancui pursed his lips, his expression disinterested. He wasn't actually here to listen to the story, but to annoy Guan Shanjin. If Wu Xingzi was upset by the story, Guan Shanjin would have to find something to cheer him up again. They were five days away from the wedding, and Rancui was sick of the smug expression on Guan Shanjin's face.

"Hm?" Wu Xingzi swept the rest of the melon seeds into the pouch hanging at his waist. He sipped on his tea, looking at Rancui in confusion.

"Ah, I don't know what I expected..." Rancui sighed. It wasn't as if he didn't know what Wu Xingzi was like. The old fellow would never get mad at such made-up stories. In fact, he thought it was quite fun.

Fine, Rancui thought. *We just came out for some fresh air.*

"Perhaps Mr. Lu will make an appearance?" Wu Xingzi asked excitedly. He was already planning on bringing Mint and Osmanthus tomorrow to listen with them.

Meanwhile, Guan Shanjin, who was still counting his dowry, suddenly sneezed. His nose turned red and he furrowed his brow. He looked around, confused. There wasn't any dust. Why did he suddenly sneeze?

"Someone must be talking about you!" Man Yue laughed.

Guan Shanjin couldn't be bothered to deal with him. Once he was married, there would be plenty of opportunities to get back at Man Yue.

The last five days passed in the blink of an eye. Soon, it was the day of the wedding. Nobody in the capital could contain their curiosity, squeezing into the street and hoping to catch a glimpse of the snowy, rabbitlike young master. Would he be as beautiful as the rumors said?

Wu Xingzi's home was all the way in Qingcheng County, so instead he stayed at the Man mansion the night before. After Guan Shanjin came to collect him, the two of them would circle around the capital before returning to the Protector General's estate to finish the rest of the ceremony. Since they were both men, they wouldn't use a traditional wedding carriage; instead, they chose a pair of beautiful horses.

When the time came, under the anticipatory gazes of the entire capital—commoners, aristocrats, and court officials alike—the gates to the Protector General's estate opened. Guan Shanjin walked out and mounted his horse with ease. One of his personal guards led the other horse, and the wedding procession made its way to the Man manor.

Dressed in his wedding robes, Guan Shanjin looked devastatingly, bewitchingly beautiful. He smiled, clearly in high spirits. Like a ball of fire, he was both scorching and mesmerizing.

Wedding music and the clopping of the horses' hooves could be heard from far away. About fifteen minutes later, they arrived at the Man family manor. Guan Shanjin jumped off his horse, and as dictated by custom, he knocked on the door. The crowd was desperate for them to complete all the rituals immediately so they could see this rabbitlike wife!

Finally, the general led a thin figure out. The onlookers could hear their hearts beating in their chests, their mouths going dry. They all wanted to turn into snake spirits just so they could use their long necks to get a good look!

Finally, the two walked out through the front door. The smaller person climbed onto the horse with the help of Guan Shanjin. He even wobbled at the top, flailing chaotically before he could steady himself.

That was when everyone managed to catch a good look...

Despite how many people were in the capital, it was silent enough to hear a pin drop.

A snow-white rabbit? Huh?! Sitting atop that horse was a thin man over the age of forty! He was skinny enough that he was practically drowning under his wedding robes. He wasn't ugly...but he wasn't pretty, either. Even his robes outshone him!

Everyone in the capital all had the same thought. *Is the general... blind?*

But no matter what the crowd thought, Guan Shanjin climbed onto his horse and held Wu Xingzi's hand. Affectionately, the two of them rode a lap around the capital together before they returned to the Protector General's estate.

They would spend the rest of their lives together; until death do they part.

THE ORIGINS OF YAN WENXIN'S LOVE – A BLESSING OR A CURSE?

Yan Wenxin stumbled forward. He only noticed that he was trembling when he picked up the brush and nearly dropped it. This brush had accompanied him for most of his career as Minister of Personnel. Whether it be messages to the emperor, orders to Huaixiu, or communications with Ping Yifan, all were written with this brush.

One way or another, his highest highs and lowest lows were all tied to this one brush...

"Ha..." Yan Wenxin looked down with a chuckle. Inside, he quaked with fear.

Yan Wenxin was born to a wealthy farming family—a family rich enough to be considered influential landlords of the area. He had an older di brother, an older shu brother, an older di sister, and two younger shu siblings, a brother and a sister.[2] He was a di son himself, and had been doted on by his father since childhood.

When Yan Wenxin first started school, his teacher discovered he had an eidetic memory and picked everything up quickly;

---

2 A man's children with multiple wives would all be considered their father's legitimate offspring. However, the children of the first or main wife (di children) were generally afforded preferential status over the children of other wives (shu children).

he predicted that Yan Wenxin would certainly do well at the imperial exams. Perhaps he could even become a court official.

Maybe the teacher had exaggerated a little to please his employers, but Yan Wenxin's father still felt very proud and held high expectations for his youngest di son. After all, the Yan family had been rich for two or three generations now; all they needed to raise the status of their family was for someone to become a court official. Yan Wenxin's older brothers were all of average intelligence—they weren't suited to academics or exams—so this hope of bringing honor to the family fell upon Yan Wenxin.

He worked hard. At nine years old, he passed the first level of examinations, and at twelve, he earned the title of xiucai. His future seemed impossibly bright; he was touted as a child genius in his village. Yan Wenxin's father doted on him more and more, bringing him all the finest things and the most sophisticated food and clothing. In his father's eyes, no other child in the family could compare. Even his eldest di son was miles behind Yan Wenxin.

Yan Wenxin studied at the local county school and always had amazing grades. His teachers only had good things to say about him. Some even secretly gossiped that the Yan family had a bright future ahead of them because Yan Wenxin would undoubtedly become an important court official and serve the emperor.

The Yan family resided in the town of Xingshan. It was not as well-developed as the nearby Goose City, but it was still one of the richer towns around. Because it was a little more remote, most people relied on farming or owning a small business to make ends meet. In the past few decades, Xingshan had only produced a dozen or so xiucai, and only two of these xiucai managed to make it to the next level and participate in the provincial exams. No wonder everyone thought Yan Wenxin was a child prodigy who would achieve great things.

Yan Wenxin also held high expectations for himself. As he studied more and more, his remote hometown slowly became too small for him. He thought of himself as a great swan, and all the people around him were endlessly gabbling ducks. He soon grew tired of them and wanted nothing but to leave his tiny hometown, to spread his wings and fly somewhere bigger and better. He threw himself into his studies and focused on nothing else. Relying on his father's love, he never had to lift a single finger when it came to eating, sleeping, changing, or bathing. His grades soared higher and higher; but unfortunately, when he took the provincial exam at the age of fifteen, he did not manage to pass.

When the news reached the Yan family, Yan Wenxin froze for a moment before letting out a shrill cry. Then, he fainted, leaving his family in a state of chaos. It took seven or eight doctors to bring him back to consciousness, and he spent months in bed before he recovered.

As he convalesced, Yan Wenxin constantly felt like his face was on fire. His father looked at him with disappointment, but he kept trying to force a smile while comforting his son. Just as horses slipped on mud, people made mistakes. He was only fifteen; no matter how talented he was, a failure or two was only natural. After all, with how large the world was, talented people were as common as the stars dotting the sky.

Everyone who came to see him had a mocking look in their eyes. Even the favored one had to fall to earth one day. The son of a duck would always be a duck—he'd never become a swan. They spoke comforting words with judgment in their eyes, and Yan Wenxin had to squeeze out a smile and thank them for their concern.

Yan Wenxin cursed the heavens; every day, he suffered through humiliation and indignity to the point of fury. It took him several months to fully recover.

But he was a determined boy. He had already fallen, and if he didn't get back up, people would laugh at him for the rest of his life. If he wanted to regain his pride, he needed to climb back up! In three years' time, he would retake the examinations, and he wouldn't suffer such a failure again. He'd force all those people mocking him to look up to him instead.

Two years passed, and the provincial examinations approached once again. Yan Wenxin was confident in himself. He knew he would succeed this time and become the youngest juren in the town of Xingshan.

However...no one could stop the weather. Rain poured down, falling harder and harder; it was as though a hole had opened in the sky for heaven's waters to spill onto the earth. After two days of relentless rain, the local dam broke. Rain and river water rushed toward the crops and houses. A dozen or so towns and cities were flooded instantly. A few of the smaller villages were immediately destroyed without a single survivor.

The flood lasted several days and nights. By the time the waters fully receded, nearly half a month had passed.

The town of Xingshan also flooded, and the Yan family didn't escape unscathed. Luckily, Yan Wenxin and his brothers all survived, but their parents were not as fortunate.

The brothers reunited in the temporary straw huts the government had built, and the future suddenly seemed bleak. The provincial exam was in three months. Yan Wenxin had already signed up, but he no longer had the money to go. In an instant, he'd gone from being the golden child to a young man with nothing to his name. The only things he had left were a book and a brush that he grabbed in a hurry while trying to escape the flood. He didn't even know how he'd managed to hold on to those two things this whole time.

It wasn't until after the flood receded that he found out his eldest brother had a special pack that their mother gave him. In it were a few property deeds and some precious accessories. It was enough for them to live on and rebuild the Yan family. Yan Wenxin was ecstatic! With this money, he could continue to study and participate in his exams. He could still become a swan and fly away from all these ducks.

But his brother wasn't planning on splitting the meager family fortune, nor on supporting Yan Wenxin in his studies. This was all that survived of the Yan family fortune—how could they squander it on a useless person who spent all his time studying and never worked? If their parents were still alive, perhaps they would've gritted their teeth and supported Yan Wenxin. But now...

His eldest brother had long harbored jealousy and hatred toward Yan Wenxin, so he made his intentions clear: If he wanted to live at home, he'd have to work just like everyone else to rebuild the family. No one was going to be a freeloader. If Yan Wenxin didn't want to work, then he'd give him a bit of money and he could go wherever he wanted. He might as well fully experience the life of a so-called starving student.

Yan Wenxin was a prideful young man; how could he bend the knee over a few coins? He took the money, made a clean break with his family, and headed off to Goose City all by himself. He found a simple house to stay in and swore that he would one day bring honor to his name. Someday, all the people who disrespected him would kneel at his feet and beg for forgiveness.

With no money and no family to rely on, Yan Wenxin went through the most difficult period of his life. His parents had always coddled him. Never mind making a living—he didn't even know how to take care of himself. If he hadn't met the young Advisor Wu, he might not have ever had the chance to partake in the exams in the capital.

He achieved the highest marks in the palace exam, and the Minister of Revenue chose him to marry his daughter. From then on, Yan Wenxin's life changed completely. He was a natural schemer, determined and ruthless. When others were good to him, he didn't always feel much gratitude—but when anyone wronged him, he never forgot it.

After he gained power, the first thing he did was get payback on his brothers, who were all still living in the village.

A few years ago, his eldest brother managed to bring the Yan family to about half its former glory using the little money their parents had left him. The town of Xingshan hadn't managed to fully recover yet, so the Yan family became the most influential family there.

Yan Wenxin was determined to destroy their success. How could he let his brothers live well? All those years ago, he'd been so poor that all he could afford to eat every day was plain rice porridge and some salty, sour pickles. If his academic achievements hadn't gotten him a government subsidy, he would've had to resort to begging or starving to death. His pride had been thrown on the ground and thoroughly trampled on.

Yan Wenxin never forgot this injustice; he'd make sure each of his brothers suffered the same way he did. He set out to slowly drain the Yan family fortune in various ways.

In the end, his brothers were forced to sell themselves as servants or beg on the streets. They were never able to return to their ancestral home, and no one ever mentioned the once glorious Yan family ever again.

Yan Wenxin finally felt vindicated. At the same time, he learned a lesson: To live in this world, you had to have both money and power.

With money and no power, you were nothing but a lamb awaiting slaughter. With power and no money, you were just a beautiful puppet waiting to be controlled. To truly succeed, Yan Wenxin needed to have both. He'd never let anyone have control over his life again.

Because of his outstanding scholarly talents, Yan Wenxin was favored by the emperor. It took him fifteen years to become the Minister of Personnel; as he gained more and more power, he gathered allies within the court. Occasionally he mused that if, one day, he really wanted to overturn the throne of Great Xia, he might even be able to choose who would sit on it next. At some point, he stopped caring about the emperor entirely.

Colluding with Nanman was really only the natural progression of things.

Nanman had plenty of valuable resources, but Guan Shanjin, who stood guard over the border, did not care about these advantageous assets whatsoever. As a border general, Guan Shanjin was a blessing for Great Xia. He was brave, skilled, and incredibly capable. He knew how to restrict imports and exports in order to control Nanman and instill fear in them, and as a result, he had total control over the border.

But a person like him was an obstacle to Yan Wenxin. Guan Shanjin was staring a pile of riches right in the eye but not allowing anyone to take it. This only fueled Yan Wenxin's determination to eradicate the Protector General's entire family line. In his opinion, even if Guan Shanjin wasn't stationed at the border, Nanman would never be able to cause much trouble. They weren't stupid; if both sides had something to gain through trade, there was no need to resort to violence.

More importantly, if Guan Shanjin were removed, Yan Wenxin could gain huge amounts of wealth from trading with Nanman as well as gain control over the general stationed at the border, which would allow him to hold military power. Then he would truly be in control of the entirety of Great Xia. Who would be able to touch him? Who wouldn't look up to him? Even the emperor would be a mere puppet in his hands.

But in the end, Yan Wenxin fell to Guan Shanjin and the emperor.

In prison, he carefully reminisced over his entire life: each deceitful scheme, each betrayal. He'd never felt an ounce of regret for making any of those choices. If he hadn't fought for his future, who would've cared for an orphan whose potential was being wasted by his own brothers? If he hadn't climbed his way up on a ladder built of other people's flesh and bones, he would've become a rung on someone else's ladder instead. He didn't regret any of it. Even if he had nothing now, he'd at least held enormous wealth and power before. At one point, no one in all of Great Xia could compare.

If he really had one regret, it was that he hadn't been ruthless enough. He tried to deal with the Protector General too late, and similarly did not control the man on the throne soon enough. Yan Wenxin should've isolated both of them two or three years ago, when he'd reached the peak of his power.

Unfortunately, there was no use in lamenting the past. If he had a second chance at life, he would not hesitate at the first opportunity.

His sentencing from the Ministry of Justice would be carried out as soon as spring arrived. The main conspirators in the collusion with Nanman—Yan Wenxin and his adopted son, Huaixiu—were sentenced to death by a thousand cuts. Yan Wenxin's two biological sons had come to say goodbye a few days ago.

Ultimately, the emperor was merciful and decided not to execute the entire Yan family. Yan Wenxin's two biological sons were to be exiled to the northwest as military slaves; they might never get the chance to return to the capital again. Whether or not they'd actually make it to the border alive was another matter entirely. The emperor appeared generous in this decision, but in truth, he was slowly wearing away at Yan Wenxin's pride and will. No matter how ruthless a man was, even a tiger looked after its cubs.

Yan Wenxin didn't have a single comforting thing to say to his haggard-looking sons when they visited him, nor did he look ready to shed a single tear. The two teenagers simply cried pitifully. They knelt on the ground for a long time without getting up. In the end, the prison guards had to drag them away.

After the cries of his sons faded into the distance, Yan Wenxin's brow creased. "What disappointments," he sighed. He had always been dissatisfied with his sons' meekness—how could he muster up any love or concern for them now? They were merely two people about to die in exile.

Winter came and went, and spring soon arrived. Although Yan Wenxin's days in prison were not comfortable, he did not suffer any torture. He ate and slept as he should every day. If he was bored, he meditated. He even recalled some of the books he'd read in the past on cultivating one's inner qi, and it really did have some effect. He lost a lot of weight, but he became a lot stronger. His complexion was flushed and full of life, not like that of a criminal in prison.

When spring came, Huaixiu was escorted in front of his cell one night. He knelt on the ground for a long time.

Although Huaixiu was young, his hair had turned white, and what could be seen of his skin was wrinkled and spotted. His hands looked like bones covered in a thin layer of flesh; clasped together, they looked like claws. "Haggard" wasn't a strong enough word to describe him.

Yan Wenxin watched his adopted son coldly, not saying a word, as though the person before him didn't even exist.

After a while, Huaixiu slowly looked up, calling out to him hoarsely, "Yifu... Yifu, I'm here to say my goodbyes..." By the end of his sentence he was wheezing, as though the sounds were coming out of an instrument with holes. His voice had long since lost its pleasing clarity.

Yan Wenxin finally furrowed his brow and said icily, "Oh...is it time?"

"Yifu, I have no way of repaying your kindness in this life. In the next life, I will do everything I can to repay you." Huaixiu still looked at Yan Wenxin with eyes full of respect and admiration. He'd never felt a sliver of resentment over the way he'd ended up in this situation.

Yan Wenxin studied his adopted son for a long time before sighing lightly. "Huaixiu, I know you are loyal to the Yan family. I wronged you in this life. Let's not meet again in the next one...or ever again."

Huaixiu froze at Yan Wenxin's words, not having expected him to say such things. He stared with eyes wide open, tears spilling forth. He desperately tried to lunge toward his father, but the guards held him back.

"Yifu! Yifu! Don't say that! Don't say that! I was wrong! I was useless! Don't be angry—don't be angry with me!" The words *or ever again* had shattered Huaixiu's soul. In the last six months he'd spent in prison, all he thought about was this last meeting with Yan Wenxin and how he would communicate his sincerity to his father. He never expected this was the response he'd receive... *Let's not meet ever again? Ever again?!*

Somehow, he summoned a burst of energy from his thin, weak body and managed to struggle out of the guards' grasp. He rushed to the bars of the cell and tried to reach in, but he couldn't touch even a corner of Yan Wenxin's robes.

"Yifu! Yifu! I was useless. Even if I have to be a horse or a cow in my next life, I will never let the Yan family suffer like this again. Yifu, please forgive me! Forgive me!" Huaixiu was so devastated it seemed he might cry tears of blood; the ends of his sentences sounded so hoarse that they were barely discernable. But no matter how Huaixiu screamed and cried, Yan Wenxin never said another word. He didn't even deign to turn and look at him.

Huaixiu cried until he shook all over, but the guards still dragged him away. His sobbing echoed through the stone walls of the prison, so pitiful that it could conjure up some sympathy in even the coldest of hearts.

Unfortunately, that did not include Yan Wenxin. He didn't even care about his own sons' lives, never mind this tool that had long since lost its usefulness.

Huaixiu's farewell did make Yan Wenxin aware that he was running out of time. In a few days, Huaixiu would be executed, and he would meet the same fate a few days after that. For some reason, Yan Wenxin didn't feel any fear; instead, he felt free, as if he'd let out a huge breath he'd been holding.

However, things did not go as he expected.

That night, as Yan Wenxin slept, he awoke for some reason. Upon waking, he was shocked to see a large man standing by his bed. Just as he was about to sit up and ask him who he was, a large palm covered his mouth.

The hand smelled even worse than Yan Wenxin did, and he'd been imprisoned for over six months. He could smell the stench of animals, as well as the scent of blood and violence. Yan Wenxin nearly choked, unable to breathe.

Yan Wenxin didn't struggle. He stared at the other men before his bed. They were all tall and large, their arms thicker than his legs.

Atop each man's head sat a large, messy braid, and nearly every one of them had a beard. Their skin was dark, slightly flushed, and very rough. The palm currently pressed to his face was riddled with scars, and they chafed a little as they rubbed against his skin.

These were definitely not people of Great Xia. If he had to guess, these were probably barbarians from the northwest. But why would they be here, in a prison inside the capital?

"Found him?" a man's low voice questioned from outside the cell. Yan Wenxin's view was blocked by a few men, so he couldn't see the speaker, but the voice sounded quite familiar. It carried a hint of a smile, like a needle wrapped in cotton.

"Yes." One of the men responded with a slight accent as he gestured for the man holding Yan Wenxin to tie him up.

"That was pretty quick." This time, the owner of the voice approached. He had a pale, round face, and he smiled as he stared at Yan Wenxin. Yan Wenxin's eyes shot wide open. It was Guan Shanjin's confidant, Man Yue!

"Oh, Lord Yan, it's been a while," Man Yue said. "You look...like you're doing well."

Yan Wenxin started struggling. What was going on? He wanted to ask, but the palm over his mouth pressed a little harder and nearly cut off his breathing altogether. He could not have been more afraid or shocked, but he dared not offend these men. He could only glare daggers at Man Yue.

"Don't stare at me like that, Lord Yan... Oh, wait, you're no longer Lord Yan, the Minister of Personnel. You're Yan Wenxin, Great Xia's criminal. Please forgive my mistake." Man Yue always grinned like a smiling buddha, but his sharp tongue could make people so angry that they wanted to rip him to pieces.

But right now, Yan Wenxin was a piece of meat on the chopping block. He couldn't even speak—how could he rip Man Yue apart? Although Man Yue had brought men from the northwestern tribes into the imperial prison, he was very relaxed. He didn't look rushed at all. Clearly, he hadn't smuggled these people in. Instead, someone... had given him permission to do this.

Yan Wenxin frowned. He was a dead man walking. Why had all these people gathered here so suddenly? They looked ready to take him away. He didn't recall having any unfinished business with them. After all, in the northwest, all that lay beyond the Yanhui Pass was frozen desert. There was nothing valuable to be found there, even if you dug up every inch of dirt. Of course he didn't want to get involved with the northwest, and he didn't want to offend them either.

Man Yue looked like he was in a great mood, and answered his unspoken question for him: "My master has already tried to convince the emperor, but the emperor doesn't want you to die still not knowing about this, so I have no choice but to pass along his message."

Message? Yan Wenxin had a bad feeling about this. He might have to face a fate worse than death by a thousand cuts.

"Listen carefully, criminal Yan Wenxin. The emperor says Great Xia needs to take a few years to recover, so we cannot go to war with any of the neighboring countries without good reason. We do not want the people to suffer. You know that only ten years ago, we fought against the northwestern Shatunu and just barely succeeded. Now, in order to avoid another battle, we can go the route of a marriage alliance...but as you are aware, the emperor does not have any daughters. Now, both Great Xia and Shatunu accept same-sex marriage, but we can't exactly give them a prince..."

Man Yue watched as the Shatunu warriors around him started laughing. Clearly, other than the person who spoke before, no one understood the language of Great Xia. As a result, Man Yue realized he didn't have to be so careful. "As they say, timing is everything," he said. "Life is just so unpredictable. You had just been arrested when the Shatunu Khan came to ask for a political alliance—they even asked for you specifically. The emperor thought about it and decided, why not? If it's for the good of the country, how could any citizen of Great Xia say no?"

How could Yan Wenxin not understand what Man Yue was saying? Clearly, the Shatunu Khan came to ask for his hand in marriage! The emperor wanted to marry him off to the northern barbarians!

Yan Wenxin's vision suddenly went dark, and he nearly passed out on the spot. He'd suffered a few humiliations and setbacks before. He'd once thought the most humiliating experience of his life was the first time he failed the provincial exam, and then when he was chased out by his brother. He worked so hard his entire life to ensure no one could control him; if anyone tried to humiliate him, he'd throw them into the mud and make sure they could never crawl back out. But clearly, the real humiliation had only just begun!

Yan Wenxin had once been the most powerful man in all of Great Xia. He was the Minister of Personnel, and he held the entire world in the palm of his hand. But in the future, he would be forced to please men...

Yan Wenxin paid no mind to the fact that he was tied up like a worm. He tried to wiggle his way to Man Yue to bite him to death, but the hands on his waist gripped him like metal clamps. If they exerted even a little force, he felt like his bones would break; additionally, his mouth was still covered.

So this was what helplessness felt like. For the first time in his life, Yan Wenxin's expression was defeated.

"Forget about Great Xia. Legally you'll be dead soon, but you aren't going to be slowly sliced to pieces in front of a crowd. Shouldn't you be grateful to your ancestors?" Man Yue gently tucked a stray strand of hair behind Yan Wenxin's ear, then lowered his voice and threatened, "You don't need to try to commit suicide, Yan Wenxin. We both know that as long as you can survive, you will do everything you can to continue living. Once you regain your bearings, I'm sure you'll try to find a way to convince the Shatunu Khan to deal with Great Xia. But you should do your best to behave. Only a truly cruel and vicious person would set their sights on you."

Yan Wenxin glared at Man Yue but did not refute him. After a while, he looked down, as though accepting his fate.

Man Yue ignored him, turning to say something to the one Shatunu warrior who knew how to speak the language of Great Xia. Then, the two of them clasped each other's hands in victory.

Yan Wenxin felt pain at the back of his neck and immediately lost consciousness.

When he woke up again, Yan Wenxin's head felt like it was splitting apart, and he was so parched that his throat burned. A layer of dry skin had already formed on his lips. He licked his lips with difficulty and felt a bit of pain. He wasn't sure when he'd last drunk any water.

After a while, he recognized that he lay in a cramped carriage. Through the thin wooden boards, he heard voices outside speaking the Shatunu language.

Yan Wenxin hissed in pain. He wanted to move, but as soon as he did, his head throbbed and his neck burned. If he hadn't been certain he was still alive, he would have thought he was a tortured ghost, the injury on the back of his neck proof of his execution.

Whoever was outside had very good hearing, because they immediately pulled the curtain open. A man gazed down at him, his head slightly tilted. "You're awake?"

"Mm—" Yan Wenxin wanted to answer, but his throat wouldn't allow him to form a sentence. He wasn't tied up, but he couldn't move. He flopped like a fish out of water, trying desperately to catch his breath in the carriage.

The man turned to say something to the others outside, then climbed into the carriage. He untied the waterskin on his waist and brought it to Yan Wenxin's lips. "Drink," he ordered.

The man's movements were very rough. Before Yan Wenxin could even fully open his mouth, he'd already choked on some water. He was so weak that he didn't even have the energy to cough. There was nothing he could do about the water trickling down his nose and throat, so he could only try to swallow some. Luckily, the man noticed him struggling and quickly removed the water pouch. He wiped Yan Wenxin's face with a sleeve that smelled like animals and hay, the rough fabric scratching Yan Wenxin's pampered skin.

"Th-thank you..." Yan Wenxin looked down, hiding the resentment in his heart. He knew the man before him wanted to torture him, but since his life was out of his own hands now, he could only submit.

In truth, Yan Wenxin was overthinking things. The Shatunu lived in a frozen desert. It was an incredibly challenging environment, and so for the sake of survival, all Shatunu people were soldiers. The women did not lose to the men. Riding, archery, hunting, fighting on the battlefield—Shatunu women were capable of all of these and more. In fact, there had even been female Shatunu generals. In their culture, women were most beautiful when they were strong and resolute. It was difficult for fragile, delicate women to survive in the harsh conditions of the northwest.

To this man, Yan Wenxin might have seemed more delicate than a Shatunu woman, but he was at least a man. If the khan hadn't warned them that the people of Great Xia were soft and weak and needed to be treated carefully, he wouldn't have even come to give him water or wipe his face.

"Are you hungry?" he asked.

Yan Wenxin still hadn't gotten up from the floor. The man was shocked by the weakness of the people of Great Xia. He carefully helped Yan Wenxin up and checked on the injury on the back of his neck. They hadn't drugged him, only hit him once before they left—he never expected Yan Wenxin to pass out for two days, or for him to be in such a sorry state upon waking. How had a nation of such feeble people managed to nearly eradicate them ten years ago?

The man picked up Yan Wenxin like a baby bird. Whenever his head moved, Yan Wenxin felt incredibly nauseated. If his stomach hadn't been empty, he might've thrown up all over the Shatunu man. He leaned against the side of the carriage weakly, listening to the noises outside. Struggling to overcome his nausea, he had absolutely no appetite.

"How long ago...did we leave the capital?" Yan Wenxin asked. He could hear vague hints of the Great Xia language outside, as well as the sound of horse hooves and carriage wheels. He guessed that they were still within Great Xia. It would take about three months to travel from the capital to the Yanhui Pass by carriage. The roads to the northwest only went as far as Long City. From there, one had to ride on horseback for five days to reach the

Yanhui Pass. He wondered if he could even survive the upcoming days.

"Two days," the man responded, brow still furrowed, and asked again, "Are you hungry?"

Yan Wenxin's stomach turned every time he heard the man say "hungry." He hadn't recovered from his bout of nausea, and his face was still very pale, but the gears in his brain were starting to turn. "What's your name?" he asked.

This man before him must've been the only person in their convoy who could speak his language. He knew he would not be afforded respect or obedience as someone who was about to become a concubine, but he had to at least establish some sort of relationship. He was completely unfamiliar with the Shatunu, so he had to use these three months to figure out a way to survive.

Just as Man Yue guessed, as long as Yan Wenxin was alive, he'd do his utmost to plan and scheme. One day, he'd exact revenge for all the misfortune and humiliation he'd suffered. They hadn't killed him this time; in the future, he would skin them all alive.

The man's brows furrowed some more, but he responded regardless. "Ge'an."

His name was easy to remember. Yan Wenxin smiled at him kindly. "Ge'an... Are you the only one who can speak my language?"

"Yes." Ge'an's brow stayed furrowed as he said, confused, "You haven't eaten in two days. If you don't eat something, you won't make it. I have some buns that you people like to eat. You probably won't want to drink kumis, but there's one more skin of water." Ge'an untied the waterskin he'd given to Yan Wenxin before and handed it over. Yan Wenxin didn't have the energy to take it, so Ge'an just laid it by Yan Wenxin's side.

"That *we* like to eat? Then what do you men eat?" Yan Wenxin's expression teemed with curiosity. He had to pretend that he didn't know Ge'an was keeping his guard up against him. He filled his tone with careful friendliness.

This confused Ge'an. He knew what Yan Wenxin was capable of, and he looked down on people who betrayed their own country, but Yan Wenxin looked too fragile and breakable to be so ruthless. He was easy on the eyes, both elegant and beautiful. Subconsciously, Ge'an lowered his defenses.

Besides, it wasn't like he couldn't answer Yan Wenxin's questions. His main duty was to take care of him. So Ge'an sat down cross-legged in the carriage and responded earnestly, "We mainly eat meat jerky, milk biscuits, and wheat pancakes. The rice and refined flours that you people eat can't be found in Shatunu. When we make it out of Long City, you'll have to eat what we eat."

"Really? I don't care that much about food..." Yan Wenxin smiled, lying through his teeth. He had been a court official for twenty years, and for the last ten, he'd held immeasurable power and authority; of course his food was as refined and exquisite as it could be. He'd never eaten unrefined barley, even when he was at his poorest.

Ge'an watched him calmly for a while. "Are all people of Great Xia as weak and delicate as you?"

Yan Wenxin froze. "Weak and delicate?"

"Yes. It's been two days since Woluhe hit you, and you look as good as dead. It'll be very difficult for you to survive in the north-west with how delicate you are. Even our women are stronger." Ge'an pointed to his own neck and shook his head. "And you won't eat. How are you going to recover? When you meet the khan, how will you please him?"

This question was far too straightforward. Yan Wenxin's face went red, then pale. In the end, he could only laugh bitterly.

"I just spent over half a year in prison, so I'm a little weaker than most. I apologize for being a burden—please forgive me." Seeing that Ge'an still didn't seem to trust him, he sighed outwardly yet clicked his tongue inwardly. "It's not that I don't want to eat. It's just that I haven't been eating much these last few days, and my stomach is not well. If I ate the buns, it might unsettle my stomach, so..."

"Then what do you want to eat? In four hours, we will reach a town. You can eat something there." Ge'an really couldn't understand the appeal of such a soft man. He didn't know what the khan saw in him. Praying to the gods was less trouble than dealing with this.

"It would be best if I could have some plain rice porridge." Yan Wenxin didn't want to suffer. He could tell the Shatunu Khan had probably instructed these people to treat him well, which meant he at least cared for him somewhat. He could take this chance to see exactly how much.

When he heard Yan Wenxin's request, some impatience showed on Ge'an's face, but he still nodded. "Got it."

As promised, once they reached town, Ge'an bought him a bowl of plain rice porridge as well as a few light dishes. Yan Wenxin was finally able to eat a hot meal, and the nausea dissipated.

While Yan Wenxin ate, Ge'an bought quite a few things. The carriage was simple and crude, and so, perhaps because Ge'an realized how delicate Yan Wenxin was, he brought back a few cushions and a blanket, as well as a side table for Yan Wenxin to eat upon. In a short while, the small, cramped carriage became a lot more comfortable. At the very least, Yan Wenxin could sleep restfully at night.

After settling into the cushions, Yan Wenxin thanked Ge'an sincerely for once. "Thank you."

"Hurry up and recover." *So you don't spoil the khan's fun.* Ge'an didn't say the last part, but Yan Wenxin could hear the implication anyway.

The rest of the journey was a lot more comfortable for Yan Wenxin. Perhaps because he looked like he had accepted his fate and didn't seem like he wanted to run away, Ge'an slowly let down his guard around him. He was happy to tell Yan Wenxin some things about the Shatunu. One day, he even warned Yan Wenxin, "The khan has five ancha, what you would call wives in Great Xia, and three anchun, who are like gongzi. But he doesn't have a hedui, which is what you'd call an empress. Of those, Ernu-ancha and Shuti-anchun hold the most favor. They were also born from the two most respected Shatunu families. After you enter the harem, remember to avoid them."

Ernu-ancha and Shuti-anchun? Yan Wenxin made note of those names and started asking about the power dynamics between the Shatunu families.

Ge'an did not respond immediately. He scrutinized Yan Wenxin for a moment, then stared into Yan Wenxin's eyes, as though he wanted to know why Yan Wenxin was asking such a question.

Yan Wenxin was a sly old fox, and he wouldn't let himself be discovered so easily. He smiled as though he wasn't bothered at all by Ge'an's probing gaze. He acted as if he had merely asked a casual question—that it would be fine if he received no answer. They were just having a friendly conversation. There was no need to insist on his innocence.

Perhaps because Yan Wenxin seemed so honest, Ge'an further let down his guard. He explained all the major Shatunu families: "We have nine major families, and each family is separated into smaller ones. Ernu-ancha is from the Na'erhe clan, and Shuti-anchun is from the Chaduoduo clan. Those two, plus the Wuhan clan, are competing rivals. Together, they are powerful enough to challenge the royal family. Na'erhe and Wuhan are both loyal to the khan, but the Chaduoduo clan has its own agenda. However, the khan is a god descended from the heavens. No one dares to start anything under his watchful eye. So you have to be particularly careful of Shuti-anchun.

"Right now, the khan has not selected a hedui, so the Chaduoduo clan is particularly set on it. A Shatunu hedui is a lot more respected than your empress. The khan discusses everything with his hedui. If Shuti-anchun becomes the hedui, the Chaduoduo clan will be able to sneak their power in."

Ge'an spoke the Great Xia language well, but he was still a Shatunu person. He couldn't go into more intricate detail. However, Yan Wenxin already understood. He couldn't help but laugh coldly inside. No matter if it was Great Xia or these barbarians, everyone still fought for power and their own advantage. Clearly, the reason the Shatunu Khan wanted a marriage alliance with Great Xia was because they could not afford to go to war with so much infighting going on. If the khan wasn't careful, he'd have a problem both with his enemies and at home. At the same time, the Shatunu had never fully recovered from that battle ten years ago. The khan's current situation was probably as precarious as the edge of a cliff next to a great abyss.

Although Ge'an said that the Na'erhe clan and Wuhan clan were loyal to the khan, how deep did that loyalty run? The Chaduoduo clan coveted the throne, but did the other clans not have a part in that as well?

Yan Wenxin had seen all sorts of plots and schemes in his life. He smiled lightly, already sniffing out the Shatunu Khan's weak points.

By now, they'd been traveling for more than two months. Soon, they would reach Long City.

The closer they got to Long City, the more Yan Wenxin felt that Ge'an was guarding him. Perhaps Ge'an was afraid he'd try to escape at the very last city before the border.

Hmph. He really was overthinking things. He, Yan Wenxin, was dead in Great Xia. If he stayed, he'd never be able to exact revenge for all the suffering and humiliation he'd endured. He might as well go see the Shatunu Khan. Although he didn't know what the khan saw in him, this was his only chance to get back up. Only a fool would let it go.

So Yan Wenxin pretended to not notice the change in Ge'an's demeanor, living his life peacefully under Ge'an's care and surveillance.

By the time they reached Long City, it was already early summer. Ge'an and a few of the other Shatunu men were clearly much happier. Evidently, the few months they'd spent in Great Xia had not been pleasant for them, and they probably weren't accustomed to the food, either. Ge'an often complained that the wine and lamb in Great Xia were tasteless, and that the people of Great Xia liked eating grass.

The road past Long City was not suitable for a carriage; riding on horseback was the fastest, most convenient way to travel. Yan Wenxin knew how to ride a horse—and besides, he'd been stuck in a carriage for a long time. Now that he could breathe some fresh air, feel the wind on his face, and see the expansive, majestic land around him, his mood lifted.

They rested in Long City for a day. The border soldiers had already received the secret order from the capital, so no one had any intention of stopping them; there were even carts of gifts from the emperor to the khan. As the representative, Ge'an was somewhat reluctant to accept the gifts, but he still felt a little smug.

Naturally, Yan Wenxin was not treated well by his fellow countrymen. News of his despicable actions had spread throughout the entirety of Great Xia. His sons were currently living here as military slaves, possibly forever. Ge'an clearly also knew that his sons were here, and he even kindly asked Yan Wenxin if he wanted to see them.

Yan Wenxin chuckled and rejected the offer. He had long since lost any affection for his sons. Now, they were nothing more than slaves and toys. It would be painful for them to see each other again, so what was the point? But outwardly, he had to pretend that he couldn't hide his melancholy as he replied. "I'll belong to the khan in the future. The children are still young and won't understand. I don't want them to worry."

Yan Wenxin's response showed some self-respect and backbone, which impressed the Shatunu man. His opinion of Yan Wenxin improved.

He had no idea that the actions of this seemingly harmless, elegant man were all carefully calculated.

The next day, they left Long City, heading toward the frozen desert where the Shatunu capital lay. After they left the Yanhui Pass, the scenery changed completely.

Even in the poor northwestern regions of Great Xia, one still saw signs of a flourishing country. But once they stepped into Shatunu territory, there was only desert as far as the eye could see, with only the occasional patch of grass. The wind wasn't cold, but it felt as sharp as a knife as it cut into the barren landscape.

It was early summer now, which Ge'an said was the best season in the desert. The grazing area for their animals was near the capital, so many people would gather there. Once it was fall, everyone other than the khan returned to their own territories for the winter. The smaller clans had to live wherever there was water and plants, so for the winter, they'd to rely on the capital or other larger clans for support—but there were some clans that had to survive the winter by themselves. Life was even harder for the nomadic clans. Every winter was a harsh test; if they couldn't survive, the only other option was death. The heavens were merciless.

They traveled as fast as possible, and, ten days after leaving the Yanhui Pass, Yan Wenxin finally arrived at the Shatunu capital. All the strength he'd recovered during the three months of traveling completely flew out the window over these last ten days.

Even though this place was the capital, it could not even begin to compare to Goose City. At most, it was comparable to Qingcheng County. The only thing impressive about it was its size. The roads and houses were large, and occasionally, a few luxurious tents appeared between the buildings. They spread out from the center in circles, and at the very edge stood a city wall. Its construction was unrestrained and free, giving it an ancient, primitive feeling. Outside of the walls were clusters of tents and animals. Many people gathered there, extending to the edges of the land.

Yan Wenxin took a glance and recognized that despite this chaotic gathering, there were indeed smaller groups of people, and they were all separated clearly—probably gathered according to their clans. He carefully memorized the flags of a few of the larger clans, planning on figuring out exactly what their relationships were to each other.

Yan Wenxin did not see any large, impressive architecture in this capital city, which left him confused. The Shatunu built this capital but did not create a palace? He soon found out why, though.

Ge'an and the others led him to the center of the capital. It was simply empty... No, that wasn't quite accurate, either. It was a large area with water and grass. A dozen beautiful, magnificent tents were scattered amid the grass, even more luxurious than the tents outside.

The largest tent in the very middle was nearly as large as two or three small houses. No matter if the tent bodies were round or square, all Shatunu tents had a round top. Something sharp poked out of each one, with smoke drifting out.

Ge'an led Yan Wenxin to the largest tent in the middle, guarded by several men outside. This was undoubtedly the khan's tent. When he saw the guards, Ge'an hugged them excitedly, patted them on the backs, and exchanged a few words with them. One of them glanced at Yan Wenxin, furrowed his brow, then walked into the tent.

"The khan is busy," Ge'an explained, turning to Yan Wenxin. "He might not see you today. But your residence has already been prepared. I will take you to rest up shortly."

"Thanks." Yan Wenxin's mood plummeted. He had come all this way to Shatunu, but he wasn't even able to see the khan on the first day. Clearly, the khan was setting an example—that he wasn't someone to be trifled with.

But the guard who entered the tent came back out quickly, confusion written all over his face. He said something to Ge'an, whose expression also morphed into shock. He turned to glance at Yan Wenxin.

"What is it?" Yan Wenxin asked. The men's actions reassured Yan Wenxin. The khan must want to see him, and this decision shocked everyone. This showed the respect the khan had for him.

"Nothing... The khan asked for you," Ge'an said, his tone hesitant. He couldn't stop himself from confirming this once again with his comrade. Upon receiving an affirmative response, he turned to Yan Wenxin. "Don't be frightened by what you see inside. To us, it's nothing, but as someone from Great Xia, you might be shocked and uncomfortable."

Ge'an was quite knowledgeable about Great Xia by now. The way he looked at Yan Wenxin was sympathetic, which only made Yan Wenxin wary. Ge'an clearly wasn't about to head in with him. He pushed Yan Wenxin gently forward and left.

The guards in front of the tent weren't planning on entering, either. They merely pulled open the entrance of the tent and signaled for Yan Wenxin to enter.

All this only served to make Yan Wenxin feel uneasy again. He was no longer sure of his previous guess. This was simply the tent of the khan, but it felt like he was entering a tiger's den. He hesitated, but the guards didn't urge him onward. They just stared at him calmly. The more they stared, the more nervous Yan Wenxin became. Ge'an had already left, and these guards didn't speak his language. He had no way of gleaning more information.

Muffled sounds came from within the tent, but he couldn't tell if these were the sounds of people speaking or not. It was just past three o'clock, so it was quite sunny outside, but the inside of the tent looked rather dim. The darkness and a thick, cloying smell made Yan Wenxin feel dizzy. He wasn't sure if it was the scent making his head spin or the fact that he hadn't eaten much for lunch.

Yan Wenxin had never feared anything in his life. Even when he was thrown in prison, with all evidence pointing against him, he had never cowered. He couldn't help but laugh at himself for his skittish behavior. If he was afraid of entering the khan's tent, how was he going to fight for a future for himself? *Yan Wenxin, think about the Emperor of Great Xia. Think about the Protector General. Think about how you landed here! Are you happy to accept all of this? Of course not!* He gritted his teeth and walked into the tent.

The guards lowered the tent's opening behind him. Taking a few steps inside, he realized the tent was not as dark as it seemed from the outside. Because of the opening at the top of the tent, plenty of areas within it looked bright and warm. The furniture inside separated different areas, and in one corner, five young women sat under the sunlight. When they heard his footsteps approach, they paused the embroidery and weaving work in their hands and looked up at him.

"Are you the anchun from Great Xia?" asked the oldest, most beautiful woman among them. She wore her long hair up on the top of her head and spoke with an accent, but her usage of the Great Xia language was articulate.

"Yes..."

Ge'an had told him before that "anchun" meant the same thing as "gongzi," but he knew that it actually signified a male wife. His face began to burn slightly.

"Ah..." The young woman studied him with her brows furrowed. "You look very weak. Can you really please the khan?"

The other women started to laugh. There was a hint of sympathy in their laughter, and Yan Wenxin almost couldn't maintain the expression on his face.

"I am Poyan of the Wuhan clan. The khan is waiting for you—go that way." Poyan didn't laugh at him. Instead, she eyed him with a kind of impatience. She pointed to a dividing screen hidden to the left.

"Thank you, Poyan." Yan Wenxin clasped his hands together in thanks, then walked slowly toward the screen. That faint fragrance he noticed earlier slowly grew thicker as he walked; it smelled so sweet that his head spun. Yan Wenxin could also clearly feel his muscles relaxing without his control, and his thoughts began to slow down... Was it an aphrodisiac?

Despite this presumption, he didn't stop. Walking around the screen, he saw a large bed covered in animal skins and furs...as well as two people intertwined upon it.

Yan Wenxin froze right beside the screen, his brain completely muddled. He couldn't look away no matter how hard he tried, completely astounded.

On the bed, a very tall, large, and muscular man lay on top of a comparably smaller person with smooth skin. The large man on top covered the person underneath completely; all Yan Wenxin could see was a pair of long legs clamped tightly around the man's strong waist, an arm tightly gripping the man's bicep, and half of a smooth shoulder.

The man's movements were harsh and powerful; each thrust elicited a sobbing whimper from the person below him. The legs around his waist tightly clenched his torso, and even the person's toes were curled. The pair of arms wrapped tightly around him the way a drowning man would grab onto the last piece of driftwood.

The sunlight filtering through the top of the tent was not as bright here as in other spots, but the muscles on the man's back visibly flexed with every thrust. They were strong, but not overly so, like a superb piece of craftsmanship. Simply looking at him made Yan Wenxin's throat go dry.

Because of the man's harsh movements, a thin sheen of sweat covered his body. Under the sunlight, it was as if he was covered in a layer of gold, making him look like a god…

The person beneath finally couldn't take it anymore and started to cry, as if begging for the man to be gentler. All they received in response was an even more violent plundering until they finally couldn't keep their legs around the man's waist any longer. They lay limply to either side of the man, twitching occasionally.

The man seemed to be nearing his peak as well. His thrusts were not as harsh as before, but they did go deeper, forcing broken moans and cries from the person below. Even the hand tightly gripping his shoulder fell to the furs on the bed.

Yan Wenxin watched all of this with a red face. This wasn't the first time he'd watched someone else have sex. Occasionally, the officials of Great Xia would throw debauched parties like this, and he'd attended a few. Every time, he thought the bodies twisting together looked like fleshy, ugly worms. After he became the Minister of Personnel, he never appeared at any such unsightly carnal banquets again.

But the sex occurring before him was unlike any he'd previously witnessed. Though he felt embarrassed, he was captivated by the man's godlike figure. He could practically feel each savage thrust right in his heart, and he could not tear his eyes away.

"Khan... Khan... *Ahhh!*"

With a few particularly harsh thrusts, the person below let out a broken scream. Yan Wenxin recognized the word he was scream-ing—*Khan*. Then, the legs on the bed twitched a few times before the person's entire body deflated from exhaustion. The man finally seemed to be satisfied and let go of his poor bedmate, then turned to look at Yan Wenxin.

Those eyes were fierce and held a beastly aura. In the sun, they were a dark, ocean blue, looking fierce and bloodthirsty, yet some-how calm. With one glance, Yan Wenxin felt the man sink hooks into his heart, and he lowered his gaze subconsciously.

The man...the Shatunu Khan chuckled from deep within his throat. Then, Yan Wenxin heard the sound of furs rustling, and a long pair of legs stepped onto the floor.

"Look up." The Shatunu Khan's voice was low and slightly hoarse, carrying a residual hint of satisfaction from his recent sexual activi-ties. It made Yan Wenxin's ears itch.

Yan Wenxin didn't want to look up. He hadn't heard the man put on any clothes, so he was probably still naked. These savages were such beasts—what a lack of propriety.

"Look up," the khan ordered once more.

Yan Wenxin was not a stubborn man. He knew what kind of situation he was in. Detecting the power in the khan's seemingly casual words, he decided to set aside his pride, looking up haughtily.

As expected, the man was naked, sitting on the edge of the bed. He clearly had just orgasmed, but his cock was still half hard and intimidating. The head was nearly as large as an infant's fist, and the veins looked thick and heavy. It was more impressive than most men's cocks; no wonder the person cried so hard when being pierced through. With how long that shaft was, he dreaded to imagine how deep it could reach.

After studying the khan's eye-catching cock, Yan Wenxin looked up at his face. The khan's eyes curved in a lazy smile, seemingly very pleased by the fact that Yan Wenxin chose to look at his cock first.

Yan Wenxin was shocked to discover that the Shatunu Khan was still very young. He must have been around twenty-five. Though he looked tough and weathered, he still seemed as dangerous as a freshly sharpened blade. He looked like he could kill with a single touch, making everyone fear him.

No wonder the Chaduoduo clan only set their sights on the hedui position, and not something more foolish.

"You've lost some weight," the khan remarked as he leisurely sat at the edge of the bed. Yan Wenxin felt like he was being stalked by a predator on the hunt.

"Thank you for your concern." Yan Wenxin wanted to look down to avoid that forceful gaze. He felt like he was being licked by a lion's rough tongue after getting stripped naked. He could barely resist the urge to run away.

"Come here. Let me take a better look at you." The khan put one thick, muscled leg on the bed, making his cock jut out even more.

But he didn't seem to care. He rested his wrist on his knee and stroked his jaw.

Yan Wenxin couldn't hide his frown. What did the khan want? To humiliate him? Or did he truly want to look at him more closely? What was going on with his weirdly familiar attitude? He had no memory of ever laying eyes on this man before.

"Come here," the khan called again.

Even though it was an order, it somehow made Yan Wenxin tingle. He trembled, feeling even more guarded toward the person in front of him. This young khan was decidedly not a man to be trifled with. If he tried to control him without a careful plan, he might get his claws pulled out. He had schemed a lot on his journey here, but he'd underestimated the khan.

Yan Wenxin couldn't just stand there. The khan didn't even try to hide the mockery in his smile. Yan Wenxin knew that if he didn't react soon, he wouldn't have the chance to anymore.

Without any other choice, he took a few steps forward. This bedroom-like space wasn't very big, and there was such a large bed in it—with just a few steps, he could clearly see each pore on the khan's face. The scent of photinias blended into the sweet fragrance in the tent, so strong that it almost hurt to smell. He reflexively sneezed a few times, making the khan laugh.

"Already can't take it anymore?" the khan asked as he gripped Yan Wenxin's chin, spreading his fingers over his throat. The rough drag of his fingers made Yan Wenxin shudder.

"You've sweated a lot just now. You should put on some clothes so you don't catch a cold," Yan Wenxin urged in a soft voice, his eyes still downcast.

"I smell. How uncomfortable would I be if I put clothes on?" The Khan laughed, pulling Yan Wenxin forward by his chin. Once they were pressed together so closely that their breaths intermingled, the khan said softly, "I like your mouth. It's a pretty mouth, and you have such a way with words. The first time I saw you, I knew I wouldn't be satisfied until I stuffed something in there."

Stuff something in there? Yan Wenxin's eyes grew wide, but he was too close to the khan. Once again, he found himself lost in those calm yet vicious blue eyes.

"Kneel," the khan demanded, his voice like that of an ethereal deity.

Yan Wenxin could not muster up any will to resist. His knees landed on the ground between the man's legs. By the time he realized what he had done, his face was right up against the man's half-hard cock. He could see each and every vein, and the thick scent of it filled his nostrils.

"Put it in your mouth."

There was no need to specify what he was to put in his mouth. Yan Wenxin shuddered, wanting nothing but to run away. He knew he was here to be the man's toy, but he had never expected he'd have to swallow such a fierce, ugly thing right upon arrival!

The khan was faster than him. He placed a hand on Yan Wenxin's shoulder casually, but it felt as immovable as the mountain that sealed the Monkey King. He could not budge, and he was forced to bend down a little more. His lips drew closer to the khan's cock than ever before; he could feel the heat emanating from it.

A scholar could be killed, but he could not be humiliated! Yan Wenxin refused to be pushed down. He stared up furiously at the khan. Whether or not he'd have to swallow this thing in the future was one thing, but he certainly wouldn't do it now! The khan had just pulled it out from inside another person. If Yan Wenxin really did put his mouth on it, he couldn't fall any lower. Never mind exacting

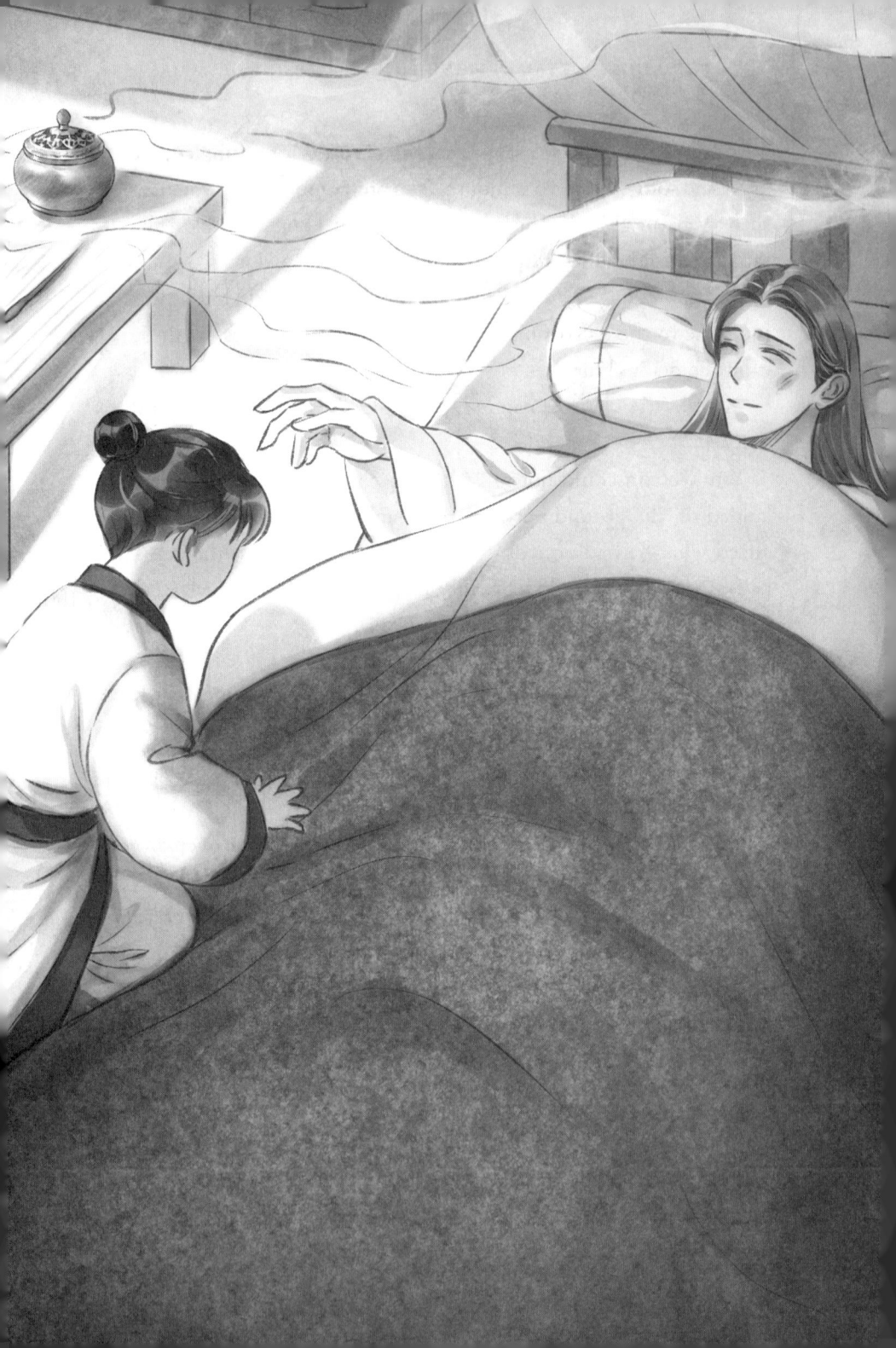

revenge on Great Xia—he wouldn't even have any status within this tent! This man before him really wanted to humiliate him.

The khan was not angered by his resistance. He repeated himself patiently: "Put it in your mouth." His words were calm, but the hand on Yan Wenxin's shoulder told a different story. It felt as heavy as a ton of bricks, as if trying to break his proud, unbending back.

Yan Wenxin still refused. His nostrils filled with the man's scent as well as the pungent aroma of photinias, making him dizzy and nauseated. If he were to live on, he refused to do so without self-respect.

"If you won't do it yourself, I'll do it for you." The khan made the words sound practically romantic, but Yan Wenxin couldn't stop shaking. The unspoken threat was clear—even if the khan had to kill him or injure him, he'd stuff his cock down his throat regardless. In order to protect his last shred of dignity, Yan Wenxin had no other choice.

"Thank you for being merciful."

Yan Wenxin quickly made his decision, no longer resisting. From the khan's standpoint, he looked well-behaved and obedient, like a courtesan used to servicing men. The only thing that gave away his unwillingness and resentment was his trembling hands.

The khan's cock was huge and feverishly hot. In order to guide it into his mouth, Yan Wenxin held it in his hands. It felt like a white-hot iron; the heat made him hesitate and muddled his thoughts.

He opened his mouth to take in the man's huge cockhead; it felt like his lips were about to tear before he managed to fit it inside. He had no idea what to do next. He was over the age of forty, but he and his wife had always treated each other with respect. In bed, they'd never done anything extreme, so of course mouths were never involved. For his reputation—and because he thought it was a hassle—he never took any other wives or women. He was quite adept at controlling other people's emotions, but when it came to sex and love, Yan Wenxin was like a blank piece of paper.

"Use your tongue."

Obediently, Yan Wenxin licked the thing in his mouth. A salty, musky flavor spread on his tongue. Instinctively, he wanted to spit it out, but the khan was one step faster, pressing down on the back of his head. The khan's grip was tight, and he had no way to escape. He could only continue to lick the huge cockhead in his mouth, humiliated, and try to swallow down more of the shaft.

"Lick it clean." The khan's voice was still gentle, making Yan Wenxin tremble. Despite his placid tone, his hand maintained a forceful grip on Yan Wenxin's head. In fact, he pushed him down even more. Soon enough, the khan had forced the man between his legs to swallow half of his length, and he grunted, almost as if in pain.

Yan Wenxin had no choice but to try to work his tongue. The khan's cock only grew harder as he licked. Soon, it poked against the roof of his mouth, pressing down on his tongue so that he could no longer move it. He could sense the man's dissatisfaction as a large hand suddenly gripped his jaw. Together with the hand on the back of his head, the khan held Yan Wenxin in place as he roughly shoved the rest of his cock into his mouth.

"*Mmph!*" The veins on the man's cock relentlessly rubbed against the sensitive roof of Yan Wenxin's mouth; then, his delicate throat was forced open. His throat bulged, the outline of the khan's cock clearly visible from the outside. Yan Wenxin gagged, unable to control his reaction. He tried to shake himself off, pushing against the khan, but the other man was too powerful.

To the khan, Yan Wenxin was barely stronger than an ant. He pulled back a bit, but before Yan Wenxin could take a breath, he forced himself back into his throat again. The khan delighted in the feeling of being tightly wrapped in a soft, smooth sleeve of flesh.

Yan Wenxin didn't even have the energy to bite down. After several thrusts, his tense throat reluctantly gave in. He continued to gag, his throat not losing any of its tightness, but the khan was able to move freely now. The man took great pleasure in each thrust, his eyes narrowing in bliss. He trailed his hand down Yan Wenxin's neck and wrapped it around his bulging throat, rubbing his own cock through Yan Wenxin's skin.

"Mmm... Nngh..." Yan Wenxin gasped like a fish out of water, struggling feebly. He could only utter a few broken sounds as the khan mercilessly toyed with him. His throat felt like it was about to be pierced through by the khan's rough thrusts, and his chin turned red as the other man's heavy balls slapped against it again and again.

Yan Wenxin's mouth was forced open so wide that he couldn't swallow. As the cock slid in and out, his saliva and the khan's fluids dripped down the corners of his mouth. Soon, his chest was soaked. The sounds of flesh slapping against flesh and the man's pleasured sighs filled the entire tent.

Yan Wenxin soon grew dazed from the fierce movements of the shockingly large cock in his throat. Most of the precum slid directly into his stomach, and his tongue had long since gone numb. Even that unpleasant flavor was bearable now.

What was left of Yan Wenxin's consciousness seemed to leave his body. It felt like he was staring at all of this from the outside. He mocked himself viciously: *You want to regain power? You want revenge on Great Xia? Look at you—even the lowest of prostitutes have more dignity!*

Suddenly, burning hot liquid filled Yan Wenxin's mouth. The khan had recently orgasmed, but he still shot out a shockingly large amount. Yan Wenxin coughed continuously, choking on the khan's cum; some even spurted out of his nose. Most of it, however, went straight into his belly. He didn't even get to decide whether or not to swallow.

It wasn't until he swallowed everything that the khan pulled his dick out of Yan Wenxin's mouth, satisfied. He wiped away the remaining wetness on Yan Wenxin's face.

Yan Wenxin, having finally been released, flopped over on the floor in a daze. His state could not be sadder. For a while, he didn't even dare to breathe heavily.

"Your mouth does not disappoint." The khan bent over to hook a finger under Yan Wenxin's chin, then swiped again at the come and spit spilling from his lips. Softly, he said, "Lick it clean." Before Yan Wenxin could catch his breath, the khan pried his mouth open and stuck his finger inside, shoving it almost all the way back to his throat. Yan Wenxin hurriedly lapped at the finger with his tongue, afraid of missing a single drop.

The khan fed him the fluids that remained on his face, which all tasted salty and bitter. Yan Wenxin felt a deep hatred in his heart, but he knew he had no other choice than to service this man.

"Good boy," the khan said, patting Yan Wenxin's face. He pulled him over to kneel between his legs, cushioned by his thighs. "I like the way you look now. Ge'an will take you to your quarters later. In order for you to feel more at home here, I've prepared two small gifts for you. I'm sure you will appreciate them."

Yan Wenxin lay against the khan's legs; all he could see was strong, firm muscles. He could barely breathe. He'd never felt so tired. All he wanted was to crawl into bed and sleep. Once he woke up, he'd have the energy to think about the next steps in his plan.

It didn't seem like the khan had any intention of toying with him further. That beauty who had passed out from being fucked earlier still lay on the bed. Now, the person let out small mewling noises, as if nearing wakefulness.

"You can go. I'll go see you in the evening." The khan pulled Yan Wenxin up from the ground easily and didn't pay him any more attention. He turned back to the person on the bed, saying something to them with a smile.

Yan Wenxin was about to leave, but he was curious who the other person on the bed was. He remembered Ge'an telling him that the Na'erhe clan's Ernu-ancha and the Chaduoduo clan's Shuti-anchun held the most favor with the khan. They were both top picks to be the hedui, especially since the Chaduoduo clan particularly coveted the position. But Ge'an hadn't mentioned the third largest clan: the Wuhan clan. Clearly, no one from the Wuhan clan had been a part of the khan's harem before—but things could've changed in the last few months.

Earlier, one of the women waiting outside said she was Poyan from the Wuhan clan...so the person on the bed was likely from the Wuhan clan as well. He had to see what they looked like. Now that he was here in the harem, Yan Wenxin needed an ally. Ernu-ancha and Shuti-anchun already held their own authority. He expected the Wuhan clan must desperately want to break apart the carefully established balance of power.

The beauty on the bed sat up lazily. That was when Yan Wenxin realized it was a young man, about seventeen or eighteen years of age. His flawless skin looked pink and tender, and his hair was a slightly lighter shade. In the sunlight, it was a light brown color.

The soft strands spilled over his body, as striking as silk. His misty eyes hid behind a layer of fog. He seemed as innocent as a fawn, but somehow still charming and seductive.

Even with such beauty, his bare upper body was still covered with muscle. The smooth, flowing lines looked soft, but he clearly didn't lack in physical strength. His arms looked as strong as willow branches; he could easily have made a great archer.

The young man also noticed Yan Wenxin. Blinking his misty eyes in curiosity, he asked something in his own language. Yan Wenxin froze and didn't answer, but the khan laughed. "He's from Great Xia—you can speak to him in that language."

The youth snorted lightly. "You're the anchun from Great Xia?" he said haughtily. "I've heard of you. You committed many crimes against your country. You're not a good person."

No matter how sly and cunning Yan Wenxin was, he couldn't stop himself from furrowing his brow at this blatant disrespect from such a young man. He quickly lowered his head to hide his expression and explained in a resigned tone. "The emperor of Great Xia has always given many explanations when it comes to his enemies. There is the saying, 'when one loves something, one wants it to live; when one hates something, one wants it to die.' Since the emperor has no use for me, he wanted me dead."

Hearing this explanation, the khan abruptly burst into laughter. The youth looked at the khan in bewilderment, trying to understand what Yan Wenxin had said. His grasp of the Great Xia language was only rudimentary, so it took him a while to parse more difficult concepts. Even after some time to take it in, he still couldn't understand why the khan had laughed.

Yan Wenxin, however, knew very well why. The khan's carefree laughter felt like mockery. He wasn't going to fall for Yan Wenxin's version of events. Clearly, he knew exactly what he'd gotten up to with Nanman. Did the khan ask someone to research Yan Wenxin specifically, or had someone betrayed him?

Either way, Yan Wenxin knew the khan only saw him as a plaything. Although he didn't know when he'd caught the khan's eye, he doubted there were any feelings involved—only a carnal desire to conquer him. The most important thing right now was to figure out how he would survive in this harem.

As soon as the khan stopped laughing, he waved Yan Wenxin away. "Yan Wenxin, you can leave. This little Wuhan youth isn't someone you can manipulate. Behave yourself in my harem, and don't forget that you're already a dead man in Great Xia." It sounded like a cold warning, but the khan spoke it with an amused smile. Yan Wenxin didn't linger for a moment longer; he glanced at the khan and left with his hands clasped together.

Walking around the screen, Yan Wenxin saw Poyan still sitting there with her embroidery. Hearing his footsteps, she looked up with a slight crease to her brow, but she didn't say anything. She pointed her chin toward the entrance of the tent.

He wasn't a man with status anymore, so no one took him seriously. Yan Wenxin smiled as he bowed toward her, then walked quickly to the exit of the tent. As soon as the guards outside saw him, they turned to call for Ge'an.

Ge'an quickly appeared before Yan Wenxin, and he even changed the way he addressed him. "Yan-anchun, please follow me."

"Thank you."

Yan Wenxin's tent was a little further away from the khan's. They passed by several clusters of tents on their way. In the end, they arrived at a group of little tents the size of a hut, their roofs edged with a grassy green color. In total, about twelve or thirteen tents were gathered here.

When he looked closely, a few of the larger tents had two smaller tents beside them, like the side rooms in the architecture of Great Xia. The large tents were spread a distance apart, but not too far away. It almost seemed a little desolate. Of these dozen or so tents, only half appeared to be occupied. It seemed that the unfavored members of the khan's harem lived here.

Ge'an led Yan Wenxin to a tent with a particularly bright green roof. "Yan-anchun, these are your quarters. Your servants are inside, so please head in."

As soon as he finished speaking, Ge'an turned to leave. Yan Wenxin hurriedly said, "Ge'an, thank you for taking care of me on the journey here. I will repay your kindness in the future."

"No need. I merely did as the khan asked," Ge'an responded flippantly. Before Yan Wenxin could react, he vanished.

Yan Wenxin was stunned, feeling a sudden helplessness well up inside his heart. He stood there for a while. It wasn't until he felt the gazes of his neighbors watching him that he walked into the tent, embarrassed.

The inside of the tent was a lot larger than it appeared on the outside. Everything he could need was already here, and the décor looked nothing like what he saw in the khan's tent. Instead of the usual style of the border tribes, everything held the elegance and intricacy of Great Xia. If it hadn't been for the furs on the bed, Yan Wenxin could almost have felt like he was back home. The table, chairs, wardrobe, mirror, shelves, and dividing screen were all the type he'd normally use. He even saw the calligraphy brush he'd used for many years hanging on the brush rack on the desk.

Yan Wenxin stumbled forward. He only noticed that he was trembling when he picked up the brush and nearly dropped it.

After a few attempts, he finally managed to hold it in his hand, observing the bristles and the handle under the sunlight filtering in through the rooftop. It looked so familiar to him.

The brush's purple-black bristles were fashioned from a wild hare's fur, glistening and as smooth as water. Despite its many years of use, the tip was still sharp and retained its flexibility. The handle was made from a special kind of bamboo. It had a magnificent, antique look, and the wood was as dark as ink. Because of how long it had been used, the wood glistened and shone with a patina.

This brush had accompanied him for most of his career as Minister of Personnel. Whether it be messages to the emperor, orders to Huaixiu, or communications with Ping Yifan, all were written with this brush. One way or another, his highest highs and lowest lows were all tied to this brush...

"Ha..." Yan Wenxin looked down and chuckled. Inside, he trembled with fear. Judging from the décor and this brush, the khan had put a lot of thought into setting up his tent. But this gift was also a knife to the gut—it was a warning to him that the khan knew everything that had happened in his past. It would be incredibly difficult for him to start any new schemes.

No wonder Guan Shanjin had never sent anyone to kill him on the way. No wonder the emperor was willing to spare his life and throw him to the Shatunu. It turned out the man he was facing wasn't someone he could control at all, and the people in the capital knew it.

"Did you think this would stop me? Ha ha ha... How many times have I been humiliated in my life? Have I backed down once? Just wait," Yan Wenxin vowed in a low voice, gripping the brush in his hand tightly. "Even as your plaything, I will make sure you never know peace!"

As he lost himself in his thoughts, the tent opened and a familiar voice called out, "Father...no, Yan-anchun, this lowly one is here to pay his respects."

This voice was so familiar that Yan Wenxin thought he'd heard it wrong. He hurried to look back, suddenly remembering that the khan said he'd prepared two gifts for him. If one of those gifts was the brush, then the other was... Cold sweat poured down his back, and he couldn't control the shudder that shook his body.

Two silhouettes stood outside the tent. They were both shorter than Shatunu men, appearing to be people of Great Xia. They were as gangly as willow trees, but those faces...

"You..." It was his sons, Yan Sinian and Yan Rixin! Yan Wenxin was so shocked that he dropped his brush. He never thought he'd reunite with his sons in this northern desert. This gift was...far too heart-wrenching!

The father and his sons did not burst into tears or comfort each other upon their reunion. Other than shock, Yan Wenxin felt some disgust. As for Yan Sinian and Yan Rixin, their expressions looked empty, as though they didn't know how to act around their father.

The two brothers looked a bit delicate. They were both wearing clothing of the Shatunu people, but the apparel was clearly too large for them. Hanging loosely on their frames, it made them seem even more weak and helpless. Their skin was already a little red from all the wind and sand, and they looked almost nothing like the rich young masters they'd once been. In comparison, Yan Wenxin was doing well—perhaps even too well. He had gotten skinnier, but his complexion still held a healthy flush. He wore his Great Xia clothing, so he still looked rather elegant and refined.

Yan Wenxin looked away, bending down to pick up his brush, then sat down at the table.

"Why are you two here?" he asked. His sons must have had a hard time in such a cold, desolate place. He regretted bringing them up in the lap of luxury. He hadn't raised them to be more capable and ambitious because he was afraid they'd be hard to control, but now he wished these two sons had more ruthlessness, so they wouldn't drag him down.

When they heard their father's question, they both shivered slightly. They looked down timidly, a red tint flooding their cheeks.

"Speak." Yan Wenxin knocked on the table impatiently.

Yan Sinian was a little older, so he responded, stuttering, after taking a few deep breaths: "F-Father... No, Yan-anchun, we... The khan asked for us from the northwestern army."

How could Yan Wenxin fail to understand the meaning hidden behind those words? He snorted.

"It's not that simple, is it? Tell me, who were you two given to?" The Shatunu men might prefer strong, muscular lovers, but everyone had their own tastes. His sons were attractive enough for some people.

Yan Sinian and Yan Rixin looked up at their perfectly composed father in shock. Their lips trembled as they struggled to respond, perhaps out of shame, or perhaps because they hadn't expected their loving father to be so heartless and blunt.

"Seems like I was correct. You two are now also... Hah, these Shatunu men..." Since they were all whores now, no one was more noble than anyone else. Yan Wenxin's twisted heart felt more at ease. "In that case, we don't need to address each other as father and son anymore. We don't need to bring any more shame to the Yan family. Don't call me Yan-anchun in the future. Call me Laoye..."[3] He sighed. "It's my fault this happened to you two." Yan Wenxin let his head fall into his hands.

---

3   A term of respect usually used for the master of the house, generally an older man.

His sons were still young and had always looked up to their father with respect. Seeing how distraught he was, they hurriedly kneeled down on either side of him.

"Father, don't say that. You were loyal to Great Xia. The emperor only placed the blame of what that bastard Yan Huaixiu did on you because he believed the lies of traitors! I was useless and couldn't do anything to help." As Yan Sinian spoke, tears spilled from his eyes. He refused to believe his father had colluded with the enemy to betray their country. The Yan family held all the power in Great Xia, and the emperor heavily relied on them. Why would their father do such a thing?

"Yes, Father, we were useless... When you went to prison, there was nothing we could do. We couldn't even preserve a single shred of dignity for the Yan family... It's all our fault!" Yan Rixin was only sixteen. Up until now, he'd only been focused on his studies, and he knew nothing about the real world; of course he fully believed in his father.

Watching his sons weep pitifully, Yan Wenxin knew he had made the right choice. If he lived by himself in the khan's harem, with no familiar faces around him, he could only be controlled by the khan.

Perhaps sending his sons to him was just another way of humiliating him, but the khan had personally delivered him two helpers. Since they had already been claimed by Shatunu men, they would be able to gather more intelligence than he could, considering he would be forced to stay within the harem. He'd raised these sons for more than a decade, putting in an endless amount of effort toward their growth. It was time for them to repay him.

He dabbed at his crocodile tears and helped his sons up from the ground as if comforting them. With restraint in his eyes, he said, "I know you're both good boys, and it won't be easy living here in Shatunu. Though we'd rather die than be humiliated, the khan has set his sights on me, so I can't just give up and die. Otherwise, it might ruin the agreement these savages have with the court and bring chaos to the northwest once again. The emperor may have been fooled by traitors, but the citizens are innocent. We must live on for the people of Great Xia. Even if we have to suffer through humiliation, we must endure. Do you understand?"

There was nothing wrong with what he said. Yan Sinian and Yan Rixin looked at their father with complicated expressions, then burst into tears. "Father, don't worry, we understand... You've suffered so much." Thinking of how his once-spirited father was now forced to pleasure another man for the sake of the people of Great Xia, Yan Sinian wanted to sprint back to the capital and annihilate the Protector General's entire family.

Yan Rixin, on the other hand, wept so forcefully that he couldn't speak. His tears and snot collected in many little puddles on the sturdy ground.

Yan Wenxin stopped speaking. With a sigh, he wiped the face of his youngest son. "The khan will come to have dinner in the evening. Do exactly as you are supposed to do," he said in a low voice. "All right, go prepare. Don't reveal anything in front of the enemy. If they do anything improper to me, just go to the side tents. Leave me some dignity."

Yan Sinian and Yan Rixin exchanged a glance, opening their mouths as if they wanted to say something. But considering how painful it was for their father to live with such humiliation already, what was the point in saying anything more?

"We understand, Father... No, Laoye. Rixin will come bring you some tea later—is that all right?" Seeing that his younger brother was starting to cry again, Yan Sinian hurriedly dragged him out of the tent.

A little while later, Yan Rixin did bring a pot of tea over. The taste was surprisingly pleasant; it was the clear tea of Great Xia, not the milk tea that the Shatunu usually drank. After sending his son away, Yan Wenxin poured himself a cup and sipped on it leisurely. The taste and fragrance were familiar; it was the exact kind of tea they often had at home. What did the khan mean by this?

Yan Wenxin was suddenly lost as he inhaled the fragrance of the tea.

At dinner, the khan came as he'd said he would.

Yan Sinian and Yan Rixin had probably suffered a lot the last few days. They used to be rich young masters who'd never labored a day in their lives. Now, they were meticulous in their assigned tasks. The table was full of roasted lamb and cakes made from milk and barley. These foods looked rough in appearance, but there were additional dishes of stir-fried lily bulbs and stewed tofu with ham. Though these dishes were made with simple ingredients, they were delicate and required an experienced chef. Yan Wenxin glanced at his sons, wondering if he should try the food or not.

The khan did not have any of his reservations, picking up a piece of lily bulb and putting it in his mouth. Then he spooned up some tofu and ate it with a piece of barley cake. Yan Wenxin grew hungry watching how heartily the khan ate, so he put aside his worries and joined in.

Contrary to his expectations, the two dishes were cooked extremely well. The refreshing lily bulb retained its crispy texture. The taste was a little strong—especially heavy on the garlic and green onions—but that was so it could hold up to the roasted meat. The stewed tofu with ham was shockingly good; Yan Wenxin hadn't tasted such delicious flavors even within the capital. Tofu was a plain ingredient, and stewing it together with ham brought out a richness and smoothness. It was seasoned perfectly, and the ham was not overcooked. The ham and tofu tasted good both together and separately. They were completely different foods, but they came together so well. Even paired with the rough barley cake, it was delicious.

Yan Wenxin was half full when the khan teased, "You lost a lot of weight on the way here, so you need to gain it all back. Otherwise, how can I shower you with my affections? Look at your wrist..." He picked up Yan Wenxin's right hand and exerted a little pressure. Yan Wenxin felt so much pain that he couldn't hold his chopsticks anymore. His face paled as he stared at the khan, not knowing what to do.

"Don't look at me like that. If you continue, I won't be able to resist snapping your delicate little bones." Yan Wenxin shuddered and looked down in a hurry, and the khan burst into laughter, very gently patting Yan Wenxin's hand. "I'm just trying to scare you. Don't take it seriously," he said softly. "Am I really such a ruthless, violent man in your eyes?"

Of course you are! "No, I'm simply afraid of offending you. Since you brought me out here from Great Xia, I'm yours. You can do whatever you want to me—I have no complaints."

His words were obedient, but the khan looked at Yan Wenxin with just the slightest smile. Yan Wenxin remained unaffected, even biting into another piece of tofu.

"Yan Wenxin, do you remember that after Shatunu lost to Great Xia ten years ago, there was a diplomatic team sent to your country?" the khan asked, knocking on the table.

"Ten years ago?" Yan Wenxin swallowed the tofu in his mouth. After pretending to think for a moment, he nodded. "Yes. At the time, I accompanied the emperor to welcome the group of Shatunu diplomats. Why are you suddenly asking about the past?"

"Do you remember the fifteen-year-old among the group at the time?"

Fifteen-year-old? Yan Wenxin furrowed his brows, thinking for even longer. After a while, he shook his head and apologized. "It was ten years ago, after all. At the time, I was just there to accompany the emperor. I did not interact with the diplomats much. I don't recall seeing this young man you speak of."

"Really?" The khan reached over to gently smooth away a stray strand of hair at the side of Yan Wenxin's face. "I've never forgotten you once in these last ten years."

Yan Wenxin's eyes grew wide. Sensing that he'd fallen into a trap, he stared incredulously at the smiling Khan, his mind racing as he tried to remember anything at all about the Shatunu diplomats. He seemed to vaguely recall a young man, but no matter how hard he tried, the man's face was a blur. He could not recall at all whether or not they'd spoken or even interacted a single time... Back then, he had only recently become the Minister of Personnel. There were so many things for him to plan for and attend to. He would not have spent an extra ounce of effort on someone who was not important. Unless...the khan was toying with him?

"You really forgot..." The khan sighed regretfully, but the way he touched Yan Wenxin only grew gentler. "That year, my only remaining older brother became ill and died. The Shatunu suffered a great loss, and we were nearly wiped out. The tribesmen who were loyal to me protected me and managed to keep me safe as the sole survivor of the royal bloodline. In order to show Great Xia our loyalty and to rest and recover, we decided to send a diplomatic team to Great Xia to meet with your emperor and discuss terms. At that time, a few of the clans had their eyes on the throne, wanting to replace me. The older subjects didn't dare leave me alone with the other clans, so they took me along."

"A smart move." Yan Wenxin smiled sincerely. The khan patted him on the cheek.

"Yan Wenxin, the first time I laid eyes on you was at the welcome banquet. The emperor of Great Xia wanted to demonstrate your country's power and prestige, so the banquet was quite casual. The host of the banquet was the Protector General, and the emperor only appeared for half an hour. We were not respected at all, but we'd lost the battle, so we were lucky to have even survived. No matter the humiliation, we had to just bear it." As the khan recalled that day, a hint of ferocity flashed in his blue eyes, but his smile was carefree.

He'd only been fifteen years old at the time.

The previous Shatunu Khan had five sons with his hedui. Out of all the past khans, he was one of the most brilliant and wise. He strove for excellence in governance, employing both literary and military strategies, and thoroughly understood Great Xia. He almost succeeded in taking a piece of the northwest. Unfortunately, all his efforts were for nothing. Not only did he lose his own life, but the lives of his wife, most of his children, and many of his tribesmen were lost too.

The current khan, at the time only a prince, was carefully protected, because of his age and because of the Shatunu custom to choose the youngest son as the next khan. As a result, he managed to survive. He watched as his home fell apart and his people were forced to flee, but he was helpless to do anything. At the time, he was too weak. Great Xia pulled back their forces, but the other powers within his tribe were waiting for this exact moment to strike.

His fourth brother, who had escaped along with him, was naturally sickly. Because of the great shock he had suffered, he died soon after. If his brother had survived, the Chaduoduo clan and the others might have sought out a way to kill him so they could control his brother as a puppet khan and eventually take over all of Shatunu. Because his fourth brother died, they behaved for a while, but it was clear they were just biding their time.

So the plan to go to Great Xia to thank them for their mercy was also a way for his loyal subjects to protect him. Without the khan's golden seal, the people lying in wait dared not make any rash moves.

That was the first time the fifteen-year-old khan saw the magnificence of Great Xia. He was in so much awe, he nearly forgot he carried the burden of revenge on his shoulders. No wonder his father wanted to take over Great Xia. In such a wonderful place, his people could live easier.

And then, at that welcome banquet, the khan laid eyes on Yan Wenxin.

At the time, he didn't know why he was drawn to Yan Wenxin. He was more than twice his age, and not the most attractive man there. At the banquet was another youth around his age and as gorgeous as a god. He could tell immediately that this young man carried the same violence and bloodthirst within him that he himself did. Later on, one of his tribespeople told him that this young man was one of the major reasons why the Shatunu had lost so completely.

Ha! His sworn enemy. No wonder he hated him at first glance. But he couldn't help but admire him regardless.

As for how Yan Wenxin caught his eye? The fifteen-year-old khan couldn't figure it out. He wasn't exactly attracted; he was just curious. The man's face was fair and angular, and his features looked as he imagined the mountains and rivers of Jiangnan—elegant to the extreme, but somehow mixed with a hint of seduction.

Yan Wenxin earnestly fulfilled his duty at the banquet. He led a round of toasts for each of the diplomats. He didn't say much, but everything he did say was pleasant and enjoyable. The khan was the youngest, so he was the last one to speak to Yan Wenxin. Before he even spoke, Yan Wenxin chuckled. "Heroes are made from young people like you. I never expected someone as young as you to attend."

"I'm not young. As you say in your language, I'm already old enough to put my hair up." At the time, he'd just experienced the pain of losing his entire family, but he was forced to muster up a smile for these "scholarly" people of Great Xia. He had to push all of his hatred down to the bottom of his heart; it truly was painful.

Yan Wenxin spoke gently, making him feel lighter.

"You have spirit. If my children could be half as ambitious as you are, I'd be satisfied." When Yan Wenxin mentioned his own children, he smiled even more gently; it felt like a little kitten pawing at the khan's heart. It made his throat dry up, so he quickly downed the rest of his wine.

Yan Wenxin found the way he gulped down his wine amusing, so he exchanged a few more words with him, asking about Shatunu culture and how he was doing. Subtly, he placed blame on that other beautiful youth for being so cruel and heartless, nearly driving the Shatunu to extinction. It wasn't something their imperial kingdom should've done.

The khan felt very reassured hearing that. After he returned to Shatunu, he'd rebuild his land as quickly as possible, just as his father did. Even if they stopped fighting Great Xia in the future, he wanted to visit as an equal next time. When that time came, would this Yan Wenxin praise him again?

"I've always thought about your words that day. How rare for a person from Great Xia to care so much for someone from Shatunu." The Khan chuckled meaningfully and brought the frozen Yan Wenxin into his arms, nipping at his earlobe. He said, in a voice so low and smooth it felt like a pool of water, "The Chaduoduo clan may have ulterior motives, but they don't have anywhere near enough power. When I was in Great Xia, you taught me many things. I always wanted to be your support so that the Protector General's family could no longer give you any trouble. Hah! Ah, but I was blind. How could the almighty Lord Yan Wenxin need anyone's support?"

Yan Wenxin's heart trembled. He turned away to avoid the khan's hot breath, but the khan suddenly gripped his chin and immobilized him.

"In that case...I've contributed at least a little to your efforts of reuniting the Shatunu," Yan Wenxin said. *How dare you repay my kindness like this!*

The khan lifted Yan Wenxin's face, hand still on his chin. He traced over Yan Wenxin's features with his gaze, finally settling on his eyes. They stared at each other, but Yan Wenxin quickly looked away. The khan's gaze was so forceful; it was as if he wanted to swallow him whole.

"Me or the Shatunu, we are all just your bait." The khan let Yan Wenxin look away, but tenderly rubbed his lip with his finger. Soon, Yan Wenxin's lips turned red.

"I wouldn't dare..." Yan Wenxin snuck a quick glance at him, looking resigned and frustrated. There were no holes in his acting, but the khan chuckled anyway.

"Yan Wenxin, if I hadn't carefully researched you all these years, I might've actually believed your 'sincerity.' Unfortunately..." The khan finally let go of Yan Wenxin. Although he hadn't used much force, he left behind two obvious marks. "Have you tried the bed I've prepared for you?"

Yan Wenxin hung his head, not answering, but he visibly tensed up.

"Go on. I've thought about you for ten years." The khan pushed his back lightly. Yan Wenxin got up shakily, walking to that large bed covered in furs. Unbidden, images of the sex he'd witnessed not long ago flashed in his mind.

While he pondered if he should get on the bed or take off his clothes first, a hot, firm body pressed into his back. The heat made him grunt slightly, and he clenched his fists so tightly that his nails could practically pierce through his palms.

"If you please me, I'll allow you to do whatever you want in the harem." The khan wrapped his arms around Yan Wenxin's thin waist, pushing him down onto the bed. His promise had come so easily, but Yan Wenxin felt both shocked and humiliated.

He was completely lost. In this desolate, northern desert, could he really accumulate enough power to follow through with his revenge, or was he destined to be a caged bird in the khan's harem?

Before he could ponder any further, the man's long, well-defined finger entered his hole with the help of some ointment.

"Mmm—!" Yan Wenxin bit his lip, unwilling to make a noise. The khan chuckled, clearly quite pleased already.

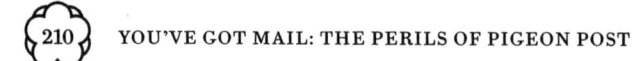

RAISING A CHILD

He pinched Wu Xingzi's nose, smiling. "What are you getting jealous for? Ever since you flew into my life, all the men you assume to be beautiful blossoms are but dust in my eyes. Your temperament has worsened recently, hm? You've learned to be jealous."

"N-no, I haven't..." Wu Xingzi was a sensitive man; after having his thoughts revealed, he stuttered and tried to defend himself, but his face was as red as a tomato.

"MOTHER..." The door opened a crack to reveal the soft, pale face of a seven- or eight-year-old boy, peering in timidly.

This was a woman's bedroom. The doors and windows were tightly closed, making it very dark. It was like a completely different world from the sunshine outside. A slight smoky haze filled the room. There was a strong medicinal scent in the air, and someone had lit up some incense in an attempt to cover it up. However, the two smells combined made a thick, cloying, soporific aroma. Anyone would instinctively cover their nose and stay away.

The room was decorated simply; the bronze mirror on the vanity was dull and lifeless. Other than a couple of jade hairpins, the table was empty, and so were the shelves. In fact, they were covered in a layer of dust. The room itself was quite large, but it seemed desolate; the large bed only made the room look emptier.

There seemed to be someone lying on the bed. At the child's soft call, a face emerged from the blankets—a face so bleak and pale, it was almost gray.

The woman looked like she was on her last breath, but when she saw her small son, she still smiled gently. With a hand that was just skin and bones, she gestured for him to come closer. "Xiao-Bao-er, come here."

The small boy's eyes lit up at the sound of his mother's voice. He pushed open the door in a hurry and closed it carefully before running to his mother, throwing himself into the blankets.

"Mother, I missed you." He didn't dare to actually crawl into her arms. Both his grandmother and stepmother had reminded him over and over that his mother was sick and needed rest. Xiao-Bao-er remembered all of these instructions. He was a good child, and he wouldn't bother his mother or throw himself at her for affection.

"Xiao-Bao-er has grown up a bit." The woman smoothed a hand over her son's soft cheeks. The smile remained on her face, but the heartache was clear in her eyes. Her baby had lost some weight; he looked even skinnier than when they last saw each other three months ago. A child his age should have been growing bigger. How much must a child suffer to become skinnier instead?

But she knew she couldn't even protect herself, never mind her son. She was close to death, so even the servants treated her as if she were nothing. If it hadn't been for the old servant who'd come with her when she got married, perhaps the grass on her grave would have grown taller than a person by now. But that servant was old now and had gone through a lot for her; she really didn't have the ability to care for the young master too. Even though she was the official wife and had given birth to the eldest di son, this was the fate of a woman without the affection of her husband.

The woman knew that her father-in-law was celebrating his birthday now. Her servant had told her that her husband had recently caught the eye of the sub-prefectural magistrate, so he was throwing this grand banquet in the hopes of meeting a socialite from high society who could help raise his status. The woman laughed coldly when she heard. Only a shortsighted man like him would treat a mere sub-prefectural magistrate like some kind of great treasure.

But the news gave her an idea. She wrote a letter and had someone secretly send it home. She couldn't protect herself, but she had to think of something to protect her son. This was the only chance she had to ask for help. She didn't know if her cousin would deign to come see her lowly little self, though, and she couldn't help but feel nervous.

"I will grow big and study hard to become a doctor and cure you," Bao-er said sincerely, holding onto his mother's hand. It was as thin as a chicken's claw. "Mother, you have to wait until I grow up."

"All right, I will wait." Even though she knew it was impossible, the woman still nodded. She knew she was at the end of her life, after all these years of illness. There was no hope for her, but how could she tell her son the cruel truth? Not wanting to talk about herself anymore, she changed the subject. "It must be fun outside, right? Why did you come here instead?"

"Mm, it's grandfather's birthday today. So many guests came! But Stepmother said I'm too young and that I should stay in my rooms and study in case I offend any of the guests. I'm a good boy, so I have to listen." He'd actually snuck a peek at the lively front hall, and saw that his stepmother was leading his brother, who was a few months younger, around the hall and greeting guests. Xiao-Bao-er had been a little confused. Why wasn't his brother staying in his rooms? But he didn't dare let his stepmother know he'd run out for a look, so he couldn't ask. Now that he was with his mother, though, he couldn't help but mention it. He didn't notice how his mother's gaze darkened.

The woman didn't explain anything to him. She only patted his cheek and told him to be good. The two of them quickly forgot about the excitement in the front hall, absorbed in their own little chat.

After a while, there came a knock on the door. The old servant's voice spoke up from outside. "My lady, your cousin from the Guan family is here to see you."

Cousin from the Guan family? The woman's eyes, lifeless from her prolonged sickness, suddenly shone. Even her cheeks seemed to gain some rosiness.

She held her son's hand tightly. "Please invite him in," she said, trying to keep her excitement under control.

"Cousin?" Xiao-Bao-er blinked curiously, looking back toward the door.

The door was pushed open. Behind the old servant's hunched body loomed a large, tall silhouette. Xiao-Bao-er had never seen such a large person before. He was so shocked that his jaw dropped, and he nearly fell over from trying to look up. After the tall man entered the room, Xiao-Bao-er noticed there was another skinny person behind him. It was difficult to see the person's face in the darkness. Xiao-Bao-er opened his eyes wide, trying his best to get a good look at the two men.

The door was closed carefully again. Smoke from the incense and herbs swirled around the dark room, making the tall man seem like he'd come from a dream.

He was a very beautiful man. He was so beautiful, in fact, that Xiao-Bao-er grew a little shy. He'd never seen such a gorgeous man! Even his stepmother, whom many people praised for her beauty, could not compare. This must be one of those immortals from the storybooks!

The man next to the immortal looked a little older. Xiao-Bao-er stared at him curiously. Even though he wasn't as pretty as the immortal, he seemed very familiar. Xiao-Bao-er wanted to get closer, his large eyes blinking as he stared at the man.

The older man noticed Xiao-Bao-er and immediately broke into a smile. He said something to the immortal, and the immortal nodded, though his brows knitted together in a frown. The older man extended his hands toward Xiao-Bao-er. "Child, what is your name?" he said in a soft voice. "Do you want to come eat candy with me?"

Xiao-Bao-er was a little nervous, but he was enticed. He looked back at his mother, and she nodded her assent and pushed his little shoulder slightly. "Go ahead. I need to speak to your uncle."

Uncle? Xiao-Bao-er snuck a glance at the immortal. "Hello, Uncle," he said obediently.

"Mm." His immortal-like uncle nodded expressionlessly, then pointed to the man next to him. "This is your aunt."

Aunt? Xiao-Bao-er's eyes grew big in his sudden confusion. Shouldn't his aunt be a woman? Despite his puzzlement, though, Xiao-Bao-er still greeted him obediently. "Hello, Aunt, my name is Bao-er."

His aunt smiled, her eyes curving into crescents. He pulled the child over and patted his head. "What a good boy. Let's go eat candy, and I'll tell you some stories. Let your mother talk to your uncle, all right?"

"All right." Xiao-Bao-er nodded and was led away by his aunt.

Once the child left, his uncle—heir to the Protector General and Great General of the Southern Garrison, Guan Shanjin—finally looked at the sickly, skinny woman on the bed. His brow furrowed. "What was that you mentioned in your letter?"

"It's been a long time, cousin." The woman smiled bitterly and tried to sit up, but Guan Shanjin stopped her. She flopped back down onto her soft pillow, panting, tears forming in her eyes. After a bout of silence, she finally said, "I didn't think you'd actually come." She let out a long sigh, as though exhaling out all the worries and unease she'd been accumulating.

"You should thank your cousin-in-law." Otherwise he'd have never bothered with a cousin he hadn't seen in years. This woman was from the Shi family. They were somewhat well-known as scholars in a midsize county. She was the youngest daughter of the younger brother of the current head of the family. Ten years ago, she was married to a merchant by the surname of Yang. This marriage hadn't been arranged by their parents; instead, the eldest son of the Yang family had run into Shi-xiaojie outside the temple. It was love at first sight, and he could not think of anything else other than her. It truly caused a stir in the family.

Though Yang-gongzi had two younger brothers, they died early in life. He only had two younger sisters born by his father's second wife, so he was considered the Yang family's precious heir. His parents treated him like a treasure, so how could they let him continue to pine like this? They did their utmost to find this Shi-xiaojie. Their efforts did not go to waste; they really did find her in the end.

As it happened, Shi-xiaojie had also seen Yang-gongzi from a distance and secretly fallen in love with him as well. Ever since that meeting, she kept thinking about that handsome, elegant young man. But she was a shy girl and didn't dare tell her family. As a result, she had lost some weight and shed quite a few tears.

But it turned out they were both yearning for each other! Although the Shi family had their doubts about this marriage and hesitated at first, when they saw how desperate their daughter was and how devoted Yang-gongzi was, they finally agreed.

It was funny; they were clearly both in love and finally got married. Their marriage should've been happy and loving. But Yang-gongzi was fickle. He could neglect his own needs for Shi-xiaojie, so naturally, he could do the same for another woman.

Not even two years into their marriage, when Shi-xiaojie was pregnant, another woman at a different city's temple caught Yang-gongzi's eye. Yang-gongzi also did everything he could to ask for her hand in marriage, but she was not as naïve as Shi-xiaojie and did not immediately agree to Yang-gongzi's request. Instead, she kept stringing him along until she had him completely ensnared. He eventually forgot about his affections for Shi-xiaojie.

Shi-xiaojie originally planned to just bear with it. She was his di wife, pregnant with his child. If the child was a boy, nothing could touch her position and status unless Yang-gongzi divorced her. Shi-xiaojie might only come from a family of scholars, but plenty of her relatives were court officials with accomplishments to their names. She could not be thrown away that easily. The Yang family were only merchants—they would not burn bridges with the Shi family.

But the new woman wasn't easy, either. With how ardently Yang-gongzi pursued her, she would only accept being his di wife. Otherwise, she would not marry him.

Yang-gongzi could not be more desperate for this new woman. Even when Shi-xiaojie was giving birth, he was still with the other woman, unwilling to return home to see his newborn child, just to prove his loyalty to his new sweetheart. When Shi-xiaojie heard, she was furious. She nearly died from blood loss. Her health never fully recovered, and within a few years, she was bedridden.

Later, Yang-gongzi still married that new woman, giving her the title of di wife as well.

Shi-xiaojie eventually found out that this woman also came from an ordinary merchant family, but her family was well-connected. They even knew the governor.

The Yang family had always wanted a foot in the door with the court officials. When they first welcomed Shi-xiaojie into the family, this was their intention as well, but the Shi family had strict rules, so the Yang family had never been successful in their pursuit of power. Gradually, they stopped caring about their honorable in-laws and decided to curry favor with the new in-laws instead.

After Shi-xiaojie found out, she couldn't help but laugh bitterly on the inside, and her feelings toward her husband faded. All she wanted now was to care for her son and live the rest of her life in peace.

Her Bao-er... As soon as she thought of her son, the rims of Shi-xiaojie's eyes reddened.

Xiao-Bao-er had already been incredibly talented at the age of five. He could read by three and write poems by five. His intelligence really did make Yang-gongzi pay more attention to him and his mother. He intended to nurture his son's talents properly.

But when he was almost six, Bao-er suddenly came down with a high fever which lasted for several days. The doctor just couldn't seem to do anything about it, and the child nearly died. In the end, he managed to survive, but his brain was affected. He became a lot slower and never recovered his intellect. Yang-gongzi immediately forgot about this child and focused all his attention on the son and daughter his other wife gave him.

Shi-xiaojie suspected that her son's illness had been the other wife's doing. How could a perfectly healthy child fall sick just like that, and why couldn't the doctor find a cure? But she didn't

have any proof. Even if she did, her husband might not care. He might even think she was jealous and trying to harm the other woman. Soon after, Shi-xiaojie herself was bedridden, and the other wife was the one looking after Bao-er. It was difficult for her to even get a chance to see him.

Now she finally realized she could not just sit here and wait any longer. Her life was a lost cause—she was the one who'd insisted on marrying Yang-gongzi in the beginning, so she only had herself to blame—but she could not let her son suffer as well.

Unfortunately, this realization came too late. By the time she decided to seek help from her family, the only person in Yang-gongzi's household who could help her was her old servant, and that servant was under careful surveillance. She could not even get a single letter out. The entire household was under the other woman's control.

Shi-xiaojie held on to her last breath, refusing to die until she had the perfect opportunity to find a path for her son. Thankfully, the heavens were merciful; in the last few years, the other woman had stopped keeping her under such tight control. After all, who would pay attention to a person who was as good as dead? And it happened to be her father-in-law's seventieth birthday. With how chaotic it was at home, she finally found the chance to get the word out to her family.

The Shi family had never produced anyone extremely rich or of high status. The highest they'd got was a district magistrate, but one daughter from the Shi family managed to marry up: Shi-xiaojie's aunt, Guan Shanjin's mother. But the Shi family never spoke of their powerful in-laws. They simply went on with their lives in peace. As a result, people in town only knew that they had a daughter who'd married someone in the capital. They had no idea she had married the Protector General.

This time, Shi-xiaojie had no other choice. If she wanted to save her son, she had to ask the most powerful person she knew—Guan Shanjin. She hadn't expected Guan Shanjin would actually come.

Guan Shanjin didn't really want to come. He'd finally managed to return to the capital from Horse-Face City for once, and he wanted to take Wu Xingzi around the country to taste the snacks from each region. They hadn't even made it halfway through their trip when he received his mother's letter asking him to go to Lijiang County to see his cousin, whom he'd only met once.

This is a nightmare, Guan Shanjin kept complaining in his head. If it weren't for the fact that Lijiang County was known for a special dish that was very difficult to make, he would have just pretended he never saw the letter.

After listening to Shi-xiaojie's story, he scratched his face in boredom. "So what do you want me to do?" he asked.

What was the point of a husband like that? His infidelity was already unforgiveable, and now he was letting his wife and son waste away. Guan Shanjin wanted to leave this disgusting place immediately.

Besides, the Yang family was truly blind. When he'd introduced himself as Shi-xiaojie's cousin, that other woman had barely greeted him. Never mind that—when she saw Wu Xingzi, there was clear mockery in her expression. Guan Shanjin didn't want to start a scene in front of so many people, or he might've taught her a lesson with his fists.

Then, he heard the old servant say that the other wife had somehow managed to invite the sub-prefectural magistrate, so the entire family was treating her like a priceless treasure. They no longer cared for Shi-xiaojie. The fact that they weren't openly mocking him in itself counted as treating him with respect.

Sub-prefectural magistrate? Guan Shanjin scoffed silently. That was only a rank five official. He couldn't even be bothered to ask for his name. He just wanted to quickly take care of this matter and continue on his trip with Wu Xingzi.

"I know you've taken a male lover—that was him, right?" Through the door, she faintly heard the sound of her son's laughter. How long had it been since she last heard Xiao-Bao-er sound so carefree? He'd clearly taken a liking to this aunt.

"Mm." Guan Shanjin could also hear the child's laughter, as well as Wu Xingzi telling a story in his soft voice. His expression immediately mellowed. "You want me to adopt Bao-er?"

"Yes... Would you be willing?" Shi-xiaojie was so nervous that she was covered in cold sweat, afraid that her long-awaited hope would vanish in the blink of an eye.

Guan Shanjin didn't answer. He crossed his arms and looked at the floor. In the darkness, he looked like a jade Guanyin statue.

Bao-er was cute. His small and dainty features clearly came from Shi-xiaojie. He almost looked like a little girl. But Guan Shanjin had seen plenty of cute kids. He himself had been a beautiful child. Whether it be Man Yue or Su Yang, they all looked like little jade dolls when they were kids. Cuteness alone was not enough to garner Guan Shanjin's sympathy. But...that old quail seemed to like children. As soon as he spotted the child, his eyes had sparkled. The way he'd looked made Guan Shanjin want to climb up to the sky and give him the moon.

Besides, the child just so happened to have a little round nose, which Guan Shanjin liked.

"I'm willing, but Bao-er is the eldest di son of the Yang family. I can't just ask for him." Guan Shanjin's alluring gaze rested on

Shi-xiaojie where she lay on the bed, something akin to a smile on his lips. His intentions were obvious.

It was true. No matter how little the Yang family cared for Bao-er, they would never let anyone just take him away. It wouldn't work out, no matter how one looked at it.

But that didn't matter to Guan Shanjin. He knew that once as they knew who he was, he'd be able to get away with any number of unreasonable things. The Yang family would not stop him. However, that would make this a big deal. If someone really wanted to report him, it could bring him trouble in the future. Guan Shanjin didn't want to deal with that—he didn't have Man Yue on hand to tidy up loose ends for him, so he had to act carefully.

It wasn't impossible, though. If the Yang family divorced Shi-xiaojie, it would be a lot easier to take away the child. Shi-xiaojie had been bedridden for many years, which meant she qualified for divorce.[4] If he exerted a little bit of pressure, he could get the Yang family to write a letter divorcing Shi-xiaojie from the family. But Guan Shanjin looked down on the Yang family. He wanted to get his cousin a mutual divorce agreement and not a one-sided one. In order for that to happen, he had to be a little more crafty.

Shi-xiaojie had a feeling she knew what Guan Shanjin meant. A relaxed smile graced her lips. "I know you want to preserve some of my dignity, but there's no need. I'm not long for this world. Whether he divorces me or it's a mutual agreement, it makes no difference to me. I just want to get Bao-er away from here as quickly as possible. What does my dignity matter?"

---

4   In ancient China, a man could legally divorce his wife for the following seven reasons: lack of filial piety toward in-laws, not bearing a son, indecent behavior, jealousy, serious illness, gossip, or committing theft. There were also three exceptions: if she had no home to return to, if she had observed the three year mourning period for an in-law, and if she'd stuck by her husband when he was poor if he was now rich.

"I see you're considering the bigger picture..." Guan Shanjin gained a little more respect for Shi-xiaojie. He nodded. "All right. I've already written a letter to Uncle. I will take care of this, and then I will send you and Bao-er to the capital to rest. Your life should be a little more comfortable after that."

"Thank you!" This assurance from her cousin made Shi-xiaojie so emotional that tears streamed down her face. Unsteadily, she started to get off the bed to bow to him, but Guan Shanjin stopped her, his lip curling in disdain. "No need to thank me. You should thank your cousin-in-law. He likes children."

"Yes, I will definitely do that!" Her heart finally settling back down, Shi-xiaojie laughed and cried at the same time. She looked slightly worse than before. Guan Shanjin couldn't take it anymore: He pressed down on an acupoint so she could take a good nap.

Outside, Wu Xingzi told Bao-er the story of Nüwa creating humans. The small child's eyes went as wide as dinner plates, and he exclaimed in all the right spots. He could not have been any more adorable. Wu Xingzi wanted nothing more than to hug the child in his arms and squish him all over.

Very quickly, the story got to the battle between Gonggong and Zhurong, after which Gonggong knocked over Mount Buzhou and tore a hole in the sky. The people below were pelted with hail and drenched by floods. With torrential winds and rain, they had nowhere to go. Wild beasts came and ate people, adding to the chaos. The cries of the people broke Nüwa's heart.

Bao-er's mouth hung open slightly. He was completely entranced in the story. All manner of expressions crossed his little face, and Wu Xingzi gained momentum as he went on.

At that moment, a soft, wicked laugh rang out.

Bao-er immediately shrank into himself, shaking. His little face—which had been rosy from listening to the story—immediately went white. Fear flooded his eyes; he looked like a scared little rabbit about to run away.

Wu Xingzi quickly gathered the child in his arms and patted him comfortingly before looking for the source of the laughter.

A young man stood beneath a tree not far away, wearing pale red robes. He had snow-white skin, a wide forehead, and rounded eyebrows. He was as beautiful as an immortal, and he almost looked a little feminine. If it weren't for the valor in his slightly upturned eyes, he could be mistaken for a woman.

"Gongzi, why are you laughing? Did I say something wrong?" Wu Xingzi shielded Bao-er behind him and cupped his hands toward the man in greeting.

Wu Xingzi had never seen the man before, but he could feel his disrespect. His gaze stabbed into him like a needle, full of judgment and contempt.

"No, I just wanted to laugh. That's all." The man pursed his lips and walked out from the shade of the tree. He looked even prettier in the sunlight—almost as pretty as Mr. Lu.

"I see." Wu Xingzi couldn't figure out the man's intentions, but since he was a guest, he needed to be careful. He looked down at Bao-er and said gently, "Bao-er, Auntie will tell you the rest of the story later. Let's go back to your mother, all right?"

Bao-er was still frozen. Hearing Wu Xingzi's words, he nodded stiffly and shrank even further back behind him.

"Auntie?" The man snorted, no longer hiding his mockery. "Does the Shi family have no one else left? You're all they sent to support that Shi woman? No wonder she's been stuck in this situation for years. What did my brother-in-law see in her all those years ago?"

Even the gentle Wu Xingzi was angered by his poisonous words. His smile disappeared from his face and he sported a rare frown. "Gongzi, any well-educated person should remember to be humble and courteous. Let's be a little more careful with our words when speaking in front of children, shall we?"

When Wu Xingzi was an adviser, he'd come across many unreasonable people, and he'd never been so stern with any of them. However, this young man had crossed a line.

On the way to Lijiang County, Guan Shanjin had given him a brief overview of his cousin's situation, but they didn't know everything at the time. Wu Xingzi wasn't sure how much Guan Shanjin's cousin was telling him right now, but he'd seen many familial disputes as an adviser. He could make a calculated guess as to what his cousin-in-law had suffered through all these years.

This man was probably very close to the other wife. When Wu Xingzi first arrived, he'd taken a look at that clever, beautiful, capable woman, and this man looked somewhat similar to her. Judging from his age, he must've been her younger brother, probably doted on by the entire family—otherwise he wouldn't spout such blatant insults.

However, Wu Xingzi had the feeling that this young man wasn't acting so rude purely because of Shi-xiaojie and Bao-er. His rudeness was clearly aimed toward Wu Xingzi. Why? This was the first time Wu Xingzi had ever been to Lijiang County, and he'd always lived a simple life. Apart from Auntie Li, he'd never gotten into any conflicts.

Unless... A thought flashed through his mind. Before Wu Xingzi could catch it, though, the door behind him opened. Out stepped Guan Shanjin, covered in the smell of medicinal herbs. He patted his sleeves, an ugly expression on his face.

"Hey, what's your name?" The young man's eyes brightened as soon as he saw Guan Shanjin. He tilted his head up proudly. "Are you really from the Shi family?"

Guan Shanjin was too lazy to even spare him a glance. Due to his martial arts training, his hearing was exceptional. He'd clearly heard the man mock and insult Wu Xingzi from inside the room. The only reason he didn't teach him a lesson as soon as he saw him was because he didn't want to deal with the aftermath. They were leaving soon, anyway—these lowly insects could hop around however they wanted.

He picked up Bao-er, then wrapped an arm around Wu Xingzi, giving him a kiss on the cheek.

"Let's go. I need to speak to Yang Baisheng. There's no good reason for the daughter of the Shi family to be tormented like this. Since he has another wife and doesn't care for my cousin or their relationship, we might as well make a clean break."

"What about Bao-er?" Wu Xingzi looked at the quiet, well-behaved boy in Guan Shanjin's arm. Bao-er was the Yang family's eldest di son. They would probably rather keep him at home and waste his potential than hand him over to his mother's family.

"I have a plan. No one's getting left behind." Guan Shanjin shook the old quail slightly. His tone was quite casual, but Wu Xingzi knew that once the general promised something, he saw it through, so he let his worries rest.

"Then should I come with you, or should I stay behind and chat with your cousin?" Wu Xingzi asked.

"With me, of course. This entire family is blind. How dare they treat you like this? Hmph." Guan Shanjin finally spared an ice-cold glance at the man. The man, having been ignored, wanted to fire back at Guan Shanjin, but the hint of sharp danger in the general's glare made him choke and look away. He recovered quickly, though, staring angrily back at Guan Shanjin.

"You're so rude! I asked you a question! Let me remind you: I'm Lady Zou's younger di brother. If you guys want to take that stupid child away, you should know who you need to curry favor with." The young man was Yang Baisheng's other wife's younger brother, Zou Yongming. He was posturing aggressively, but he was intensely focused on Guan Shanjin.

Wu Xingzi finally understood his intentions. Had this man taken a liking to Guan Shanjin? He glanced at Zou Yongming, whose admiration was quite obvious, then stared at Guan Shanjin for a while. Then, he smiled at Guan Shanjin in realization.

How could Wu Xingzi forget? In the capital and in Horse-Face City, Guan Shanjin's reputation preceded him. Even when someone had romantic interest in him, his fame stopped anyone from approaching him. Not to mention that the men of the Guan family only took one lover. This was a pattern over several generations; all of Great Xia knew the Guan men's reputation as faithful life partners.

After Guan Shanjin officially married Wu Xingzi, following all of the correct rites and procedures, no one dared say anything to try to ruin their marriage. If they actually succeeded, fine, but what would happen to them if they didn't? Everybody remembered how Guan Shanjin bullied all the officials in the capital, even the aristocracy. Yan Wenxin, the most powerful official in the capital, wasn't an exception either! Even a first rank official couldn't oppose the great Guan Shanjin!

Now that they were in Lijiang County, though, Guan Shanjin's appearance attracted all sorts of attention. Zou Yongming had good taste. Wu Xingzi thought it was amusing, but it also left a bad taste in his mouth.

He'd been with Guan Shanjin for a few years now. He was no longer that lonely adviser from a little town who was too afraid to ask for anything. When Guan Shanjin doted on someone, he knew no bounds, showering him with all the affection in the world. If Wu Xingzi wanted anything at all, Guan Shanjin would give it to him, even if it meant moving mountains or draining the sea.

Those who were loved often gained confidence from it. Wu Xingzi's personality would never allow him to let the attention get to his head, but he was no longer as self-deprecating when it came to romance. At least he was confident now that Guan Shanjin would never do anything to hurt him. If he were sad, Guan Shanjin would become even more upset in response.

But knowing was one thing, and seeing was another. When someone eyed Guan Shanjin right in front of him, Wu Xingzi still felt a little glum. Subconsciously, he scrunched his nose at Guan Shanjin.

Guan Shanjin could tell what was going through Wu Xingzi's head. His delight sparked like a firework going off in the sky. This silly old fellow had no flaws, but his personality was so gentle. They had been together for so long, and Wu Xingzi never got jealous. He, on the other hand, had to occasionally swallow his jealousy at Wu Xingzi's collection of pengornis drawings...

Unexpectedly, this annoying task was bringing him some benefit.

Even though flowers bloomed furiously in his heart at Wu Xingzi finally, for once, feeling jealousy because of him, Guan Shanjin couldn't bear to let Wu Xingzi suffer for too long. He pinched Wu Xingzi's nose, smiling. "What are you getting jealous for? Ever since you flew into my life, all men whom you assume to be beautiful blossoms are but dust in my eyes. Your temperament has worsened recently, hm? You've learned to be jealous."

"N-no, I haven't..." Wu Xingzi was a sensitive man; after having his thoughts revealed, he stuttered and tried to defend himself, but his face was as red as a tomato.

Guan Shanjin and Wu Xingzi were clearly a loving couple. Even Xiao-Bao-er could feel it; he covered his face, peeking out between his fingers. Zou Yongming, however, was clenching his teeth furiously. If looks could kill, Wu Xingzi would have been full of holes by now.

Guan Shanjin couldn't be bothered to deal with Zou Yongming. He put down Xiao-Bao-er and pushed him into the room, telling him to talk to his mother some more. Then, he turned and led Wu Xingzi away to find Yang Baisheng.

When they passed Zou Yongming, the young man raised his chin and glared at him. He was biting his lip so hard that it looked like it might bleed. His sorry state did garner sympathy, but unfortunately, neither Wu Xingzi nor Guan Shanjin cared that much. Wu Xingzi shoot him an apologetic glance, which only made Zou Yongming nearly furious enough to spit blood.

How dare this ugly thing pity him?

The two of them left in a hurry. Zou Yongming stomped his feet, glaring at Shi-xiaojie's door. He decided to go tell his sister about Guan Shanjin's intentions to take the child. They had to teach that sickly woman and stupid boy a lesson. The Shi family needed to know that their beloved daughter and grandson's lives were in his hands! See if that man dared ignore him after that!

The fury in his heart calmed a little. Zou Yongming spat in the direction of Shi-xiaojie's quarters and turned to leave. He had no idea that to Guan Shanjin, his little plan was a joke. There was nothing in the world that Guan Shanjin couldn't accomplish.

Yang Baisheng stood in the front hall, welcoming guests to the banquet. The old family steward did not spare a glance for anyone from the Shi family. He just left Guan Shanjin there, not letting the head of the household know that his wife's cousin was here to see him.

How could Guan Shanjin endure such a slight? With an alluring smile, and the sudden sound of something slicing through the air, he rested a shining sword on the old steward's shoulder. The sword was so sharp that even the steward's hairs trembled. Even though the sword was not actually touching the old man's neck, his whole body shuddered. He looked ready to piss himself from fear.

"Tell Yang Baisheng to come see me." Guan Shanjin didn't have much patience to begin with, but the Yang family was going too far, forcing him to pull out his Chenyuan Sword.

"Yes, yes…" The steward clearly had to obey the man's orders. He'd drag Yang-gongzi here if he needed to! But he dared not breathe too harshly with this sword by his neck, never mind move. How was he going to get Yang-gongzi?

"Thank you." Having achieved the desired result, Guan Shanjin quickly sheathed his sword. He was wearing a casual outfit; without careful inspection, one couldn't even tell where his sword was stowed.

Wu Xingzi was curious as well. He'd seen Chenyuan many times—usually when Guan Shanjin and Man Yue got into a fight out of nowhere—but Guan Shanjin's waist was quite trim, and it really didn't seem like he had a sword strapped there. All he knew was that Guan Shanjin always carried his sword with him.

While the old steward went to fetch the head of the house, Wu Xingzi circled Guan Shanjin once, then circled him again in the other direction. He really couldn't tell where he hid the sword. Guan Shanjin knew he was curious, but he didn't want to tell him. He just smiled, letting Wu Xingzi circle around him. In the end, he took the old man into his arms and gave him a kiss, then rubbed his nose into the side of his neck.

"Stop looking. I have my own ways of hiding my sword. It's to protect my life—I can't let anyone spot it, can I?"

Wu Xingzi wasn't that determined to find the sword anyway, so he nodded obediently and kissed Guan Shanjin back.

The old steward took so long that Wu Xingzi got hungry. From his robes, he procured a packet wrapped in wax paper and opened it up, revealing a few walnut cookies. He picked one up and started nibbling on it with his front teeth like a mouse. Guan Shanjin watched him lovingly. He adored it when he did that. Occasionally, he reached out to brush away the crumbs around Wu Xingzi's lips.

Unfortunately, this peaceful moment didn't last very long. The steward dragged Yang Baisheng over in a huff. He'd only just entered his study when he spotted these two shameless men. Privately, he felt even more disdain for the Shi family.

"To whom do I owe the pleasure?" Yang Baisheng asked. He knew Guan Shanjin was Shi-xiaojie's cousin, but he hadn't asked for his name before. It was clear how little respect he afforded him.

Guan Shanjin glanced at Yang Baisheng coldly. With just that look, this arrogant man started to feel uneasy. His shoulders shrank slightly, and even the old steward took a few steps back, wanting to flee from the study.

"You should call me biaoge," Guan Shanjin said lazily. These simple words angered Yang Baisheng so much that his face turned red—this man really wanted the respect afforded to an elder cousin?!—but he dared not say anything. Yang Baisheng looked down on Shi-xiaojie's family, but he wasn't stupid. He recognized Guan Shanjin's hostility.

"Hello, cousin." Yang Baisheng's smile did not reach his eyes. He gritted his teeth as he cupped his hands together in greeting. "How may I be of service?"

Wu Xingzi finished the walnut cookie in his hand. Guan Shanjin immediately poured him a cup of tea in case his throat was dry and felt uncomfortable, intending to lift the cup to Wu Xingzi's lips himself. He had completely forgotten about Yang Baisheng.

But Wu Xingzi was directly facing Yang Baisheng. He couldn't disrespect the host so openly, even if Guan Shanjin could.

"I can do that myself—your cousin is waiting for you to respond." Wu Xingzi wanted to take the cup from Guan Shanjin, but Guan Shanjin wouldn't let him. The man was a battle-hardened general, so how could Wu Xingzi take anything from him by force? He could only accept Guan Shanjin's help, embarrassed. He knew Guan Shanjin was purposefully ignoring Yang Baisheng to show him his place.

Yang Baisheng had never been treated so coldly his entire life. He wanted to cuss Guan Shanjin out. The old steward had been shooting him warning glances, but Yang Baisheng missed his signals entirely. This time, however, he reached out to stop Yang Baisheng. Guan Shanjin finished giving Wu Xingzi the tea, and the old steward managed to keep Yang Baisheng's head on his shoulders.

"When I'm done here, I'll take you out to eat. Bear with it for a bit, hmm?" Guan Shanjin said, wiping away the tea at the corner of Wu Xingzi's lips. The old quail nodded, face red, which only turned Guan Shanjin on. He couldn't help but blame his mother for keeping him away from Wu Xingzi. He should be cuddled together with him right now, but instead, he was here taking care of someone else's family matters.

Since he couldn't take his anger out on his mother, he found the next best thing. The thing in question, Yang Baisheng, had no idea what kind of wrath awaited him.

Guan Shanjin smiled lightly. "I have nothing to say," he said. "Write a divorce letter."

Yang Baisheng's eyes went wide. He wasn't expecting 'divorce letter' to be the first thing out of his mouth. He dug into his ears, thinking he'd heard wrong, and laughed angrily. "Cousin, what are you talking about? You want me to divorce my wife? Are you trying to say I don't treat her well?"

"You know very well whether or not you do. My uncle is overly pedantic and doesn't want to meddle in his daughter's private affairs, but she's close to death. Who cares about dignity and courtesy? This is much more than you deserve—we're not even asking for a mutual divorce. You must divorce her." Guan Shanjin did not bother being polite. He slammed his Chenyuan Sword down on the table. Yang Baisheng jolted, his face deathly pale, so shocked that he swallowed down all the curses he'd been about to let out.

"I didn't want to use force," said Guan Shanjin, "but asking nicely clearly didn't work, so now you've forced my hand."

Yang Baisheng's face went from white to almost blue, then settled on a sickly gray. His lips trembled before he finally said, "D-do you even care about the law? She's just a married-off daughter..."

"Of course I care. That's why I'm asking you to write the divorce letter. Since you already have another wife and you haven't cared for my cousin in many years, what difference does it make to divorce her? She's sick enough that you have reason to. You're not the one losing face here." Guan Shanjin's voice contained a hint of amusement. Everything he said sounded like he had the best interests of the Yang family in mind, but no matter what, it just felt wrong.

Yang Baisheng felt like he'd been slapped in the face, but he didn't know how to defend himself. He'd ignored Shi-xiaojie for a while now, and since Bao-er had never recovered his cleverness after the illness, he only felt more resentment toward her. His last shred of pity had run out, and the only reason he hadn't divorced her was to uphold his reputation. Deep inside, he hoped Shi-xiaojie would just hurry up and die.

Originally, he'd thought the Shi family no longer cared for their daughter. After all, scholars rarely wanted to kick up a fuss, so it was unlikely they'd come to defend her. But unexpectedly, the very first time they did, they sent someone incredibly difficult to deal with—he couldn't just ignore him.

Yang Baisheng didn't want to draft the divorce letter, but he knew it was futile to go against this man. It didn't matter what kind of status this cousin had; if his sword pierced through him, nothing else would matter anymore. As he quickly weighed the costs and benefits, Yang Baisheng's expression turned ugly.

"Cousin, since you've already considered everything for my family, then..." He sighed. "I can only regretfully divorce her. I hope she understands that our relationship is still very dear to me."

His implication was that Shi-xiaojie better not ask her brothers and father to come for the Yang family and start trouble. After all, the Yang family had not mistreated the Shi family. All these years, they'd dutifully taken care of all her medical costs.

Of course Guan Shanjin understood what the man meant. He scoffed coldly, languidly smoothing a finger down the Chenyuan Sword. His careless action was beyond beautiful, but Yang Baisheng shivered, afraid to say or do anything.

Even though he was unwilling, Yang Baisheng had no choice but to write the divorce letter. Before the ink had even dried, Guan Shanjin snatched it away for Wu Xingzi to examine.

The letter was very simple, and even followed the standard formatting. If it fell under one of the seven qualifications, the husband could divorce the wife without going to court. The husband only needed to sign with his fingerprint. In three days, the wife had to leave the husband's house, all she was allowed to take with her was her dowry. But that didn't mean there wasn't the possibility to play around with the wording of the letter. If the letter was deemed unacceptable, it was possible for the decision to be rendered null.

Wu Xingzi had seen many divorce letters in his time. With a quick glance, he spotted quite a few errors; in a soft voice, he asked Yang Baisheng to correct them. Guan Shanjin stood to the side with something akin to a smile on his lips as he stared at his haggard cousin-in-law. He knocked on his sword slightly, and everyone in the room except Wu Xingzi shook like frightened birds.

Yang Baisheng had indeed tried to pull a few tricks. It wasn't that he didn't want to part with his wife—he just didn't want to part with his wife's dowry. The dowry wasn't worth much, but a penny was a penny, and he was loath to part with even a single coin. He intended to make a few mistakes in the divorce letter, then destroy it after this fearsome cousin-in-law left. That way, he wouldn't have to lose anything; he might even gain the upper hand over his father-in-law.

But...Yang Baisheng was too afraid to even look at Guan Shanjin, so he could only glare at Wu Xingzi. This old thing looked soft and meek. As soon as Yang Baisheng glared at him, he retracted his hand, his actions hesitant. He looked up at the man next to him in uncertainty.

"What is it?" Guan Shanjin asked.

"Why don't I draft the divorce agreement for our cousin-in-law?" That way, they could stop editing it back and forth. He was afraid Guan Shanjin would lose his patience and resort to violence.

Yang Baisheng's expression stiffened. "How could I ask such a thing of you?"

"It's no trouble. I've written many a divorce letter in my time. I just need your fingerprint afterward." Wu Xingzi smiled bashfully at Yang Baisheng, and with a wave of his brush, the divorce letter was finished.

With Guan Shanjin pressuring him, Yang Baisheng had no choice. Shaking, he pressed his finger to the paper.

Once Guan Shanjin saw Wu Xingzi blow the ink dry on the divorce paper and carefully tuck it into his robe, he clasped his hands together and made the pretense of showing respect as he bade farewell to Yang Baisheng. "Since cousin-in-law…I mean, since Yang-gongzi has agreed so readily, I will take my cousin away within a couple of days, and we'll keep out of the way of your father's birthday celebration. There's no need to see us out. Oh, right… Xiao-Bao-er is still young. Since you already have a wife and many children, why don't we take the child with us? That way, your wife won't have to see him around anymore."

Yang Baisheng nearly jumped three feet into the air. Even with the presence of the Chenyuan Sword, he grew red in the face. "Cousin-in-law, aren't you going too far?!" he exclaimed angrily. "Bao-er is a child of the Yang family. Have you ever heard of a divorced wife taking her child with her? Since you have the divorce letter, leave!" With a wave of his sleeve, he turned to summon the steward to chase them out.

At that moment, the soft voice of a woman emanated from outside the study. "Husband, can I come in? This lowly one has something to discuss with you."

"Come in quickly!" Yang Baisheng beckoned her in hurriedly. He knew his wife was smart and capable. If she wanted to see him now, she must have some way to deal with this cousin-in-law.

When he opened the study door, his wife Lady Zou and her brother Zou Yongming were standing outside, just as expected.

Clearly, Zou Yongming had already told Lady Zou everything, from when Guan Shanjin met with Shi-xiaojie in her room to have a secret discussion to what had happened after. Now, his chin was practically pointing in the air as he stared smugly at Guan Shanjin, as though waiting for Guan Shanjin to cower. Of course, he didn't get so much as a glance. Wu Xingzi sighed at him instead, a little resigned, and looked down to nibble on another walnut cookie.

Zou Yongming grew so angry he started to huff and puff, and his pale skin flushed with fury. If Lady Zou hadn't stopped him, who knew what sorts of ugly words would've come from his mouth.

"Husband, I heard that Lady Shi's cousin came to visit, and that he wants to take Bao-er away for a while. Is this true?" Lady Zou looked radiant and gorgeous; her smile was enchanting. She acted like Guan Shanjin and Wu Xingzi didn't exist. Her actions and behavior were a lot more gracious than the men around her.

"That's right. First, they forced me to divorce her, and now they want to take away Bao-er. Hmph! Such behavior is simply an insult!" Yang Baisheng glared at Wu Xingzi, gritting his teeth, but he dared not look at Guan Shanjin.

Lady Zou took note of her husband's actions and started to secretly observe this shockingly beautiful stranger who looked so at ease. He didn't seem to care about anything, staring gently down at the old man in his arms as though he could stay like that forever.

"Cousin-in-law, Bao-er is a child of the Yang family after all, and I will take care of him as if he were my own. How could you..." Lady Zou hadn't finished speaking when Guan Shanjin raised a hand to interrupt her.

"I really must have too much time on my hands, to be dealing with you lowlifes." Guan Shanjin's patience had run out. He regretted trying to stay subtle. "Lijiang County is under the Lu Prefecture, right? I know the prefect of the Lu Prefecture is Xiang Chang'an, and he's about four hours away. Go! Send someone to bring Xiang Chang'an. Just say Guan Shanjin wants to see him."

Everyone from the Yang family was stunned. They didn't know who Guan Shanjin was, but considering the careless way he'd mentioned the prefect, he must be someone with a lot of power. Had they offended someone they couldn't afford to offend?

But the Shi family had been so easy to bully for all these years, and Yang Baisheng and Lady Zou still felt hopeful. Perhaps this man was just bluffing. The couple exchanged glances, then nodded at each other without saying anything. They ordered the steward to send someone to summon the prefect.

For the next four hours, Guan Shanjin and Wu Xingzi returned to Shi-xiaojie's courtyard. Wu Xingzi really liked Bao-er. Although this beautiful child was a little slow, he was not stupid. As long as you gave him enough time to think and practice, his results were shockingly astute compared to other children his age.

Wu Xingzi was not a man with any astonishing talent. Ever since he was young, he'd had to spend more time than his peers to memorize his books, but his father never once scolded him. If he couldn't remember by reading it once, he'd read it three, ten, or even a dozen times. It didn't matter if he walked a little slower; reaching the finish line was what mattered.

Before Bao-er's intelligence had been affected by his illness, he'd read all the books that a child was expected to read to start school. He'd already started to read the Four Books and Five Classics. Now, Wu Xingzi grabbed a copy of the *Analects* and sat the child in his lap, reading it to him word by word. Bao-er behaved himself well, carefully reading the book along with Wu Xingzi. Even if they read it ten times, he didn't get bored. A few hours later, he'd managed to memorize Xue Er, the first book of the *Analects*.

"Bao-er, you're doing great." Wu Xingzi complimented the child, pleased and surprised. Bao-er hadn't been praised like that in a while, and his face flushed with delight. He couldn't have been any cuter if he tried.

After his mother fell sick, everyone—whether it be his younger siblings, his stepmother, his father, or his beautiful but mean second uncle—all said he was stupid. No one bothered to hire a teacher to teach him anything. He wanted to read, and although his stepmother never said he couldn't, he never heard anything about the matter again. It was as though she'd forgotten. So Bao-er could only read those books he'd already read, the ones he could already recite with ease.

Eventually, the prefect arrived. The Yang family chaotically rushed to welcome him, but the prefect was even more panicked than they were. After asking where Guan Shanjin was, he ran over in a hurry, nearly falling flat on his face.

"G-General of the Southern Garrison! Why didn't you tell this lowly one that you were coming to the Lu Prefecture?" The prefect rubbed his hands, an ingratiating smile on his face. The Yang family, who'd rushed in after him, were drenched in cold sweat when they saw the prefect's attitude.

Guan Shanjin waved a hand, a bored expression on his face. "Originally, I just wanted to take care of some family business and didn't want to bother you, but unfortunately...I have a short temper. In order not to cause a huge mess, I had to invite you out here."

"It's my honor to be of assistance!" The prefect's smile did not reach his eyes. He was a secondary class, rank four official—where was the pride that an official of his station should have had? He could not have been more humble.

"It's not a big deal," said Guan Shanjin. "I just have a cousin who married into the Yang family and had a child. But the Yang family tormented them for many years, and now Yang-gongzi has another wife and other children. Clearly, these two are not necessary to the Yang family. As such, I figured it would be best not to disturb the peace in the Yang household, and so I asked Yang-gongzi to divorce my cousin." Guan Shanjin was speaking diplomatically for once. Wu Xingzi, watching from the side, thought this was both surprising and amusing.

"Yes, yes, the general is very noble, keeping the best interests of the Yang family at heart. Quite admirable."

Guan Shanjin smiled, then stared at the members of the Yang family, who were kneeling on the ground and shaking. "My cousin's son has been treated poorly all these years," the general said. "Now that his mother is leaving, how could I rest easy knowing I let him stay in a family where he no longer has a mother to look after him? I heard that a few years ago, he mysteriously fell ill..." At that moment, Guan Shanjin noticed that Yang Baisheng's mother and Lady Zou both shrank into themselves a little. A mocking light shone in his eyes. "I want to take the child with me, but the Yang family won't agree. As a result, I called you here to be a witness. I want to adopt Bao-er as my son. Will the Yang family let him go or not?"

The Great General of the Southern Garrison wanted to adopt Bao-er? The Yang family were already up to no good. Upon hearing this, they realized Bao-er was a hot commodity! There was no way they could let him go now! The Zou family or a sub-prefectural magistrate were nothing compared to Guan Shanjin. They had already divorced Shi-xiaojie. If they wanted a relationship with Guan Shanjin, they had to hold onto Bao-er!

"General! Great General! Bao-er is, after all..." Yang Baisheng looked up in a hurry, wanting to play the emotional card. Bao-er was an obedient child. As long as he had the child, there was no way he'd come out of this empty-handed.

But Guan Shanjin had no patience to listen to him. He tapped on a pressure point, rendering Yang Baisheng unable to speak. He knocked on the table again and again, causing the entire Yang family to break out in cold sweat. Lady Zou wanted desperately to shrink into nothingness; she wanted nothing more than to tunnel underground and disappear.

"Let me remind you: Whether or not you like it, I will be taking Bao-er away today. But if you displease me, things will be even worse for your family. Isn't old Mr. Yang celebrating his birthday?"

At this point, what could the Yang family do? Even the prefect was here as a witness. This wasn't merely just a difference in power anymore—one sneeze from Guan Shanjin could ruin the entire family.

No matter how much hate and regret Yang Baisheng felt, it was no use. He never would've expected Shi-xiaojie to have such a powerful cousin. Later, when he found out Shi-xiaojie's uncle was the Protector General, he nearly lost the ability to breathe. He passed out on the spot, and fell sick for several months. The regret he felt... He'd chased after power and fortune his entire life, yet he threw away his most useful chess piece! But all of this was only clear in hindsight.

Guan Shanjin cut off all of the Yang family's ties to Bao-er with the prefect as witness, then adopted him himself. Finally, he could report back to his mother.

With this matter taken care of, there was no need to stay in Lijiang County any longer. After he took Wu Xingzi to go eat that special dish, they continued on their journey.

After Shi-xiaojie was sent to the capital to recuperate, she lived for another two years. When she closed her eyes for the final time, she looked nothing like that thin, haggard, sickly woman from before. Her face was rosy and her mood was good; she died with a smile.

Bao-er was named Guan Chenliang, and every day, he followed behind Wu Xingzi like his little shadow.

Wu Xingzi couldn't possibly have loved the child more. He taught him every day, told him stories, and took him to the magistrate's office. Bao-er wasn't as clever as most other kids, but he was well-behaved and considerate.

By the time Guan Shanjin quit his job standing guard over Horse-Face City and returned to the capital to inherit the title of Protector General, nearly half the people in Horse-Face City knew of Bao-er or had met him. No matter anyone's age or status, everyone heaped praises onto the child—they all adored him.

Originally, Man Yue and Guan Shanjin's other confidants thought Guan Shanjin would get jealous of this child stealing all of Wu Xingzi's attention, but Guan Shanjin doted on Bao-er, too, attentively raising this son he'd stolen.

What more could one ask for in life?

At one point in his life, Wu Xingzi had planned to commit suicide when he turned forty. He had no family and no hope, only endless loneliness.

Now, he had a child to hold as he taught him to read and write, and a warm, firm chest to protect him from the wind and rain. Perhaps this was the light at the end of the tunnel.

STEPFATHER AND STEPSON

EVERYONE KNEW that the Chief of General Affairs was the company chairman's stepfather. Everyone also knew that the chairman had never liked the Chief of General Affairs. And because he disliked him, the chairman would summon the Chief of General Affairs into his office to humiliate him on a daily basis.

Each day, the Chief of General Affairs left the chairman's office slightly dazed and red-eyed. Everyone concluded that the chairman must constantly be giving him a hard time. After all, even though the chairman was young, handsome, capable, and looked gentle and refined, when he yelled at someone, he could make them wish they'd never been born.

No one knew what the chief had done to offend the chairman. The stepfather and stepson had once lived together for many years. Even if they weren't close, how had their conflict escalated to this point?

The chief always treated the chairman with respect, not acting like his father at all, while the chairman always spoke to the chief coldly. Nine tenths of the chairman's words were thinly veiled insults. As for the remaining tenth of the time, the chairman didn't take his stepfather seriously.

Today, the chief was resting at home, apparently suffering from a summer cold, and the chairman's mood seemed better. During

the weekly meeting, his expression was gentle, a smile curling his lips. His beauty practically doubled, which distracted all the female employees and made all the male employees secretly blush.

Once the weekly meeting was over, Chairman Guan Shanjin returned to his office. When he pushed open the door to his lounge, the mechanical sound of vibrations was deafening in the otherwise quiet room. Accompanying the vibrations was the sound of a man's weak, broken moans. The air filled with the stench of obscenity, and a beautiful smile broke out on Guan Shanjin's face.

"Father," Guan Shanjin said, taking off his suit jacket and loosening his tie. As leisurely as a cat, he ambled to the side of the enormous bed. The bedframe was a European antique, covered in intricately carved metal flowers that were beautiful and delicate. Currently, a pair of hands were bound to this ornate bedframe. The handcuffs jangled softly as the thin, pale wrists trembled.

"X-Xiao-Jin..."

The middle-aged man on the bed was covered in an unhealthy flush, his naked legs spread and tied to a stand at the foot of the bed. The mechanical whirring sound emanated from between his legs, and the sheets beneath him were so wet that liquid could have been wrung from them.

Upon closer inspection, one would find a furry, tail-like thing peeking out from between the man's legs, vibrating slightly. It was also soaking wet.

"Do you like your gift, Father?" Guan Shanjin asked, sitting down on the edge of the bed. A slender, jade-like finger slid up one of the man's legs. His touch, though light as a feather, made the man tremble violently and elicited a low cry from deep in his throat.

"What's the matter? You don't like it?"

"N-no..." The middle-aged man tried to hide, but he was tied too securely. Instead, his movements made it seem like he was begging for more. "Xiao-Jin... Xiao-Jin... Untie me, all right? Please, I'm begging you..."

Guan Shanjin's alluring eyes narrowed slightly, and the small smile on his lips was cold. "Father, does this mean you don't like it? I'm disappointed. After all, I asked a craftsman from overseas to make this little toy as a special gift for your birthday."

At this point, Guan Shanjin's finger had reached the sensitive skin of the other man's inner thigh. His snow-white legs were dotted with finger marks, some dark, some light. It seemed that he had been grabbed there many times. Guan Shanjin's hand wrapped around the pale thigh and easily lifted up the man's lower half.

This position made it feel like his bound ankles were about to come off. The old man cried out, but Guan Shanjin didn't seem to hear him. He forcibly revealed his ass as well as the base of that tail—or rather, a vibrator shaped like a tail.

The older man had a full, perky behind, and a soft, tender bud lay in the middle. Originally, it had been pink and tightly furled, but the vibrator now stretched it to a bright, lewd red. It looked ready to tear; the flesh was almost translucent. As the tail vibrated, juices burst from his hole—it was no wonder the bedsheets were drenched.

Guan Shanjin's long finger pressed down on the man's hole and fragrant fluid immediately covered his hand. The old man let out a broken whimper, and the leg that wasn't in Guan Shanjin's grasp kicked out against the bed, the muscles of his inner thigh trembling and twitching.

"What a slutty old thing..." Guan Shanjin let go of the man's leg and brought his hand, covered in the older man's juices, to his lips. Under the man's shameful gaze, he smiled and slowly licked his hand clean. He looked ethereal as his pink tongue laved his jade-like fingers; the old man could not tear his eyes away. He swallowed reflexively, then opened his mouth, his tongue peeking out slightly.

He looked stupid, yet lascivious all the same. Guan Shanjin snorted, then slowly picked up a small remote from the bedside table. "It seems your mouth is not very honest," he told the other man gently. "Since you *are* enjoying it, how could I not fulfill my duties as a son? Don't worry, there's plenty more where that came from."

The old man's face went white. Trembling, he opened his mouth to beg for mercy, but Guan Shanjin pushed a button on the remote and increased the vibrator's speed from the lowest setting all the way to the highest. The sounds of the vibrations mingled with the wet noises from the man's body. His eyes rolled to the back of his head; even his stomach twitched. He arched his back, feeling like he couldn't get any air into his lungs. His cock, which once lay limp on his stomach, was now so wet it looked like he had pissed himself.

"Look at you. Could you fall any further?" Guan Shanjin furrowed his brow in disgust, then grabbed the man's cotton shirt—which Guan Shanjin had ripped previously—to wipe his stomach. After wiping away the musky, clear fluid, he brought the shirt to his nose and chuckled. "Smell yourself," he demanded. "If I take this outside, everyone will know you're begging to be fucked. Why don't I just throw you onto the street like this so that the dirty vagrants can line up and fuck you one after another? You'll never be able to live without a dick inside you again."

The man hiccupped. "Dragon's pearl," he sobbed.

These completely unrelated words made Guan Shanjin freeze for a moment. Then, sighing, he turned off the vibrator and carefully untied his stepfather.

"Giving up so quickly?"

The man on the bed was crying so hard his face looked splotchy. Pitifully, he stared at the tent in Guan Shanjin's pants with a little resentment. He pouted, not answering.

"I told you this sort of thing isn't for everyone, but you just had to try it after we watched that movie," Guan Shanjin said as he tenderly pulled the man into his arms, leaving kiss after kiss on his haggard face.

"You're so mean," the old man complained. Inside, he still felt unhappy. It had felt good, but his son's words scared him. He couldn't take it anymore and said his safeword, but now, he was trying to play tough. "Next time... Next time, I'll get used to it!"

"There's still going to be a next time?" Guan Shanjin laughed, exasperated. He grabbed the man's hand and put it on his dick. A bright red tongue peeked out as he licked his lips. "Why don't you help me with this problem first?"

The old man's face blushed red as he glanced at him. Trembling, he unzipped Guan Shanjin's pants and pulled his hard, dripping cock out through the fly of his underwear. Suddenly, his mouth went dry, and he couldn't help but lick his lips.

Just as he was about to lean down to wrap his mouth around that full head, the room's intercom buzzed to life.

"Chairman, Vice President Man is looking for you." The secretary's sweet, beautiful voice made the old man's shoulders slump in disappointment.

"Don't worry, you can suck to your heart's content." Guan Shanjin smiled as brilliantly as a blooming flower, and he carried his stepfather out of the room.

By the time the old man realized what was going on, he'd already been pushed into the small space beneath the desk, forced to curl up into a ball. His chin just so happened to rest on his stepson's knees as he sat down at the desk, and he was now directly facing the bulge

in his pants. Before he could even blush, those long, powerful legs parted, and Guan Shanjin patted him on the cheek.

"Didn't you want to suck me off, Father? Remember to be quiet."

Charmed by his son's soft, gentle voice, the older man didn't even hear the office door open or the footsteps that followed. All he could focus on was the heavy warmth he could sense through his son's pants. Mouth dry, he swallowed, then slowly brought his face closer. Gripping the zipper with his teeth, he slowly pulled it down.

Guan Shanjin quickly gave his father an encouraging look, then turned his attention to Man Yue as his chubby body jiggled over to the desk.

"Where's your dad?" Man Yue asked as he looked around, not finding the person he expected to see. He vaguely felt that something was amiss.

"You came to look for him?" Guan Shanjin coldly quirked up his lips, scaring his childhood friend and confidant.

Under the table, the old man had already pulled out Guan Shanjin's dick and was stroking it with his soft hands. Entranced, he pressed his face into the younger man's crotch, breathing in his scent.

What a fucking slut, Guan Shanjin thought.

"Your face is a little red." Man Yue was about to report on his work when he just so happened to glance at Guan Shanjin's reddened ears. His question came out unbidden; once he realized what he'd asked, his face went red as well. Angrily, he glared at his friend. "Holy shit, you're an *animal*. Don't tell me anything—I'll come back later."

"No need. Go ahead." Guan Shanjin grabbed Man Yue, forcing him to stay. His beautiful smile was like a bloodthirsty beast's, wild yet alluring. Even though Man Yue was used to Guan Shanjin's beauty, his own ears felt a little warm.

"Fine." Spitting angrily, Man Yue looked down, pretending he hadn't noticed anything. Word by word, he mechanically read out the report in his hands.

Meanwhile, things were heating up under the desk. The old man held his son's thick cock, his hands barely able to close around it. The veins on the shaft almost seemed to throb as precum beaded at the tip and slowly slid down. As he stroked it, the entire meaty cock felt hot and wet, giving off the thick scent of pheromones.

He swallowed, no longer able to resist. He reached forward to lick it, and a musky, slightly bitter taste spread over his tastebuds; it was unbelievably delicious. He sucked on it bit by bit, his tongue moving along the tip. He occasionally licked downward to the ridge of the head. The taste was slightly stronger and saltier in the area around the foreskin, but he loved it. He kept pressing down, nibbling, and sometimes even licking under the foreskin, stimulating that extremely sensitive area.

"Mn!" Guan Shanjin grunted. His beautiful brows furrowed, the image of a worried beauty.

Man Yue—who happened to look up at that very moment—felt queasy. Did this father-son duo have to go so hard at it? Did they care about the mental well-being of the single people around here?

"Continue," Guan Shanjin said.

If Man Yue could ignore Guan Shanjin's slight breathiness, he would have seemed extremely calm and collected—no different from his typical serious demeanor as Chairman... *Calm and collected, my ass!*

Man Yue backed up a couple of steps, then continued reading the second page of the report in a loud voice.

Underneath the desk, the old man seemed to have had enough of licking his son's big cock. His mouth tingled, and his throat—

which had been thoroughly trained—was desperate for something thick and hot to fill it. Even if he choked, even if uncontrollable tears flowed down his face, nothing could quell his desire.

The best thing was, of course, his stepson's huge, thick cock.

The old man sucked on his son's wet slit, completely enraptured. Then, he opened his mouth wide and took most of his length into his mouth in one movement. When it reached the back of his throat, he reflexively gagged. Tears were smeared all over his face and drool escaped from the corners of his mouth, mixing with Guan Shanjin's precum and making the thick length even wetter.

He pressed his tongue into the slit, then hollowed out his cheeks and sucked, even though his mouth was already stuffed full. He managed to slowly swallow the rest of the length down his tight throat, and a large bump appeared through his thin neck. The vague shape of Guan Shanjin's cock could be seen under the thin flesh as it moved.

His mouth was stuffed and he couldn't move his tongue. All he could do was press it against the hefty cock and feel the thick veins. His chin had already reached the heavy, round balls, and he reached out to gently squeeze them.

The old man had no gag reflex. He took a few breaths, and all he could smell was the potent virility of his son. His brain, which was already quite muddled, felt even more like mush. Finally recovering a little, he tightened his throat, squeezing the cock inside. Then, he started to bob his head up and down.

After deepthroating his stepson for a while, he let up a little bit and used his teeth to scrape lightly against the sensitive ridge of the cockhead, feeling his son's trembling thighs. Then, he sucked on the head itself for a while, licking at the slit and swallowing down precum.

As the old man concentrated fully on his task, Guan Shanjin could no longer maintain his calm demeanor. Thin beads of sweat appeared on his forehead, and his alluring eyes misted over slightly. His breathing grew hot and heavy, and his hands clenched tightly together atop the desk; the report in his hands crinkled from the force.

Man Yue stood with his back pressed against the office door, wishing desperately to be anywhere else. He wanted to leave but couldn't. His boss had said before that if he ran away, he'd lose two months of bonuses—how could he be so cruel?! Besides, showering his father with affection like *this*... Did he have a problem?!

Guan Shanjin made a valiant attempt to curtail his response, but the old man was diving in with more and more enthusiasm. He swallowed the entire length down, burying his nose into Guan Shanjin's neatly trimmed pubic hair. Unable to withstand it anymore, Guan Shanjin clamped down on his father's head and thrust deeply, as though he were a mere sex toy.

The old man felt like his throat was about to burst, and he sobbed as he looked up pitifully at his son. He could not have looked any more obscene. Guan Shanjin's heart immediately went soft, but he couldn't control himself—he thrust in deeply and came straight into his father's stomach.

When the still-hard cock was pulled out of his throat, the old man lay atop his son's knees and coughed uncontrollably. A drop of cum still stained the corner of his lips. His son wiped it off, then fed it to him.

"Does it taste good, Father?" he asked, smiling.

He gazed at his son's beautiful face and smiled back almost drunkenly. "Yes... I want more..."

The office door suddenly slammed shut, startling the secretary. Looking up, she saw the round man was red in the face, and his usually smiling expression was ugly. He loosened his tie aggressively, then said roughly, "Clear the Chairman's schedule until two p.m.! *He's* in there."

As one of the Chairman's confidants, the secretary immediately understood who "he" was. Her expression turned sympathetic, and she carefully nodded in understanding.

They both knew very well that the Chairman and the Chief of General Affairs were not, in fact, enemies who could not stand each other. Instead, they were very close and got along swimmingly. The secretary was a single lady about to turn thirty, and she'd witnessed the pornographic scenes of the Chairman fucking his stepfather into his desk a few times already. Hearing the hurried, fierce sounds of slapping bodies, the secretary sometimes worried the Chief's stomach would be pierced through. How ruthless and violent!

Watching as Vice President Man stomped off in a huff, the secretary picked up the phone and started to rearrange the day's schedule.

Meanwhile, inside the office, the couple who only brought trouble to their employees had already stripped each other bare. In front of a large stretch of floor-to-ceiling windows, they were tangled together passionately and kissing noisily.

The old man's well-used hole was bright red and debauched. He was so turned on from that blowjob that his hole was already wet, and it kept clenching and unclenching, eager and insatiable. His entire pale body was flushed pink, and as his son kissed him deeply, suffocatingly, it felt like he could no longer keep up.

But Guan Shanjin knew well that his stepfather was just a hungry kitten. He looked shy and bashful, but when he got in the mood, there was no limit to his debauchery—even prostitutes would have a hard time keeping up. But that was exactly what he liked about his father. He practically wanted to swallow him whole.

As Guan Shanjin kissed him, he touched him everywhere. He pressed the thin body into the glass of the window and pulled a slender, pale leg up to wrap around his waist. The old thing couldn't keep his balance, leaning all his weight into him. Cupping Guan Shanjin's face, he begged, "Come inside... Quickly... There's an itch I need you to scratch... I need your huge cock..."

How could he be such a slut? Did have no shame?!

The young man gritted his teeth and did not answer. Instead, he rubbed his hard dick against the man's perineum, then toward his winking hole, making slick, wet sounds along the way.

The older man was clearly impatient. He shook his ass excitedly, eager to take in the hard length. But Guan Shanjin refused to do as his father asked. He slightly pressed the head of his cock inside before pulling back out. In and out, this continued a few times until the old man clung to him tightly and kissed his face and neck. "Fuck me," he cried and begged, "Fuck me to death!"

Guan Shanjin's chest burned. His father's lewd words were more potent than any drug. His cock stiffened even further. He slid into the hungry, wet hole, wanting to tease him some more, but he couldn't bring himself to pull out. It felt like a hundred little mouths were sucking at his cock. It was so good that he let out a low grunt, his charming eyes reddening slightly.

"As you wish!" Since the old thing dared to play with fire, Guan Shanjin wouldn't stop until he was pumped full of cum!

Guan Shanjin had always been a little aggressive when it came to sex, and his stepfather had always brought out the most sadistic side of him. He forcefully grabbed the older man's other leg, and with a single thrust, his entire length burrowed inside.

The old man felt like his stepson's cock was nearly in his stomach. Deeper inside, Guan Shanjin's cock reached somewhere that should have been far too deep, but through many years of passion, the pair had found a suitable angle. That area was even tighter and hotter, and it tightly clamped down onto a third of Guan Shanjin's dick as it sucked him in, trembling.

The older man threw his head back, revealing his thin neck. His delicate throat bobbed as he mewled weakly. The pleasure was so intense that for a moment he blacked out.

Guan Shanjin did not wait for him to adjust. He immediately began fucking into him in earnest.

The old man's belly protruded with the shape of Guan Shanjin's dick. His son held him in midair, fucking him against the window with his huge cock as the only point of support. It felt like every thrust was deeper than the last, the young man's firm body pressing more and more into his until there was absolutely no space left between them. His belly, swelling with the outline of Guan Shanjin's massive cock, brushed up against his son's tight abs; even his own tiny dick would rub against that taut stomach from the force of their fucking.

"T-too deep... Xiao-Jin, Xiao-Jin... You're going to break me— *ahhh*!"

His small dick could not take the friction any longer; he suddenly released everything onto his son's belly. His cum was already as clear as water, and it had a musky, sweet scent. Stimulated by the scent, the young man fucked him even harder.

The older man's cries became sweeter, and he could not stop kissing his son. He felt his own belly with a free hand, as though wanting to flatten the bump, but with each of his son's harsh thrusts, his hand fell away.

The hot, hard cock reached new depths, rubbing powerfully against his soft, sensitive insides to the point where his channel almost seemed to lose its elasticity. He allowed his son to use him like a fucktoy, the harsh thrusts leaving his insides swollen. Even the narrowest part of his passage was stretched open.

Within the pain was unparalleled pleasure, pouring over the man in waves until he cried out. His entire body trembled and twitched as more wetness poured out of him. His climax never seemed to end, and the pleasure pushed the old man to another peak. He couldn't breathe, his eyes rolling into the back of his head as strands of saliva coated his lips. His fingers weakly scrambled for purchase as he clung to his son's muscular shoulders. Several times, he thought he might pass out, but he was pulled back to reality each time, trembling and screaming from his orgasms.

White foam frothed up where the two men's bodies were connected. It was beautiful and filthy, and plenty of the fluids stained the windows. The old man slid across the glass with a harmonious yet peculiar sound.

Guan Shanjin leaned down to bite ferociously at his father's pale, delicate neck. The adrenaline of having his life in someone else's hands, as well as the excitement and pleasure that followed, made the older man convulse. The slit of his half-hard cock gaped open, but only a few drops came out. In the chaotic excitement, he could only manage a dry orgasm.

Guan Shanjin was about to continue fucking his father when the secretary suddenly called. Her tone was very even, as though she had no idea what kinds of erotic, devious things were happening inside the office, as if she hadn't heard the old man's moans.

"Chairman, you have a meeting with the Nanyang Group in an hour," she said.

In an hour? Guan Shanjin clicked his tongue and glanced at the clock on his desk. He was very disappointed that he hadn't fucked his father into pissing himself yet, but the meeting with the Nanyang Group was about their collaboration over the next three seasons... As Chairman, he had to attend.

The old man's eyes were half closed. He shivered as he leaned against his son's shoulders and tried to catch his breath, still recovering from his orgasm.

Leaning forward to kiss his eyelids, Guan Shanjin pressed down into his father as he fucked him forcefully again and again. The old man—who had yet to catch his breath—was fucked until he could no longer control his legs. He cried and screamed as waves of lewd juices poured out of him, completely dirtying the windows. His eyes rolled back into his head and his tongue lolled out. He was about to faint.

The young man finally mustered all his courage to go as deeply as he could. It felt like he'd nearly pierced through his stepfather's stomach. The older man arched his neck and trembled uncontrollably as Guan Shanjin filled him.

Guan Shanjin came deep inside, so when he pulled out, not much of his cum spilled out; it was mostly his father's juices. Most of his cum was safely locked away inside his father's belly, so much of it that his stomach bulged. He patted his stepfather's belly, satisfied, then pushed himself inside once more. "Father," he said in a low voice, biting his stepfather's ear, "Father, you should give me a child. Would it call me Dad, or brother?"

Feeling his own stomach, the old man responded, dazed, "I'm a man. I can't give birth..."

"Who knows? I come inside you so much every day that it leaks out of you when you walk. How could you not get pregnant?" Guan Shanjin smiled, his eyes narrowing slightly. He patted his father's round ass, then wrapped his legs more firmly around his waist. "Hold on tight. I'll carry you to the other room."

"Mm..." The older man whined as he did his best to wrap his legs around Guan Shanjin's torso, but the movement made his son's large cock slide further inside of him. With the fat head caught within him, he nearly came again.

"Slut." Pressing his stepfather's ass firmly against his pelvis, Guan Shanjin carried him back to the lounge room. It was a short journey, but the old man cried out nonstop, breathing harshly. His belly sloshed with the mixture of his own juices and Guan Shanjin's cum.

By the time he fell back on the bed, the older man was nearly half dead. His eyes rolled into the back of his skull, and all of his limbs trembled. His awareness had flown clear out the window.

Guan Shanjin was very pleased. He retrieved a large buttplug from the bedside table. At its widest point, it was even thicker than his own cock. Weighing the plug in his hand, he lightly shook his father awake. "Father, I'm going to plug you up so my cum stays inside you and gets you pregnant, all right?" he said sweetly.

The old man took a groggy look at the teardrop-shaped object in his son's hand and nodded without fully understanding what he was agreeing to. By the time his son positioned him so he was forced to watch the huge plug enter his hole, it was too late to change his mind.

"Xiao-Jin... Xiao-Jin," he sobbed, unable to tell if what he felt was fear or excitement. He called out his son's nickname as he cried, and the ends of his sentences sounded as sticky as syrup. Guan Shanjin hesitated, his heart softening. In the end, he gritted his teeth and continued.

Until his father said his safeword, the scene would continue—that was their agreement. His father had used his safeword not too long ago before expressing that he wanted to continue, so Guan Shanjin didn't dare go too far. His words and actions weren't that much different from the norm; he was just a little rougher.

He hadn't planned on using this plug so soon. His father's hole was so soft and tight. If it stretched too much and tore, his heart would ache. But...truthfully, he felt a little excited. He wanted to see exactly how far this slutty, leaking hole could stretch. When he thought about his cum staying inside his stepfather, filling him up until the next time he fucked into him, Guan Shanjin could not contain his sadistic side.

"Be good and take a deep breath." He raised his father's hips even more and bent him well past a ninety-degree angle, pushing his pale, slender thighs nearly to his chest.

Even though he was lying on the bed, the old man could very clearly see his own swollen hole. Each wrinkle was bright red, and it gave the occasional uneasy clench. Every time it tensed up, a little bit of liquid dripped out, making the bud seem even more delicate and wet.

Guan Shanjin's left hand pressed down on the inside of his father's right knee, letting his left leg dangle. In this position, the small hole opened up a little more, and he immediately pressed the tip of the plug in. Taking advantage of the trickling slick, he slowly pushed the plug further inside.

"Mm... Hurts..." The plug was too thick. The thinner part at the beginning felt all right, but as it went in further, his small hole was completely stretched out. The skin around the plug went white, and it looked like it could tear at any moment. The older man wept from the pain. He wiggled around, wanting to hide, but of course his son mercilessly stopped any attempts.

"Just bear with it, hm?" Sweat beaded on Guan Shanjin's forehead. His movements were gentle but unyielding as he continued to push the plug deeper inside.

The older man's passage had always been tight. When he fucked into him, the tightness sometimes hurt. Now, it clung tightly onto the plug, and the resistance was obvious. Guan Shanjin chuckled and pulled the plug out slightly.

As expected, the old, greedy thing desperately clung onto the plug. Suddenly, it was impossible to pull the toy out. Instead, when Guan Shanjin let go, the greedy hole sucked in quite a large portion of the plug; much more of it was inside than before. "You filthy old thing. I knew you were hungry."

The thickest part of the plug stretched the older man open. The well-fucked hole did not rip or tear; it just looked paler than usual. Feeling the pain of the stretch, he couldn't help but beg and cry pitifully. "Xiao-Jin... It hurts..."

"Give me a child, hm?" Those long fingers held onto the base of the plug and pulled it out slightly. The rim of the older man's hole started to stretch along with it. It was stretched so thin that it almost felt like one could see the flesh on the inside.

"I can't... I can't do it... Xiao-Jin, stop bullying me..." He sobbed as he thrashed his one free leg. As he trembled and twitched, it was hard to tell if he was feeling pain or pleasure.

"Okay, I'll stop." Guan Shanjin smiled lightly but enchantingly. As his father stared up at him, enamored, he stuffed the entire plug in until only the base peeked out.

"Ah!" the old man screamed, tears streaming down his face. Clutching his stomach, he lay limply on the bed, spasming. He looked broken, which only gave his ordinary appearance a lascivious edge.

Guan Shanjin's chest felt hot. He leaned down and sucked the older man's tongue into his mouth. He kissed him feverishly and twisted their tongues together. He plundered his sensitive mouth and nearly reached his throat. He didn't stop until the older man hit him on the shoulder, desperately needing to breathe.

"Once the meeting is over, I'm taking you home. I'll make sure you get pregnant today." Guan Shanjin smiled. He was so handsome that it took the older man's breath away. He nodded, dazed.

"Be good."

By the time the older man was woken again, the sky outside the window had gone dark. His stomach was full and bloated; even when he rolled over, he could feel just how full his belly was. His limbs felt weak as he lay feebly in his son's arms, staring at the set of women's clothing before him, lost.

"Can you wear this for me, Dad?" The man caressed his father's cheek, planting several kisses on his face.

"B-but this is..." Slowly, starting from the base of his ears, the older man's entire body flushed red. Tears swam in his eyes as he begged his son with his gaze.

"Don't you want your master to be happy, you little slut?" Guan Shanjin smiled with narrowed eyes, his voice going cold. It was not a question—it was a command.

The old man shrank into himself and smiled ingratiatingly. "O-of course I do... C-can you help me up?" His expression was innocent and pitiful, but he didn't put up much resistance.

Satisfied, Guan Shanjin patted his firm ass. He helped his father up from the bed and handed him the clothes. "Put these on. You've acted like a bitch in heat the whole day—do you even remember that you're human?"

His rough words made the older man's face go pale. His brows knit together, and he looked like he was about to cry.

His son raised a brow. "Hurry up," he demanded. "I've had a long day. I don't have time to watch you squirm."

The outfit wasn't difficult to put on, but he got the order wrong.

He first put on the shirt, then the skirt, but then he realized there was no way he could get the stockings on. They were caught around his knees. The skirt reached just past his knees, but it was tight, squeezing his ass so that it looked even rounder and perkier than usual. With all his stepson's semen and his own juices still plugged up inside of him, he nearly couldn't pull the zipper up. He almost looked three months pregnant.

He awkwardly sat on the edge of the bed and nearly fell over, one foot in the tights and one foot out. He looked to his son for help.

Guan Shanjin sighed. "Did I fuck your brains out?" he chided him impatiently. "If you can't get the tights on with the skirt, then take off the skirt and put it on. Stupid thing. If you lose any more brain cells, I don't want you anymore."

"Ah... Oh..." The old man shrank into himself and hurriedly removed the tight skirt. Finally, he managed to get the entire outfit on.

The old man was average in appearance, but he had a beautiful figure. He was on the smaller side, with pale skin, and his son had spoiled him until he was pink and flushed everywhere. His slender legs were particularly eye-catching in the sheer black tights. His well-proportioned calves stretched out from beneath the skirt, and his ankles were thin and delicate. Because he was not used to wearing women's clothes—and because he was embarrassed—his round little toes squirmed inside the tights.

Guan Shanjin's chest suddenly felt hot. Without thinking about it, he loosened his tie, and his charming eyes darkened a little. He brought out a pair of plain black heels.

"Put these on."

"Huh?" The older man accepted the shoes. Although the heels weren't too tall, they were at least a couple of inches high, and they were so thin that he wasn't confident he could even walk in them.

Seeing him hesitate, Guan Shanjin pushed the man down to sit on the edge of the bed. He helped him into the shoes, first the right foot, then the left. When he was done, he couldn't resist biting the inside of his ankle.

"Hey!" The old man panted lightly, his cheeks blushing bright red. He looked at his son in a hazy stupor. He felt embarrassed and obscene as he slowly stood. The heels were exactly his size, and easier to walk in than he'd thought. Although his steps weren't too stable, he was in no danger of falling.

"Let's go." As the finishing touch, Guan Shanjin placed a long, straight black wig on his father's head.

Guan Shanjin was very satisfied with the sight before him. Reaching out to pull the older man into his arms, he went down to the parking lot through his own private elevator.

When they left the office, they just so happened to run into the secretary. The older man was so embarrassed that he wanted to dig a hole and throw himself into it. The secretary, however, was unfazed. Without a change in her expression, she stood up to send them off. It wasn't until the elevator doors had closed that she covered her face and let out an exhausted sigh.

Because he was wearing heels, the old man swayed as he walked, and so did his tight ass. He looked like he was inviting everyone around to press him down into the floor, rip his skirt to pieces, and fuck him. Guan Shanjin purposefully stayed a step behind his stepfather, unable to tear his eyes away from his voluptuous ass. His gorgeous and expressive eyes now looked like that of a starved wolf; he could not bear to look away.

"Xiao-Jin?" Stumbling a few times, the old man looked back pitifully to see his son. The tight skirt meant he had to take tiny steps, and with the heels, his balance was even worse. He had to squeeze his ass together to walk, but he was hindered by that large thing stuffed inside of him. Whenever he clenched, the plug would settle right against all his most sensitive spots. In just five short minutes, he had leaked so much that the plug couldn't keep it all contained. Droplets seeped out from around the plug, and his crotch was now wet.

"Hm?" Guan Shanjin's throat went dry and his breathing grew slightly heavier. He procured a cigarette before glancing at his father, signaling for him to continue.

The old man bit his lip. "Help me. My tights are all soaked..."

Guan Shanjin didn't know if he was doing it on purpose or not, but when the older man spoke, he kept shaking his ass. How could he remain indifferent to that? If he didn't do something about this right now, either he couldn't get it up, or he wasn't a man!

"You asked for it." With two large steps, Guan Shanjin reached his father and scooped the man into his arms, dragging him toward his car. The rough movement made the older man scream in alarm. In his panic, he even lost a shoe.

In less than a minute, they arrived at Guan Shanjin's car, a black Maserati. The car was very low to the ground, and its front hood was slightly slanted. The car reflected a dim light, looking like a black panther waiting to pounce.

The old man let out a slight scream as Guan Shanjin pushed him onto the hood of his car. He violently ripped off his wig and threw it to the ground. Due to his stepfather's squirming, his skirt was starting to ride up, revealing half of his thigh. Guan Shanjin stared at the slightly thin leg, lit his cigarette, and took a drag. Then, he slowly exhaled all the smoke. The man on the hood looked back at him just in time to see him exhale. Guan Shanjin looked elegant yet dangerous, with slightly narrowed, charming eyes. Almost anyone would fall at his feet and beg him to fuck them.

The old man's ass suddenly felt itchy. Whimpering, he moaned lewdly, dragging the noise out. He really could not have made for a filthier sight.

"If I don't fuck you to death here, we're not leaving." Guan Shanjin reached for his father's exposed thigh. With a loud sound, the sheer tights came apart, slowly ripping up toward his ass. The crotch area really was wet. Caught between shreds of sheer fabric, the older man's pale asscheeks were particularly eye-catching.

Guan Shanjin aggressively kneaded his father's full rear, the tight flesh jiggling in his palms. Then, he spread apart his legs, which were curled up tightly to maintain balance, and exposed his entire crotch. The plastic buttplug peeked out of his asshole. The rim seemed to constantly shrink into itself, rosy and slightly swollen.

Following the curve of his father's thigh, Guan Shanjin's hand slowly slid toward the base of that plug. It was ring-shaped; the perfect fit for a finger.

"Father," he said, his soft voice full of emotion.

The old man trembled slightly. From his awkward position, he looked back at Guan Shanjin and answered him in a soft voice. "Yes?"

"Take a deep breath."

A deep breath?

Before he could react, the younger man harshly tugged on the ring, ripping out the plug in one movement. With it came all the cum and fluids trapped inside, shooting over a foot away.

"*Ah!*" the older man cried shrilly. He tried to clench his asshole shut, but after being toyed with the entire day, the ring of muscle had lost its elasticity, gaping half-open. It seemed he could not even work those muscles. They would not tighten nor clench.

He didn't want to face the reality of the situation. He put his head in his hands, but nothing could cover up the scent or the wet, dripping feeling.

Guan Shanjin's eyes were red as he stared like a hungry wolf at his father's red, swollen hole that wouldn't close up anymore. Covered in all kinds of fluids, the older man could not have been in a sorrier state. Guan Shanjin didn't even care that his own leather shoes were now wet. Even his pant legs felt damp.

"Dirty slut..."

He pressed down on the man half sprawled on his car hood. Other than the hiked-up skirt and the torn tights, his clothes were still pristine, which only increased the sexy but forbidden feeling. Heat surged within Guan Shanjin, and he aggressively kneaded that soft, bouncy ass.

The older man wanted to bury himself in his shame. He called out to his son and cried as Guan Shanjin spanked his ass. "Xiao-Jin... Xiao-Jin..."

"Good boy." The younger man yanked down his zipper, revealing his hard, leaking cock. Without any resistance, he shoved his way into his father's body.

"No—!" The old man cried out in pain again, but it only made him seem more salacious.

His son forcefully spread his cheeks apart, the large cock managing to sheathe itself almost entirely in one go. It rubbed against every inch of delicate flesh. After the hard cockhead made its way past his prostate, it stabbed directly into the deepest parts of him. He was so swollen there that it almost hurt when Guan Shanjin reached it.

The old man shrank into himself, wanting to hide, but the hood of the sports car was slanted. He could not maintain his balance at all; he kept sliding down the hood and onto his son's cock.

Then, the force of a thrust would push him back up the hood before he slid down again. After a few times, he lay limply on the hood with absolutely no energy left. Guan Shanjin fucked his most sensitive spots, and it felt both amazing and painful at the same time; his voice went hoarse from all the screaming.

A few dozen thrusts later, Guan Shanjin's large cockhead finally made it past that tight ring of muscle deep within him. At this point, his father was covered in all kinds of sweat and fluids, and he looked like an overripe fruit. Every time he fucked into him, more juices spilled out, thoroughly soaking the place where they were joined.

"Ahhh, Xiao-jin, ahhhh!" the old man screamed as he struggled on the hood.

The waxed car looked very smooth, but there was a lot of friction as his body dragged along it. He felt like his half-hard little cock might lose a layer of skin from all the rubbing; it hurt like hell. But combined with the pleasure of being fucked so brutally by his son, this pain only intensified the pleasure. He arched his neck, unable to catch his breath. His small, delicate Adam's apple bobbed; in the darkness of the underground parking lot, it looked like a small butterfly.

This only urged Guan Shanjin on more, but he was afraid that his father would get hurt, so he turned him around and held him up by the crooks of his knees. The old man let out a surprised yelp, but it soon turned into a prolonged moan. As he slumped into his son's arms, there were only three points of support between them: his son's dick, and the two arms clamped around his legs.

The thick, fierce length jostled his pale, thin body up and down, and the outline of the cock could be seen through his stomach. Separated by a thin layer of flesh, his own tiny cock and his son's monstrous one rubbed against his stomach from both sides. He arched his back and cried out lasciviously. His mouth hung half-open, tongue peeking out; he could not have looked any more debauched.

His spread thighs trembled, and even his toes curled up in pleasure. His expression, deep in the throes of passion, was utterly captivating. Guan Shanjin couldn't help but capture that lolling tongue with his own lips, kissing him aggressively.

He was kissed nearly to the point of suffocation, but he just couldn't get away. The pleasure was too much, and he couldn't take any more; quivering, he came.

After he was fucked to his last breath, the older man's little cock was so dry that not even urine would come out of it anymore—but his son would not let him rest. Once again, he pressed him into the hood of the car and swallowed all of his broken screams. His thick cock reached deeper and deeper with each thrust, forcing orgasm after orgasm from the old man. It was like he had molded even his deepest parts into a cocksleeve. His father twitched and jerked, his eyes rolling into the back of his head. He nearly passed out, but because of all the overwhelming pleasure and how sensitive his body was, he remained conscious.

The old man opened his lips to beg for mercy but was instead locked into a kiss. Clamping down firmly on his hips, his son continued to fuck him fiercely.

His hole was now thoroughly fucked and bright red, and with each thrust, peeks of the rosy flesh could be seen. Even though his stepson had freed his lips, he still couldn't make any sound. His mouth hung open and drool dripped out. It felt like he was now completely useless, like there was no other point to his existence than taking his son's huge cock.

Suddenly, Guan Shanjin clamped down harshly on his waist, and with a few deep, fierce thrusts, he came like a geyser deep inside his father's ass. There was so much cum, and it was so deep. The older man shuddered from the heat of it all and finally fainted.

Lying atop his father, Guan Shanjin panted heavily for a while. Due to the immense pleasure, he felt a little dizzy. They truly had indulged too much in debauchery today—his father looked broken.

A large patch of Guan Shanjin's slacks was wet from his father's juices, but he didn't mind. He wiped the various fluids off of his dick and tucked it back into his pants, then pulled his father's tights off all the way. He stuffed the plug back into the older man's hole and smoothed his skirt back down. After that, he couldn't resist kissing his father's delicate, naked ankle.

"Father, let's go home." Guan Shanjin gathered the older man into his arms and gave him a kiss. Despite having passed out, the old man still occasionally twitched in his arms.

The old man still had plenty of vacation days to use. Perhaps he could rearrange his work and the two of them could go on a trip. Having sex with the ocean breeze blowing over them would be a whole new experience!

The pale and skinny middle-aged man slept on a huge king bed. Although it was a cold night, the heat was turned to a comfortable temperature. He was only covered in a thin blanket, nearly swallowed up by the soft mattress.

When Guan Shanjin walked into the room, rubbing his nose, exhaustion was evident on his face. However, when he saw the soft heap on the bed, his expression immediately relaxed. His father was deep asleep, his small face nestled crookedly into the pillow. He looked foolish but endearing.

The temperature was perfect for the older man, but it was a little too warm for Guan Shanjin. Very quickly, he removed his sweater, revealing a muscled torso that looked as though it was carved from marble. His legs were clad in a pair of sweatpants, making them seem long and powerful.

If the old man was awake, he'd surely cry out for his son in desperation, but unfortunately, he was deep asleep right now. He didn't wake even when his son climbed onto the bed and flipped back an edge of the blanket. He only mumbled sleepily, rubbing his face into the pillow. His mouth fell open slightly from the movement.

Guan Shanjin chuckled lightly as he rubbed his father's lips with long, callused fingers. When he entered his stepfather's half-open mouth and played with the tongue inside, the old man let out a muffled grunt. In his sleep, he obediently sucked on the fingers inside his mouth. He was still asleep, but his soft tongue was already starting to act lewdly. He licked at the pad of Guan Shanjin's fingers, then at his knuckles. Occasionally, he would even softly bite down, then go back to suckling. His stepfather's tongue set Guan Shanjin's heart ablaze. He cursed under his breath as his huge cock hardened, tenting his sweatpants.

He knew his father slept deeply. Even if he was fucked into harshly, he would not immediately awaken. A wicked idea formed in his head: He was going to fuck his father awake.

Pulling his slightly tingling fingers out from his father's mouth, Guan Shanjin dragged him out from under the blanket. His father was wearing a set of white silk pajamas, his birthday gift to him last year. He'd worn them too often, and the collar was a little loose. The old man turned over, stretching out the collar and revealing pale, delicate skin and collarbones.

Guan Shanjin breathed deeply, leaning down to kiss and suck at his collarbones. Because the older man was skinny, his collarbones protruded quite a bit. He had a small frame and delicate bone structure, and the dip between his collarbones looked round and smooth. Soon, several marks appeared on them.

The man remained deeply asleep. Moaning a few times, he puffed his chest up toward his son, asking for more.

"Dirty thing..." No matter how much affection Guan Shanjin showered upon his father, he could not tamp down the sadistic urge rising within him. This old thing looked shy and modest, always wearing a dark, old-fashioned suit paired with a discounted white shirt from a random market and a plain-colored tie. If he hadn't been the Chairman's stepfather, who knew what kind of bullying he'd suffer at the hands of his colleagues. But when faced with his son, his shyness, modesty, and chastity all flew out the window. He would beg for his son's large cock, leaking from both ends, and he was willing to try all sorts of kinks—sometimes he even enjoyed them more than Guan Shanjin.

Cursing under his breath, Guan Shanjin quickly undressed his father. Soon he lay naked atop the blankets. Goosebumps appeared on his delicate, white skin, and he kept trying to burrow back under the blankets. After Guan Shanjin dragged him back out again, he pressed the man into the mattress with his body and started to pinch at his father's soft, slightly round chest.

On his pale chest were two peachy nipples, perky and stiff. They used to be tiny, almost too small to lick, but after several years of being played with, they had become swollen and large. They were each about the size of a red bean, and if he didn't wear an under-shirt, the redness would even peek through his clothes. He'd worn nipple clamps before, but because Guan Shanjin was afraid it'd hurt

too much, they didn't keep the jewelry on for more than a couple of days before they removed it. They'd never tried it since.

Guan Shanjin pinched the large, swollen nipples, entranced. They were soft but bouncy. He leaned in and sucked the left nipple so that even the areola was in his mouth. He licked at the bud with the flat of his tongue, then started to poke at it with the tip. After a while, he bit at it a little. The slightly rough treatment made the nipple go from the size of a red bean to the size of a soybean. He sucked harshly a few more times before letting it go, leaving the nipple nearly rubbed raw.

After all the attention he poured onto the left nipple, of course he couldn't just ignore the right one. Soon, both of the old man's nipples were wet and swollen. His breathing grew heavier as he panted slightly, and a beautiful rosy flush appeared on his skin.

Guan Shanjin's mouth was busy, and his hands were not idle either. He stroked his father's soft, small dick with his rough palm, then rubbed at the slit with his callused fingers. He'd deliberately trained his father's urethra so that it was slightly wider than the average person's, and also slightly looser. It was several times more sensitive than it had been before, too. With just a few casual touches, the sleeping man furrowed his brow and whimpered wantonly. He thrashed his torso around like he couldn't get enough.

Guan Shanjin scoffed, then pulled his father's hand over to stuff his pinky into his urethra. It was an awkward position for the old man, and he subconsciously wanted to pull his hand back, but his son used the opportunity to fuck his pinky into his dick. Precum flowed out like he was pissing himself, and soon, the old man's entire hand was wet.

Either from the stimulation or the awkwardness of the position, the older man's eyelids twitched like he was about to wake up.

Guan Shanjin immediately pulled his finger out from his cock with a *pop*. Another gush of precum immediately gushed out, the smell even stronger than piss. Even a section of the mattress was drenched.

He couldn't let his father wake up now. Guan Shanjin leaned down to gently smooth a finger over his father's brow. Gently, he stroked his small, flushed cock, and was able to soothe him.

The old man slept soundly. His son doted on him, taking care of his every need, from food and clothing to shelter and travel. He never hesitated when it came to spending money on his stepfather. If the older man ever wanted to save money, his son would become unhappy. If it weren't for the fact that he wanted to fly under the radar at work, he might not have been able to convince his son to let him wear regularly priced suits.

Although he and his son each had their own rooms in Guan Shanjin's spacious mansion, they usually slept in the same bed. There was central AC in the building, and it was usually set to a comfortable 77 degrees. It was warm in the winter and cool in the summer, and he never got too hot or too cold. All of their bed linens were made from the softest, smoothest, highest quality silk, and the comforter was filled with fluffy down. Lying on the bed felt like being surrounded by water.

How could he not sleep soundly?

But today, the more he slept, the hotter he felt. A flush had already appeared on his cheeks, and his clothes had long since been removed by his son. He curled up in the silk blanket, his entire body a rosy hue. His hands were wet from his own precum, and even the bedsheets beneath him were damp.

Half asleep, the old man rubbed his face against the soft goose-feather pillow, unaware that his stepson was playing with him.

Guan Shanjin stood with one knee on the bed as he stared down at his father's naked body.

The old man was very skinny, short, and small. He was only about five foot four, but his proportions were very appealing. His thin, white legs were very long and his ass was perky and full, which only made his waist seem smaller. The cock between his legs was a soft pink color, and looked shy and unused. The slit on his cockhead gaped wide enough to fit a fingertip. As it twitched, fluids leaked out and dripped onto his delicate balls and slid back toward his perineum. Some of it landed on the bedsheets, and some disappeared down his crack. He was the perfect picture of debauchery.

The younger man leaned down to kiss his stepfather on the mouth. As he did so, his tongue poked into the older man's soft, pouty lips, wrapping itself around his tongue, licking and sucking. His kisses were harsh and demanding, as though he wanted to swallow the man beneath him whole. He was so deep in the other man's mouth that he could nearly reach his throat.

The old man wanted to turn away and avoid Guan Shanjin, but he put a firm hand on the back of his head to prevent him from escaping. Soon, the older man was trembling all over, his eyelids opening slightly to reveal his eyes rolling into the back of his skull— but he wasn't awake yet. He was merely breathing unsteadily and unable to fully close his eyes.

Guan Shanjin reluctantly released his father's lips and instead pecked at them sweetly. The hand he placed on his father's thin waist started to misbehave as well. Following the curve of his spine, he ended up near the older man's tailbone. With a squeeze, his hands were full of soft, bouncy flesh. He couldn't resist getting in a few good squeezes, which only made his father whimper in his sleep. With a sway of his hips, the older man's soft belly came in contact with Guan Shanjin's painfully hard cock, somehow managing to make it even harder.

Guan Shanjin chuckled lowly, finally ready to let go of his father's kiss-swollen lips. He flipped the older man around so that he lay face down, knees bent, and ass up. He looked incredibly obscene.

The older man's breathing had not fully recovered, and he panted slightly. There were still bright-red finger marks on his ass left there by his son, covered in a layer of sweat and precum. Guan Shanjin spread his cheeks slightly to reveal his hole. The folds of his rim were a soft shade of red. It was a very cute hole, and it had been well-loved by his son throughout the years. Despite years of use, it maintained its tightness; it clenched and unclenched slightly.

"Father..." Guan Shanjin called out softly. His low whisper was like strong liquor—mellow, rich, and intoxicating.

The old man curled in on himself, his lewd hole clenching tightly for a moment before relaxing again.

Guan Shanjin knew his father hadn't woken up yet, but he was getting there. Perhaps he thought he was dreaming right now. In that case, Guan Shanjin might as well go even further, especially considering his dick had been so hard for so long that it hurt.

He opened the drawer on the bedside table and pulled out some lube. The applicator was shaped like a syringe, about the thickness of a pinky finger. He first squeezed out a little onto his finger, then spread it out on his father's hole. With just a few touches, the hole started furl open by itself. Guan Shanjin immediately stuffed the tip of the lube applicator inside and squeezed out half of the bottle in one go.

The older man vaguely felt a coldness in his ass and something filling him up. Then, he felt something about the thickness of a finger pull out of his ass. He shuddered, not knowing if he was dreaming or awake. Someone kneaded his ass, and the movement felt incredibly familiar. Unable to bear it anymore, he let a soft moan escape from his throat.

Before he could figure out whose hand it was, his hole was stretched open by a thick, long shaft. It was so hard that it felt like a steel bar wrapped in silk. When the tip of it rubbed right against his prostate, pleasure shot to his brain like a bolt of lightning. He breathed in harshly but still wasn't able to wake up completely.

His son had no plans to wake him up gently.

With the help of the lube, as soon as Guan Shanjin's cock entered his father's hole, it started to leak. He thrust a few times, but his cock was still not fully inside. The older man opened his eyes halfway, looking lost.

"How slutty, Father..." Guan Shanjin clenched his teeth, savoring the feeling of the warm, wet hole. He pressed down harshly on his father's pelvis and stuffed the rest of his cock into his hole.

"Ahh!" The old man arched his back and screamed uncontrollably. Tears spilled down, wetting half his face.

His son's huge dick was frighteningly hard. He still wasn't fully awake, but he was already being fucked so hard that he couldn't stop the filthy moans from spilling out of his lips.

"Xiao-Jin, Xiao-Jin—it's so hot, so hot, *ah*—" The old man realized he was in an incredibly depraved position on the bed. His ass was up in the air, and the impact of each thrust made it bounce. With the relentless sound of flesh slapping against flesh, juices started leaking out of his hole.

His son's cock was scorching, thrusting inside his passage like a hot iron. The older man shuddered all over and moaned all sorts of nonsense, unsure if he wanted to meet his son's thrusts so that he could go even deeper or crawl away to catch his breath.

Soon the large cockhead reached even greater depths than before. The tightest parts of his channel were now soft and malleable from all the stimulation and soon opened up. The almost twelve-inch dick was now fully sheathed, and the shape of it could be seen through his stomach.

"I'm gonna break... Xiao-Jin, I'm going to break," the old man moaned, saying any filthy thing that came to mind. He held his stomach, carefully squeezing the dick inside of him through the thin layer of flesh.

He was asking for it.

Guan Shanjin took a deep breath, his gaze going dark. Clamping down harder on his father's waist, he started to thrust even harder. He really was going to fuck him to death.

Guan Shanjin was tall and strong, covered in tight, intricate muscles. He locked his stepfather in his embrace and forced his chin up to kiss him. The old man was completely soaked down there, dripping wet from all the fucking. The flesh of his ass, pale from constantly being covered, rippled and bloomed a soft red from the impact of Guan Shanjin's thrusts. He cried out, asking his son to be gentler. It was as if he was his son's personal blow-up doll.

"You dirty thing..." Sweat beaded on Guan Shanjin's forehead. With his lips pressed against the old man's swollen mouth, he smiled. His father's passage was tight and slick as it sucked his dick vigorously. Occasionally, it would tremble a few times and suck him in harder. When he pulled out, the soft pink flesh refused to let go.

His stepfather moaned out lustfully, his eyes half closed. "Xiao-Jin! Harder, harder—I'm all yours! Ahh—"

Guan Shanjin thrust even deeper, past his father's prostate, swollen from all the fucking, and entered an even tighter passage. It was tight and wet and sucked on his large cockhead. It squeezed his huge cock pitifully but eagerly, and Guan Shanjin's rationality was slowly withering away. Furrowing his beautiful brow, he held his father's hips down forcefully and fucked into him even harder. His father's lewd hole trembled, and he let out a broken scream.

The older man's stomach was completely full of his son's large cock, and his son had great technique. When he really put his mind to it, he was nearly inhuman. When he pulled out, he would leave just the head inside, and when he thrust in, he changed the angle so that he reached every single inch of the passage within. The old man's juices completely drenched his insides. As the pleasure increased and overlapped, he shook his head desperately and cried out, "Xiao-Jin! Please, no more! You're going to pierce straight through me! Ahhhh!"

Obscene, wet noises mixed with the sounds of flesh slapping against flesh and filled the entire bedroom. The old man could not swallow down his screams. His stepson stretched his hole wide open, the rim a bright red, and his juices spilled out and soaked his son's belly.

But Guan Shanjin was not finished. He plowed forward, his hard cockhead pressing into every inch of his father's ass, his balls tightly pressed up against his hole. He panted a few times, then leaned down to take his father's tongue in his mouth.

They kissed loudly for a while, his rough tongue nearly licking into the older man's throat, making it hard for him to breathe. He stared blankly at the sheets below, completely undone.

"Father..." Guan Shanjin sucked on his father's earlobe and left a few bite marks.

"Mm..." The old man's entire body trembled, lost in a sex-drunk haze. He was just about to reach his peak, but his son abruptly stopped moving. The overwhelming pleasure made him feel like he was a high-pressure cooker, and he had no capacity to think about what would happen after he exploded. All he could focus on was the hot fullness inside of him and the cock-shaped bump on his belly.

"Can I go even deeper?" Guan Shanjin asked. His soft, low voice was very seductive. The older man's brain wasn't working properly to begin with, but hearing his voice dizzied him more. Without even hesitating, he nodded dumbly.

"Dirty thing." Guan Shanjin chuckled. Through the thin layer of flesh, he pressed down on his own large cockhead.

"Ahhh! Xiao-Jin, Xiao-Jin—!" The pitiful old thing was trapped entirely in his son's arms. His hole twitched a few times, sucking so hard on Guan Shanjin's cock that his eyes went red.

This old man was so salacious, he had to fuck him to death!

Guan Shanjin roughly pulled his father's pelvis toward his own. He didn't think his cock could go in any further, but somehow it did. It felt like even his balls could fit inside. His father's tight passageway had completely opened up; the older man screamed out erotically yet pitifully. His legs could no longer support his weight, and with a twitch, the slit of his little cock opened up as he pissed all over the bed.

SECRET ROOM

WHAT KIND of fucked up situation was this?!

Guan Shanjin panted, striking the dark, black walls with all his strength. A few moments ago, a doorway opened, and he and Wu Xingzi had been brought inside. Then, the doorway disappeared without a trace, as if it never even existed.

Everything had happened too quickly; even now, Guan Shanjin was still stunned. He had no idea how they'd fallen into this trap, or who dared to spring such a thing on them.

"If I get out of here, I'll repay you a hundred, a thousand times over!" Guan Shanjin was so angry his chest hurt, and he forcefully swallowed down a mouthful of blood before it made its way out. His teeth creaked as he ground them together.

Since he didn't know where he was, and Wu Xingzi was passed out next to him, he didn't dare use his martial arts powers to try and break down the wall. Instead, he forced himself to calm down. With one hand, he held Wu Xingzi tightly, and with the other, he felt up and down the wall.

There was no light in the room, as though they were in an airtight metal box. The wall was bone-chillingly cold. It felt like black steel.

Guan Shanjin's heart dropped.

There weren't many places in Great Xia where the walls were built from black steel. Usually, the aristocratic families built their private dungeons or storage cellars with walls like this. Or...this could be one of the many hidden rooms within the palace.

Good! Very good! He knew what was going on now.

"Are you asking me to commit regicide?!" Guan Shanjin pounded against the wall forcefully, uncaring if there were spying eunuchs or guards standing outside. Screw being polite—he practically wanted to pierce the man on the throne straight through. He'd only leave him with enough breath to write the edict to pass down the throne.

"Haiwang... Haiwang..." Perhaps sensing Guan Shanjin's anger, Wu Xingzi mumbled pitifully, finally managing to bring Guan Shanjin's focus back.

"Xingzi, are you awake? Do you feel all right?" Since he knew where he was now, Guan Shanjin didn't have to worry about leaving immediately. The emperor would not kill the Great General of the Southern Garrison here in a random corner of the palace.

"Haiwang..." Wu Xingzi didn't seem to be completely awake. He sniffed at the familiar scent next to him, then buried his face into Guan Shanjin's chest, wiggling slightly.

"What is it? What's wrong?" Guan Shanjin quickly realized something was going on with Wu Xingzi. The old quail was always quite shy outside of the bedroom. There was no way he'd initiate such intimate contact with him when he had no idea where he was. Besides... "Why do you feel so hot?" Guan Shanjin's brows furrowed.

They were in the middle of the hottest days of the summer. Not only were the temperatures high, there had been no rain recently. As soon as the sun came out, a fierce heat covered the streets, making everything seem a little hazy. Wu Xingzi was from the south, but he could not take the hot summers of the capital. During the hottest days, he always wore thin robes, and through these robes, Guan Shanjin could feel how hot his skin was.

He felt much hotter than normal, almost so hot Guan Shanjin couldn't keep holding him. The heat traveled through his fingers and into his chest. Combined with his anger, it felt like he couldn't breathe.

Had he been drugged? Guan Shanjin thought about it for a moment and checked on himself. As he channeled energy through his body, a spark in his belly suddenly burst into flame, and it felt like the fire burned everywhere.

"You old bastard, are you tired of sitting on the throne...?" Guan Shanjin felt dizzy. Using all of his martial arts strength, he struck the wall. There was a loud *bang*, and he left behind half a handprint in the metal.

Guan Shanjin wanted to keep hitting the wall. There was no way the old man on the throne wouldn't notice all this ruckus. But as he raised his hand again, the person in his arms started moving. He kept trying to burrow further and further into Guan Shanjin's chest, mumbling, "Haiwang... I'm so hot... I feel so hot... Touch me..."

"Xingzi, get a hold of yourself. You've been drugged. Be good, hmm? After we get out, I'll do whatever you say, all right?" Guan Shanjin couldn't see what state the old fellow was in, but from his scorching flesh, he could imagine exactly how red his face was now! These were fierce side effects. He didn't want to think about what kind of drug it was, but just from Wu Xingzi's reactions, he already had an idea.

Good! Very good! That old man gave him an aphrodisiac!

"It's so hot... Haiwang, it hurts... Touch me, touch me." Wu Xingzi didn't have Guan Shanjin's years of martial arts training, so he couldn't mitigate the effects of the aphrodisiac. He woke up from the discomfort, and now it was even harder to bear. His limbs felt as soft as jelly, and his entire torso burned with heat. It was like a

fire blazed inside of him, making him unable to think clearly. His clothes felt like they were biting into his skin, and he couldn't keep them on. He twisted about, wanting to get rid of them, but Guan Shanjin held on to him so tightly that he was unable to move.

For some reason, Wu Xingzi started to cry. He sniffed, feeling sorry for himself. "Haiwang, let go. I feel so hot. It's too hot. If I keep these clothes on, I'll burn. I'll burn to death... Haiwang...Haiwang..."

"Don't be silly." Guan Shanjin gritted his teeth. He was also suffering the effects of the drug. He hadn't realized before that the burning heat in his chest was desire and not anger.

It had been a few days since he'd last taken Wu Xingzi to bed. In order to return to the capital from Horse-Face City, they'd been on the road for a few months. When they arrived, it just so happened to be the emperor's birthday, so they'd celebrated the grand occasion. As a result, they dared not delay their trip whatsoever; naturally, they'd had no alone time.

Guan Shanjin had been keeping his desire in check to begin with. Now, with the influence of the drug, he almost couldn't resist anymore.

But Wu Xingzi had no idea how hard Guan Shanjin was holding himself back. Apart from the heat, he felt like there were bugs crawling under his skin. The tingling itchiness was torturous. Why wouldn't Guan Shanjin touch him?

"Haiwang, do you...do you...not like me anymore?" He sniffled, and tears started to spill from his eyes.

"Do you even hear what you're saying?!" Guan Shanjin gnashed his teeth, wanting to take a few bites out of Wu Xingzi to vent his anger. Wu Xingzi had never said anything like that to him. What exactly was this drug, and why was it so potent? They were both rapidly losing their ability to think properly.

"But you won't touch me," Wu Xingzi complained pitifully, still rubbing his cheek into Guan Shanjin's chest. "You smell so good... Haiwang, you smell so good... Can I lick you?"

"No." Guan Shanjin pushed his head away. If it weren't for the fact that he couldn't see, he'd be worried there were other traps in here. He wanted to settle Wu Xingzi into a corner so he'd stop trying to wrap himself around him.

"Not even a tiny lick? J-just a taste?" Wu Xingzi refused to let go of Guan Shanjin. Even though his limbs were held down, his head was free! With a little rub here and a little push there, he quickly made his way to Guan Shanjin's neck. He opened his mouth and took a bite.

"Wu Xingzi, you old fool, when did you become a dog?" Guan Shanjin hissed in pain. Keeping a tight hold on his rationality, he cursed under his breath. He knew that Wu Xingzi's current wanton state was only because of the drug. If he really did as the old thing wanted, after the effects of the drug passed, Wu Xingzi might drown him in the garden pond.

"Haiwang, you smell so good, so sweet... Hee hee, how can you taste so sweet?" Wu Xingzi happily gnawed on Guan Shanjin. Every time he took a bite, he'd lick the spot he bit, then suck on it. A row of purple-blue splotches now marked Guan Shanjin's neck.

There was nothing Guan Shanjin could do. All he could feel was helplessness and desire. The lust burned brighter and brighter, swallowing up his sanity. He clenched his teeth, pushed away the old quail who was ravaging his neck, and kissed him on the lips a few times.

"Haiwang... Haiwang! Kiss me more... Kiss me..." It was like Guan Shanjin was Wu Xingzi's oasis in a desert. Unabashed, Wu Xingzi puckered his lips, asking for kiss after kiss. All he could smell and taste was Guan Shanjin, as sweet as osmanthus candy.

Although he was shy by nature, Wu Xingzi was always honest when it came to desire. Since his life partner was the one in front of him, there was no reason to shy away or hide. Besides, Haiwang was so enticing right now. He couldn't wait for another kiss—he leaned in to bite Guan Shanjin's neck again.

"Wu Xingzi!" Guan Shanjin pushed at his head, annoyed, but didn't dare use any real strength. He was also still fighting against the drug, so his mind was quite occupied on multiple fronts.

"Haiwang, Haiwang...kiss me. Don't you want to taste me?"

I do! I really do! Guan Shanjin panted, using all of his martial arts training to quell the effects of the drug. He leaned into Wu Xingzi and bit harshly into his cheek to let off some steam.

"Ah..." Wu Xingzi let out a pained noise.

"If you don't behave, I'll have to tie you up," Guan Shanjin threatened fiercely.

Despite the fact that the old man's brain wasn't working from the drug, Guan Shanjin's words still scared him. Admonished, he licked the neck he'd marked up and shoved his head into Guan Shanjin's feverishly hot chest.

The two of them quietly held each other for a while. If it weren't for their erratic breathing, it would even have felt a little cozy.

Suddenly, some sort of mechanism within the wall made a slight noise. Furrowing his brows, Guan Shanjin looked in the direction of the sound. A small window the size of half his face opened up, allowing them to see the outside. Through the dim candlelight, they could vaguely see that it was a eunuch.

"Is the Great General of the Southern Garrison, heir to the Protector General, inside?" The eunuch's voice was small, weak, and shaking with fear.

Guan Shanjin didn't respond; he only laughed coldly.

The eunuch outside shuddered at the sound of his laughter, wanting to run away right then and there, but he couldn't. He clearly must've opened the window because he had a task to accomplish.

As expected, the little eunuch swallowed a few times before saying pitifully, "Great General, what goes around... No, no, no, I mean..." He took a deep breath before continuing again: "As they say... As they say... Anyway, there's no such thing as coincidence. There will always be some evidence left behind!"

"Hm?" Guan Shanjin scoffed.

The little eunuch shuddered again, licked his lips, then continued: "Th-this aphrodisiac is actually... Anyway, if you would like to come out with your wife in one piece, you'll have to wait until six forty-five tomorrow morning. The door will open then, and you may go wherever you please!"

"Oh? And?" Guan Shanjin didn't believe that things would be so easy.

"Uh... The general is w-wise... Um... The emperor, uh... Anyway, this room is unique. There's a special enchantment on this room. If the people inside are to copulate, the room will be locked forever and cannot be opened again. So..."

"You think I believe that?" Guan Shanjin had never believed in such things. He stopped Wu Xingzi's wandering hands, then glared coldly at the eunuch. "I remember now. You're the last student of the Head of the Imperial Household Department."

The eunuch gasped. He hadn't been expecting his identity to be exposed like that. "General, whether you believe it or not, your fate is in your own hands!" he yelled, panicking. "This lowly one is taking his leave!" He slammed the little window shut with a bang, running back to report to either his teacher or the emperor.

To believe it or not...

Guan Shanjin laughed coldly. He had to admit, he was in quite the pickle.

"Haiwang... Haiwang..." Wu Xingzi started struggling again. Since he couldn't feel Guan Shanjin, he started taking off his own clothes. In the blink of an eye, he was nearly half naked as he lay pliable and boneless in Guan Shanjin's arms.

Guan Shanjin gritted his teeth and pressed his palm directly onto Wu Xingzi's burning skin. It was hot and smooth. He couldn't retract his hand even if he bit a hole through his tongue.

"You're killing me, Xingzi..."

It was like Guan Shanjin's arms were made of metal as they clamped down tightly on Wu Xingzi's body. No matter how much he struggled, he couldn't break free. Other than his neck and head, he couldn't move at all.

Wu Xingzi was desperate. He really couldn't understand why Guan Shanjin wouldn't touch him, despite how desperately he begged and how horrible he felt. It was like being burned alive!

He wiggled even more forcefully, rubbing his thigh against the other man's erection. Soon he felt it right up against his stomach.

"Haiwang, clearly you are also..." The feathery softness of his breath burned hot against Guan Shanjin's neck.

The general didn't even flinch when faced with death on the battlefield, but those few breaths made him tremble.

"Haiwang..." Wu Xingzi knew he had a chance. He blew on Guan Shanjin's face a few more times.

"Wu Xingzi, you're playing with fire..." Guan Shanjin squeezed the threat out from between his teeth, but his clenched fists and haggard breathing did not faze the old man one bit. He'd been doted on too much to be scared of the general. Instead of shrinking away in fear, he kissed Guan Shanjin's jaw and laughed.

As the saying went: Three days without a beating, and a child will rip out the roof tiles. Wu Xingzi wasn't just ripping out the roof tiles at this point, he was practically flying through the sky!

Guan Shanjin held his breath, but his grip on Wu Xingzi loosened quite a bit. With how fierce its effects were, the damned emperor's aphrodisiac must have been some hidden drug specially developed at the palace. Guan Shanjin was relying entirely on his martial arts training and the resilience he'd developed on the battlefield to keep a clear head, but he was nearing the end of his rope.

As soon as Wu Xingzi freed himself from Guan Shanjin's hold, he was as excited as a bird. He wrapped both arms around Guan Shanjin's neck and puckered his lips, planting them on Guan Shanjin's with extraordinary accuracy considering how dark it was in the room.

"You taste so sweet… Haiwang, you're so sweet…like osmanthus candy…" Wu Xingzi mumbled as he licked and sucked. His soft tongue didn't show any of his usual shyness, licking eagerly into Guan Shanjin's mouth.

Wu Xingzi had always been a shy kisser. Even though he was honest when it came to sex, there was still a certain bashfulness within his bones. Guan Shanjin always liked to tease him and force kisses from him. He would lick at his teeth and at the softest places within his mouth. Wu Xingzi's slutty yet shy kissing always riled him up, and after a few licks, he'd fiercely kiss him back. He wouldn't let up until the old thing was dizzy and unable to close his mouth.

But now, the man trying to deny his desires was Guan Shanjin. As soon as Wu Xingzi's tongue touched his, he backed away, unwilling to get tangled up with him. This only made Wu Xingzi more insistent. He chased after his tongue, unwilling to let go. He needed to suck and bite until he took the almighty general's breath away.

This old fellow... *Once we get out, I'll really have to discipline him!* Despite his furious thoughts, Guan Shanjin couldn't stop his hands wandering as he started to strip the two of them. Even their underwear soon joined their other clothes on the floor.

The secret room filled with the wet sounds of kissing. Wu Xingzi grew even more excited, licking Guan Shanjin like a piece of candy. He lapped at him everywhere and wanted to suck everything. When he had his fill, Wu Xingzi leaned back reluctantly, but he still licked at Guan Shanjin's lips a few more times before he was truly satisfied.

"Haiwang... Can I lick you some more?" Wu Xingzi clearly wanted to say something dirty, but he'd been a well-behaved adviser his entire life. Everything that came out of his mind was gentle. How would he be able to say anything filthy? After thinking about it, this was all he could come up with. But Guan Shanjin was turned on by his words. The eunuch's warning was lost in the back of his mind.

"Where else do you want to lick, hm?" He reached out to pinch the back of Wu Xingzi's neck, and the last of his rationality and sympathy was finally destroyed by the aphrodisiac. Resisting the drug any further might result in harm to his body, and this was what Wu Xingzi wanted, after all.

"I want to lick y-your..." The last few words remained on Wu Xingzi's lips. He was still too shy to say it out loud.

"Hm? I didn't quite catch that." Guan Shanjin leaned in, first rubbing Wu Xingzi's earlobe, then nibbling on it with his teeth. Wu Xingzi trembled all over, then fell limply into his arms. "Xingzi, you know I care for you. If you tell me exactly what you want, I'll let you lick me," he said, with a hint of a laugh.

Wu Xingzi thought he was melting into a puddle of water, starting from where Guan Shanjin was licking. Lost in sensation, he said, "I want to lick your h-huge cock..."

Guan Shanjin burst into laughter, then kissed him on the cheek. "All right, go ahead." This old quail truly was something else.

Wu Xingzi slid down from Guan Shanjin's arms. They were already undressed, and when they pressed together, their skin burned with heat and felt sticky. They wanted to hold each other like this for the rest of their lives and never part.

But Wu Xingzi didn't want to give up on the thick, heavy cock that had been poking his stomach for a while now. He'd wanted to put it in his mouth for ages.

"Wu Xingzi...you sure...have learned..." Guan Shanjin's usually pleasant voice sounded tight and somewhat hoarse. It went straight to Wu Xingzi's heart, making him feel hot and tingly.

He kissed down the man's body until he reached the edge of his underwear. Taking it into his teeth, he started pulling it downward. Guan Shanjin's cock was incredibly hard, so despite many attempts, Wu Xingzi could not get his underwear down his thighs. Incredibly frustrated, he looked up at Haiwang with a pitiful expression. "Haiwang, help me..."

"If you can't get it off, I'm not letting you lick me. Do you really want me to help you?"

Guan Shanjin felt a little mischievous, and there was nothing Wu Xingzi could do about it. He whined a few times but saw that Guan Shanjin really wasn't going to help him. Left with no other choice, he ripped the garment off with his hands.

"Impatient old thing..." Guan Shanjin scolded him with a chuckle, but he didn't stop him. He let Wu Xingzi strip him bare. Then, Wu Xingzi returned to his spot between his legs and rubbed his face against his long, thick cock as it stood up tall.

Although Wu Xingzi couldn't see it in the dark, they had been together long enough that he didn't need to. He could clearly imagine its thickness and girth as it curved up, its full head, and the way the veins wrapped around it.

Wu Xingzi swallowed down his saliva, desperate for a taste. He couldn't resist anymore, and he reached out with his tongue for a lick. In an instant, a musky, bitter flavor spread across his tongue. It was indescribably delicious.

Sucking gently, his tongue moved all around the head. Occasionally, he licked at the ridge right underneath, where the taste was the strongest and a little saltier. Wu Xingzi loved it, and he kept nibbling at the skin there. Sometimes, he even dipped his tongue inside the slit, massaging the most sensitive area.

"Mm!" Guan Shanjin grunted, his brows knitting together. Clearly, he was enjoying himself. His hand made its way to the back of Wu Xingzi's head, ripping apart his already messy bun. A curtain of black hair streaked with white strands brushed against his inner thigh. It felt like little bugs biting his heart, itchy and tingly.

Wu Xingzi huffed out a breath, deeply engrossed in his task. Perhaps it was because of the drug, but he kept feeling like this wasn't enough. He rubbed his tongue almost roughly against the veins on Guan Shanjin's dick. He did his best to open his mouth wider so the heavy, thick length could enter his throat.

"Xingzi... Xingzi..." Guan Shanjin hadn't been treated like this by Wu Xingzi in a long time. His powerful body trembled like a leopard waiting to pounce. He tangled his fingers in the old man's hair, feeling his thick cock slide deeper and deeper into the wet heat.

Wu Xingzi pressed his tongue against the slit and sucked on it like he was kissing it. Then, he sucked on it even harder. Before Guan Shanjin could react, Wu Xingzi had stuffed the whole thing down his throat, filling his mouth completely, his nose reaching the thick hairs at the base.

He'd swallowed a little too much of it, and started to cough like he was choking. He almost couldn't breathe. He wanted to back up a bit, but now that Guan Shanjin had gotten a taste, how could he just let Wu Xingzi go? Suddenly, the hand gently playing with the hair on the back of his head pressed down forcefully, making Wu Xingzi swallow him down even further. Without a care for Wu Xingzi's poor throat, Guan Shanjin only desired to force himself in deeper.

Wu Xingzi coughed and struggled, but he was no match for Guan Shanjin's strength. He could only allow the man to move his head up and down on his suffocating cock. It felt like his neck was being stretched out. If there'd been any light in this room, one could have seen the shape of a cock down his throat. It bulged out and then sank back in with Guan Shanjin's thrusts. Saliva he couldn't swallow down kept leaking out of his mouth and dripping down the general's dick. The entire room filled with wet, filthy sounds.

Under the effects of the drug, Guan Shanjin had long since forgotten what it meant to be gentle and careful. He only wanted to be deeper inside Wu Xingzi, not letting go of any part of him. Wu Xingzi could not withstand such an attack. After a few dozen thrusts, he was about to pass out. But even so, he sucked greedily on the huge cock. He tried to relax his throat, allowing his lover to do as he wished.

His tight throat convulsed from the stretch. Instead of a throat, it was more like a sleeve, squeezing and stimulating Guan Shanjin's dick. He panted heavily, pressing down more and more fiercely on Wu Xingzi's head. In the end, he was practically holding Wu Xingzi's head down as he thrusted. It felt like he was about to break Wu Xingzi's delicate throat. The older man started to cry, but it only added fuel to the fire.

The drug delayed Guan Shanjin's orgasm; it took him a while to reach his climax. He stuffed his entire length down the old man's throat and finally released months of pent up cum.

Wu Xingzi, already in a daze, was shocked even further by the warm liquid. It felt like his brain had burned to a crisp. He sobbed, and his face shone with streaks of tears and saliva. He had no way to resist. He could only swallow down all of Guan Shanjin's cum.

Guan Shanjin's huge length did not soften after he came—it was still scarily hard. He also didn't immediately pull away. Instead, he thrust a few more times into Wu Xingzi's mouth before slowly backing out.

Wu Xingzi fell onto Guan Shanjin's legs, panting and coughing like a broken doll. Before he could catch his breath, the man swept him up into his strong arms. At the same time, he pulled down the older man's pants and aimed a few harsh slaps on his ass. The old thing sobbed and whined from the impact, nearly losing his breath.

"H-Haiwang..." Wu Xingzi's throat was numb; he couldn't speak properly. All he could do was call out Guan Shanjin's name pitifully.

"Good boy. Let me please you next, hm?" Guan Shanjin smiled and kissed him on the cheek. His gentle, deep voice sounded as smooth as silk, enchanting Wu Xingzi. He didn't notice that this man was exactly the same as when they first met.

Guan Shanjin hadn't always doted on Wu Xingzi like he did now. When they first met, the two of them were always doing unspeakable, shameless things to each other. Guan Shanjin, who was quite experienced, had many exciting and cruel tricks up his sleeve. It was not an exaggeration to say that after experiencing such pleasure, Wu Xingzi felt about to die on the man's cock.

Through the years, Guan Shanjin thoroughly pampered his old quail. He didn't have enough opportunities to spoil him, so how could he treat him roughly in any way? Even their sex had become gentler, losing the fire and heat of their earlier encounters.

Wu Xingzi never thought he'd be able to relive such an experience again.

Inside this secret room, things were heating up. The smell of sex permeated the space along with desperate moans and harsh breaths. The sound of flesh slapping against flesh was never-ending.

Wu Xingzi thought he'd be fucked to death in this place, where he'd never see the sun again.

"Haiwang... Haiwang, slow down... *Ah!*"

It was as if the younger man could not hear his pleas. He pressed the old quail down against the cold, hard ground, his strong hips constantly moving as he fucked into him harshly.

Wu Xingzi's hole was now red and swollen. It had been a long time since they'd last had sex. Being fucked so suddenly and fiercely, it began to stretch a little. It held onto the man's hardness pitifully, sucking on it as if trying to please him.

His willingness only made Guan Shanjin lose more of his control and fuck him even harder. Slick gushed out of Wu Xingzi's ass like he was an overripe fruit.

They fucked for quite some time, but because of the drug, it was like Guan Shanjin didn't know what it meant to be tired. In fact, it didn't seem to matter that he'd already come; his cock seemed to grow even bigger. Wu Xingzi climaxed so many times that a puddle formed on the floor.

Wu Xingzi thought he'd died and come back to life at least two or three times. He was flushed all over and trembling. Guan Shanjin kept hitting his most sensitive spots, and his belly protruded with every thrust.

"Haiwang, Haiwang, *ahhh*!" Wu Xingzi screamed, his body quaking so hard that Guan Shanjin nearly couldn't keep his grip on him. The slit of Wu Xingzi's cock winked open a few times, letting out a few drops of cum and nothing more.

His cock hurt from orgasming so much. He really couldn't take it anymore. With snot all over his face, he cried and begged for Guan Shanjin to have mercy on him. He was afraid. He'd forgotten how scary the man could be. No wonder greed was a sin—this truly was endless!

"Be good. Didn't you want me to touch and kiss you? Don't you like it when I do this?" Guan Shanjin clamped down on Wu Xingzi's soft hips and pressed him down onto his cock. At the same time, he thrust forward, completely opening up Wu Xingzi's passage.

Wu Xingzi's mouth hung open, desperately gasping for air, but his brain could no longer process any of it. He threw his head back, shaking like a leaf, as he vaguely felt that Guan Shanjin was playing with the part of his belly that bulged out from his cock.

The general chuckled. "Do you like this?"

"I-I do... Haiwang, l-let me rest for a while... *Ah—!*" Wu Xingzi finally managed to squeeze out a hoarse plea from his throat, but Guan Shanjin wouldn't listen. He pulled out his large cock, and as Wu Xingzi took a breath, he thrust back in. Wu Xingzi cried out, his ass convulsing.

"Don't cry. You know how much I care for you, right? Let me kiss you." The man's deep whisper carried his scorching breath. It was enough to captivate anyone! Wu Xingzi's face was splotchy from crying, and his brain was a mess. Even though his body trembled, he rubbed his face against Guan Shanjin's cheek.

"Kiss me..." He'd always loved Guan Shanjin's gentle, loving kisses. He'd been willing to leave his home in Qingcheng County for this kiss.

"Good boy..." Guan Shanjin wrapped an arm around his waist and placed the other on his jaw. As their lips met, he thrust his cock inside him some more, reaching even further depths.

As he was kissed, Wu Xingzi couldn't make a noise, nor did he have any energy to struggle. Guan Shanjin tangled their tongues together, and it felt like he was sucking his soul away.

Since the man in his arms was on the verge of passing out, Guan Shanjin ended this dominating kiss. Pulling away slightly, he gently said, "Bear with it for a little longer, hm? Let me have my fill."

"All right..." Wu Xingzi was in a daze and didn't really know what he was agreeing to. By the time Guan Shanjin started moving again, his mouth dropped open and his eyes rolled into the back of his head. He could only let Guan Shanjin have his way with him.

Every time, the man would pull out until just the head of his cock was still inside, then thrust back in fiercely. When he reached the end, he'd thrust in just a little more, as though wanting to pierce him through. Wu Xingzi's juices gushed out with wet noises as Guan Shanjin moved, and soon, he managed to reach even deeper inside Wu Xingzi.

Guan Shanjin almost couldn't take how tightly Wu Xingzi's ass gripped onto him. He sighed in satisfaction, then leaned down to kiss the old man, who had been fucked senseless. Then, he started thrusting in earnest again.

He really was putting all his strength into this bout of fucking. He didn't stop until Wu Xingzi pissed himself and was barely breathing. It seemed like he'd simply become a sex toy for Guan Shanjin. When he finally thrust deeply inside for the last time, he released all of his thick cum deep inside Wu Xingzi's belly.

The sensation only stimulated Wu Xingzi to piss himself once again.

Now that he'd climaxed, Guan Shanjin's mind was a lot clearer. Panting harshly, he tightly held the old quail, who was shaking all over.

Wu Xingzi's hole felt too good. Even though he'd been fucked so harshly, his soft, delicate passageway still tightly gripped Guan Shanjin's thick cock, sucking him in. It really was going to be the death of him.

"Xingzi..." Kissing the limp man in his arms, Guan Shanjin hesitated for a moment. After a moment's respite, the fire in his belly was rekindling. Apparently, one orgasm was not enough.

Realizing that Guan Shanjin was getting hard again, Wu Xingzi moaned a few times, twisting his hips as he tried to get away. That movement, however, was the beginning of the end.

At first, Guan Shanjin had wanted to be good to the old quail, but now...it was better to be good to himself.

With his decision made, Guan Shanjin no longer held back. He pressed Wu Xingzi into the wall and fucked him savagely once again.

At a quarter to seven in the morning, the little eunuch was forced by his master to check on the hidden room. His master said that the aphrodisiac that had been used on the general's lover was a secret drug from the palace. It didn't even have a name; the recipe was only passed down through word of mouth from imperial physician to imperial physician.

The effects of the drug were far too potent, and it was impossible to determine which emperor had ordered the imperial physicians to create such a cursed potion. In any case, only the head of the Imperial Hospital still knew how to make it.

He knew how to make it, but he did not know how to make the antidote. Only copulation would alleviate the effects.

Wasn't this just a trick? Everyone said the secret room held an array. The little eunuch believed it; after all, what didn't the palace have? Would the Great General of the Southern Garrison really be able to resist devouring his wife? The entire nation knew that the general and his partner were deeply in love and always together. It must be very difficult to resist.

The eunuch's head filled with all sorts of thoughts. Dragging his feet, he finally made his way into the room. As soon as he arrived, he froze, staring at the scene before him in disbelief.

"G-General of the S-S-S-Southern—"

Under the flickering moonlight, the man seemed even taller and larger; his aura was overwhelming. Even in such a sorry state, he still seemed like a sharp blade, glinting with a cold light. He was entirely capable of committing murder at any moment.

The eunuch stumbled back several steps, then fell to the floor. He immediately burst into tears.

He didn't even want to know how the general had managed to break out. He only knew that he didn't want to die here! The way the general looked at him was no different than the way he looked at a dead man!

"P-p-p-please spare me!" he begged, trembling. His voice was stuck in his throat; the only sounds he could make were hoarse noises.

Guan Shanjin gave him a cold glance and recognized him as the eunuch who'd come last time.

He was too lazy to waste time on a little shrimp like him. He could always deal with the person behind all of this after he recovered. "Man Yue?"

"Yes." A round body walked out from the shadows. That was when the little eunuch realized there was someone else here.

"Go tell the emperor that I will bring a gift to thank him for his favor in a few days. Tell him to wait." His tone was very rude—almost like he was about to start a coup.

"Got it." Man Yue pursed his lips. Looking at the man wrapped tightly in Guan Shanjin's embrace, he chuckled. "The prized blade has never dulled."

Guan Shanjin's expression went stiff. He shot him a dangerous look. "Watch your mouth. Don't give me a reason to go bother Su Yang."

Those words stabbed Man Yue right where it hurt. He wasn't afraid of anything, but Su Yang was his only weakness. He rubbed his nose and gave up on teasing his boss. Taking a few steps to walk to the eunuch's side, he led the shaking man away.

After Man Yue's footsteps could no longer be heard, Guan Shanjin tightened his hold on Wu Xingzi, then glanced back at the sex-soaked room that had held them for a night. He sighed.

"Aren't you playing with fire?" he said, sounding helpless. But when he looked at Wu Xingzi's peacefully sleeping face, his heart melted into a puddle. "Never mind. It was my fault for neglecting you for so long."

Guan Shanjin had fucked Wu Xingzi the entire night, over and over, until the drug ran its course and he could think clearly again. The old man obviously could not stop him, and nearly lost half his life in the process. If it weren't for the fact that he'd been really looking after his health these last few years, it might take him over half a year to recover.

As soon as he returned to his senses, Guan Shanjin immediately knew who it was who'd dared to set this trap. Regardless of how unreliable the person on the throne was, so long as Great Xia needed Guan Shanjin to stand guard over the southern border, there was no way the emperor would offend him—that would be the same as hanging a knife over his own head.

It was even less likely for it to be anyone else. Guan Shanjin's reputation was infamous; no one in the entire country dared to trifle with him. After all, the one man who'd dared to before had his entire family killed or exiled.

Besides, he grew up on the battlefield and was vigilant against everyone, even Man Yue and his own parents to a degree. Who would be able to drug him without his knowledge? Sighing again, he leaned down to nip at Wu Xingzi's nose.

Wu Xingzi.

Wu Xingzi was the only person who could've done this. At most, the emperor knew about it but didn't say anything, and lent him the drug and the room.

Had he figured it out?

"Let's see if you have the courage to try this again." In the end, Guan Shanjin could only threaten the sleeping Wu Xingzi with those words to recover some of his pride.

Clearly, he could no longer be too restrained when it came to sex. The old thing was so starved he'd resorted to drugging them both!

Guan Shanjin chuckled.

Wu Xingzi, still deeply asleep, suddenly felt a chill run down his spine. He burrowed further into that familiar embrace, trembling a little.

By the time he woke up and realized exactly what the aftermath of his drugging attempt was, it was already too late.

But that all came after.

MAY ALL LOVERS BE PAST LOVERS

"**M**ISTRESS! MISTRESS!**" Mint and Osmanthus ran to the back vegetable garden with their skirts hiked up. Their shouts were so loud, they could have been heard from the heavens.

Wu Xingzi was digging in the garden with his child. The weather was turning colder, and the originally green patch now looked a little gloomy. The only things left in the garden were a few cold-resistant plants, waving their branches gently in the winter sun.

The child heard Osmanthus and Mint's shouting from a distance and glanced at Wu Xingzi with his large, black eyes. "Father?" He was well-acquainted with Mint and Osmanthus. They were always so well-behaved and capable. He'd never seen them act so chaotically. Did something monumental happen?

"Hm?" Wu Xingzi's hearing wasn't as sharp as the child's, and he only vaguely noticed some noise in the distance. He hadn't realized his two servants were running toward him and screaming their lungs out.

"Mint-jiejie and Osmanthus-jiejie are calling for you." The child looked up obediently, pointing to the outside. Helpfully, he added, "It sounds quite urgent. Something might've happened. Do you want to wash your hands and feet first?"

"They're yelling for me?" This surprised Wu Xingzi. He'd been with the girls for nearly ten years now—they rarely ever shouted.

"Yes, they're yelling..." The child paused and listened for a while. "'Mistress, Mistress, something has happened!'" He repeated what he heard in his still baby-toned voice. "I also hear Steward Yuan's voice."

"Steward Yuan is calling for me too?" Wu Xingzi was even more shocked. Steward Yuan was an old, expressionless man. In the ten years they'd known each other, Wu Xingzi hadn't seen him smile even once. He really was as solid as a rock; his expression never changed.

Realizing something was probably wrong, Wu Xingzi forgot about his chive sprouts and washed his hands and feet with his son. Putting on his shoes, he hurried toward the voices.

Upon seeing Wu Xingzi, Mint and Osmanthus called out to him. "Mistress, Mistress!" They bit their lips, panting.

"What's wrong? What happened?" Wu Xingzi hurried to help the two girls catch their breath. At the same time, he signaled to his son to bring tea to soothe the girls' throats.

Although the boy was technically a young master, he'd been brought up by Wu Xingzi, and he didn't have any of the arrogance of an aristocratic child. He quickly poured two cups of tea, then handed them carefully to the two girls.

Mint and Osmanthus seemed to have something to say but didn't know how to say it. They accepted the tea and quickly drained the cups.

"Feeling better now?" Seeing that the girls had calmed down a bit, Wu Xingzi asked them again, "Why were you yelling for me so unexpectedly?"

"The entire garden could hear," the child said, a little teasingly. Never mind what exactly had happened—with how loudly Mint and Osmanthus were yelling, what if outsiders had heard? Rumors often spread like they had wings. In the blink of an eye, it could have traveled across the entire capital, or even the entire nation. It would be terrible if the great Protector General became the hot gossip of the country!

"I wasn't careful enough. Please forgive me, young master," Mint and Osmanthus apologized in unison, looking a little tired.

"It's not a big deal. I know you girls well. Don't worry about it." Wu Xingzi hurriedly comforted the two girls. "Tell me what happened."

They'd drunk their tea and learned their lesson, but they still hadn't said what they came here to say. Even Wu Xingzi was losing his patience.

"Um..." Mint opened her mouth hesitantly, then glanced at her sister. Osmanthus nodded at her, so she took a deep breath. "Mistress, i-it's...the general..."

The general? As soon as those words came out of Mint's mouth, Wu Xingzi's expression changed immediately. Worried, he pulled on her hand and asked, "What's wrong with the general? Aren't we in the capital? How could anything happen right under the emperor's nose?"

In recent years, the emperor had heavily favored the Protector General. The Protector General's family now stood at the top of Great Xia's food chain. Besides, Guan Shanjin was older now, and he had a spouse and child. He was no longer as arrogant as he used to be, and didn't show off so brazenly anymore. As a result, he didn't really have any conflicts with any court officials; logically, no one should be out to get him.

"The general was in an accident, but..." Osmanthus hesitated once again.

The child had run out of patience. "Hurry up!"

Mint grit her teeth and finally explained the situation. "The general fell off his horse. Vice General Man said he's hurt his head. Right now... Right now..."

Wu Xingzi felt the world spin. He stumbled back a few steps and nearly fell over—it was lucky his son put an arm out to help him before he did.

"Is he badly hurt? Has a doctor seen him yet?"

The child was only seven or eight years old. Hearing that his father was hurt, he panicked a little. A tear nearly escaped the corner of his eye, but he managed to stop it. "Father, should we go see Dad?"

Osmanthus hurried to stop the father and son, who were getting ready to leave. "Hold on!" she said. "Um... The general's injury isn't serious. A doctor already looked at it. He said the general just has to rest for five or six days."

"But I should still go and take care of Haiwang." Wu Xingzi's brow furrowed, and he stared in confusion at Osmanthus and Mint, who were blocking his path. He was slightly angry now. "Move out of the way. Did Haiwang say something?"

This wasn't the first time something like this had happened. Guan Shanjin was the Great General of the Southern Garrison. Even though the borders had been peaceful in recent years, the occasional conflict still arose. Over the last few years, a few minor skirmishes with Nanman had occurred. If a fight broke out, there was no way he'd return completely unharmed.

Whenever Guan Shanjin suffered an injury, he wouldn't let anyone tell Wu Xingzi or let him take care of his injuries. He would suffer alone, pretend nothing had happened, or have someone lie to Wu Xingzi so he could hide and recover.

Throughout the years, Wu Xingzi had gotten angry with him twice. Finally, Guan Shanjin relented, allowing his subordinates to let Wu Xingzi know when he'd gotten injured. But knowing was one thing; taking care of him was another. To this day, they hadn't managed to find a compromise that both men could agree on.

"He hurt his head. He's not going to the battlefield—am I not allowed to see such an injury?" Wu Xingzi's breath caught in his throat, and his eyes went red.

"It's not that..." Mint grit her teeth. She sighed again and said, "Mistress, y-you...should have some tea first and calm down. I'll explain things to you clearly."

How was he supposed to drink tea at a time like this? Wu Xingzi was so angry that his mind went blank for a moment. He grabbed the pot on the table, then gulped down all of the tea directly from the spout. He threw the pot back down, wiped his lips boldly, and said, "Go ahead!"

Osmanthus closed her eyes, having no choice but to reveal the truth: "The general, h-he has amnesia!"

"Amnesia?" Wu Xingzi froze, then inhaled sharply. "So h-he doesn't remember us? Does he remember who he is?"

"The general still remembers himself, but..." Mint and Osmanthus exchanged a look before they stammered, "Amnesia is not quite right. The general remembers lots of things, except..."

"Except?"

"He only has memories from when he was twenty-five years old..." Osmanthus sighed, deciding to throw caution to the wind. "So the general wants to see Mr. Lu right now, and he's angry at Vice General Man."

"Mr. Lu?" Wu Xingzi paused, then nodded. "That's to be expected. He did like Mr. Lu around that time."

"Mistress, aren't you angry? The general has forgotten all about you and your child!" Since everything was out in the open now, Mint couldn't keep her anger tamped down anymore.

"Is the general even human? He hit his head and only forgot you!" Osmanthus chimed in.

"Steward Yuan asked you two to come see me because he has something to ask, right?" Wu Xingzi prompted them. Compared to the girls' indignant anger, Wu Xingzi was very calm. He pulled his son to the table and sat down. He picked up a sweet cake from the food box on the table, broke it in two, and shared it with the boy.

"Yes..." Osmanthus pouted, growing angrier than before as she thought of Steward Yuan's request. She rubbed her chest before saying, "Steward Yuan wanted us to ask you if he should bring Mr. Lu to see the general."

"That's fine..." Wu Xingzi took a few bites of the cake, then sighed. "But would Mr. Lu be willing?"

After all, it had been ten years since Mr. Lu was unceremoniously thrown out of the Protector General's estate. Apparently, he almost hadn't even made it to his home. If it weren't for the fact that Guan Shanjin had been the one who'd had a property prepared for him, they wouldn't even know where to go looking for him.

"Steward Yuan said as long as you're all right with it, he has his ways." Osmanthus pursed her lips. She'd never liked that Mr. Lu fellow. Even ten years later, she still disliked him. She really didn't know what Steward Yuan was thinking. And why didn't Vice General Man stop him?

"All right, then." Wu Xingzi nodded and stuffed the cake in his mouth. "Can I go see him now?" he asked.

Man Yue sat by the table, drinking tea and eating snacks. He watched coldly as the man on the bed held his head in his hands, clearly in pain. Internally, he was snickering.

What was wrong with him? He could've hit anything, but he just had to hit his head. Fine, he hit his head. But he couldn't even properly forget! He just had to go back to that time when he lost his brains over Lu Zezhi.

Back then, Guan Shanjin had doted on Lu Zezhi relentlessly. If Lu Zezhi asked for the stars, he would give him nothing else. "Apple of his eye" wasn't a strong enough term to describe the general's affections.

And never mind how many good young men Guan Shanjin had trifled with at that time. According to Manager Rancui, he'd been gifted no less than two dowry cakes from the men whose hearts Guan Shanjin had broken.

Tch. What a beast, Man Yue thought.

At the time, Man Yue thought that maybe Guan Shanjin's misguided feelings for Mr. Lu would be his one mistake. If Man Yue couldn't get rid of Lu Zezhi, he might as well help his boss with him. But he just couldn't get used to that pure, otherworldly way Lu Zezhi carried himself. He got so angry back then that he gained weight.

But then, Guan Shanjin met his true match. He fell headfirst and landed in Wu Xingzi's gentle embrace, never to walk out of it again.

"Man Yue," Guan Shanjin called to him hoarsely, still holding his throbbing head.

"Yes, sir." Man Yue shoved the last two candied plums into his mouth and walked over, smiling. He shoved Guan Shanjin, who was about to stand up, back into his blankets with perfect timing.

"Don't get off the bed. The most precious thing about you is your head. Now that there's a huge dent in it, you've probably lost a few hundred taels. You'd better take it easy and save up for your future."

Guan Shanjin spat at him. He wanted to struggle, but his head really did hurt. He couldn't escape from Man Yue's chubby arms, so he had no choice but to lie back down, glaring at the round, smiling face.

Sighing, Guan Shanjin touched his injured head through the bandages with his brows furrowed. "Where's Teacher? Doesn't he know I'm hurt?"

"Hah," responded Man Yue, his smile not reaching his eyes.

"What are you being passive-aggressive for?" Guan Shanjin's head hurt. And his neck, shoulders, eyebrows, eyes—basically everything ached, so he had no patience for Man Yue's attitude. "I don't understand what you have against him. You'd better be nicer to him."

"Have I not been nice enough to him? What has he even done to warrant me calling him 'Mr. Lu'?" Man Yue complained, pursing his lips. This was ridiculous. It'd been ten years; why was he still holding a grudge?

"Didn't you tell him that I'm hurt?" Guan Shanjin asked again. The anticipation in his voice was palpable.

It'd been a long time since he last saw this version of his boss: stupid in love. Man Yue kind of missed it.

"I sent someone to tell him already." It wasn't exactly a lie. Mint had just passed Wu Xingzi's word to Steward Yuan not long ago, saying he was allowing Lu Zezhi to come see the general. Steward Yuan immediately sent someone to let Lu Zezhi know.

But Lu Zezhi lived about half a month's travel away from the capital. Even if he rushed here fast enough to make it in ten days, the back and forth would take twenty days at the earliest. Guan Shanjin might even have recovered by then. If he did, then what happened next would be very interesting.

Man Yue smiled.

Guan Shanjin's brow furrowed even more. He knew something was up with Man Yue, but he couldn't put his finger on what. It felt like Man Yue was waiting to see something happen to him, which made Guan Shanjin feel a little panicky.

"Stop holding me down. Since you've already told him, I'll just wait here for him." Guan Shanjin finally managed to get rid of the chubby hand on top of him, but that movement sent his head into another fit of pain. Gritting his teeth, he took a while to recover.

Man Yue returned to the table and took a few sips of his tea. Seeing that the general's complexion was improving, he said with a chuckle, "I don't know when Mr. Lu will come, but there's someone else who's desperate to see you. You'll see them, right?"

Guan Shanjin frowned, and his heart randomly skipped a few beats. He wanted to say no, but he forced himself to remain calm. "Who?"

"A..." Man Yue stuffed a candied plum in his mouth, thinking. Guan Shanjin nearly lost his patience before he continued, "An old friend."

Those three words seemed to hold a lot of meaning. Guan Shanjin's brows knit together even further.

Guan Shanjin knew Man Yue too well. He was too clever for his own good and way too hard to deal with. "What are you planning?"

Man Yue pursed his lips. "Will you see him or not?"

"I will not... I know that's what you expect me to say." Guan Shanjin glared at him, then reached up to touch the bandages on his head. "Since you say it's an old friend, what do I have to fear?" he said coldly.

Man Yue shrugged. He could tell Guan Shanjin did not actually want to see him. Even though his brain wasn't at full capacity right now, his habit of hiding his injuries from Wu Xingzi still persisted. Look at his frustrated expression. Where was his usual calmness? Where was his domineering attitude? Man Yue felt satisfied just looking at him!

"Then I'll send him in." Man Yue didn't forget to ask considerately, "Do you want a hat to cover up your injury?"

"No. You're never up to any good. Go get him, and then you can fuck off. Stop being an eyesore," Guan Shanjin spat at him moodily. His head felt like someone was chiseling into his skull. He really didn't have the energy to deal with the sly Man Yue.

"Getting rid of me once I'm no longer useful? I'm hurt!" shouted Man Yue, putting a hand to his chest exaggeratedly. He scrunched up his face so much that he looked like a steamed bun.

Guan Shanjin couldn't help but laugh at him, and felt a little better. "Fuck off. Go do whatever you're supposed to be doing. I'm recovering from an injury, but you're so unconcerned you're here eating my snacks and making fun of me? Hmph."

"I'm just taking what I can get." Man Yue shrugged, not bothering to squabble with his boss any longer. "General," he said earnestly, "you've hurt your head and there are things you can't remember, so don't go doing anything rash. If you sense that something is wrong, stop and reconsider. Otherwise, you might find that your troubles have only just started once you recover."

That was quite thoughtful and considerate of him. Guan Shanjin opened his mouth, but didn't end up saying anything. He just made a noise of acknowledgment and took his words to heart.

Man Yue had only just left when several footsteps—some heavy, some light, some quick, some slow—approached. They stopped in front of his door. From the sound of it, there were four or five people: One was a child, one was older, and then there were two girls.

What were they doing in the general's estate? Were they guests? Had the news of his injury already made its way out...? Guan Shanjin immediately shook his head. There was no way. Man Yue was handling things, and everyone in the manor was either his personal guard or in the Protector General's private army. They would've kept their mouths shut about the news. Not even a mosquito, not even a single willow leaf, would be able to make its way out of this estate.

Then who were these people?

Before he could give it some more thought, someone outside knocked on his door. He could tell the person was impatient, yet careful, like he was unsure how Guan Shanjin was going to respond. For some reason, his heart melted at the sound.

"Come in." Guan Shanjin hadn't thought he could be this gentle to anyone other than Mr. Lu. It was as if he was afraid of scaring the person outside, but he didn't even know who it was.

"Then I'm coming in." The person outside spoke in a gentle southern accent, but it was not from Horse-Face City. It sounded more like a soft, sweet piece of osmanthus cake. Even Guan Shanjin's heart felt sweet.

As he finished speaking, the person pushed open the door. He seemed to hesitate for a moment before entering, then walked in slowly.

Judging from the footsteps, only the child followed. The two girls stood outside waiting; Guan Shanjin guessed that they were servants. They must have been very close to their master.

Since this wasn't someone trying to marry his daughters into the Protector General's prestigious family, Guan Shanjin calmed down a little. In fact, he now felt a little relaxed, waiting for the guest to approach.

"Be good and wait here for me," the man said to the child in a soft voice. The two of them had stopped just before the dividing screen in the room.

"I want to go see him too." The child's voice was soft; he sounded very young. His accent was a mix between that of the capital and that of a southern region. Somehow, it sounded very familiar.

Guan Shanjin couldn't help but furrow his brow. There was something not quite right with what he was feeling. It was just a few words—why was he getting emotional?

"There's no rush. Be good, all right?" the man with the southern accent said patiently. It sounded like he patted the child on the head.

Perhaps because his tone was gentle, the child sighed. "All right, I'll be good," he said in a resigned tone too mature for his age.

Guan Shanjin nearly laughed out loud. He guessed the child was only about seven or eight, but he spoke like a little old man. Perhaps his chubby little face was twisted into a steamed bun, but he still couldn't win against his father.

Wait. Chubby little face?

How did he know the boy would have a chubby face just from his voice? Guan Shanjin's chest suddenly went tight, and pain blossomed in his head again. He gripped the bedsheets tightly, forcing down the pained expression on his face. He nearly shredded the linens before he managed to control himself.

Outside the man and the child came to an agreement, and the man headed inside alone.

It was noon, and the warm winter sunlight shone in through the window. Guan Shanjin hadn't noticed how lovely the sunlight was today. His head hurt and his mind was occupied with Mr. Lu, so when could he have noticed something like that? But now, he saw the brilliance of the winter sun as it covered everything in a thin layer of gold, including the man walking toward him.

The navy blue robes he wore looked quite old, but they appeared to be made from a high-quality fabric: Yinyue silk from the Li Prefecture. The patterned fabric shimmered in the light, and even though it was old, it had a certain simple charm to it. Because the weather was cold, only the man's hands, part of his neck, and his face were exposed. They were quite pale and tinged with pink. Under the sunlight, he gave off a warm, fuzzy feeling.

Guan Shanjin sighed.

"Who are you?" he asked, resting his gaze on the man. His brows scrunched so tightly together that they might knot.

The man wasn't young; there was some gray and white hair at his temples. His ordinary appearance made the gray seem extra visible. The man looked like a wet quail who'd shrunk itself into a ball and was poking a head out of its wing, shaking, quivering, and lost.

"I am..." The man shrank in on himself a little more, like the question had startled him. He hesitated for a moment, and then finally answered carefully, "I'm Wu Xingzi."

"Wu Xingzi?" Guan Shanjin snorted. He'd either gone blind for a moment or his head was acting up again. For a second, he'd thought this old thing was rather pleasing to look at. "Where do you come from?"

"Uh..." Wu Xingzi rubbed his nose. He studied Guan Shanjin with a frown. Seeing that the general was getting impatient, he could only sigh inwardly. "I'm from Qingcheng County. General, do you know of Qingcheng County?"

"No." Guan Shanjin pursed his lips, covering his injury with his hand. His tone grew sharp as he said, "Man Yue told me you were an old friend. I don't remember being friends with an old thing like you."

His words were a little too harsh. Guan Shanjin felt somewhat guilty as soon as they left his mouth, but he couldn't understand why. He'd always been arrogant. He was capable enough and his family had enough status for him to look down on everyone. He'd said many things in the past worse than this, and he'd never felt guilty or regretful.

Guan Shanjin grew even more annoyed, and his headache worsened. He gripped the sheets so hard they tore, but his expression didn't change.

"What are you here for?" he asked the stranger impatiently. It was clear he wanted this guest to leave immediately.

"Um... You see... I'm planning on going back to Qingcheng County for a while. Is that all right?"

Guan Shanjin watched as the man rubbed his nose with his callused fingers. He nearly didn't hear him.

"What did you say?" By the time he worked out what the man had said, his tone darkened, and he sounded even more aggressive than he realized.

"I want to go back to Qingcheng County for a while. Is that all right?" Wu Xingzi repeated himself slowly, his eyes full of anticipation.

"No," Guan Shanjin said with gritted teeth, not knowing why he was refusing. The old thing was about to open his mouth when Guan Shanjin pointed outside. "Get out. Go back to where you came from!"

"Yes." Wu Xingzi nodded obediently, and was ready to walk out with his head bowed.

A thought suddenly occurred to Guan Shanjin and he raised his voice. "Not back to Qingcheng County. Go back to the manor. We can decide after I recover." He felt like if he didn't add that, this old fellow really would go all the way back to where he came from and happily return to Qingcheng County.

It was odd. He didn't even know this old man. How did he anticipate what he would be thinking?

"All right." It was like someone had pulled on Wu Xingzi's tail. He nodded and walked out of the room with his head down, deflated.

Mr. Lu arrived earlier than anyone expected. Never mind twenty days—it took him less than ten. Just six days later, Steward Yuan led him into the Protector General's estate.

Mr. Lu looked exactly the same as he had ten years ago. He was not the most beautiful man, but in his pure white robes, he looked as gentle as water and seemed slightly otherworldly. When he stood in Guan Shanjin's yard, Man Yue couldn't resist the urge to rub his eyes. It was like this person had never left Guan Shanjin's protection; he still shone like a ray of moonlight.

Guan Shanjin had just fallen asleep. The wound on his head was doing all right, but his internal injuries were more serious. His amnesia wasn't simply caused by hitting his head; there was blood collecting at the base of his skull. He'd lost his memories because it was pressing into his brain.

Other than Man Yue, Steward Yuan, and the doctor, no one else knew this. Even Guan Shanjin himself was unaware of the severity of his injuries. He just knew that he was sleeping more than usual—in fact, he spent nearly half the day sleeping.

And Mr. Lu just so happened to arrive right at that moment.

"Mr. Lu." Man Yue cupped his hands at him in greeting. He smiled at him, but did not hide the judgment in his eyes.

"Vice General Man." Mr. Lu returned the greeting. His expression was mild, but there was a hint of anger in his brows that he wasn't able to hide.

Man Yue was slightly surprised; it seemed like he really had changed in these last ten years. Lu Zezhi didn't look as soft and helpless as before. He also didn't seem as eager to throw himself at Guan Shanjin. In fact, he seemed a little impatient.

"You...sure came fast?" The statement slipped out of Man Yue's mouth as a question.

"Yes." Lu Zezhi nodded, the impatience on his face deepening somewhat. "You don't need to try me like that. I've already heard the news from A-Fan... I mean, Steward Yuan. But I didn't think you'd allow me to come."

A-Fan? Man Yue's ears twitched. With one brow raised, he glanced at Steward Yuan, who was standing to the side with his head down, his expression serious. If he remembered correctly, Steward Yuan's name was a single character, Fan, and it was the previous Protector General who'd given it to him.

"Oh, A-Fan." Man Yue's curiosity instantly piqued. New, exciting things sure did happen every day! No wonder Lu Zezhi had arrived in six days. Perhaps he could've arrived even earlier—someone must've delayed him.

Even though Man Yue had pointed out his relationship with Lu Zezhi, Steward Yuan's expression remained unmoved. He didn't even blink. "Young Master Man," he said in a low voice, "where should I arrange for Mr. Lu to stay?"

"You can't ask me that. I'm merely the Vice General. I have no say over the matters of the Protector General's residence." Man Yue spread his hands out and shrugged. His smile grew more sincere. "Why don't you take Mr. Lu to see the Mistress? Ask him to decide." He had to find something for Wu Xingzi to do, otherwise he might just disappear from the Protector General's residence at some point.

As soon as the thought crossed his mind, Man Yue grew annoyed. He suspected that despite his calm demeanor, Wu Xingzi was fuming inside. Apparently, once he found out Guan Shanjin's life was not in danger, he didn't want to stay a moment longer in the Protector General's estate. He'd even packed bags for long-distance travel. All he was missing was an opportunity to leave.

Now that Lu Zezhi was here, perhaps Man Yue could trick him into staying.

"Mistress?" Lu Zezhi's face twitched. Clearly, this title bothered him.

"Yes, Mistress." Man Yue blinked as he smiled. Although Lu Zezhi was different from ten years ago, Man Yue still hated him. His mood improved when he saw that Lu Zezhi was bothered.

"Yes." It was as if Steward Yuan couldn't see the tension between Man Yue and Lu Zezhi, nor remember how much they'd hated each other ten years ago. He waved at Lu Zezhi. "Mr. Lu, please follow me."

"Oh." Lu Zezhi immediately abandoned Man Yue once Steward Yuan summoned him. He knew very well that even if he grew two more brains, he still wouldn't win at anything if his opponent was Man Yue. He might even be mocked for trying. What was the point?

Man Yue didn't chase after him. Instead, he got out some melon seeds and started snacking.

He watched as Steward Yuan led the way for Lu Zezhi. At first, Lu Zezhi still put on a facade of superiority. But once he thought there was no one else watching, his shoulders came down and he jogged to Steward Yuan's side, stuffing his hand into the other man's and holding it tightly.

Not even the normally unbothered Steward Yuan could maintain his expression. He stopped walking, looking like he wanted to pull his hand back. Lu Zezhi clearly knew what he wanted to do, and brought his other hand over to join the first. Steward Yuan trembled slightly and glanced back in Man Yue's direction. Their eyes met.

Man Yue smiled broadly, spat out the melon seeds in his mouth, and waved to him. He was surprised to see that the man whom everyone at the Protector General's estate called "Iron Mask" was actually blushing.

"Tch. Why did he fall for him?" Man Yue mused.

Steward Yuan ran off with Lu Zezhi in a bit of a panic as Man Yue sighed judgmentally.

Before Man Yue could figure out if he was simply observing the situation, here for the show, or just wanted to join in on the fun, Steward Yuan had already led Lu Zezhi to Wu Xingzi's yard.

Wu Xingzi was peeling chestnuts with his son in the yard. As he stepped on the spiky, pointy shells, he instructed the child to grab the flesh out with tongs. The two of them joked and laughed as they went about the task, and there was even a fire crackling next to them—they would roast the nuts later.

"Mistress." Steward Yuan lowered his head respectfully. "Vice General Man asked me to bring Mr. Lu to come see you. Could you please decide where Mr. Lu will be staying?"

The instant his eyes landed on Lu Zezhi, Wu Xingzi's smile froze for a moment, but he very quickly regained his previous warmth. A little embarrassed, he let down the hem of his robes.

"Mr. Lu, it's been a while." He rubbed his nose and lowered his head slightly, unsure what to do.

"Yes, it's been a while." Lu Zezhi also seemed a bit uneasy. The last time he saw Wu Xingzi, he hadn't been in the best state. It was when Guan Shanjin had thrown him out of the Protector General's residence. He truly hadn't spared any of his dignity.

Lu Zezhi had thought he would never have to see either of them again after that. After all, Guan Shanjin had said so himself, and he knew how decisive that man was. Perhaps fate was just toying with them.

"Mr. Lu, are you tired? Do you want to come in and have a cup of tea? I'll ask Steward Yuan to tidy up that yard you used to stay in."

"The yard I used to stay in?" Lu Zezhi's brow furrowed, and his mood turned sour. "What do you mean? You want me to go back there? As expected of the wife of the Great General of the Southern Garrison. You've gotten craftier in these past ten years."

Wu Xingzi froze for a moment, his mouth agape. He hadn't expected Mr. Lu to react like that. "No, no, no, Mr. Lu, you've misunderstood me!" he said, shaking his head hurriedly. "I don't mean anything by that! It's just, it's just…Haiwang has always thought you should live there, so I can't just…I can't just…"

"Because of you, I was stuck in that little yard for several months. And in the end, that was where he chased me away. If you want to, you can go live there, but I will not." Lu Zezhi pursed his lips and glared at Wu Xingzi. Before Wu Xingzi could say anything in reply, he turned to ask Steward Yuan, "Can't you decide? Even before, not everything was decided by the Protector General's wife. Besides, as of now, he's only the wife of the General of the Southern Garrison."

"The Protector General and his wife are out traveling right now," Steward Yuan told him calmly. This meant that Wu Xingzi was essentially the one in charge of the household right now. As a lowly steward, his job was to listen to his master.

Lu Zezhi wasn't the same foolish, naïve caged bird from ten years ago. "So you plan on locking me up there?" he scoffed coldly. "What power the Protector General's family has! You locked me up ten years ago, and now you want to lock me up again?"

"Ah, Mr. Lu, you're mistaken," Wu Xingzi said. "That's not what I mean. I just…"

"Teacher!"

Before Wu Xingzi could explain himself, Guan Shanjin's unusually cheerful greeting boomed from afar. In the blink of an eye, he was in the yard.

"Teacher! You're finally back!"

Perhaps his brain really was broken. Guan Shanjin swept Lu Zezhi into his arms, a bright smile on his face.

"H-Haiwang!" Lu Zezhi yelped. He reached out to push him away, his cheeks burning.

"Sorry, that was rude of me." Guan Shanjin could clearly feel Lu Zezhi's stiffness and rejection. Cursing himself for not being patient enough, he hurriedly let him go.

Almost no one saw Steward Yuan's shoulders shaking, or the way his fingers twitched as if they were about to curl into fists. The only person who noticed was Man Yue, who was following behind Guan Shanjin. He almost got his melon seeds out again, but he managed to hold back. He stood by the gate to the yard, smiling at the five people inside.

"No... It wasn't that serious." Lu Zezhi coughed a few times, then suddenly smelled the cold fragrance emanating from Guan Shanjin. He couldn't help the blush creeping up his cheeks. "Steward Yuan said you were injured?"

"Yes..." Guan Shanjin was about to respond, but he suddenly remembered something, glancing at Wu Xingzi. Whatever he was about to say, he swallowed it all back down for some reason. "It's not exactly an injury. I just bumped my head a bit."

Man Yue couldn't resist anymore. He started snacking again.

"Oh..." Lu Zezhi followed Guan Shanjin's gaze and glanced at Wu Xingzi as well.

Wu Xingzi, who was quietly discussing with his child whether or not they should go dig up a sweet potato from the back garden and roast it along with their chestnuts, suddenly found himself being stared at by two people. He shivered slightly, then looked up, unsure of the situation.

"Ah... What is it?"

"Who's that child?" Guan Shanjin's expression turned very ugly. It was as if he'd forgotten all about his beloved teacher. He aggressively approached the old quail and the little quail next to him.

"This child is..." Wu Xingzi opened his mouth but didn't know exactly how to explain to Guan Shanjin.

The child wasn't shy. Since his dad asked, he'd react honestly. "Hi, Daddy."

"Daddy?" Guan Shanjin froze, his eyes big. He pointed at Wu Xingzi. "You called him Father earlier, right?" He recognized this voice! It was the kid Wu Xingzi had brought with him the other day! He did have a chubby face, and an expression like an old man.

"Yes." The child nodded, then smiled brightly. "You were the one that told me to call him that, Daddy."

"I did?" Confusion washed over Guan Shanjin's face. After thinking about it for a while, he suddenly gasped, "So you're my child?"

"Yes. Did you forget?" The kid blinked his black, crystal-like eyes, and his expression turned a little gloomy. Guan Shanjin's heart ached, but he didn't know this kid. He'd never even held a woman in his life—how could a man birth his child?

But this kid was quite clever. He clearly took after him.

No, wait... Man Yue said this old quail was an old friend of his, even though he had no memories of him. And this kid said he was his... They did have somewhat similar brows, and he did have a chubby little nose... Guan Shanjin suddenly felt dizzy and couldn't think about it any further. "Can you...bear children?" he blurted out, looking at Wu Xingzi.

There were many people in the yard, but it was silent enough to hear a pin drop...

"A ha ha ha ha hah!" Man Yue abruptly burst into laughter. Then he choked on a melon seed casing and nearly coughed up a lung.

"No..." Wu Xingzi rubbed his nose. He was always so gentle and well-mannered, speaking in a soft tone of voice. "I did not give birth to this child. In terms of blood, he is more related to you, General."

There was a small, slightly shy smile on the old quail's face. For some reason, Guan Shanjin felt somewhat uneasy.

For once, Wu Xingzi slept late.

When he woke again, it was already bright out. The rare winter sunlight peeked in through the curtains on his bed, bringing with it a sense of warmth.

His eyes were half open and he still felt a little lethargic, so he didn't move for a while. His brain hadn't quite woken up yet. Sleepily, he wondered why he'd slept in so late. Had he ever woken up this late?

Ah...he had. The night of their wedding, Guan Shanjin was like a wild beast that had been starved for a long time. He had gobbled him up bite by bite until there was nothing left. If he could, he might've even sucked his marrow dry.

Wu Xingzi had been tormented all night and didn't wake up until noon the next day. It took him ten days of bed rest to recover.

After that, Guan Shanjin kept himself in check. Perhaps he was worried Wu Xingzi was no longer young. It wasn't like he could wait until something really happened to Wu Xingzi to curb his desires.

Thinking about that, Wu Xingzi chuckled lightly, hugging the blanket. Then, he stopped and sighed instead.

"Mistress? Are you awake?" Mint's voice came from outside the curtains.

"Yes," Wu Xingzi responded. Emerging from the blankets, he looked down at his body. He was properly dressed and nothing was showing. He let out a sigh of relief before he slowly got up, pulling apart the curtains.

"What time is it?"

"It's not too late. It's eight forty-five," Osmanthus responded from the side. She was holding the water for Wu Xingzi to wash his face and the tea for him to rinse his mouth.

"It's already eight forty-five?" Wu Xingzi asked, shocked. By this time, he'd normally already have eaten breakfast, be finished gardening, and would be getting ready for lessons with his child!

"Yes." Mint and Osmanthus were quite calm. They didn't ask how Wu Xingzi was feeling. In fact, they didn't even blink. They simply busied themselves with their tasks.

Something was up.

Wu Xingzi could only sigh inwardly. There was no need to ask. These two had been with him for many years now, so he understood their behavior. If anything big had happened, they would've told him already. But if it was their master's order or it had to do with his privacy, they would never open their mouths.

The only person who could command them to be silent other than himself was Guan Shanjin.

Right... Wu Xingzi took a sniff. Among the scent of longevity flowers filling the room, he also detected hint of a coldness. It was chilling yet alluring and seemed to surround him, even though it was faint enough that he wondered if it was really there.

So last night wasn't a dream... Wu Xingzi took a deep, careful breath, inhaling that icy fragrance.

"Mistress, would you like some breakfast?" asked Osmanthus.

"Yes, it'll be good to eat something." Wu Xingzi did not reject her. But it was a little unfortunate that Guan Shanjin's scent did end up dissipating. In the last breath he took, he could only smell the longevity flowers.

Mint and Osmanthus left to prepare breakfast.

Finally, Wu Xingzi got out of bed to ready himself for the day. He was still wearing the old gray-blue robes. Sitting down at the table with his head in his hand, he thought back over the last few days...especially what had happened last night.

Guan Shanjin had hurt his head and become a lot more emotional and impatient. Even Man Yue was at a loss as to why he was like this. After discussing it with the doctor, they had no answers.

"Master has never been this erratic, even as a child. Thinking of what he said that day, and how he even hugged Lu Zezhi... I don't have any explanation other than that his mind is broken." Man Yue spread his hands out in resignation, then took a sip of his tea. He drummed his fingers on the table, slightly bored.

"What do you mean, 'even hugging' me?" Beside them, Lu Zezhi immediately became unhappy. He first glanced at Steward Yuan, then glared at Man Yue. If they were judging the most innocent person in the room, Lu Zezhi was sure that if he was second, no one else would dare come first.

The rest of the people in the room were Man Yue, Steward Yuan, Wu Xingzi, and that kid named Guan Chenliang. These were all people of the Guan family, and he was the only outsider. However, he was stuck in this room, unable to go anywhere.

And the person they spoke of was currently asleep due to his injuries. That was why they were able to gather to discuss the situation.

That wasn't quite correct, though. Lu Zezhi was here because when Guan Shanjin was awake, he had to be cautious around Steward Yuan, drawing a careful line between them. He couldn't let anything slip—not even a glance—so he was quite tired of putting on the act. Now that they had the chance, he didn't want to separate from Steward Yuan for even a moment.

Wu Xingzi and his child, on the other hand, were forced to come by Man Yue. Asking the lady of the house to come keep an eye on things was one way of spinning it, but in actuality, Man Yue needed to keep an eye on Wu Xingzi. After all, Wu Xingzi had been quite active these last few days. The tall walls of the Protector General's estate might not be enough to contain him for much longer.

Meanwhile, the leashed old quail blinked his little eyes and a small, gentle smile appeared on his lips. "He once liked Mr. Lu very much. This is just a reflection of how he felt." He sighed, then, somewhat emotionally.

If it had been anyone else, Man Yue and Steward Yuan would have knocked the teeth out of anyone who dared say such a thing. But they both knew perfectly well that Wu Xingzi's tone did not hold an ounce of sarcasm.

Man Yue smiled bitterly and rubbed his jaw. "Mistress, aren't you curious why the general fell off his horse?"

Guan Shanjin was, after all, the Great General of the Southern Garrison and Great Xia's god of war. He spent half his life on the battlefield, and his horseback riding skills were practically unmatched. He'd never fallen off his horse before. How did he fall in a place like the capital and manage to hit his head in the process? There was no way Man Yue could believe in such a coincidence.

Wu Xingzi pursed his lips, his brows knitting together slightly.

Of course he'd considered it. This was the capital, where the emperor lived. The stone slabs on the road were perfectly aligned and flat. Even he would have a hard time tripping when walking on those roads, never mind Guan Shanjin, an experienced rider trained in martial arts. Even if something happened to the horse, the horse might be injured, but Guan Shanjin wouldn't lose a single hair.

For some reason, his heart felt like it was burning. His lips twitched, and he finally nodded. "It is a little strange... What are you thinking, Vice General Man?"

They didn't spend much time at the capital. Usually, they stayed in Horse-Face City, Qingcheng County, or Goose City instead. Wu Xingzi wasn't too familiar with the grudges and relationships between the noble families of the capital, so he couldn't examine the possibilities as thoroughly as Man Yue. For now, he really couldn't think of anyone who would dare to harm Guan Shanjin.

But to his surprise, Man Yue shook his head as well. "I'm stumped on this. Right now, the Protector General's entire family is favored by the emperor. They've never been corrupt. None of the princes or their supporters would try anything so rash. Why would they bring trouble upon themselves for no reason? It's not worth it."

Wu Xingzi nodded in agreement.

"I need to look into this further. I'll also ask the doctor to treat the general more carefully and see whether his brain was damaged by accident, or if someone did something deliberately," said Man Yue.

"I think he just hurt himself..." Lu Zezhi muttered, then sighed, holding Steward Yuan's hands even tighter.

Perhaps he really was just hurt, Wu Xingzi thought as he was escorted back to his yard.

After having dinner with his child, he looked over his homework. Then, Mint and Osmanthus led the little heir to his own rooms. Now, Wu Xingzi was the only one left in the large, empty room.

He grabbed a piece of flaky pancake, taking small bites. The fragrance of the yak butter and the sweetness of the sugar filling spread across his tongue. The flaky layers broke in his mouth, landing on the wax paper on the table. Once he was done, he'd scrape up all the crumbs and eat them too.

Guan Shanjin had taken him on a ride a few days ago to a nearby town to get them. Apparently, it was a local treat. It used to only be known among the neighboring villages, but somehow, these last few years, its fame had spread to the capital. It had become a trendy snack, and many people went to the town just to get them.

It was delicious, but as Wu Xingzi ate, it slowly started to lose its taste in his mouth. Sighing, he put down the half that was left. After wiping his hands, he slowly moved to the basket where he kept his clothes. He thought about it for a while before opening the lid and rustling around the bottom. He pulled out a large pack.

"What's that?" A voice like jade beads suddenly rang out from behind him. Wu Xingzi shrank into himself in shock, and the pack in his hands fell to the floor.

The pack landed with a *smack* and somehow came undone. A piece of paper floated out, and then another, and another—the... penises...that were drawn on them were clear to see.

Guan Shanjin gasped in disbelief. "What is all this?"

"Um... This... Um..." Wu Xingzi's face flushed bright red. He couldn't bring himself to say a thing. How was he supposed to explain this? *Uh, Haiwang, don't be mad. These are just my pengornis drawings. Look! Yours is right there! See? Right there! The one by the foot of the table, closest to you! Isn't that yours? It's straight, thick, and beautiful.*

All these years, there has never been another pengornis that can hold a candle to yours! You know this!

"They're all drawings of men's..." Guan Shanjin glared at him with narrowed eyes. Not even he could utter such crass words. "Man Yue said you're my wife? Why would my spouse be looking at such things?"

"You look at them too..." Wu Xingzi had no idea why that was his response, but he was telling the truth. Guan Shanjin always respected him. He knew that he liked collecting penis pictures, so he'd always look through them with him. As a result, this carefully curated selection of pengornises was a collaborative effort between the two of them!

"I do too? Why would I look at such things?" Guan Shanjin glared at the shaking yet indignant old quail, fury bursting forth in his heart. He wanted to stomp on those drawings and tear them to shreds.

However, even though he lifted his foot, it did not land on any of the drawings. Instead, it landed next to one of the drawings harmlessly and stomped down twice.

He couldn't understand what was wrong with him! He was so angry that his chest hurt, but he was trying to tamp down his anger. This push and pull made his head ache, as though his wound was about to reopen.

He put a hand to his chest and stumbled a couple of steps back.

"A-are you all right?" asked Wu Xingzi. "Does your head hurt? Do you want me to call the doctor?" Guan Shanjin's face was ashy pale, and sweat beaded on his forehead. Wu Xingzi was both worried and pained seeing him in this state. He immediately rushed forward to hold him, but was pushed away.

Guan Shanjin was still furious. He was angry at all the pengornis drawings on the ground, but he was also angry that he was mad at the old quail. This old man could go looking at anyone's prick as he pleased! What did it have to do with him? Why was he angry? The one he admired was obviously Mr. Lu!

Wu Xingzi's outstretched hands didn't land on anything, so he retracted them, dejected, and rubbed his own nose. "Then why don't you sit here for a while? I'll go get Man Yue and the doctor."

"Don't you dare!" Guan Shanjin glared at the phalluses on the floor. Even though there were now dark spots in his vision, he counted roughly a hundred drawings. How did Wu Xingzi manage to collect so many? His head hurt, his chest hurt, and he could taste a hint of metallic sweetness at the back of his throat, but he managed to swallow it down.

"All right," Wu Xingzi answered obediently, and stood there with his head hanging. He kept playing with the perfume pouch hanging at his waist.

"Clean all this up. I don't want to look at such filthy things." Guan Shanjin really didn't know who Wu Xingzi was, but was certain he must be here to test him.

"All right." Wu Xingzi rushed to nod, then carefully cleaned up the drawings spread out on the floor. He meticulously blew the dust off of every single page. After he'd smoothed them out, he sorted them in some specific order before putting them back in the cypress box and tying the whole package back up.

"You keep these things in a box made of cypress?" Guan Shanjin's fury skyrocketed once again. It felt like someone kept stabbing into his skull with a needle. His skin dripped with cold sweat.

But even so, he wasn't going to leave. Perhaps because of what Wu Xingzi had done to him, he refused to leave until he got his revenge.

"Yes. Cypress boxes are great. They smell good and repel insects. Wouldn't it be a shame if these drawings were eaten? It's not like I can go ask for replacements." Wu Xingzi's eyes shone brightly as he stroked his precious cypress box. "Besides..." He glanced at Guan Shanjin. "You're the one that gave me this box."

Guan Shanjin didn't believe him. "Even if I was the one who gave it to you, it definitely wasn't for this kind of disgusting purpose."

Wu Xingzi sighed. He usually avoided conflict like this, and there was even less reason to fight with his husband when he had a head injury. So he nodded dutifully and tried to comfort him. "Perhaps I remembered wrong. It wasn't you who gave it to me."

"Hmph." Seeing him acquiesce, Guan Shanjin finally calmed down a bit. He sat down on the chair and took a few deep breaths. His injury finally didn't hurt as much anymore. "Come here."

"Huh?" Wu Xingzi looked up at him, blinking in confusion.

"Come here." Guan Shanjin didn't even know what he was planning on doing. He just called out to Wu Xingzi in a cold voice.

"All right, all right." Wu Xingzi finally moved toward him slowly. When he was about half an arm's length away, Guan Shanjin, patience running out, grabbed him by the hand and pulled him into his arms. Wu Xingzi's nose smushed into the man's solid, thick chest, and he let out a sound of pain.

"Hmph, can't even take this much pain? You're surprisingly delicate, hm?" Guan Shanjin's nasal, smiling tone made Wu Xingzi's ears hot. Between that and Guan Shanjin's scent, it was enough to make Wu Xingzi's legs go soft.

But the general didn't plan on letting him go. He leaned down, nibbling on his earlobe. "Since you said I also look at your pengornis drawings, why don't you show me how mighty yours is?" he said with a smile.

"N-no, no, no..." Wu Xingzi wanted to resist. Not only was he still angry at Guan Shanjin, but wasn't this Guan Shanjin in love with Mr. Lu? Why was he making moves on him? Although...back then, when they first played with each other's pengornises, Mr. Lu was still in the picture...

"Why do I feel like your mouth is saying one thing, but your heart is saying another? I bet you're secretly delighted." Guan Shanjin chuckled and nimbly removed Wu Xingzi's pants.

Guan Shanjin had also seen countless "pengornises."

He'd spent most of his life in the army, after all. He'd climbed up from the lowest ranks all the way to being a general through his own merit. His life constantly hung by a thread.

The battlefields and border both were harsh environments. Just having food to eat and a place to sleep was good enough. Hygiene was never a high priority. They would only clean themselves up if they passed by a river or lake, and they always did so in groups—so of course they saw plenty of penises.

Long, short, girthy, skinny; they were all men, so they didn't pay much mind. Even if some of them were gay, they didn't resort to sneaking peeks at their comrades to fantasize about it later.

But Guan Shanjin was certain he'd never seen such a delicate, cute cock.

Perhaps because he was a little scared, Wu Xingzi's dick lay there softly. It wasn't that small—about the length of Guan Shanjin's pointer finger—but the foreskin was on the long side. It covered up the head completely, giving it a smooth, round appearance. It was flushed pink, which was not a color an old man like him should have.

Setting aside whether or not the two of them really did enjoy pengornis pictures together, the one in front of him right now certainly suited his tastes.

Guan Shanjin smiled and glanced at the old man, whose eyes and brows were tightly scrunched together. He flicked his poor little prick with a finger.

"No wonder I always think you look like a quail. You really do resemble one."

Wu Xingzi hissed. Guan Shanjin's body temperature was running quite hot. Now that he was playing with Wu Xingzi's dick, it felt like a flame licking at it. The old man's hips shook uncontrollably, wanting to move away, but Guan Shanjin grabbed them with his callused hand and easily held him there.

"D-don't play with me." Wu Xingzi had no choice but to beg, but he was so embarrassed he couldn't even open his eyes; his voice caught in his throat.

Guan Shanjin had excellent ears, though, and heard him clearly. He chuckled lowly, then flicked the trembling member in his hand. "No wonder you like looking at those drawings. They're to tide you over, huh?"

When he glanced at them earlier, Guan Shanjin noticed that all the pengornises that this old man collected were quite large. As soon as he had that thought, he began to feel annoyed again.

"N-not quite. I just, I just..." Wu Xingzi opened one eye and snuck a glance at Guan Shanjin. Unexpectedly, Guan Shanjin was looking right at him, with a smile on his lips that didn't reach his eyes. Wu Xingzi suddenly couldn't find a single excuse. All he could do was blush furiously.

"Hm?" Seeing him like this, Guan Shanjin felt his heart itch terribly. Some unfamiliar emotion, like a pot of boiling sweet soup, raged in his chest and slowly spread to his limbs.

"Nothing..." Wu Xingzi hung his head. This time, he saw Guan Shanjin's hands, as beautiful as jade, holding his little pengornis.

He sucked in a breath, then looked up in a hurry. "D-don't hold my...my..."

"You really don't want me to?" Guan Shanjin was in a great mood. He wanted to do so much more than just hold the little thing.

"Yes, please, let go—ah!" Wu Xingzi suddenly yelped. He watched with large, disbelieving eyes as Guan Shanjin bent down and buried his face in Wu Xingzi's crotch. A warm, wet sensation traveled straight from his dick to his brain, and he froze.

G-Guan Shanjin is a-actually...swallowing me down?

It felt quite good. His thick, soft tongue enveloped Wu Xingzi's pink length as he sucked, and he moved all the way from the base to the tip many times. Then, he took his balls into his mouth as well. Wu Xingzi jerked harshly, reaching down to push away Guan Shanjin's head.

"Stop, don't! Ah! No—Mm..." *Don't suck me!* Wu Xingzi's face flushed bright red, and he panted so harshly he couldn't even speak properly.

Guan Shanjin's beautiful mouth was very cruel. With his nimble tongue, he fully demonstrated what it meant to "press lightly, slowly, then pluck again and again."[5] Wu Xingzi felt like his soul was about to be sucked out of his body.

But Guan Shanjin didn't seem to notice. He was preoccupied starting to use his teeth to nibble on Wu Xingzi's cockhead. He was very gentle, but it felt tingly and a little painful. The sensation went all the way to Wu Xingzi's heart. Out of fear that he'd accidentally bite, Wu Xingzi's hand shrank back, and his legs, wrapped around Guan Shanjin's shoulders, started trembling.

---

5   From the poem *Song of the Pipa* (琵琶行) *by Bai Juyi* (白居易). *This line talks about various pipa techniques.*

"Haiwang... Haiwang..." Wu Xingzi had always been honest when it came to sex, and he could never resist Guan Shanjin. At first, he struggled shyly, but now, he was screaming his name.

For some reason, Guan Shanjin was really getting into sucking Wu Xingzi's cock. Each time, he sucked harder than the last. The old man's dick wasn't very large, but it slowly hardened under his efforts. It was now big enough to fill his mouth, so he had to let go of Wu Xingzi's balls to focus on the shaft. He licked and nibbled, making Wu Xingzi pant and cry out again and again. His waist would give out, tremble, and stiffen; he was completely at Guan Shanjin's mercy.

From what Guan Shanjin could recall, he'd never serviced a man like this. In bed, he was always the one on top. Other than Mr. Lu, whom he loved, he thought it was dirty to touch anyone, whether it be their sweat or other fluids. It was sticky and smelly. He didn't like it when others sucked his dick, so it was even more absurd that he had someone else's dick in his mouth right now.

Why was this old man so different? Guan Shanjin clamped down even harder on the thin, struggling waist in his hands. Not caring if he left behind marks, he pressed the older man harshly down into the chair and maliciously bit down on the trembling length in his mouth. Wu Xingzi cried out, begging him pitifully to be gentle. He finally slowed down and comforted him with his tongue, softly licking over the faint bite marks, then sucked a few times.

Wu Xingzi once again felt like his soul was not his own. His trembling fingers wrapped around Guan Shanjin's hair. He almost couldn't take it, wanting to push the man away, but he also couldn't bear to do it. Before his mushy brain could make a decision, Guan Shanjin had started flicking his foreskin with his tongue.

"Haiwang, no... It's t-too dirty..." Wu Xingzi was jolted back to reality. Blushing, he tried to push Guan Shanjin away. It was only shortly after noon, and the weather was cold. He hadn't bathed in a few days, so the taste must be...! How could he let Guan Shanjin lick him there?

It wasn't like Guan Shanjin had never sucked him off before, but each time, he'd always washed himself clean before he let Guan Shanjin's mouth near his cock. They'd never done it like this.

But Guan Shanjin ignored him. He even patted Wu Xingzi's butt in warning. Even more nimbly, he used his tongue to stretch Wu Xingzi's foreskin a little, poking his tongue in between.

"Ahhhh!" Wu Xingzi screamed. His legs, hanging off of Guan Shanjin's shoulders, jerked a few times before going limp.

Guan Shanjin sucked out all of the cum from his dick and swallowed it down.

"You... You..." Wu Xingzi's gaze was slightly lost as he recovered from his orgasm. He watched as Guan Shanjin looked up. His neck tensed, and with a bob of his throat, he swallowed all of Wu Xingzi's semen. His bright red tongue even licked his wet lips, then spread into a small smile.

It was over for him! Wu Xingzi's head buzzed. His waist was sore, his legs were sore, even his cock was sore. But the person before him was so tempting and delicious. As the general's wife, he had no way to resist. He practically wanted to throw himself onto the sly demon and kiss him!

"Why did you swallow it?" he asked shyly. Even though it wasn't the first time, and Guan Shanjin was his husband, wasn't Mr. Lu the one currently in his heart?

Guan Shanjin spat lightly, wiping away the leftover cum on his lips. Under Wu Xingzi's lost gaze, he stuffed his finger into the old man's mouth, a little roughly. Before Wu Xingzi could react, he pinched Wu Xingzi's tongue and wiped the cum on it.

"Ughh!" Wu Xingzi's eyes went wide. A salty bitterness flooded his mouth. That was fine, but Guan Shanjin didn't stop. He moved his finger deeper in his mouth, even to his throat. Wu Xingzi tried to push him away with his tongue, but how could a soft tongue compete with Guan Shanjin's finger? Never mind pushing him away, Guan Shanjin thoroughly played with his mouth to the point where he couldn't even keep all the saliva in. It started to drip down the corners of his mouth, and tears started to leak from his eyes.

"Does it taste good?" Guan Shanjin asked, chuckling.

"Mmmmph!" The general was still playing with Wu Xingzi's tongue, so Wu Xingzi couldn't say anything.

"Seems like it. It tastes so good that you're crying." As he spoke, he reached over to wipe the tears on Wu Xingzi's face, finally pulling his fingers out. He pulled out his handkerchief and wiped his hands clean. "If I catch your eyes wandering again, don't blame me for what comes next."

"What...exactly will come next?" Wu Xingzi couldn't quite close his mouth. His tongue hurt from what Guan Shanjin did, and he didn't realize he had spoken his question out loud.

Guan Shanjin raised a brow at that. "You're quite strong-willed for your age, hm?"

Wu Xingzi went limp at those words. He blushed—not just his face, but across nearly half his body. Panicked, he looked down, trying to find his handkerchief in his sleeve to wipe his face, but Guan Shanjin was one step ahead and wiped his face for him.

"How did I fall for such an ugly thing?" Guan Shanjin hooked a finger under Wu Xingzi's chin, carefully observing him from his eyebrows to his neck, his brow furrowed in confusion.

Wu Xingzi wasn't exactly ugly, but he was very plain and un-exciting. If you compared him to food, he was more boring than plain rice porridge and small side dishes. How could he, Guan Shanjin, give up the pearl that was Mr. Lu and choose this fish's eyeball instead? His previous self must've been the one who'd hit his head!

Even though he always felt an inexplicable stirring whenever he saw Wu Xingzi, Guan Shanjin tamped down the urge and ignored it. His feelings toward Mr. Lu were deeper than just lust or beauty. He would always remember that Lantern Festival. With all the lanterns in the trees, it was like the stars had fallen to the mortal realm.

He had walked slowly within the lanterns, coldly watching as passersby either laughed, gasped, whispered, or yelled to each other. He seemed somehow completely disconnected from these living beings. He was separated from this world, but he felt nothing.

Until a figure in white suddenly appeared before him. In that moment, he was part of the world once again.

Even though Man Yue said he'd hit his head and lost more than a decade's memories, his feelings toward Mr. Lu were deeper than love. How could he forget?

Wu Xingzi's face felt a little raw from the rubbing, so he reached up to stop Guan Shanjin.

"Perhaps it's because my waist is supple?" After all, their relationship had started with sex. He also couldn't understand why Guan Shanjin chose to swallow him, an old quail, but after some consideration, what other explanation was there? He was flexible, so he could be twisted any which way.

Guan Shanjin stopped, his brows knitting even further as an inexplicable feeling entered his heart. He didn't know why, but he was angry all of a sudden.

"I've seen plenty of people with softer waists than you," he scoffed, glaring at the man before him.

"Really?" Wu Xingzi didn't really care, nodding along. He scrunched his face up, a little frustrated. "Then why?"

Why had this question come back to him? Guan Shanjin took a deep breath and smiled insincerely. "Sometimes I do have my blind moments."

"Oh." Wu Xingzi snuck a glance at him, seeming to hesitate about something.

Guan Shanjin knew he shouldn't ask him what he was thinking, but he just couldn't hold it in. "What do you want to say?" In the end, he still ended up asking. It wasn't like the old thing could say anything more ridiculous. He was the Great General of the Southern Garrison; he couldn't show fear in a moment like this.

"Nothing..."

"Speak."

Since the general insisted, and seemed a little annoyed, Wu Xingzi had no choice but to respond. "Um... In order for you to stop being blind," he said, rubbing his nose, "can I return to Qingcheng..."

"No!" Guan Shanjin pressed a hand to his chest without waiting for Wu Xingzi to finish. He practically wanted to pinch his mouth shut. Seeing as Wu Xingzi was about to open his mouth again, he clenched his teeth and repeated, "No!"

He needed to tell Man Yue to send someone to watch over this courtyard. He could not let this old thing get away!

As much as Guan Shanjin wanted to lock Wu Xingzi up in his yard, or even the Protector General's estate, it just wasn't possible.

But Guan Shanjin's head wasn't working properly, so he didn't know that. Placing his faith in Steward Yuan and Man Yue, he ordered them to keep an eye on Wu Xingzi, then delved into investigating why he had fallen from his horse.

He didn't know that after he'd held Wu Xingzi in such high regard for ten years, there was nothing Wu Xingzi couldn't do. If he didn't do something, it was merely because he didn't want to. He had earned a great reputation in the Protector General's estate, as well as in Guan Shanjin's own manor. Even Guan Shanjin's two most loyal men, Steward Yuan and Man Yue, knew that the best way to show loyalty to Guan Shanjin was to make sure his wife was happy.

If it weren't for the fact that Wu Xingzi was an honest man with a good head on his shoulders, he would have been totally capable of acting as a beautiful face who brought the downfall of the country.

So Man Yue sent someone to stand guard over Wu Xingzi's yard. He didn't just send anyone—he sent two of Guan Shanjin's closest bodyguards. But even so, they could not come between the mistress and his desire for House of Taotie's new rose dumplings.

Bright and early, Wu Xingzi didn't even eat a proper breakfast. He just had two bowls of plain rice porridge paired with some eggs and fried chives. Then, he led the little heir out to wander.

The capital was located far enough north that the weather turned cold quite early. As a southerner, Wu Xingzi still wasn't very used to it. It wasn't as piercingly cold as the south, where the humidity brought the cold straight to one's bones, but the wind was fierce, and it felt like spikes blowing across his face. Soon his cheeks and nose were both bright red, and he couldn't even keep his eyes open.

The weather wasn't great today, so Wu Xingzi didn't wear an old robe like usual. If there was one lesson he'd learned in the last few years, it was how to be good to himself. At the very least, he no longer treasured his new clothes and refused to wear them. When he put on his coat, he felt warm and toasty all over save for his exposed face.

The coat was brand new. It was made of plain cotton, but the work was meticulous. There were subtle patterns on the collar, sleeve cuffs, and hem, the same kind Guan Shanjin liked to wear. Wu Xingzi never understood what the patterns meant; he just thought they looked good, especially on Guan Shanjin. It gave him a special elegance.

Guan Chenliang did not fear the cold like his father did. He just wore a slightly thicker robe. His bright red cheeks were quite cute. Obviously, they didn't travel alone; the guard that Man Yue had assigned to them had to come along no matter what. However, Osmanthus and Mint, who were always by Wu Xingzi's side, weren't there because Steward Yuan needed them for something. With no other choice, they asked the little heir's servant to follow along. Dianzi was only twelve or thirteen this year, and he had a square head and large ears. Despite looking slightly slow, he was rather clever, and the two sisters trusted him quite a lot.

Right before they left, Wu Xingzi just so happened to run into an ugly-faced Lu Zezhi, who was meticulously avoiding Guan Shanjin. This Mr. Lu, who was once treated like a treasure within the Protector General's residence, now showed an expression like a bitter melon.

Wu Xingzi saw him hiding pitifully behind a grove of trees, munching on a dry piece of flatbread. He didn't even have any tea with him. Wu Xingzi truly felt sorry, so he asked Lu Zezhi if he'd like to head out with them.

Lu Zezhi swallowed down his bread and sighed, his face scrunching up. "You realize that I hate it the most when you pity me?"

Before, Man Yue had laughed at him for putting on the act of an untainted white lotus flower despite growing out of the mud, but he did not deny it. Whether it be a white lotus flower or a sesame ball, he never regretted his decision to rely on Guan Shanjin. After all, he did have true feelings for him, and he did try his best.

But this man before Lu Zezhi had always looked like the wild grass growing on the side of the road. Who would've thought he'd bloom into a little white flower? He looked gentle and slow, well-behaved and meek, obedient and well-mannered...but he could incite such fury.

"I'm not pitying you..." Wu Xingzi explained hesitantly, scratching his nose. Everything that had happened was in the past now. He just thought that right now, he felt apologetic toward Mr. Lu. Why did Steward Yuan agree for Mr. Lu to come? Guan Shanjin yelled for Mr. Lu sometimes, but most of the time, he just forgot about him.

"Mr. Lu isn't coming with us?" Guan Chenliang asked. He didn't know the history between his father and this Mr. Lu, but he was also sympathetic since Mr. Lu was stuck in the manor, unable to leave.

"House of Taotie has these new rose dumplings. Su-shushu got us a private room."

Lu Zezhi took another bite of his dry bread, chewing on it bitterly. It took him a while before he could swallow it down successfully without choking. He let out a long sigh and put away his food before standing up. "All right, since I am bored with this place, and A-Fan is busy, I might as well go take my mind off of things with you two."

He also knew that if he randomly ran off, Guan Shanjin would be displeased. But if he stuck with Wu Xingzi, no matter how angry Guan Shanjin was, he'd have to keep it to himself. Lu Zezhi had such an effective shield now—he couldn't just let it get away.

"Very good, very good." Wu Xingzi smiled and led the group out of the Protector General's estate.

The group slowly wandered down the street, not in a rush to get to House of Taotie. They followed Xiaotianshui Street and started shopping on the near side of the road. This was usually when the food stalls opened up for business, selling all kinds of snacks, breakfast foods, and desserts, and Wu Xingzi stopped at almost every stall to take a look. He didn't make any big purchases, but he did not leave behind a single snack.

House of Taotie was in the middle of Xiaotianshui Street. By the time they arrived there, all of them, even the unwilling Mr. Lu, had their hands full of food.

The manager was familiar with Wu Xingzi, and he was also familiar with the way Wu Xingzi would always appear laden with food. Seeing him, he welcomed him with a smile, and even called for a few employees to come help.

"Isn't this Mr. Wu? You're here so early! The boss isn't here yet."

"Oh, don't bother him. I came because I remembered your rose dumplings are available starting today, so I came to have a taste."

"Mr. Wu has a good memory." The manager gave him a thumbs-up and led the group up to the private room on the second floor.

It was early, but House of Taotie was already full. Although the prices here were quite high, this was the capital, and plenty of aristocrats and rich people lived here. There were no open seats on the first floor, and the private rooms on the second floor were all full too. The only room left was the one Su Yang had booked for Wu Xingzi.

The manager was just about to open the door when a clear voice rang out behind them in accusation. "Wait! Manager, isn't there a room right here? Why did you say there weren't any before?"

The group stopped. The person who spoke was a young master just past twenty. He had two or three servants with him. His little face was white and soft like butter, and his eyes and brows were so delicate, they looked like they'd been drawn on. Underneath his left eye was a mole, bringing a seductive charm to his otherwise pure looks. Right now, his appearance was also colored by fury, like a spicy dish—though the taste was harsh, some people wouldn't be able to eat enough.

"Luo-gongzi." The manager clasped his hands in apology. "Luo-gongzi, our boss leaves this room open specifically for himself. These are the boss's dear friends."

This explanation did not appease Luo-gongzi; instead, he only grew angrier. "Are you saying I'm not worthy of using Mr. Su's room?" His almond eyes glared at the manager as his cheeks flushed in indignation. "Is this how House of Taotie treats its guests? He's just a lowly businessman! How dare he slight the di son of a second rank official?"

Hearing that, the manager nearly lost control of his pleasant expression. His smile didn't change, but there was a spark in his eyes. He remained smiling with his hands still cupped. "Luo-gongzi, you've misunderstood! This is just a little misunderstanding. Our boss had promised these gentlemen this room earlier! It's been reserved. See? The third east room and the fifth west room are the same: Guests reserved them a few days ago. We're here to do business, and all the guests are very valuable to us. We don't offend anyone, right?"

Luo-gongzi was not placated. He became even more rude. "The Vice Minister of Revenue's family are in the third east room and the Third Prince's family are in the fifth west room. They are powerful officials—I'm not blind. But tell me! This old man, this backwater hick...what is he supposed to be?"

"Um..." The manager was just about to answer when Luo-gongzi walked up and pointed his folded fan at Wu Xingzi.

"I don't want to speak to the likes of you. Since you're an honored guest, why don't you say whose family you are from?"

What a domineering attitude, Wu Xingzi thought, sighing inwardly. When it came to numbers, he actually had more people than

Luo-gongzi, and two of them were even soldiers who'd seen battle. It was just a room; there was no need to make such a big fuss.

He smiled and cupped his hands toward Luo-gongzi. "I'm just a lowly commoner. Since Luo-gongzi was here first, I should leave this room to you."

It didn't matter to him where he ate. Although he could admire the views of the capital from the room, wasn't the kitchen a much more convenient place to eat? It wasn't as if he'd never done that before.

When he saw that Wu Xingzi was giving in, a smug, disdainful smile spread on Luo-gongzi's face. He pointed his chin toward the manager slightly. "Even your honored guest is saying so. Can I use this room or not?"

The manager knew Wu Xingzi's character. Although he disliked this arrogant Luo-gongzi, he still smiled. "Of course, of course. Please follow me."

As he turned away, he glanced at a server to bring Wu Xingzi and the others to the kitchens.

The smoke from the battle dissipated. Luo-gongzi was like a victorious peacock, smug and pleased. He opened up his tail feathers and strutted into the room. When he passed by Wu Xingzi, he spat quietly, "How dare you try to fight with me, you old fool? Hmph!"

Even Wu Xingzi understood the hostility in his words. But it was odd. Wu Xingzi scratched his nose, lost. He didn't know which official's son this was, but they definitely had never met. Why did he have such a grudge against him?

After the group went down the stairs, Fang He, who had a large beard, suddenly piped up, "That was Assistant Administrator Luo's di son."

"Assistant Administrator Luo?" A second rank official was indeed someone with authority, and Wu Xingzi just so happened to have met him before. On this trip back to the capital, Guan Shanjin had taken him to several palace banquets, through which he'd met this Assistant Administrator Luo.

"I know him too." Guan Chenliang pulled on his father's sleeve. With a serious expression on his chubby little face, he said quietly, "Daddy said we must not run into this person."

Must not run into this person? Wu Xingzi blinked, a little surprised. Guan Shanjin was a proud man. He'd didn't have much respect for most of the capital. Of course, there weren't many people whom he'd view as a threat either. In fact, he didn't care enough to even form an opinion on most people. "We must not run into this person" was probably one of his harsher opinions. After all, Guan Shanjin was usually too lazy to fight with his mouth. He'd much rather just fight with his fists.

"He never mentioned that to me..." Wu Xingzi didn't know what to feel. His chest felt a little stuffy.

"Why would he tell you?" Lu Zezhi handed the food he had over to the House of Taotie servers and was now sneering coldly. "He practically keeps you on his palm, in his heart. He wouldn't even let the wind or rain touch you."

"Ah..." Wu Xingzi wasn't embarrassed by his words. Instead, he felt a little lonely, and his shoulders slumped.

"What? Haven't you noticed?" Lu Zezhi could not help but roll his eyes when he saw Wu Xingzi like that. "I can't speak on anything else, but I am definitely qualified to comment on these things."

"These things?" Wu Xingzi was confused.

"Didn't you see? That Luo-gongzi just now was wearing an old gray robe that was a few sizes too big for him. It was loose around his shoulders, arms, and waist."

Now that he'd mentioned it, Wu Xingzi realized he was right.

Luo-gongzi acted so powerful and intimidating, like a peacock showing off its tail. Even if he didn't care about the way he dressed, there was no way he'd wear such an old, simple robe.

And why did that color and style seem so familiar?

"Ah!" Wu Xingzi's brain was still turning when the child by his side came to a conclusion. "He's copying the way Father dresses?"

"Copying me?" Wu Xingzi paused for a moment, his expression becoming even more lost. "Why would he copy me? I'm old and don't care about my appearance. I don't even go outside that much. Why would he want to copy me?"

Lu Zezhi smiled coldly, too lazy to say anything else. They had arrived at the table in the kitchens. In order to avoid the smoke from cooking, two guards moved the table and chairs into the garden.

Sitting down at the table, Lu Zezhi opened up the osmanthus-flavored melon seeds he'd bought, poured himself a cup of tea, and started enjoying himself.

"Probably because..." Guan Chenliang's expression was serious, and his delicate brow furrowed. "That gongzi likes Daddy."

Wu Xingzi finally realized.

In that case, Guan Shanjin really was someone who caught the eyes of others.

It really wasn't Wu Xingzi's fault that he didn't know Luo-gongzi liked Guan Shanjin.

If Guan Shanjin was just as he appeared—a beautiful gongzi with power, authority, a noble family, and the attention of the emperor—Wu Xingzi might have been able to find out about Luo-gongzi's intentions. Perhaps he might've gotten jealous.

But Guan Shanjin was the Great General of the Southern Garrison! Nobody in the capital dared to challenge him, and the

Protector General's family was full of righteous court officials. Guan Shanjin himself was also technically an official who worked alone and far away.

He was the Emperor of Great Xia's sharpest blade. Apart from his role guarding the border, Guan Shanjin was the man the emperor relied on whenever he wanted to get rid of anyone.

Ten years ago, Yan Wenxin's downfall had proved a lot, and the emperor was happy Guan Shanjin had no allies in the court. Guan Shanjin himself was born proud and arrogant. He'd truly never taken any of the court officials seriously.

Perhaps things would be different if there was a new emperor, but Guan Shanjin held the army in his hands, and the northwestern tribes' military was on friendly terms with him. Altogether, he wielded nearly half the military power in all of Great Xia. Why wouldn't the emperor just happily live his life like this? There was no reason to fight with Guan Shanjin and risk his country and power.

All the court officials in the capital had the same thought. With such a powerful god to keep the emperor in check, they were all well-behaved.

Some people wanted to form an alliance with Guan Shanjin. After all, Guan Shanjin's reputation was enough to make a child cry, and he had enough power to inspire jealousy in other people. Sure, he only liked men, but who didn't have a handsome son or two?

Ten years ago, Guan Shanjin married a little adviser from who-knew-where, and the wedding was utterly extravagant. Everyone in the capital knew that the general's wife was over forty and had a plain appearance, and no one understood what Guan Shanjin saw in him.

Lots of people guessed that this was Guan Shanjin purposefully demonstrating his loyalty to the emperor by picking a spouse with a poor family background. He'd probably had no choice. So plenty of people started scheming. At first, they subtly tried to get into Guan Shanjin's good graces. Then, they started getting bolder and began trying to push the general's wife out of the picture.

And so chaos and bloodshed ensued, and the court was greatly affected.

After everything, both of the Grand Councilors were replaced. Half of the officials above rank four were dismissed. A few particularly involved young masters were either forced to leave the capital or had to become monks to avoid any further trouble.

To the people of the capital, Guan Shanjin was even more fearsome than a natural disaster. And everyone knew exactly how much Guan Shanjin doted on his wife.

To be honest, Wu Xingzi had forgotten that Guan Shanjin was a huge temptation for everyone. The reason why people stayed away from him was because Guan Shanjin had instilled fear in them. But if someone had never suffered at his hand, it made sense that they would be enticed.

"Doesn't Assistant Administrator Luo know how Haiwang is?" Wu Xingzi asked curiously. They were waiting for the rose dumplings, so Wu Xingzi ate a few water chestnut cakes.

The two guards looked back at their mistress helplessly. If it weren't for the fact that they knew their general and his lover had a strong relationship, they'd almost take this as a jab at Guan Shanjin.

"Four years ago, Assistant Administrator Luo scored third place in the Palace Examinations and entered the Hanlin Academy," responded Fang He.

"Four years ago..."

Wu Xingzi nodded. No wonder. They left the capital five years ago. If the Protector General and his wife hadn't been traveling right now, forcing Guan Shanjin to return to the capital to report to the emperor, they might not have come back until Guan Shanjin inherited the title.

"Besides, he's just an assistant administrator." Lu Zezhi snorted lightly. It was clear he looked down on him.

"Isn't an assistant administrator quite a high position?" Wu Xingzi was not familiar with the various court official positions. After all, he'd spent his life in Qingcheng County. He only needed to know who the district magistrate was and what he had to do.

"Second rank does sound high," Lu Zezhi chuckled, then took a sip of tea. He poked Guan Chenliang, who was imitating Wu Xingzi, taking bites of the water chestnut cake like a little mouse. "Ask this child what kind of position an assistant administrator is."

Guan Chenliang wasn't expecting to be picked. With his cheeks puffed out, he blinked, looking a little lost.

"Do you know?" Wu Xingzi asked with a smile, poking him on the nose as well.

Guan Chenliang swallowed the snack in his mouth hurriedly, then took a sip of tea. "I do. Although the assistant administrator is a second rank position, it holds no real power."

It was hardly surprising. Assistant Administrator Luo had only been an official for four years, but he was already sitting at rank two. That was a shocking speed to be climbing up the ranks. Not even Guan Shanjin ascended that fast through the army with all his achievements.

In recent years, the court of Great Xia had been peaceful and calm. Although Nanman did attack a few times, it never amounted to much. This meant Assistant Administrator Luo hadn't been promoted because he'd done a great job on something. Getting promoted time and time again... It was probably because he had underhanded ways of getting promoted.

No wonder.

"But Assistant Administrator Luo doesn't seem like an impatient man." Wu Xingzi thought back to the few times he'd met him. He was proud, but there was no friction between them. He interacted warmly with his colleagues, and he seemed to have a good reputation.

"I have no idea how patient he is, but his son is somewhat famous within the capital." Seeing as the two guards didn't know what to say, Lu Zezhi decided to start gossiping. "Do you know who Luo-gongzi's mother is?"

"Luo-gongzi's mother?" Of course Wu Xingzi had no idea. His head hurt. It was just a private room—why was there so much involved?

"Her father was the last emperor's Grand Councilor of the Left, Yu-gong."[6]

Who? Wu Xingzi blinked, then blinked again.

Who was the Grand Councilor of the Left? Who was Yu-gong? Everyone else's faces, including Guan Chenliang's, revealed expressions of realization. Wu Xingzi could only pick up a mung bean cake to munch on to calm his nerves. After all, he came from a small town. Back when the previous emperor passed away, it took nearly half a year for the news to reach Qingcheng County.

"Father, he's a very famous old man," Guan Chenliang explained. "He was only Councilor for five years before he retired and returned to his hometown, but he taught many brilliant students. He only had five children, all daughters, and they all married well."

"So..." Wu Xingzi seemed to have figured something out. But this was a matter involving Guan Shanjin—he couldn't imagine anyone who'd be so willing to play with fire. Shouldn't it be common sense to avoid danger?

---

6   "Gong" (公) is a suffix sometimes used for very well-respected old men.

"Ha." Lu Zezhi rolled his eyes at him and dusted off the crumbs on his hands. "Perhaps Assistant Administrator Luo wants to take things slowly. After all, he's never seen Guan Shanjin truly take someone down. Haiwang has been lying low in recent years, so it's not a surprise that fools are out there champing at the bit."

"This is...too much," Wu Xingzi sighed.

If Guan Shanjin hadn't hurt his head, everything would be fine. At most, he'd give Luo-gongzi and Assistant Administrator Luo a warning. That old Mr. Yu had probably witnessed Guan Shanjin's past methods of conflict resolution. After a warning from Guan Shanjin, he'd definitely make sure to keep his son in check.

However, Guan Shanjin had hurt his head. Wu Xingzi hadn't been around when Guan Shanjin was twenty-five, but thinking back to how things ended with Yan Wenxin and the effects it had on the court, Wu Xingzi started to feel bad for Luo-gongzi.

After all, it was Haiwang's nature. When he loved someone, he wanted them to live well. If he hated someone, he wanted them to die. Assistant Administrator Luo probably had plenty of mistakes for him to target.

At that moment, the rose dumplings arrived, along with lamb soup.

The manager smiled warmly. "Mr. Wu, the lamb soup won't be on the menu for another few days, but since things didn't go to plan today, this is a small apology on our part. Please have a taste!"

"Ah, I'm very sorry for the trouble," Wu Xingzi responded politely, his eyes bright.

House of Taotie's lamb soup was really something. They only sold it for three months out of the year, and only fifty portions were available per day. Even he, the Great General's spouse, sometimes had a hard time ordering it! This was all thanks to Luo-gongzi's outburst!

After drinking a little and eating a couple of pieces of lamb stomach, Wu Xingzi was thoroughly delighted by the lamb soup. "Don't tell Haiwang about what happened today with Luo-gongzi," he said happily to the guards, Dianzi, and Guan Chenliang. "He's young—it's normal to have a crush on a beauty."

Since Wu Xingzi himself had nothing to say about the beauty being the Wu family's son-in-law, nobody else needed to say anything either.

Lu Zezhi ate a dumpling and a bowl of soup, and didn't react to Wu Xingzi's words. He wouldn't tell Haiwang. After all, he couldn't get away from him fast enough. It would be fine to mention it to A-Fan, though, right? Would A-Fan tell his master?

Mr. Lu decided it was not his problem.

As Wu Xingzi's group happily ate the House of Taotie's rose dumplings and lamb soup, Guan Shanjin was in bed at the residence, leaning against the headboard as he observed the doctor taking his pulse.

Doctor Xia and his family had been friendly with the Protector General's family for generations. Years ago, he'd even gone to the battlefield with Guan Shanjin to take care of his injuries. Now he lived in Horse-Face City and followed Guan Shanjin wherever he went.

After taking his pulse and treating him with some acupuncture, the doctor said in a soft voice, "The wound is healed up now."

"Oh?" Guan Shanjin looked at him, the smile on his lips not reaching his eyes, and waited for the rest of the doctor's evaluation. Doctor Xia always liked to take breaks while talking, and his sentences were like a rollercoaster. Until he reached the very end, it was hard to tell if the conclusion was good or bad.

"The herb did its job," Doctor Xia said. He pointed to one of the herbs on the paper and explained, "Lily of the Nile can suppress the effects of wolfsbane, but because it dissipates faster when paired with tengjiao, its effects will be delayed by a day or two."

"How thoughtful of the person who poisoned me," Guan Shanjin sighed, giving the doctor a slight smile.

"How fearless as well," the doctor remarked.

Doctor Xia picked up his tea to take a sip. Neither of them knew who'd done this to Guan Shanjin. Seeing the general smile so warmly made a cold shiver go up the doctor's spine. The hair all over his body stood on end; not even the floor heating could dispel the chill.

Guan Shanjin smiled. "Does this person want to control me or kill me?" It really had been too long since he'd returned to the capital, if some people had started to think they could extend their claws toward him without losing an arm in the process.

"At most, control you. It seems like the purpose of this drug was to make you bedridden for a few days. But it just so happened that you were on horseback, which resulted in you hitting your head." Doctor Xia shook his head and clicked his tongue at this unknown culprit. He really didn't know what he was up against.

"Then I should thank him, hmm?" Guan Shanjin chuckled. Doctor Xia was terrified. The doctor clasped his hands together in farewell, eager to leave, but Guan Shanjin stopped him. "You didn't say anything to Wu Xingzi, right?"

Doctor Xia wasn't expecting this question. He stilled, then hurriedly shook his head when Guan Shanjin narrowed his eyes at him. "No, no, no, I wouldn't dare. Even if the heavens lent me the courage, I would not dare go against your orders! I have not breathed a single word of this to the mistress."

"Really?" Guan Shanjin's brows furrowed as he thought back to his interactions with Wu Xingzi. Something didn't feel quite right. But Doctor Xia had no reason to lie to him. The doctor hadn't even told Man Yue or Steward Yuan that the general had been drugged, so obviously Wu Xingzi would never find out.

"Don't think too much about it. The mistress is just like that. He once even angered you to the point of spitting blood!" Doctor Xia truly respected Wu Xingzi. There was no one else in the world with the power to make Guan Shanjin suffer like that.

"He's just like that..." Guan Shanjin sighed, rubbing his temples. "All right, you can tell Man Yue."

"Understood." Doctor Xia nodded repeatedly. Guan Shanjin's eyes began to close; he was about to fall asleep. "General, get some rest," the doctor said, noticing his weariness. "I'll take care of this for you. Don't worry—I won't let the mistress know."

"Mm." Guan Shanjin felt slightly uneasy, but Doctor Xia's acupuncture was starting to take effect. He couldn't stay awake anymore and drifted off to sleep.

The doctor shifted him so he could sleep comfortably. He was just about to leave to find Man Yue when a voice came from behind him. The voice sounded cheerful, but it instilled a deep terror in him.

"What's the deal with the wolfsbane?"

Doctor Xia jerked in shock and quickly shuffled two steps back before he could face the speaker.

"Ah—Man Yue." Doctor Xia smiled, ingratiating.

"You'd better explain yourself." Man Yue was too lazy to waste any words on this comrade. He cracked his knuckles, the threat palpable without having to verbalize it.

Doctor Xia gulped, forcing the smile to remain on his face. "Please don't act rashly! I was following the general's orders!"

Man Yue remembered how Wu Xingzi had once told him Guan Shanjin was indeed ruthless and cold. Not only to others—he was even more cruel to himself. In dire times, whatever he did to his enemies, he was also willing to do to himself.

Back when they set a trap for Yan Wenxin, he had not cared one jot about his own reputation. He was willing to sacrifice the impeccable reputation that the Protector General's family had accumulated over several generations. He even threw himself into prison!

However, all of it was planned with the emperor and was for the benefit of the country. Reputation was external and unimportant, something one could gain or lose in an instant.

Man Yue was not surprised Wu Xingzi knew Guan Shanjin so well. This small town adviser truly saw the world very clearly.

But what stuck with Man Yue was what Wu Xingzi said after he sighed. "I know he's doing this for me," the older man said sadly, "but why won't he ask me if I want to do something for him too?"

Wu Xingzi didn't even care about himself, so who *could* he care for? Wu Xingzi wasn't afraid of Guan Shanjin dying on the battle-field or in a court struggle. What he truly feared was Guan Shanjin dying a silent death after fighting so hard for him.

They were married, so they should be together through thick and thin, two halves of a whole, living and dying together. Guan Shanjin had taken on too much of that burden. Wu Xingzi's heart ached for him, but he was also angry. No matter what, he couldn't change Guan Shanjin's mind once it was set on something.

Guan Shanjin had started killing on the battlefield at twelve years old. His determination was truly forged in flame. There was no way to break it.

No wonder Wu Xingzi is angry, thought Man Yue. Even he was angry enough that he could vaguely taste blood.

Doctor Xia knew exactly how to protect himself. Before Man Yue could ask, he explained everything, his words pouring out like spilled peas.

He explained that the first time Guan Shanjin woke up after hurting his head, they confirmed he'd lost all his memories past the age of twenty-five. All of that was true. He did demand to see Lu Zezhi. But after seeing Man Yue, Steward Yuan, and his other confidants—and after receiving Doctor Xia's acupuncture—the second time he woke up, he pretty much recovered his memories.

But recovering his memories was only one piece of the puzzle. Guan Shanjin was a clever man; he knew there must be something suspicious going on that caused him to fall off his horse. He just didn't know if the person was after him, the Protector General, or perhaps Great Xia itself. Before he got to the bottom of it, he couldn't waste this golden opportunity.

He sent Man Yue to investigate while he asked Doctor Xia to figure out what was going on with his body. He was afraid he wouldn't be able to keep up the act, so he asked the doctor to make him forget his memories every day through acupuncture. That way, he could maintain the same state as when he first woke up.

"The general trusts you." The doctor wiped the sweat from his forehead, trying to comfort Man Yue, who was no longer smiling. If only someone could understand what a difficult position he was in!

"He made himself forget so he could fish out the culprit behind everything?" Man Yue was silent for a moment. Then he gave an ugly smile. "Fuck that shit!" he spat. He pointed at Guan Shanjin, so angry that his finger trembled. "Since he lost his memory, he hasn't even left the Protector General's estate! Is he trying to catch worms or maggots? Does the person who drugged him even know he's lost his memories? Huh? Not even the emperor knows he fell off his horse the other day!"

Doctor Xia continued to plead his innocence. "I don't know. I'm just following orders."

"In the end, his brain is just broken! There's no way he'd come up with such a stupid idea if it wasn't! He hid this from me! What is he supposed to accomplish with only your help? You figured out the drug, but can you find out who did it?" Man Yue's face shook with the force of his yelling. If it wasn't for the fact that Guan Shanjin had hurt his head, he'd strangle him!

"I can't! I really can't! That's what I told the general!" Doctor Xia tried to defend himself. Of course he'd mentioned to Guan Shanjin that continuing to fake his memory loss through acupuncture was a stupid idea. Who was he trying to fool? The person who drugged him had no idea what was going on. Meanwhile, the Protector General's estate was in complete disarray.

But Guan Shanjin insisted! What was he supposed to do? He was just a doctor. There was no way he could win against a general who was highly skilled in martial arts!

"You could've told me in secret," said Man Yue, squeezing the words out between his clenched teeth. His fury made Doctor Xia shrink in on himself and shiver.

Fearing for his life, Doctor Xia put aside his pride and tried his best to explain. "I mean...I'm telling you now. It's not too late."

"That's because the general told you to tell me." Man Yue rudely rolled his eyes. He'd overheard them talking about the wolfsbane, so of course he heard Guan Shanjin's orders before he fell asleep.

"A ha ha ha..." Doctor Xia scratched his face as he laughed awkwardly.

Man Yue knew there was no point in being angry with the doctor. He knew why Guan Shanjin was hiding all of this—it was because he didn't want Wu Xingzi to worry. Knowing Wu Xingzi, if Guan Shanjin hadn't lost his memories but was still injured, Wu Xingzi would stay at his side to take care of him, waiting on him with soups and medicines. But if Guan Shanjin was no longer the Guan Shanjin who fell in love with Wu Xingzi, Wu Xingzi definitely wouldn't care as much. As long as someone was there to take care of Guan Shanjin, that would be enough for Wu Xingzi.

And when Wu Xingzi wasn't in a good mood, he'd take a walk outside on the street. At that point, whoever had drugged Guan Shanjin might show themselves again. After all, if they couldn't find Guan Shanjin, they'd try to get close to Wu Xingzi instead. Man Yue would definitely be able to protect Wu Xingzi. Like that, the culprit would be caught in their trap.

But why go through all that?

Man Yue's chest felt tight and painful. What did he do in his past life to deserve such an insufferable boss?!

"Since I've passed on the message, I'm leaving. No need to send me off!" Doctor Xia picked up his medical kit and ran off as quick as a hare, terrified that Man Yue would take his anger out on him.

Man Yue watched coldly as Doctor Xia ran away. He took a few deep breaths before he finally managed to calm the anger inside of him. Then, he closed the door, pulled up a chair, and sat down by the bed. With his brow furrowed, he stared at Guan Shanjin, who was either sleeping or unconscious.

Compared to Man Yue—whose head was exploding from suddenly finding out he'd been deceived by his master who might've really hurt his head, then came up with a stupid idea—Wu Xingzi felt satisfied, both in mind and belly. Not a single drop of the lamb soup remained, and they also finished all the snacks they'd bought on the street.

On the way back to the Protector General's estate, he remembered to buy some freshly steamed sweets and date cakes.

No one knew what Mr. Lu had said to Steward Yuan, or how Luo-gongzi felt after getting the private room in the House of Taotie. But the next morning, right after Wu Xingzi finished up in his garden, he heard that an invitation had arrived from Luo-gongzi.

"An invitation from Luo-gongzi?" Wu Xingzi swallowed the fried wonton in his mouth, wiped his hands, then accepted the paper that Steward Yuan handed over.

"It's written on pink paper…" The paper was smooth and smelled faintly of gardenias. It sure made an impression.

Written in Luo-gongzi's beautiful and somewhat grandiose script was an invitation to the Great General of the Southern Garrison and his wife to visit Suiyu Pond two days from now to view the snow.

The snow? Wu Xingzi glanced outside the window. It was quite cold now, but snow probably wouldn't come for a while yet.

Perhaps seeing his confusion, Steward Yuan explained, "Suiyu Pond lies on Xiaolanting Mountain, about half a day's journey from the capital. It's very cold, and at this time of year, it's usually snowing there already."

"What an elegant activity Luo-gongzi has chosen..." Wu Xingzi nodded, placing the invitation on the table. He sighed. "But is it all right for Haiwang to accept in his current state?"

Steward Yuan paused for a moment before answering. "Why don't you ask the general himself?"

"He'll probably want to go..." Wu Xingzi picked up the invitation and looked at it again, then sighed, "All right, I'll go ask him."

He didn't even finish his breakfast. Holding the invitation, Wu Xingzi headed to the yard where Guan Shanjin had been staying in recent days.

Steward Yuan froze. He hadn't expected Wu Xingzi to be so efficient. After a moment, he rushed to follow Wu Xingzi.

Steward Yuan trailed Wu Xingzi to Guan Shanjin's study, which was where he was recuperating. He was currently working, so the doors were shut. Through the thin doors, they vaguely heard Man Yue and a few other guards speaking inside.

Wu Xingzi did not approach the door. Instead, he stood and stared from a distance, holding the invitation. He let out a soft sigh.

"Mistress, aren't you going in?" Steward Yuan asked.

Yesterday, Man Yue had revealed to Steward Yuan that the general hadn't really lost his memories, so Steward Yuan's emotions were still slightly delicate at the moment.

Steward Yuan and Man Yue both agreed that their master must've really hurt his head. If one day he recovered, how would he comment on his actions over these last few days?

But no matter what they thought, they knew they could not let the mistress know. Wu Xingzi seemed as gentle as water, but if you stepped on his tail, you might end up getting splashed.

Man Yue said it was unfortunate that Wu Xingzi ended up with Guan Shanjin, but Steward Yuan didn't agree. Wu Xingzi always did things perfectly. All those years ago, Yan Wenxin probably never expected to fall at the hands of a man like Wu Xingzi.

In Steward Yuan's opinion, the lid fit the pot. In order for a couple to get along, their personalities had to be similar in some way.

"No..." Wu Xingzi shook his head. Turning, he left the yard and headed in a different direction. Instead of going back to his own quarters, it seemed like he was heading toward Doctor Xia.

Steward Yuan immediately became alarmed and uneasy.

Doctor Xia lived on the edge of the property to the north, very far from the main courtyard. It was about a fifteen-minute walk. When Wu Xingzi arrived, Doctor Xia was sitting in his yard, sipping on tea as he read a book. His little student was reciting a medical text, and he would occasionally correct him. If the student made too many mistakes, he hit the student's calf a couple of times. Tears swam in the small twelve- or thirteen-year-old boy's eyes, but he didn't dare to cry.

"Doctor Xia."

Doctor Xia jumped up from his chair, then stumbled. "Aiyayayaya, Mistress, to what do I owe the pleasure?"

"Doctor Xia, when will you be treating Haiwang again?" Wu Xingzi got straight to the point.

"Um..." Doctor Xia scratched his face, his smile stiff. He snuck a glance at Steward Yuan standing behind Wu Xingzi. After a bit of hesitation, he finally answered, "Um, I usually go in the afternoon after the general eats lunch."

Steward Yuan furrowed his brows, seemingly unhappy with his honesty. But what could Doctor Xia do? There were four people in this yard right now. Everyone here had more power than he did, except for his little student. He had no choice but to protect himself.

"Then I'll accompany you today," Wu Xingzi said. His tone was light and gentle, but for some reason, it sounded slightly hard. Doctor Xia obviously couldn't refuse.

"I'm fine with it. It's only natural for you to want to see the general. But...the general might not cooperate with the treatment if you're there." Doctor Xia gave Steward Yuan a look.

They both knew that Guan Shanjin was faking his amnesia. Which meant today, the doctor wouldn't suppress Guan Shanjin's memories through acupuncture anymore. Instead, he'd make Guan Shanjin remember them.

He should've gone earlier today, but Man Yue stopped him for some reason, saying he should just go at the regular time. It didn't really matter if Guan Shanjin had his memories for his work in the morning. He'd done it several days now and it all went fine, so there was no rush for him to remember.

It felt like Man Yue was actually just getting back at Guan Shanjin.

Doctor Xia, however, was afraid of conflict—and even more afraid of Man Yue—so he decided not to involve himself further. But he'd already walked through the rosebushes so many times; how could he avoid getting a few thorns stuck to him?

Besides, whatever one feared the most always ended up knocking at the door. Wasn't Wu Xingzi here now?

Doctor Xia didn't delude himself that Wu Xingzi was coming along out of boredom. If he truly was bored, he'd go on a stroll with his child or try to find some way to return to Qingcheng County.

"Mistress, what are you planning?" Steward Yuan had to ask.

"I just want to go see Haiwang." Wu Xingzi smiled shyly. "He didn't even come see me yesterday."

Steward Yuan furrowed his brows, then quickly recovered. "I'm sure the general will be happy to hear that you miss him."

"Really?" Wu Xingzi chuckled.

That chuckle made Doctor Xia's shoulders tremble. He felt like something was about to happen. He couldn't ask Steward Yuan for his thoughts. Had Wu Xingzi figured something out?

After Wu Xingzi made his plans with Doctor Xia, he did not stay for long. He returned to his own quarters with Steward Yuan in tow, resuming his daily routine. He spent the morning studying with his child, and left the invitation by the window.

Time passed quickly. After lunch, Wu Xingzi asked Dianzi to take Guan Chenliang back to his room. Then, he headed off alone to find Doctor Xia.

He and Doctor Xia planned to meet outside Guan Shanjin's yard and head in together. Doctor Xia arrived quite early. From a distance, Wu Xingzi could already see him pacing in front of the gate, looking troubled.

"Doctor Xia." Wu Xingzi rushed forward, slightly apologetic. "I'm late."

"No, no, no, Mistress, you're much too polite. I'm just early." Doctor Xia rubbed his nose and adjusted the medicine kit he carried on his back. "Shall we head in?"

"All right." Wu Xingzi nodded, walking into the yard first and heading straight for Guan Shanjin's study. He spared no sympathy for Doctor Xia's nervousness. The doctor followed behind him.

At the door, Wu Xingzi took a deep breath before lightly knocking on the door. "Haiwang? I'm coming in with Doctor Xia, all right?"

"Come in." Through the doors, Guan Shanjin's voice sounded slightly dark.

Wu Xingzi gulped, wiping his palms on his robes before taking another deep breath and pushing the door open.

"Mistress." Man Yue was inside as well. When he saw Wu Xingzi, he greeted the older man with a smile.

Guan Shanjin was sitting at the desk. He looked a little tired, resting his chin on his hand as he read a book.

The general glanced at Wu Xingzi. "What are you doing here?" he asked.

"Haiwang, you really don't remember me?" Wu Xingzi walked to him, disregarding his cold attitude.

At Wu Xingzi's words, the hand that Guan Shanjin was using to hold the book trembled slightly, but he quickly recovered. Even Man Yue almost missed it.

"How could I not remember you, you old quail?" Guan Shanjin pursed his lips, then threw his book down on the table. "Steward Yuan said you complained that I didn't go see you yesterday."

"I wasn't complaining..."

"Yesterday, didn't you take Mr. Lu and that kid to House of Taotie to eat rose dumplings and lamb soup?" Guan Shanjin interrupted the older man's explanation. The old fellow looked kind and honest, but he was actually evil on the inside! Guan Shanjin huffed. He'd clearly told Man Yue to keep an eye on Wu Xingzi, and look at what happened! He ended up wandering the streets and didn't return until almost six in the evening! He didn't even eat dinner at home!

Why didn't his subordinates listen to him? Guan Shanjin couldn't have been more upset. He'd wanted to confront Wu Xingzi last night, but when he arrived outside, he happened to see Wu Xingzi napping with his cheek in hand. For some reason, his heart softened, so he could only rub his nose and return to his study, having achieved nothing.

And now this old fool dared to say he missed him? Missed him how? He didn't have lamb soup or rose dumplings. What was there to miss?

"Ah...You already know?" Wu Xingzi suddenly turned red. He smiled shyly. "I just wanted to have a taste. Besides, aren't you busy during the day?"

"How considerate of you." Guan Shanjin really wanted to grab him and squish him everywhere! He wanted to teach him a lesson! This old fool didn't act like his wife at all. Mr. Lu wasn't like this—he would never randomly just leave. He stayed in his yard obediently and lived each day in peace.

Meanwhile, this old quail clearly knew that he'd been injured, but he never came to take care of his husband. That was fine. But how many days had it been? Other than the very first day, this was the only time he'd come to visit!

"Forget all that. You keep wanting to go back to Qingcheng County. I said no! If you won't give it a rest, I'll tie you up! Let's see who dares to let you out after that!" Guan Shanjin said all in one breath. He felt a lot better, like he'd let go of something that had been bothering him. He stared at Wu Xingzi smugly.

Wu Xingzi's expression was pained. "It's not that I have to go back to Qingcheng County, but..." Wu Xingzi hesitated, unable to finish his sentence. After a while, he turned to Doctor Xia and said, "Doctor Xia, weren't you going to take a look at Haiwang? Why don't you do that first?"

"Say what you were going to say. You're not allowed to be here during my checkup." Guan Shanjin didn't know why he'd said that. He always hoped Mr. Lu would stay by his side when he was injured. But when it came to Wu Xingzi, he never wanted to see a thread of worry on his face, regardless of the circumstances.

This inexplicable feeling annoyed him.

"No. I have to be here today." Wu Xingzi stood his ground for once. Seeing Guan Shanjin about to scold him, he frowned and stammered out, "D-don't try to chase me away. I-I know...I know everything. You... You've had your memories this whole time."

Like a bolt of lightning, this statement struck everyone in the room speechless. Everyone's expression stiffened.

Guan Shanjin froze for a moment, then his face went blank. He put a hand to his head, his wound hurting so much he broke out in a cold sweat. However, his expression remained terrifyingly cold.

Gritting his teeth, he said, pausing after each word, "What. Did. You. Say?"

"I-I... Um, I mean..." Wu Xingzi shrank into himself a bit, perhaps because it had been a long time since he'd seen Guan Shanjin look so terrifying. He did his best to steady his voice. "I know you have always retained your memories. B-because you were trying to fish out the person behind this..." *You did something so stupid.* Wu Xingzi swallowed down the last part of his sentence. After all, he was worried about Guan Shanjin's head injury. Besides, even before he got hurt, he was already hiding things from Wu Xingzi!

"Oho," Man Yue chuckled from behind them.

"You know? What else do you know? I—" Guan Shanjin hissed, pressing a hand into his wound. His face went so white it looked nearly gray. Oh, how Wu Xingzi's heart ached! He wanted to go to Guan Shanjin but didn't know what to do. He was forced to stay back by Guan Shanjin's glare. With no other choice, he could only turn to Doctor Xia for help.

"Doctor Xia! Come take a look at Haiwang's injuries! Please bring his memories back."

"U-u-uh... I'm afraid that if I go, the general will be angry with me!" Doctor Xia exclaimed, worried. He knew that Guan Shanjin's memories were in conflict with the needles. Most people would've already passed out from the pain. Originally, he'd planned on taking care of it after Guan Shanjin passed out, but Guan Shanjin refused! Was he planning on keeping up the pretense to the very end?

"Haiwang! You know that I planned on killing myself on the day that I turned forty, right?" Wu Xingzi asked, walking to Guan Shanjin. Guan Shanjin's eyes were bloodshot from the pain. Veins popped on his hands, forehead, and neck. Wu Xingzi's heart ached at the sight, and he almost couldn't breathe.

"I don't..." Guan Shanjin clenched his teeth so hard that they made crackling noises. Even so, he held on through sheer willpower, refusing to let go.

"Well, I'm telling you now." Wu Xingzi approached him carefully. One step, two steps, three steps... Slowly, they drew close enough to feel each other's breaths. "That year I met you, I was about to turn forty. At that time, I had no one. My parents had died many years ago, and I was the only one left in the Wu family. Day after day, night after night, I only had myself for company."

"Nonsense..." Guan Shanjin kept trying to scoot back as Wu Xingzi approached, but the desk was only so big, and he was in so much pain that his bones felt like they were shattering. Where could he hide? Besides, Wu Xingzi's smell was somehow both comforting and something he longed for, so he couldn't even bear to move too far from him.

"It's not nonsense." Wu Xingzi smiled with his lips closed, having arrived at Guan Shanjin's side. He knelt down next to Guan Shanjin's legs, which trembled from pain. He grabbed Guan Shanjin's hand where it rested on his knee and held it tightly, rubbing it on his cheek. "Although Auntie Liu's family was looking after me, they had their own lives to live, and I had mine. We weren't truly family. And they weren't very well-off. But they were willing to look after me as I grew up in a place like Qingcheng County, and that's a debt I'll always owe."

"They're good people…" Guan Shanjin didn't seem to be in as much pain anymore. He hesitated, but in the end, he was unable to resist. He moved his other hand from his wound to the back of Wu Xingzi's neck, massaging it slightly.

"Yes, they're good people. I will never be able to repay their kindness, nor will I be able to forget it. Good thing I've had you these past few years to help them. Their lives are better now, so I'm happy." Wu Xingzi closed his eyes slightly, like a fat quail who had eaten and drank his fill. He curled up into a fuzzy ball, making the general's heart go soft. "But I was too lonely. Haiwang… I was so lonely. After all those years, there wasn't a single trace of my parents left in that house. The flood had destroyed my family, and now I truly was the only one left."

Guan Shanjin felt a buzzing in his head. He didn't understand what this person kneeling at his feet was saying, but his heart hurt. He felt like he should provide a safe haven for this old thing so that he could be happy, free, and untroubled for the rest of his life.

Without thinking, he promised, "You're not alone. I'll stay with you." His head didn't hurt that much anymore.

"Yes, you'll stay with me." Wu Xingzi smiled shyly, rubbing his cheek on Guan Shanjin's rough hand again. "So if anything were to happen to you… Haiwang, you said you'd stay with me. Then, I have to…"

"You have to?"

Wu Xingzi closed his eyes slightly, sighed, then said, "To go find you."

Guan Shanjin's eyes grew wide, as though he couldn't believe what he was hearing. He moved his lips, but pain suddenly stung the back of his neck like the stab of a needle…

Actually, Doctor Xia had stabbed him.

The general's smoky, alluring eyes started to droop against his will. He wanted to struggle but didn't have the energy. After a few blinks, he fell asleep.

Wu Xingzi immediately held up Guan Shanjin, who had fallen toward him, and smoothed a hand over his pale yet still unbelievably handsome face.

"I'll wait for you to wake up."

Doctor Xia watched the hugging couple, wondering who would be the one to suffer next.

Luo-gongzi's given name was Xiuyu, and his courtesy name was Yanzhi. He'd turned twenty not long ago and was the only son in his family, the treasure of his parents. He had a delicate, beautiful appearance and was doted on by all the elders in his family, which resulted in an arrogant, spoiled personality.

If he wanted the moon, he had to have it. The sun or stars simply would not do. It had to be the thing that he wanted, and he didn't care if it didn't make sense or if it was difficult to obtain. He wanted it.

Guan Shanjin was the moon that he wanted.

He could never forget where he first met Guan Shanjin. He remembered the scenery and the weather. He could even remember what he was wearing and each strand of his hair. The moment was carved into his memory in detail. Every time he thought back to it, his heart filled with sweetness.

Unfortunately, the sweetness came with bitterness, because Guan Shanjin already had someone by his side. It was an ugly old man who looked like he came from a poor family. Apparently, he was Guan Shanjin's wife. Ten years ago, they'd thrown a grand wedding in the capital, and even the emperor had personally sent a gift to congratulate them.

Why? Luo-gongzi's chest hurt from the hatred he felt. He'd seen the old man from a distance a few times. Calling him plain was a compliment. He looked like a joke standing next to Guan Shanjin, like a duck standing next to a phoenix. He was so ugly it hurt Luo-gongzi's eyes.

Luo-gongzi fell into an obsession. He despised that old duck, but he loved the phoenix that was Guan Shanjin. However, for some reason, those two were a couple. He hated everything he saw, but he couldn't stop looking. He kept trying to find out what the two were up to so he could secretly follow them.

The more he saw, the more he thought he was far better than that old duck. He could step all over Wu Xingzi on the strength of his family and education alone, to say nothing of his age and appearance. That man was just an adviser from a small town with no parents. He had only passed the academy exams, and he radiated poverty.

How did Guan Shanjin settle for such a thing? Luo-gongzi could not understand. Guan Shanjin must treat him so coldly! Even though they were always together, they never acted very affectionate. Guan Shanjin always stayed a few steps behind the old duck, watching as he strolled down the streets buying snacks. Guan Shanjin never even paid for anything. Luo-gongzi could not help but smile at how distanced they were.

Guan Shanjin must've been forced to marry such a vulgar, crude person. Everyone said a relationship with the emperor was as treacherous as a relationship with a tiger. Even though Guan Shanjin held the emperor's favor, the emperor probably didn't want to see him wield too much power. If he let Guan Shanjin marry a high-ranking official, Guan Shanjin would become like a fish bone stuck in the emperor's throat.

Luo-gongzi had been spoiled by his family, so he only ever thought of things from his own point of view. He never considered any other possibility.

At one point, he could think of nothing else other than Guan Shanjin. He stopped studying, and he spent all his time thinking about how he could save Guan Shanjin from his marriage. Maybe that way, they could get married instead and spend the rest of their lives together.

But it was so difficult to get close to Guan Shanjin. He always took the old duck to the outskirts of the capital on vacation, but the closest Luo-gongzi got to them in the last two months was a distant glance. Not only could he not approach Guan Shanjin, he couldn't even bribe the servants of the Protector General's residence.

He was so frustrated! Especially since his father mentioned that Guan Shanjin would be leaving the capital again in about a month. It would be five or six years before he returned.

That just wouldn't do. How could he endure that old duck being around Guan Shanjin for another five or six years while Luo-gongzi could only pine away?

So he decided he had to find some way to get close to Guan Shanjin, or at least show his face to him so Guan Shanjin would remember who he was.

The timing was too tight. After careful consideration, he still couldn't think of any good ideas, and Guan Shanjin's departure drew closer by the day. He really had no other choice...

He had heard about wolfsbane and lily of the Nile from his aunt. Apparently, it could induce someone to pass out for a few days, and upon waking, their thoughts would be jumbled for a while. Even Guan Shanjin, with such strong willpower, would not be able to resist the effects of such a drug, and he'd be more vulnerable to his true desires.

That was exactly what Luo-gongzi wanted! If Guan Shanjin could follow his heart, he'd definitely get rid of that old duck! Luo-gongzi heard from his father that Guan Shanjin held practically half of the military power in all of Great Xia in his hands. The emperor probably needed to be careful around him, too, in case he pulled him from the throne with the excuse of "protecting" him.

It was to be expected of someone Luo-gongzi fancied. Guan Shanjin truly was an extraordinary man with the ability to rule the world.

Of course, Luo-gongzi couldn't drug Guan Shanjin on his own. The Protector General's estate was as well-protected as an iron fortress. Never mind an outsider, not even a pair of sparrows could fly in.

He couldn't go inside, but Guan Shanjin would have to come out at some point. Especially when he had to attend a palace banquet, where his security was slightly more lax. Luo-gongzi would find an opportunity somehow.

Although Luo-gongzi couldn't attend a banquet himself, he could bribe the eunuchs and servants. After all, his father, his grandfather, and several of his uncles all held powerful positions in the court. Those servants would more or less respect him just because of his powerful relatives.

The drug was finally put into Guan Shanjin's cup at one of these banquets through the hands of a wine-pouring eunuch.

Luo-gongzi had no idea if it had worked or not. He heard that a few days ago, Guan Shanjin had gone out but quickly returned. It was so fast that he hadn't even managed to get out there to "run into him." And for once, the old duck wasn't there with him!

In the next few days, absolutely no news came from the Protector General's estate. Neither Guan Shanjin nor his old duck went out. Luo-gongzi grew more excited by the day, guessing that his drug had worked after all. In a few days' time, once Guan Shanjin awoke, that old duck's days would be numbered!

The wait was painful, and there was no news in the capital at all. He tried to subtly ask his father, but all he heard was that Guan Shanjin was sick and wasn't seeing guests. Even the emperor's head eunuch had been politely turned away when he came around to convey the emperor's well wishes.

When he heard that, Luo-gongzi nearly laughed out loud. He knew his plan had succeeded! If he waited patiently for a few days, he might just be the person that Guan Shanjin left the capital with!

After waiting patiently for several days, he heard that House of Taotie was coming out with a new dish: rose dumplings. He also heard that the old duck was an honored guest of the owner of House of Taotie, so he would surely show up at the restaurant.

He had to take advantage of this opportunity! Luo-gongzi took his time to get dressed up, then went to House of Taotie to wait for Wu Xingzi. Guan Shanjin wasn't there—it was just the old duck and several rough-looking servants. In just a few sentences, he'd intimidated the old duck so much that he didn't dare speak. It was so satisfying!

Enough days had passed now that it was about time for Guan Shanjin to wake, which meant it was time to go see him. No one could understand exactly how fervently he yearned for him!

He'd sent an invitation over to the Protector General's estate yesterday, inviting them to view the snow at Suiyu Pond.

Luo-gongzi did not care that he didn't receive a response. He thought perhaps the old duck was too afraid to tell Guan Shanjin about the invitation. But no matter. If nobody came to Suiyu Pond, he'd have an excuse to visit the general's residence. Either way, no matter how the old duck tried to cling onto Guan Shanjin, he'd already made his move.

It was about time. Luo-gongzi checked his appearance once more. He imitated the old duck's way of dress on purpose, wearing an old blue-gray robe with a somewhat worn jacket on top. Everything was slightly large and loose on him. When other people dressed like this, they looked ugly and poor. But Luo-gongzi was pretty, so he looked cute and simple instead. It was quite attractive. He spun in front of the bronze mirror and smiled smugly.

He'd dressed like this so that he could fully demonstrate the difference between him and the old duck. That old man should go back to whatever mountain he came from!

On the way to Suiyu Pond, Luo-gongzi felt like he'd swallowed butterflies, equal parts excited and uneasy. He wanted Guan Shanjin to come, but he also didn't. His emotions were all over the place, and his palms even started to sweat a little.

Finally, he arrived at Xiaolanting Mountain, where Suiyu Pond was located. Luo-gongzi noticed that something wasn't quite right. Silently, the excitement in his heart was replaced with fear. In the end, he stopped the driver and asked his servant to go ahead to see what was going on.

It was way too quiet here.

Because it got colder earlier in the mountains, plenty of people with elegant, refined tastes spent the early winter days at Xiaolanting Mountain. Normally, at this time of year, the mountain would be full of life by now, with tea parties, poetry readings, and other scholarly gatherings. He'd never seen this road so empty, without a horse, ox-drawn cart, or even a single human in sight!

What was going on? Luo-gongzi's unease only grew, but he couldn't turn back. He'd spent so many days planning this, and he was about to get what he wanted! How could he give up so easily? He waited for his servant to report back, but he was still impatient enough that he kept peeking outside.

Finally, the servant returned, a panicked expression on his face. "Master! Master!"

"What are you shouting for? Come in first," scolded Luo-gongzi. His servant acting so hastily was an embarrassment to him.

"My mistake..." The servant swallowed, then hurriedly climbed up into the carriage. "Master, the road has been blocked off up ahead! Apparently, the general brought his wife up here to enjoy some wine and the snowy scenery. He will not allow anyone to disturb them."

Luo-gongzi gasped, his composure slipping. With an expression as dark as the bottom of a scorched pot, he asked in a harsh voice, "The general is with his wife? Who told you that?!"

Not expecting his master to look so scary, the servant trembled. He shrank in on himself and said with a hoarse voice, "U-um, I saw Vice General Man standing guard over the road, so I didn't dare approach him to ask. I walked around for a bit and ran into a few hunters about to deliver some game to them and chatted with them instead. That's how I found out."

"Those hunters told you the general brought his wife to Suiyu Pond to enjoy wine and the scenery?" Luo-gongzi gnashed his teeth together. If that old duck was here in front of him, he'd bite him to death!

"Yes... That's what I heard. I waited until they delivered the game and came back out to chat with them again. According to them, a beautiful, godlike gongzi was fishing on the pond with another man, and they looked like a phoenix and an old quail. They didn't look like a good match, but they were very affectionate with each other." The servant forced himself to finish the story, afraid to look up at his master.

"You're lying! You're lying!" Luo-gongzi's face twisted. He couldn't stand to hear about Guan Shanjin being affectionate with that old duck! Impossible! Guan Shanjin was obviously very cold toward him—he might even feel disdain for him! He should be following his true desires now—how could he be getting along with the old duck?

"Some other slut must've taken the chance instead!" Luo-gongzi exclaimed. "I'll rip that bitch to pieces!"

Luo-gongzi then jumped down from his carriage in a huff, disregarding his servants' shouts. He headed straight for Suiyu Pond, ignoring everything else.

He was so angry that his brain felt like a pile of mush, incapable of any thought—not that he wanted to think, anyway. There was only one thing occupying his mind: to see Guan Shanjin and to chase away anyone by his side! In the future, when he stood firmly by Guan Shanjin's side, he'd find them all again and teach them a lesson!

Luo-gongzi only paid attention to moving forward. He'd completely forgotten his servant's report that there were people guarding the road. Right now, not a single person could be seen, and he made it to Suiyu Pond unhindered. None of his servants could catch up to him.

Up here in the mountains, small snowflakes floated down atop Suiyu Pond. The plants surrounding the lake were all dusted in a layer of white. Through the gloomy winter sky, a few dazzling rays of sunlight shone down, scattering a golden haze on the ground.

The edges of the pond were slightly frozen. The water was so still that it looked like a mirror, reflecting the mountain scenery and warm winter sun. It looked like a beautiful, ethereal realm.

In the middle of the pond sat a small boat. Inside it, Luo-gongzi saw two silhouettes intimately wrapped around each other as they fished.

Luo-gongzi immediately recognized the taller of the two. It was the man he'd been admiring all this time, Guan Shanjin. His complexion was a little pale; it made his hair, as dark as crow feathers, seem like spun silk.

Probably because they had cordoned off the area, there was nobody else around aside from the person in his arms. Guan Shanjin's hair was not done up, and it fell loosely over his shoulders. His expression was cold, but he was so charming that it was hard to breathe. Luo-gongzi could not look away.

The small figure in his arms was mostly covered up. All Luo-gongzi could tell was that it was indeed a man. His hair was done up properly with not a single strand out of place, and he held a fishing rod in his tanned hand. From a distance, his silhouette could not be considered pretty, but for some reason, Guan Shanjin looked like he was holding a precious gem. He held that pair of hands softly and carefully as they fished together.

Luo-gongzi's eyeballs were about to fall out from how hard he was staring, and he could not stop panting. Of course he recognized who it was in Guan Shanjin's arms—that old duck!

How could that be?! How could that be possible?! Guan Shanjin should've been acting very cold toward him!

Luo-gongzi had followed them around for several months. Every time they were in front of other people, Guan Shanjin always treated the old duck coldly, following behind him at a slight distance. As he

watched him flit from food stall to food stall, he never even lifted a finger to pay.

They never went anywhere quiet; instead, they always walked on the streets where the hustle and bustle of commoners was most prevalent. It was not worthy of the status Guan Shanjin held.

But now...when Guan Shanjin should be listening to his heart the most, why was he being so gentle toward the old duck? Luo-gongzi's vision went red, and a breath caught in his chest, making him choke. A loud buzzing noise filled his ears.

He stumbled forward a few steps, refusing to believe his own eyes. At that moment, the old duck raised his head and said something, his eyes full of surprise. And Guan Shanjin...Guan Shanjin's lips curved up into a doting smile at the sight of him.

Luo-gongzi did not see that under Guan Shanjin's guidance, Wu Xingzi had reeled in a huge fish. Wu Xingzi's laughter could be heard across the entire lake, as well as Guan Shanjin's light chuckle.

Luo-gongzi's eyes rolled into the back of his head and he fainted.

Luo-gongzi's servants cried and screamed after they caught up to their passed-out master, and they had to be dragged out by Man Yue.

Wu Xingzi wanted to check out what all the commotion was about, but Guan Shanjin pulled the fish up, weighed it in his hand, and smiled. "What a big fish."

"Yes..." Wu Xingzi's attention was immediately drawn away, his eyes glittering as he looked at the nearly twenty-pound fish. He swallowed hungrily.

Because Suiyu Pond was in a valley, it was rather cold all year round. Its winters came early and lasted longer, and the waters froze for three months out of the year. As a result, the fish in the pond grew large and fat. Even their scales looked thin and delicate, as if covered in a layer of silver foil. According to Guan Shanjin, these fish's scales were soft, and their fat was thick and smooth. The best way to cook one was to bake it like beggar's chicken or fry it to bring out all its flavors.

The larger this kind of fish grew, the more tender its flesh became. It didn't have a lot of bones, so it could be eaten without having to worry about getting anything stuck in one's throat...

Although he knew Guan Shanjin was trying to distract him, Wu Xingzi accepted it without putting up a fight.

"We don't need to worry about Luo-gongzi?" Wu Xingzi tied the fish up with straw and peeked in Luo-gongzi's direction while Guan Shanjin rowed the boat.

He didn't ask how Luo-gongzi had managed to reach Suiyu Pond under such heavy surveillance. It must've been Guan Shanjin and Man Yue's plan to allow him to come to Suiyu Pond so he'd see something and pass out from fury and shock.

"Don't worry, soon he won't have the energy for all his antics anymore." Guan Shanjin snorted coldly, then pulled Wu Xingzi further into his arms. "Are you still mad at me?"

Wu Xingzi just smiled, looking down at the fishing rod and not answering.

Guan Shanjin knew immediately that the old quail in his arms was still angry. He sighed inwardly; for once, he didn't know what to do.

Yesterday, under Doctor Xia's care, the general had finally woken up fully. His head still hurt, and his heart felt uncomfortable, but the worst thing of all was that the first person he saw when he woke up wasn't Doctor Xia. It was Wu Xingzi, eating a chestnut bun with his cheeks puffed up.

Shock and confusion couldn't describe how Guan Shanjin felt. He subconsciously avoided Wu Xingzi's gaze and searched for Doctor Xia instead. He aimed a fierce glare at him.

"General, I truly am innocent!" Doctor Xia was so shrewd. Guan Shanjin had only just aimed a look at him, and he was already down on his knees with his shoulders slumped. His expression looked like the embodiment of a bitter melon. "You gave an absolute order, so how could I disobey? But...Mistress found out ages ago. I had no other choice!"

He found out? Guan Shanjin's heart stopped beating. Slowly, he turned to look at Wu Xingzi, who was still chewing on his chestnut bun.

Seeing Guan Shanjin finally look at him, Wu Xingzi gave a small, shy smile. He swallowed his food and took a sip of tea, then finally said in a soft tone, "Don't blame Doctor Xia. The first day I came to visit you, you wouldn't let me go back to Qingcheng County. I was thinking maybe you'd regret it the next day. After all, Mr. Lu was about to arrive, and I would only get in the way. Besides, you didn't know me anymore. Xiao-Bao-er has never been to Qingcheng County. I wanted to take him to go see Auntie Liu."

Wu Xingzi wasn't actually an ineloquent speaker; he just wanted to avoid unnecessary conflict. He didn't mind being disrespected. Sometimes, he'd just let it roll off his back. If it was too much, he could fight for himself. But if he really cared, he could also speak as smoothly as a needle slipping through cotton. There wasn't anything wrong with what he said, but every word was sharp.

Because he'd just woken up, Guan Shanjin's brain still felt a bit muddy, and he couldn't come up with a response. Lost, he stared at Wu Xingzi as he finished his chestnut bun and drank some tea.

"But when I came the next day, Man Yue was busy. You know that I've never been barred from entering your area. That day, I was a little impatient, so I didn't ask anyone to announce my arrival." Wu Xingzi sighed. "I don't know if it was a coincidence or what, but Doctor Xia just so happened to be checking over you at the time. I heard you speak. You had just woken up, and asked Doctor Xia to prolong your memory loss through acupuncture until after you found out who was responsible for drugging you."

So he'd heard everything. "You... You already knew everything then?" Guan Shanjin finally managed to ask in a hoarse voice. His entire body felt uncomfortable, especially his chest, which was particularly tight. He didn't dare move his gaze from Wu Xingzi.

"Yes, I probably heard most of it." Wu Xingzi nodded, then poured himself another cup of tea. At the same time, he opened up the food box next to him, focusing his attention on choosing his next snack. After a while, he picked up a rice cake.

The small, bite-sized cake had a sesame paste filling. Once it was in his mouth, the fragrance of sesame and rice filled his nostrils. Wu Xingzi closed his eyes and let out a satisfied sigh.

"You..." Guan Shanjin's shirt was soaked through with sweat.

"Hm?" Wu Xingzi had another piece. He smiled that shy smile that Guan Shanjin loved so much as he stared at the general, waiting for him to continue.

What kind of person was Guan Shanjin right now? He had hurt his head, and he was probably still affected by that drug. His brain wasn't working at full capacity, and he might even have been a little slow at the moment. But no matter how slow he was, he was still smart. With just a bit of thought, he understood everything.

Wu Xingzi had been waiting for him to tell the truth—to stop pretending and come clean on his own.

But it never happened. This time, Guan Shanjin had even lied to Man Yue.

"I did it for your sake..." After a while, Guan Shanjin tried explaining, stumbling over his words.

"Oh." The corners of Wu Xingzi's mouth dropped down. His gentle brows drew together for once. "Haiwang, is it that you want to be good to me, or do you just not trust me?"

They'd been together for ten years, so of course they loved each other. Even Wu Xingzi thought that their feelings for each other ran deeply. Guan Shanjin truly doted on him. When he was good to someone, the general truly was willing to pick the stars and moon from the sky for them. He'd even dig out his heart and present it with both hands. He could really spoil someone rotten, and Wu Xingzi believed he was no exception.

But what Wu Xingzi wanted was for them to be truly connected and to trust each other. After all, they were the only ones keeping one other company in this life, and they would be buried together at the end.

The words he'd said before Guan Shanjin passed out weren't a lie. Even though they were words of anger, they were sincere. Haiwang was his family, and he was no longer alone. Naturally, he wanted to be the same for Haiwang!

The man before him probably couldn't even understand where he was coming from. It was a discouraging line of thought.

A little frustrated, Wu Xingzi saw that Guan Shanjin still looked rather out of it. Perhaps he needed to rest for a while. He took out Luo-gongzi's invitation and waved it in front of Guan Shanjin. "The fish you were looking for has bitten."

"The fish I was looking for?" Guan Shanjin's brows twisted together. He finally recovered a bit and got up from the bed, immediately pulling the old quail into his arms and rubbing his cheek into the crook of Wu Xingzi's neck. It was clear he was trying to get back into Wu Xingzi's good graces.

"Didn't you ask Doctor Xia to look into who drugged you? So I took Xiao-Bao-er out to town yesterday. Don't you want to take a look at this invitation?"

"Who's it from?" Guan Shanjin's head still throbbed in pain. Wu Xingzi sure could be heartless when he wanted to be. Guan Shanjin recently passed out from the pain.

"Assistant Administrator Luo's di son. Do you know of him?" Wu Xingzi didn't try to escape from Guan Shanjin's embrace. He'd missed the man's smell and warmth.

"I do." Guan Shanjin's brows furrowed. He cursed under his breath. "He's been sneakily following us these past few months. I have no idea what he's up to."

Guan Shanjin had been aware of Luo-gongzi for quite some time, and he even asked Man Yue to look into him. Assistant Administrator Luo had been doing very well in court these last five years. He didn't have deep roots, so he had no real power. He and his wife only had one di son, and his shu children were all daughters, so of course Luo-gongzi was viewed as a treasure and spoiled to high heaven. Luo-gongzi's reputation wasn't very good in the capital.

Neither Guan Shanjin nor Man Yue had been able to figure out why Luo-gongzi had been following them these past few months. At first, they thought he was hatching some sort of plot, but Assistant Administrator Luo wasn't aware of Luo-gongzi's actions, and Luo-gongzi himself was not part of the court. He technically had no connection to Guan Shanjin. They just couldn't figure out a reason.

Hearing the impatience and confusion in Guan Shanjin's voice, Wu Xingzi felt a little better. He cleared his throat and pulled out a thousand-layer cake from the food box. He bit half of it off and put the other half in Guan Shanjin's mouth.

"Luo-gongzi fancies you," he said evenly.

Guan Shanjin froze, the dessert in his mouth melting away and nearly choking him. He coughed heavily, his head buzzing even louder. It felt like he might cough up a lung, and he nearly lost his grip on Wu Xingzi. Meanwhile, the culprit just stood there and chuckled.

This old quail is truly fearless now! Guan Shanjin thought, his emotions all jumbled. After regaining his breath, he hugged Wu Xingzi tightly and kissed the old thing on the cheek a few times. "You've learned to be sneaky, huh? You know how to bully me now?"

"You're the one who's spoiled me," Wu Xingzi responded in his soft voice.

"Yes, this is exactly what I wanted."

Nonsense! Wu Xingzi huffed, not believing him.

"I don't need to be spoiled. I just want you to have me in your heart. Stop pushing me away."

Guan Shanjin knew they wouldn't be able to reach a compromise here, but what could he do? This was all his fault, so he had to deal with the consequences. He could only hold Wu Xingzi even closer. After thinking for a while, he said a little reluctantly, "Then, do you want to join me when I deal with the Luo family?"

Of course I do! Wu Xingzi nodded, his smile so large that his eyes curved into crescents.

Thus, Guan Shanjin brought Wu Xingzi to Suiyu Pond to fish. They weren't just here for the fish in the pond—they were also here to fish out the son of the Luo family.

Luo-gongzi never saw this coming. He thought his plan was flawless, so he never would've expected that the very duck he looked down upon would be the one to fish him out.

Wu Xingzi didn't know who had drugged Guan Shanjin, but Doctor Xia said the drug was not fatal, so the perpetrator's goal was not to kill him. But why would someone spend so much effort to drug him if they didn't want to kill him? Clearly, they were after Guan Shanjin himself.

At first, he hadn't even considered romance as a possibility—he thought someone just wanted something from the general.

In order to lure the suspect out, Wu Xingzi kept acting like he wanted to leave. After all, the culprit probably had a constant eye on him. Wu Xingzi knew that he was Guan Shanjin's weak spot, so if the culprit couldn't find Guan Shanjin, they'd definitely try to go after him instead.

It wasn't until he met Luo-gongzi at House of Taotie that he realized the culprit was actually after Guan Shanjin's body! What a dangerous beauty!

If this was the case, things would be much easier to deal with.

As expected, Luo-gongzi passed out from anger when he saw Guan Shanjin. Things probably weren't going to go very well for the Luo family in the future.

"How do you want to eat this fish?" Although Wu Xingzi hadn't fully forgiven Guan Shanjin, they still had to eat the fish. With Guan Shanjin's skills in the kitchen, Wu Xingzi drooled just thinking about it.

"We can't exactly fry it here, so let's make it into beggar's fish. I asked Steward Yuan to bring wax paper. The mud around the lake is smooth and clean—it'll work well."

Guan Shanjin rowed the boat to shore. After taking the fish from Wu Xingzi, he gathered Wu Xingzi up in his arms and jumped to land.

Steward Yuan immediately came up to greet them. "Mistress, there are a few mountain delicacies here. How would you like to eat them?"

Wu Xingzi looked at the food and swallowed. "Let's barbecue them!" Ah, they'd really managed to strike his weak spot. How could he stay mad at Haiwang?

"Have some snacks and hot tea first, all right?" Guan Shanjin looked at the greedy old thing, thinking that he had to be even more careful with his actions in the future.

Guan Shanjin and Wu Xingzi happily enjoyed the snowy view and freshly barbecued meat. Meanwhile, the Luo family had exploded into chaos.

Luo-gongzi, who had been dragged home, was on his last breath. After he finally woke up, he was in a complete daze. No matter how Madam Luo called out to him, he did not respond. Terrified and alarmed, she spent a huge amount of gold to ask an imperial physician to see Luo-gongzi.

When Assistant Administrator Luo returned home and heard the news from his various servants, his face turned completely white. Without even going to see his son, he ran back out. No one knew where he went.

Luo-gongzi ended up falling so sick, he was nearly half dead. His scholarly career took a turn, and slowly, he seemed to fade out of existence.

Three days after they enjoyed the snowy, mountainous view of Suiyu Pond, Wu Xingzi and Guan Shanjin were chatting with each other when Steward Yuan brought them a visit notice. When Guan Shanjin opened it to see who it was from, he burst into laughter.

"That sure was quick."

"Who's coming?" Wu Xingzi asked, craning his neck to look. It was a guest with the surname Yu.

"Yu Yu, the Grand Chancellor to the previous emperor." Guan Shanjin's lips quirked up in a smile; then he threw the notice back to Steward Yuan. "Tell him to come in."

"Here?" Wu Xingzi shrank into himself a bit, wanting to extricate himself from Guan Shanjin's arms. But the man held him tightly, not letting go. "Haiwang, I should leave."

"No. Don't you want to know how I'll deal with the Luo family in the end? Yu Yu has come all this way; why are you shying away?" Guan Shanjin kissed Wu Xingzi on the cheek, keeping him wrapped up in his arms.

"Even so, we don't need to be hugging..." Wu Xingzi mumbled, slightly embarrassed. Even though his mouth said one thing, his body was honest. He leaned into Guan Shanjin, snuggling into his embrace even further.

Soon, an old man with white hair and a beard walked into the room after Steward Yuan. When he first spotted Guan Shanjin holding Wu Xingzi, his footsteps faltered slightly, but his expression remained unchanged. He was even smiling a little. He cupped his hands toward Wu Xingzi in greeting. "Is this the general's wife? It's an honor to finally met you."

Who knew whether or not it was truly an honor, but "the general's wife" were words chosen specifically to slight Wu Xingzi.

Wu Xingzi was not offended at all. Instead, he smiled shyly, accepting the greeting. He cupped his hands toward the old man as well. "You're Yu-gong, right? It's an honor."

His words were as unexpectedly sharp as a needle wrapped in cotton. Yu Yu's expression nearly slipped. He could only chuckle in response. Under Steward Yuan's invitation, he sat down to the side.

Seeing he was about to speak, Guan Shanjin stopped him with a wave of his hand and said lightly, "If you want to beg for mercy on behalf of the Luo family, you can save your breath. I've already been very lenient with them."

Assistant Administrator Luo had been stripped of his title yesterday, demoted four ranks, and nearly kicked out of the capital. Originally, Guan Shanjin wanted him exiled to the northwestern border to be an official with actual authority over there, but the emperor still had plans for him. Thus, he was allowed to stay in the capital. This had struck Assistant Administrator Luo like lightning from the sky, so he went to his father-in-law to beg him for help.

Yu Yu didn't expect Guan Shanjin to be so cold. He hadn't even opened his mouth to ask anything yet, and his words were already forced back inside his throat. At first he wasn't able to say anything, but when he thought of his daughter and her family, he could only forge ahead.

"I've already heard everything from my son-in-law. That child, Yanzhi, indeed went too far. He'll discipline the child however you see fit. Although he is guilty of not educating his son properly, the punishment doesn't fit the crime..."

"Sir Yu, you've witnessed my methods before." Guan Shanjin interrupted Yu Yu and smiled lightly. "Since you're forcing me to spell everything out for you, I won't hold back anymore."

"What do you mean, general? I don't understand..." Yu Yu's expression stiffened, but he still held on to a shred of hope.

"Luo Yanzhi said he bribed the eunuch responsible for pouring wine, but the person he spoke of has far too low a rank in the palace.

There's no way he should have been allowed to serve at the banquet. You should know the rules of the palace, right? Who was the one that planted the poison? Who has the ability to bribe a eunuch with enough status?"

Yu Yu's back broke out in a cold sweat, but it was too late for him to leave now.

Guan Shanjin picked up a mung bean cake and fed it to Wu Xingzi, then said casually, "Have I left the capital for so long that even clever people like you have forgotten how I dealt with those traitors all those years ago?"

"No, I... Yanzhi is just infatuated with you, and my son-in-law was just..."

"His feelings are real, but who knows their true nature? Assistant Administrator Luo... Oh, I forgot. Now he's Secretary Luo. He wanted Yanzhi to enter the Guan family to elevate his status in court, no? Luo Yanzhi was crazy enough to acquire wolfsbane and lily of the Nile, and he successfully managed to bribe someone to put it in my wine. Ah, it's not easy being a parent." Guan Shanjin chuckled, but his smile did not reach his eyes. He stared coldly at Yu Yu, making the old man tremble. He couldn't even sit still.

"When some people get too ambitious, they forget their own worth. Wouldn't you agree?" the general asked. This was a pointed comment. Yu Yu's face trembled, and it took him a few tries to stand up from the chair to bid his goodbyes.

"Poor Luo-gongzi..." Wu Xingzi sighed as he watched Yu Yu leave.

Guan Shanjin didn't comment, just hugged Wu Xingzi even tighter.

Finally, the smoke had dissipated.

ABSOLUTE LOVERS (OMEGAVERSE)

LONG AGO, humanity was divided into only two sexes: Male and female. Humans on ancient Earth relied on these two sexes to produce great quantities of offspring—until the day finally came that their planet no longer had enough natural resources to support so many lives. With their planet drained of resources, humanity needed to find a way to expand the territory in which they lived, or else face the extinction of their species.

Fortunately for mankind, at this critical moment, they were ultimately able to develop a warp engine. The test flights were successful, marking the beginning of humanity's spread into the greater cosmos. In the course of their migration, they met with friendly and highly intelligent races, as well as ruthless foes. Humanity itself was just as brutal, seizing planets already occupied by intelligent life to develop them into colonies.

Science, technology, and society as a whole advanced rapidly. Humanity finally solidified their place within the universe, and curbed that brutal side of theirs as they attempted to form more positive relations with their neighbors.

In any neighborhood, however, you could never count on all your neighbors being good people. There'd always be a few bad eggs which the rest of the neighborhood hated but couldn't do anything about. One example of this was the Insectoid race.

Nobody knew where the Insectoids came from; they simply appeared out of the blue one day. Their race was divided into a great variety of different types, but there were common characteristics shared between all of them—namely, they were all tough-skinned, rude, and violent. And worst of all, they weren't stupid. Among all the known intelligent lifeforms in the universe, in fact, the Insectoids could be ranked first in terms of IQ. Most lifeforms with high intelligence and technology tended to have a relatively weak reproductive ability, but the Insectoids didn't abide by this rule either; they were extremely prolific because, in an extraordinary defiance of the natural order, their method of reproduction had the same high yield as ordinary, less advanced insects. A female Insectoid could lay hundreds or thousands of eggs at a time with a reproductive cycle as short as a shocking three months per clutch, and an adult Insectoid could continue to reproduce for as long as ten years.

The Insectoids were ruled by a queen who, though fortunately not responsible for reproduction, acted as the brain for the entire Insectoid race. Perhaps the best term to describe the Insectoids was *hive mind*.

If not for the low survival rate of their larvae, and the fact they had to return to their original planet to successfully mate and birth offspring, it would only be a matter of time before a race like this took over the entire universe.

All the same, the Insectoids still caused problems for a great number of other intelligent lifeforms. After all, they were violent, warlike, naturally disposed to pillaging, and found joy in destruction. No grass grew in the places they'd razed, and a thriving planet like Earth would become a dead star in the space of three days if it failed to fend off an Insectoid attack in time.

And so it was that many of these intelligent creatures banded together in an alliance to fend off the Insectoid invasion together, hoping they would one day be able to drive the Insectoids back to their original galaxy, never to harm the universe again.

In the subsequent battles, humans became an extremely important military power.

For one thing, human fertility was exceptionally strong for an intelligent life form; their reproductive period could last twenty to thirty years, and thanks to advancements in medical care and genetic engineering, this period ended up being extended up to fifty years. There were only one or two children per pregnancy, but the conception rate was extremely high, it took less than a year to produce a child, and the human would become capable of pregnancy again immediately after giving birth. All this was incredible enough, but they were also reproductively compatible with many other intelligent lifeforms, and the resulting offspring would retain the reproductive advantages humans possessed.

Humanity's advantage in this respect became all the more obvious in the face of the Insectoid threat. Many of those races capable of reproducing with humans, once they started living together with them, accidentally sparked the flames of love, and *boom*! Newborns popped out one after the other. Before anyone noticed, they'd spread to quite a few different galaxies, truly becoming the foundational pillar of the anti-Insectoid forces, and slowly pushing humankind into the position of leader of the Galactic Alliance.

During this drawn-out war against the Insectoids, the human race gradually mixed with the bloodlines of many other intelligent lifeforms, and in the process their sexes began to undergo a strange division that damaged their reproductive advantage to a certain extent.

At the time our story takes place, most of humanity had established an empire outside of the Galactic Alliance, and they continued to be the main force in the war against the Insectoids. Their sexes had also divided into six different types: Along with the original male and female sexes, they were further divided into the Alpha, Beta, and Omega sexes. Among these, Alphas and Omegas had the greatest fertility rate when paired together, whereas Betas were relatively lacking in reproductive ability, making it extremely difficult for them to give birth to the next generation. Despite this, Betas numbered the most amidst the three types, and with their gentle and obedient natures, they were quite suited for acting as a social lubricant between the hot-headed, sturdy, and physically strong Alphas, and the fertile, yet soft and fragile Omegas.

It was a mystery which bloodline Alphas and Omegas had inherited heat and rut cycles and pheromones from, but the moment they entered their cycle, pheromones would gush uncontrollably out into the air, affecting all Alphas and Omegas in the area, whereas very few Betas would feel anything at all. Under the effect of these pheromones, these Alphas and Omegas would fall into a mindless frenzy of desire regardless of how unfamiliar they might have been with each other, and it became impossible for them to have thoughts of anything besides sex. Reproduction became the only thing that mattered.

This was a seriously bum deal.

So Guan Shanjin thought, panting heavily as he rolled up the sleeve of his military uniform to reveal fair yet muscular and well-defined arms, trying to inject the pheromone inhibitor into his body and failing repeatedly.

As a general of the empire's Third Legion, he'd spent the last few days fighting constantly on the very front line, and in the chaos his approaching rut had slipped his mind. The battlefield had given him the opportunity to heartily vent the brutal energy which preceded the coming of those passionate urges—in the process he'd actually managed to pick off tens of millions of Insectoids and push the front line forward by the distance of two planets.

It wasn't until he finally had the chance to breathe that he realized his rut had arrived. In fact, it had reached its peak. His head swam with thoughts of copulation and violence, leaving only a small corner of his mind to hold onto his last shred of reason. He hurriedly retreated to his cabin and changed the ventilation to a single-room cycle in order to prevent his pheromones from spreading to his troops and throwing the legion into chaos.

He couldn't have hated his reputation as the Alpha with the most perfect and powerful genes in the Empire any more than he did in this moment. Indeed, there were only three or four registered Alphas as powerful as he was, and he was the youngest of them all; the entirety of the Empire's upper class had their eyes on him, hoping to offer their own Omegas to him in marriage so that they could give rise to even more powerful offspring.

But Guan Shanjin had no interest whatsoever in those soft Omegas; he was now at prime age to have children, yet still refused to marry. Assessing gazes surrounded him on all sides, wondering whether they should take the opportunity to destroy him, or use coercion to force him to take their Omegas.

"Fuck!" Guan Shanjin couldn't resist cursing aloud after another failed attempt at injection. His temples were throbbing, several blood vessels surfacing on his forehead; he looked as if he were about to explode.

"This worthless excuse of a bullshit needle!" He glared at the syringe with reddened eyes, wanting nothing more than to destroy its manufacturer. If it weren't for the fact the syringe contained his much-needed medication, he would have thrown it to the ground and crushed it under his feet.

This calamity would be entirely undeserved for the syringe, however. The fact of the matter was that during the peak of their rut period, an Alpha's skin and muscles would become extraordinarily strong, enough to deflect attack from any ordinary blade. They had evolved this trait to ensure that an Alpha and Omega's intercourse could not be interrupted by external interference. As such, there was no way this syringe's needle would be able to penetrate the skin of the Alpha it was faced with now—the fact it hadn't broken was itself a testament to how well-made it was.

But Guan Shanjin refused to give up—he simply couldn't believe that this damn needle was so beyond his ability to handle. If he didn't inject the inhibitor soon, the only option left to him would be to simply endure the rut period. For an Alpha who'd just come off the battlefield, and whose mind was still active, such an outcome could be fatal. If an Alpha's overactive physical and mental faculties could not be calmed, they would enter a state akin to an out-of-body experience; if this state lasted for more than twenty-four hours, the Alpha's mind would collapse.

He, the next marshal of the Third Legion, eldest son and successor of the Guan family—one of the top families in the Empire—would die miserably yet laughably in the middle of his triumphant return home, and with his parents already too old to bear another child!

All the people with their eyes on the Guan family and the Third Legion would doubtless laugh so hard they dislocated their jaws, and the emperor would surely jump at the chance to raise a national celebration over the loss of such a major worry! There was no way he could let something so stupid and disgraceful happen!

However, this latest rough attempt was too much for the syringe, and the needle broke right off. The body of the syringe, too, was cracked by the Alpha's extraordinarily strong grip, and the medicine inside almost spilled out.

Guan Shanjin glared at the syringe with reddened eyes, finally forced to accept the fact that he would not be able to use the inhibitor.

There were many Omegas on the ship, all of clean background and outstanding ability. Many of them had yet to be marked, having chosen to focus on their careers, and had no objection to the occasional unmarked, passionate rut-period tumble with an Alpha. As long as they made sure to take all the necessary protective measures, an Alpha and Omega could still enjoy sex without fear of any unwanted complications.

But this wasn't an appealing option for Guan Shanjin, because all of those Omegas were his subordinates. Sleeping with a subordinate would cause far too many troubles down the line, and it wouldn't look good if news got out either. It could even be used to create scandals by someone with ulterior motives. Even if Guan Shanjin's brain broke from lust, he still wouldn't do something so dangerous.

It was right at this moment that the communicator on the table rang. Guan Shanjin had no interest in answering this call. Instead, feeling somewhat defeated, as he used what little remained of his rationality to ponder what to write in his will.

But the communicator kept on ringing—it seemed like it wouldn't stop until he answered it. Guan Shanjin was irritated beyond belief, but had no other option than to pick up the communicator.

"Who is it?" he panted out between heavy breaths.

"General! It's me, Man Yue." The voice on the other end was that of Guan Shanjin's Staff Officer and friend, Man Yue. Man Yue was an Omega, and, true to his name, he was as round as the moon. He was already in talks with an Alpha for marriage, and he'd been marked a long time ago besides, so he wasn't affected by Guan Shanjin's pheromones.

It was also Man Yue who'd noticed Guan Shanjin's abnormal state and hurriedly dragged him back to the residential floor.

"What's the matter?" Guan Shanjin asked grumpily. At present there was no possible way for him fuck any Omegas, and couldn't do anything about the inhibitor either, leaving his tyrannical urges to steadily grow in intensity—more than enough for him to pick off another few million low-level Insectoids.

"I was just thinking, it's impossible for you to inject the inhibitor right now, isn't it? You'd break the needle without even trying." It was clear from his tone that Man Yue was trying to ease the atmosphere, but he couldn't hide his concern.

Man Yue understood Guan Shanjin's concerns perfectly well: There was no solution to this problem other than Guan Shanjin agreeing to mark one of the ship's Omegas. There was no way he'd be able to reach the nearest branch of the Imperial Academy of Sciences in time, and even if he did, they might not be able to relieve the rut effects for an Alpha of Guan Shanjin's level. It could only end in him dying from that out-of-body state.

"This is a fucking miserable situation..."

It had to be said that the differentiation of the three secondary sexes had enabled humanity to evolve their battle strength to an unprecedented degree. Whether it was in combat awareness, physical strength, or mental ability, Alphas were far superior to primitive humans in every respect. While it was true that they were violent and bellicose, they were able to vent these urges on the Insectoids, so no harm ever came to human society. This trait only further cemented humanity's position in the Galactic Alliance.

However, they also had to bear the original sins of pheromones and rut periods.

"I just got an idea—did you know they came out with an oral inhibitor a while back?" Man Yue's tone was hopeful, and he became noticeably more energetic as he explained, "The oral medication might not be as effective as the injection, but it'll be enough to get you through this rut period safely...in theory."

Guan Shanjin felt his temples throb again at those last two words. "In theory?"

"Yeah, in theory. The oral medication only just went on the market, you see, so all we have is the lab data on exactly how effective it is. Now, laboratory data is more than enough for your average person, but for *you*...I don't know how much it might fall short of standards." Man Yue was helpless on this front; he didn't want to dump cold water on his superior and friend, but it'd be even more irresponsible to casually give him baseless hope.

"Forget all that, just let me take the medicine. Even if it falls short by a lot, it should be enough for us to make it to the Warren Galaxy's branch of the Imperial Academy of Sciences, right?" Guan Shanjin had always been a decisive man; he was not the kind of person to be overcautious. An opportunity had presented itself before him, so what reason did he have to let it pass him by?

"Okay, I'll have someone deliver the medicine over to you," Man Yue said with a nod. He was just about to hang up when Guan Shanjin spoke up to stop him.

"Have someone deliver it? Why don't you bring it over yourself?" Man Yue had his own Alpha, so reasonably speaking he shouldn't be afraid of Guan Shanjin's pheromones at all. The two of them trusted one another implicitly, besides, making Man Yue the best candidate for the task.

"I can't... Su Yang's about to go into rut, and if I get another Alpha's pheromones on me he'll lose his mind. But I'll happily deliver the medicine for you if you're willing to let me take maternity leave." Man Yue's exasperated yet doting smile was genuinely beyond annoying. Guan Shanjin rudely rolled his eyes, but didn't dare offer his friend the proposed maternity leave.

This wasn't out of selfishness, but because their fleet was still set to patrol the front line for another eighteen months. He couldn't do without his capable assistant Man Yue right now, and neither could the empire.

"But my current condition might affect whoever brings the medicine." Even Guan Shanjin himself couldn't explain how he was still managing to remain calm and rational; it was extremely hard to say when this precarious lucidity might suddenly snap.

"You don't need to worry about that, I'll have a Beta deliver the medicine." Man Yue seemed to have everything planned out, leaving Guan Shanjin with no choice but to go along with his friend's arrangements.

Indeed, having a Beta deliver the medicine was the safest option at this point. Betas weren't affected by Alpha or Omega pheromones, being closer to ancient earthlings in their bodily functions. Alphas and Omegas also rarely showed interest in Betas, because Betas had barely any scent. The only exception to this was if their compatibility score was over ninety percent, in which case they would hit it off immediately regardless of their sex. It was incredibly rare for that to happen, though; in the hundreds of years since the empire's founding, no more than three hundred A/B or B/O pairs had occurred who were an above-90-percent match.

With that in mind, Guan Shanjin finally relaxed enough to half-lie down on the sofa. His military uniform was soaked with sweat and sticking uncomfortably to his skin. He thought a moment, then stripped off his coat and shirt, the nakedness of his upper body bringing him some relief.

The person with the medicine didn't take long to arrive; it was probably a little over ten minutes before the doorbell rang, and a soft, gentle, somewhat timid voice came in through the loudspeaker: "General, this is clerk Wu Xingzi, here to deliver your medicine for you."

This voice was such an incredibly beautiful one that it made Guan Shanjin's ears go a little numb. Because of his fierce and resolute nature, Guan Shanjin disliked soft and weak-willed people, which was why to this day he'd always turned his nose up at all those Omegas so carefully cultivated by aristocratic families. His ideal partner could be meek, but had to have their own personality as well. They certainly couldn't be someone who bored him. However, the voice he heard in this moment was comfortable and pleasing to the ears, enough so that he found himself softening his own tone in response: "Come in."

"All right," Clerk Wu Xingzi responded in that sticky-soft voice of his, before pressing the button to open the bedroom door and walking in. He then quickly shut the door again to prevent Guan Shanjin's pheromones from spreading outside.

Though Guan Shanjin's pheromones did not spread, he smelled an incredibly alluring scent. It was a very light, refreshing scent, unlike the cloying sweetness particular to Omegas, elusively vague yet somehow able to ignite the Alpha's full sensory focus. He felt as if he'd entered the most beautiful dream, one where the agony of his rut was instantly soothed only to rise up again even more fiercely than before. And yet, this change inexplicably made Guan Shanjin feel at ease, giving him an indescribable, unexpected, and unreasonable sense of security.

He opened his eyes, turning his head to look in the direction the footsteps were coming from.

What entered his field of vision was a slender figure with a face so ordinary that one might forget it immediately upon seeing it. This average and far-from-youthful male Beta was the one giving off the pleasant aroma. If an Alpha could smell a Beta's pheromones, that meant the two of them were at least a 90 percent match; not only could this Beta's scent be picked up by an Alpha, but it was even managing to soothe an Alpha at the peak of his rut, meaning that their compatibility must be over 95 percent...

Guan Shanjin suddenly laughed. He'd been forced to submit a partner application to the Imperial Academy of Sciences a few years previous, and he'd gone to matchmaking meetings with a good number of Omegas under the control of a variety of different forces. Because he was the highest level of Alpha, those Omegas who were introduced to him all had a compatibility score of at least 80 percent, with quite a few even managing to hit the 90 percent mark.

But his pheromones and vitality were both far too strong; he'd lost track of how many Omegas he'd frightened to tears, and he'd even made some of them faint. This made him quite a popular topic of conversation with certain nuisances among the upper class.

His family had never cared about sex or bloodline. Whether it was A, O, or B, nobility or commoner, what mattered most to them was the attraction of pheromones—in other words, their compatibility. Successive Guan family heads throughout history had had 100 percent compatibility with their partners, and they'd never gone to the Imperial Academy of Sciences to make that match. Guan Shanjin's parents were in no hurry at all; they believed whole-heartedly that their son would find his one and only in his own time.

And indeed he had.

In his time of greatest need, when he was at his most downtrodden, Guan Shanjin met the one with whom he'd fall in love at first sight. The draw of the other man's pheromones was so strong. He knew they were meant to be together.

This certainly wasn't a one-sided attraction, either. When Wu Xingzi first stepped into the general's room, he felt somewhat nervously helpless—after all, though he worked on the ship, as a clerk he was at the absolute lowest level of the chain of authority. He was in charge of logistics-related matters, and it was unlikely he'd ever meet the highest commanding officer.

So when he was suddenly tasked with delivering medicine, conflicting feelings of joy and unease arose simultaneously within his heart. While it was true that he lacked the authority to meet their commanding officer in person, there had been nothing stopping him from taking advantage of all kinds of video recordings to admire the sight of the most handsome and powerful Alpha in the empire. He was much older than Guan Shanjin, yet had unconsciously found himself carrying the faintest sliver of a hidden crush on this peerlessly, unforgettably handsome general.

However, he also understood that—being an old man, and a mere rank and file clerk as well—there was probably about a fifty million light-year distance between him and the general, rendering any wishful thinking entirely pointless. He was content simply to watch the man secretly from the sidelines.

No one could possibly have imagined that this single medicine delivery would completely change the course of Wu Xingzi's life.

As soon as he closed the door and turned around, Wu Xingzi found himself meeting the general's deep, beautiful eyes; they were somewhat reddened due to his rut, but that didn't make him look like he was struggling very much; in fact they held a bewitching sort of charm to them. The general lay on the sofa with his torso bared to the world. His muscular body was indescribably beautiful, and along with his naturally fair skin, it made him look almost as if he were carved from marble. Wu Xingzi felt inexplicably hot at the sight, and his breathing grew heavier as well, as if he were somewhat out of breath.

The scent filling the air was cool, yet so sexual as to make a person blush. He couldn't tell exactly what scent it was, something like a mix of white sandalwood and orange blossom—not a particularly invasive combination, yet it still gradually seeped into his consciousness. Little by little, before he knew it, this seemingly harmless and elegant aroma had silently invaded all of his senses, wrapping him up so firmly in it that he was unable to extricate himself.

"G-General...this is your medicine..." Wu Xingzi felt as if he were walking on clouds, barely even able to speak clearly. His voice was so soft it was like he was half-holding it in his mouth.

"Bring it here..." Guan Shanjin's voice was husky and magnetic, making those three short and simple words sound like a declaration of love. Wu Xingzi unconsciously gave a little shiver, his mind almost entirely devoured.

He didn't know how he'd walked over to Guan Shanjin, nor how he'd fed the medicine to him; all Wu Xingzi knew was that when he came to his senses, his lips were already pressed against Guan Shanjin's elegant, rosy, extremely kissable mouth. His tongue shyly probed into the other man's hot mouth, and there definitely seemed to be a pill lying on the tip of it.

Guan Shangjin's tongue quickly stretched out to entangle itself with Wu Xingzi's, the pill rolling around between their two tongues. Perhaps because of the inhibitor, it was slightly sweet rather than bitter; that sweetness soothed Guan Shanjin's violent mind, but also made him all the more certain that his genes had not misjudged the degree of compatibility he held with the person before him.

They definitely had to be 100 percent compatible. Guan Shanjin was sure: All he wanted in this moment was to completely devour the ordinary old Beta now lying limp in his arms and pitifully panting for breath. He was eager to form a knot in the old Beta's womb and use any means possible to mark him, ensuring that he could never leave him for the rest of his life.

This goddamned genetic instinct!

Guan Shanjin spared some energy to complain, but his strong, sturdy arms had already wrapped around Wu Xingzi's slender waist, firmly trapping the man in his embrace. He gnawed at those pleasantly sweet lips and the soft tongue within, stubbornly refusing to pull away, until the old Beta was struggling to breathe under his kiss, weakly and pitifully struggling in his arms. Only then did he reluctantly part long enough to let the man breathe—and then he immediately kissed him again.

An Alpha in rut was incapable of holding on to rationality. Even knowing that the one before him was a Beta—not physically fit to bear an Alpha's passion, not as soft as an Omega, and unable to secrete enough slick to properly lubricate himself the way an Omega could, so that the Alpha could plunder him more easily—Guan Shanjin didn't care. He was the highest level of Alpha, full of love and patience for his partner, and opening up a Beta was no difficulty for him. Besides, they had a lifetime to get familiar with each other.

As for now... Guan Shanjin ended the long and unbroken kiss. That new oral inhibitor had melted amidst their entangled lips and tongues, and it had definitely had some effect; it'd gotten him out of the peak period, at least, so he wouldn't be entirely controlled by his desire. The old Beta in his arms, meanwhile, looked as if he'd just undergone an intense bout of lovemaking; he was flushed from head to toe, sweat beading his temples, his lips swollen. Saliva he'd been unable to swallow hung at the corner of his mouth as he gazed at the alpha obediently, dazedly, his thin frame trembling slightly.

It was true that he was on the older side. He appeared to be at least around forty, and had very plain looks as well, not at all like the people of the empire with their history of genetic selection. That fleshy nose was hard to miss. Guan Shanjin would have been turned off by it if he'd seen it on anyone else's face. On this Beta's face, however, he found it nothing short of adorable, and had the irresistible urge to pinch it.

"Wu Xingzi." Guan Shanjin could still remember that the Beta had announced his name before coming in, and wanted to properly confirm their respective identities in this lull before his rut returned at full force.

"Ai..." Wu Xingzi clearly hadn't recovered yet from that overly passionate kiss, responding in a somewhat dazed tone of voice.

"Where are you from?" Guan Shanjin shook the man in his arms, only to realize that he was half-kneeling beside the sofa. Weren't his knees in terrible pain, kneeling there for so long? Guan Shanjin quickly lifted the man up onto the sofa to lie within his arms, then clumsily gave a comforting pat to that back with its protruding shoulder blades.

"Where?" Being jostled around like that finally jolted Wu Xingzi back to his senses. His cheeks flushed despite himself, and he tried to break free from Guan Shanjin's embrace, but was powerless to resist the Alpha's strength. "G-General, I'm just, just here to...deliver your medicine, and you've already taken it, so shouldn't I be—ah, ow..."

The Alpha grumpily bit him before he could finish speaking. Those arms around his waist were like an iron vise, wrapping around him so tightly that he could barely breathe; all he could do was lie obediently against the man's chest, smelling the cool scent of white sandalwood mixed with orange blossom, and secretly rejoicing over his situation.

Wu Xingzi wasn't thinking anything untoward. He assumed Guan Shanjin had only tried to devour his mouth like that because he'd lost his mind in the peak of his rut. Once the medicine kicked in, Guan Shanjin would realize that the person he was holding in his old arms was an ordinary Beta rather than a soft, agreeable Omega, and he'd naturally let him go.

"Do you want to leave my side that badly?" Alphas developed a strong sense of possessiveness when faced with their chosen mate. This desire was so powerful that it was impossible to control, even with a rational mind. Even Guan Shanjin was unable to except himself from this rule, especially not now that he was in rut!

"Leave? No, no, no, that's not what I mean… It's just that I'm still on the clock, so I can't leave my post for too long, plus I have to report your condition to Staff Officer Man, so…" Wu Xingzi unconsciously, uncontrollably rubbed his cheeks against the general's sturdy pectorals, his eyes in a docile half-squint as he listened to that powerful heartbeat through a layer of muscle.

As a Beta, his senses weren't nearly as sharp as Guan Shanjin's. Though he was curious why exactly he was able to smell the general's rut pheromones, his sense of inferiority prevented him from thinking too much of it. *It's probably because the general is the highest level of Alpha that his pheromones are so strong,* he thought to himself. *Ai… it really is such a pleasant aroma.*

The Alpha was begrudgingly appeased by the old Beta's explanation. He pursed his lips. "That's not an issue," he murmured, planting a few scorching hot kisses on the shell of the Beta's ear. "Your job is to take care of me. Then once I mark you later, you can stay by my side forever... As for Man Yue..." Thinking of his friend, Guan Shanjin clicked his tongue in impatience, then asked the man in his arms, "Do you have a personal terminal on you?"

The Alpha's pheromones had the Beta in a daze, his mind turned entirely to mush; if it hadn't been for his deeply rooted inferiority complex, he'd have already tried to bite the beautifully voluptuous muscles of the man beneath him. He blinked his misty eyes, then obediently held up the hand wearing the personal terminal.

This submissive behavior was so satisfying that the Alpha practically melted at the sight. He gently gripped the Beta's slender wrist, flipping it over to place two kisses on the thin, soft palm of his hand before finally switching on the personal terminal and contacting Man Yue.

The call connected barely seconds after it went out, and Man Yue's face appeared on the screen. He'd been wearing the serious expression one would expect of a high-level government official, but when he saw Guan Shanjin and Wu Xingzi tangled together in an embrace his eyes widened in dumbstruck shock.

"This is... Guan Shanjin! You beast!" a flustered Man Yue roared angrily. There was a limit to what he could see, but what he *could* see was plenty—in fact, it was enough to make him explode. Guan Shanjin was naked, while Wu Xingzi's lips had been bitten until they were red and swollen, his entire body limp and boneless; their limbs were so entangled it was as if they wanted nothing more than to fuse into one...

"Wu Xingzi is a Beta! I can't believe a high-level Alpha like you would actually put your hands on him! Are you planning to fuck him to death?" Man Yue lost all restraint in his anger.

Guan Shanjin frowned at those words. He didn't like other people scolding him and his partner; even if he hadn't officially marked him yet, that would change in a couple of hours.

"I haven't made a move on Wu Xingzi yet. Send over some lube, I don't want to hurt him on his first time." Guan Shanjin had already forgotten what he'd originally called Man Yue to say. All he knew was that he needed to mark the man in his arms as soon as possible; that way, nobody could gossip about their relationship.

"So you really *are* planning to do it with a Beta? Guan Shanjin, he doesn't have the constitution to handle you!" Man Yue was regretting having chosen Wu Xingzi to deliver the medicine. He'd combed through the DNA database of all the staff on the ship in search of the individual with the least attractive genes to ensure the safest possible trip for the person delivering the medicine.

The planet Wu Xingzi was born on was a relatively remote one, and due to local customs there, he had barely gone through any genetic screening. He could even be considered to have especially pure genes in comparison with his fellow Betas, and his light scent was the least likely to catch anyone's attention, making him the safest option to face a rutting Alpha.

How could such a huge mistake occur? Was there an issue with the data in the DNA database?

"I don't care. He and I are a 100 percent genetic match; I can smell his pheromones, and he can smell mine. So as long as he's lubricated well enough, he should definitely be able to handle me." When an Alpha got stubborn, nobody could make them change their mind. Guan Shanjin knew he was going to enter another peak in his rut in ten minutes. He needed to properly open up the Beta before then, in order to avoid causing irreversible damage to him.

"Could you at least let me confirm whether or not he has a partner, then?" There was nothing Man Yue could do in the face of Guan Shanjin's earnest, solemn expression. At most, he could have their onboard military doctor make all necessary preparations to avoid the worst possible outcome.

If a clerk got injured, they could deal with that. If the general of a military legion died in an out-of-body state, it would be a loss to the entire empire. Selfish and unfair though it was, Man Yue immediately made up his mind.

"Of course he doesn't, he's mine," the Alpha said, then pulled the Beta's head up from where it was buried in his breast, bit into those soft, sweet lips, and started noisily sucking away. He seemed so excited it was as if he wanted nothing more than to swallow the other man into his stomach, skin, bones and all.

Man Yue rolled his eyes, quickly pulled up every detail of Wu Xingzi's life, then breathed a sigh of relief. "Congratulations, he really doesn't have a partner. I'll have someone send lubricant over right away... And please, don't eat the delivery man again this time."

Man Yue had a huge headache, but on the other end of the communicator, Guan Shanjin was already inescapably intoxicated by the Beta's scent, and was barely paying any attention to what he said.

He wanted to devour this old Beta, make him bear his children, and ensure he stayed by his side for the rest of his life.

He naturally encountered no more opposition once he finally managed to abduct the old Beta back to his home.

The Guan family heads had always been free to choose their partners; they didn't care a whit about bloodlines or backgrounds, and paid far more attention to the person's character and compatibility.

Yet the old Beta was severely lacking in confidence, and at first he'd been reluctant to enter the Guan family's door. He was much older than Guan Shanjin, close in age to the wife of the Third Legion's marshal—he was basically a cradle-snatcher! How could he ever have the nerve to imagine he was qualified to be with Guan Shanjin?

Besides, it wouldn't be easy for him to have children at this age, and he was a Beta as well; he wouldn't mind giving birth to a little Beta, but he didn't think the empire's foremost Alpha could accept having a Beta child. If Guan Shanjin regretted it... Well, it was one thing for Wu Xingzi's feelings to be hurt, but the poor child wouldn't be having a good time of it either!

After thinking it over, though the old Beta had already been marked by the Alpha during his rut, he secretly slipped off the warship once they returned to the imperial capital. He proceeded to hide there for a full ten months. When Guan Shanjin found him those ten months later, he threw him over his shoulder without another word, carried him back to his official residence, and forced him to register for marriage right then and there.

He fucked him repeatedly that night; it wasn't until the old Beta was practically on his last breath that Guan Shanjin's desires were finally satisfied.

Guan Shanjin really wanted to stay, work on building his relationship with his Beta, and develop his body while he was at it, so that he wouldn't have to worry about hurting the old Beta every time they made love. It didn't matter so much if he couldn't fully enjoy himself, but he wouldn't be able to stand it if he couldn't make Wu Xingzi feel good.

However, he still had ten months of patrol left. He hadn't been to the front lines in the past ten months because he was busy looking for the runaway old Beta. There was no way he could carry on being so willful for another ten months.

The Alpha had no other choice. He was forced to leave his Beta at home, and hope that his mother could help break down some of the man's emotional defenses while he was away.

And so, the moment his ten-month front-line patrol was complete, Guan Shanjin made three consecutive wormhole jumps back to the imperial capital. He didn't care whether it would overload the engine. He'd been given a year and a half of vacation, which was more than enough time to have the old Beta birth an heir for him and tie the man firmly to his side.

"You're back?" That light, soft voice immediately relieved his tense mood; a slender man stood in the entranceway, head half-lowered as he peeked nervously and shyly up at him.

"Why are you standing here?" Guan Shanjin frowned as he reached over to pull that thin body into his arms. He tightened his embrace. "Have you lost weight again?" His dissatisfaction was obvious.

"Er..." The man docilely lowered his head, unable to work up the courage to answer that question.

"Have you been eating properly?" The moment that question left his lips, Guan Shanjin was already answering himself with a sigh. "I'm sure you *have* been eating well, so why aren't you gaining any weight?" he murmured to himself with a hint of exasperation.

"Heh heh..." The man's ears reddened as he cast a furtive glance at Guan Shanjin, and he stutteringly changed the topic. "You can touch me and, and s-s-s-see if I have or not...'"

Guan Shanjin laughed softly. He tilted up the man's face to look at his acutely bashful, embarrassed expression. The sight filled him with delight. "Just a few days apart, and already you've learned to seduce me? All right then, let's go to our room right now—I hope you can handle my idea of a good time."

"Are, aren't you going to eat first?" Wu Xingzi grew flustered, not having expected Guan Shanjin to jump into doing it right away. He repeatedly gazed back in the direction of the dining room, but instead found himself steered into the bedroom by the man who was soon to become the youngest marshal in the empire. Before he could figure out what was going on, he'd already been pushed down onto the room's humongous bed.

Er...is it just me, or does my situation look like a bad one right now? He belatedly shrank back and gave Guan Shanjin a pitiful smile in hopes of appeasing him.

"Don't be scared, I'll be gentle." Guan Shanjin's eyes curved in a charming smile that could only be described with the classic phrase, *a single smiling glance overflows with every sweetness.* Regardless of whether the phrase was right or not, Wu Xingzi was stunned by the sight. He looked like a smooth, tender, freshly-peeled boiled egg that was ready to be eaten at any time.

It wasn't long before obscene, wet noises began emitting from the large bed.

Guan Shanjin had stripped the older male Beta completely naked by now. This male Beta had very fair skin, and was quite thin as well; you could see the traces of protruding ribs in the warm light of the lamp. His waist, of course, was slender enough that it could almost be fully encircled with a single hand—which accentuated the perky plumpness of his rear. His ass felt amazing to the touch.

While his partner was nude, Guan Shanjin only unzipped his pants and pulled out his thick, long, savage, heavy cock. He half-lowered his eyes to watch as the Beta took the head into his tiny mouth, doing his best to relax his throat as he tried to swallow it deeper.

"Take it slowly, there's no need to rush." As Guan Shanjin reached out to stroke that head of fluffy hair, the Beta cast a pitiful glance up at him, his cheeks bulging with the shape of the glans. His soft black eyes were filled with such gentleness and trust as to make a man lose his mind.

He'd had practice at this by now; he used his small pink tongue to lick the young marshal's glans. He was very meticulous about it, first licking around the circumference of that umbrella-shaped head before following its shape upwards to lick the half-opened urethra. Alpha penises were always thick, but Guan Shanjin's cock was even thicker and longer than most; when Wu Xingzi took it into his mouth, it filled up so much space that his tongue barely had room to move.

The powerful Alpha's pheromones began to spread out into the air. Even the precum flowing from his urethra carried their scent. It was an incredibly erotic, seductive, and refreshing scent, mixed with white sandalwood, orange blossom, citron and cedar, so charming that it didn't seem like it should belong to an Alpha at all.

Pheromone-laden fluids flowed onto the tip of the Beta's tongue. With a flushed face and an intoxicated expression, he reached out to grip that erect penis—as thick now as a child's arm—and lick eagerly at the urethra. The Alpha's breathing grew heavier, and the fingers tangled in Wu Xingzi's soft black hair grew rough, tugging at it to press his face into his crotch.

The egg-sized glans suddenly pushed against the Beta's fragile throat, causing him to gag, and he unconsciously pushed against Guan Shanjin's thigh in an attempt to give himself space to breathe. His mouth was stuffed too full for his tongue to move, and that cock was pressing too roughly against the back of his throat, making it spasm on reflex. The tight squeeze made the Alpha groan in pleasure, and he became even more violent than before, grabbing the Beta's head to use his tiny mouth as a sheath of flesh to thrust rapidly into. The continual mix of precum and saliva made his throat sticky and slippery, and Guan Shanjin's cock felt even thicker and more robust than before.

The thrusts of Guan Shanjin's waist and the increasingly out-of-control movement of his hands sent that savage, impossibly thick shaft deeper and deeper into the Beta's narrow throat until Wu Xingzi started to struggle in response. His gag reflex had been almost completely obliterated by the Alpha's violent thrusting, and the fear of suffocation filled his eyes with tears as that heavy cock plunged far too deep into his throat, but his mind was also blank from the lack of oxygen. He fruitlessly slapped a hand against Guan Shanjin's strong, slender thighs.

However, despite his struggles, his lips still touched those heavy balls, the tip of his nose burying itself in a neatly-trimmed lawn filled with the enticing scent of a man's flesh mixed with pheromones. The Beta spasmed despite himself, saliva spilling from the corners of his fucked-out mouth; his throat contracted violently, making his partner gasp and groan in pleasure. Guan Shanjin wanted nothing more than to cram himself so far into the Beta's warm, supple throat that he made him swallow his balls.

The Alpha didn't wait for him to catch his breath. He stroked that slender neck which had been pushed into the shape of his penis, then began to thrust.

He plunged in and out with the ferocity of a storm, each thrust slamming the head of his cock into Wu Xingzi's throat hard enough to make it bulge. His tongue burned from the friction of rubbing against the blood vessels and veins which covered that meaty shaft, leaving it painful and numb. It made him feel as if his entire body were nothing but a sheath made to accommodate the Alpha's powerful cock. Saliva flowed ceaselessly from the Beta's mouth, and his vision blurred with tears as he tried, with muffled cries, to beg for mercy. But there was no mercy. He was fucked so hard that his eyes started to roll up into his head.

Guan Shanjin's movements were powerful and fast-paced, and his eyes were faintly bloodshot, like a wild beast teetering on the edge of madness. Panting heavily, the hand clasped around that slender neck pressed harder. Between that and the palm against the back of the Beta's head, he managed to thrust himself so deep that even his balls got halfway in, stuffing that little mouth so full that it nearly split open and blood began to ooze from the corners of his lips.

The Beta sobbed brokenly, but he was unable to call out. The intense, suffocating feeling had his consciousness fading, and he fell limp as a dead man. He didn't even have the strength to support himself against Guan Shanjin's thighs.

"Slut..." The Alpha thrust a few more times, then pulled out his massively swollen cock and sprayed an obscene amount of fishy-smelling spunk all over the Beta's dazed face. After making a mess of his face, the liquid slid down the soft lines of his cheeks and nose. Much of it made its way into his mouth, which still hung half-open, red and swollen from being fucked so hard.

Twitching slightly, the Beta unconsciously stuck out his pink tongue, licking away the turbid white liquid around his mouth and swallowing it. This sight made the Alpha's eyes redden, his expression turning savage. His senses sharpened acutely.

The near imperceptibly faint scent of green grass and spring water, mixed with a hint of osmanthus, floated past the Alpha's nose.

It was the Beta's pheromones.

Guan Shanjin pressed his face against the gland on the back of the Beta's neck, sniffing at the faint scent that emitted from it. This belonged to him and him alone; no one else could touch it. This scent could soothe his violent emotions, and it could also bring out his rough side. There was a bite mark on the gland that had already scabbed over; in a few days only a faint scar would remain. It was a pity that Betas couldn't be truly marked, meaning his scent would never be tainted by Guan Shanjin's, but the Alpha didn't care in the slightest.

After panting for a good while with the slack-faced Beta in his arms, Guan Shanjin got up to grab a towel from the bathroom, which he used to wipe the fishy-smelling semen from his face. While he was at it, he also wiped the man down from head to toe, kneading his soft muscles as he went. The Beta was left sprawled on the bed, twisting and moaning from his ministrations, his skin turning an enchanting light pink color.

"You slutty darling..." Guan Shanjin couldn't resist leaning in to kiss him. His tongue licked over every sensitive inch of his mouth, nearly licking the uvula before hooking around the Beta's soft tongue and loudly sucking away. The Beta, who still had yet to recover from the previous round of pleasure, trembled and nearly fainted from this prolonged kiss.

"Still so weak to teasing," Guan Shanjin said with a sigh. Alphas' sexual desires tended to be strong and highly demanding; the more powerful the Alpha, the more urgently they needed sex to relieve the restlessness in their bodies, and generally it was only Omegas who were capable of keeping up with them. But all Guan Shanjin wanted was to fuck the Beta in front of him, and so he had no choice but to endure the boiling-hot feeling of his blood racing through his veins as he patiently trained this unripe body.

After giving the man another deep kiss and caressing him all over, Guan Shanjin reluctantly withdrew. He went over to the spacious dressing room and rummaged in it for a while before coming back to the bed with an exquisitely decorated box in his hands, took the half-asleep Beta into his arms, and coaxed him to open it.

"Th-this is…" There was a puzzled look on the Beta's face when he first opened the box, but when he saws what was inside he became so embarrassed that he wanted nothing more than to hide.

It wasn't that this object was something particularly strange, but it wasn't something you normally came into contact with on an average day, either.

At first glance, it was a perfectly ordinary massager. But on closer inspection, that hideously thick, long shape and the veiny details along its length all gave him a sense of déjà vu. The old man stared blankly at it for a few seconds before realizing with a start: this was an exact imitation of Guan Shanjin's penis!

He carefully reached out a hand; while he had no idea what the toy was made of, it felt smooth and warm to the touch. He wasn't sure whether to call this strange or impressive.

"This will be thrust into your belly in a little while. Come, I'll show you how much fun it is." The Alpha urged the Beta to take the massager, and despite his embarrassment, the old man still obediently picked it up as instructed. Guan Shanjin covered his hands with his own so that they were holding the massager together. "Look, the head area is a little different, isn't it?" he said lovingly.

The head area? The Beta inspected it closely for a moment, then cried out, his face turning nearly blood-red. He tried to toss aside the massager, but Guan Shanjin was holding his hands, leaving him entirely under his control.

"You, you…" The Beta was stuttering too hard to speak. The head part of the massager had a mechanism installed; he wasn't sure how the Alpha had activated it, but the urethra part opened up, becoming much more conspicuous than in a normal cock, and a rod covered in soft fur poked out from inside it. It would be one thing if all it did was poke out, but it was spinning and vibrating too. Just the thought of what this thing would do to his innards filled the Beta with a conflicting mix of fear and anticipation.

"This is a tool specially used to train the womb." Guan Shanjin nibbled at the sensitive earlobe of the man in his arms as he whispered to him softly. "My cock was always able to reach your womb, but you *are* a Beta, after all. Your womb has signs of degeneration, so it can't handle an Alpha's knot. This little toy can help redevelop your womb, so that in the future it will be able to swallow my cock entirely."

Swallow it entirely? The Beta timidly reached out to touch that little stick, only to hastily retract his hand again, turning his head to give his Alpha a pleading look. But all he got in response was a cheerful kiss, followed by a question which made all the fine hairs on his body stand on end: "Why don't we give it a try?"

There was naturally no room for refusal here. Guan Shanjin first retracted that tool for training reproductive cavities, then coated the massager in a great deal of lubricant. No matter how much he teased the Beta's body, if they didn't train his womb, sex would only become more and more difficult for them in the future.

"I-I..." The old man was pushed down onto the bed before he could start to struggle. The slippery, moist massager rubbed a few times against the outside of his hole, making his tight sphincter itch, and he began to moan and gasp as well. That gargantuan glans slowly yet firmly pushed open the fleshy pink folds, pressing into the thin passage beyond.

The feelings of being stretched open and filled up were far too intense. The Beta took a deep breath, trembling all over as he tried to cooperate by relaxing his body, but the massager was so smooth and warm, its every bump so familiar, that it suddenly felt as if he really were being entered by his Alpha. He bit his lips, grunting softly; without realizing it, he'd forgotten all that talk about his womb.

Guan Shanjin had used more than enough lubricant for the task, making the daunting massager's entrance a smooth one. It wasn't long before it was pressing against the tiny entrance of the womb with all the familiarity of a frequent visitor—but a full third of the thick shaft was still left outside.

"Take a deep breath." The Alpha gave his Beta a kiss on the cheek, and as the other man opened his mouth obediently to breathe, he pulled out the massager, then thrust it back in again, hard. The huge, unyielding head pressed roughly against the opening of the Beta's womb, and he cried out at the sharp pain it caused, cold sweat covering his body as he trembled uncontrollably.

It really did hurt far too much!

While Beta males did have a womb, they'd more or less lost their reproductive ability over the long years of evolution. That cavity entrance was like a scar deep within his body, one so extremely sensitive that he couldn't bear for it to be touched.

"It hurts... It hurts so much... Gentle, could you be gentle, please?" The old man sobbed noisily, his nose, eyes, and cheeks all red. He looded a different sort of attractive than usual. The pain had stimulated his pheromones, causing what was originally a nearly unnoticeably faint scent to become more intense; it falteringly surrounded the Alpha. This intensified scent was both an ingratiating move and a show of weakness, and it did indeed elicit feelings of pity.

"How can it get in if I'm gentle?" Guan Shanjin's tone of voice was a tender and loving one, yet the words were terrifying enough to make one's hair stand on end. The Beta started trembling even more violently than before, his face paling, and he shut his eyes tightly as he waited for the next thrust.

"Don't be scared. If you endure the pain this once, there won't be any more discomfort in the future." With that, the Alpha pulled out the massager once more, then shoved it even harder into the womb.

"Aaah—!" The Beta screamed. The pain this time was worse than before. It was like a wound being torn open. Cold sweat poured so uncontrollably from his body that it was as if he'd just been pulled out of the water. The Alpha could barely hold onto him.

"It hurts! Please... Please... Weeehhh..."

Frowning, Guan Shanjin tightened his grip around his tearfully hiccupping partner, his resolution beginning to waver. He didn't need a child, but he wanted to be more closely connected with his Beta; for an Alpha, sex where he couldn't expand his knot wasn't nearly enough to fully vent his restlessness. While he could endure it for a short time, the longer this went on, the more likely it became that he might lose control of his rationality and end up hurting the man in his arms.

And so he lowered his head to carefully lick the tears from the old man's face. His tongue passed over the tear-cooled cheeks, the pointed corners of his eyes, the thin yet downy lashes, before finally kissing those tightly-shut eyes. His lips could feel the uneasy rolling of eyeballs beneath those lids, and his heart softened at how cute it was.

"You have to endure it this once." He moved towards the Beta's trembling, cold lips, kissing him deeply. The tip of his tongue hooked around the old man's bashful one, and he sucked at it noisily.

The painful twitching quickly calmed down, and that inexperienced body softened as Wu Xingzi became absorbed in the kiss.

Taking care with his timing, the Alpha repeatedly pressed the massager against the Beta's womb, kissing him whenever he whimpered. The kisses made him feel a mix of both pleasure and pain; his mind grew blank, and he melted like warm butter.

Under the continuous assault, the sharp, stinging pain at the opening of his womb soon became a numbness mixed with just a hint of pain. His inner passage, which normally struggled to get wet, unexpectedly began to secrete pheromone-scented slick, mixing wetly with the melted lubricant to flow out in a slippery stream. The massager made a loud squelching noise as it thrust in and out; the fluid even dripped onto the sheets and wetting a large portion of the bed.

"You dirty boy, you're totally soaked down there," the Alpha said with a satisfied smile.

He moved his wrist slightly, pressing the massager against the womb's entrance. The head touched right against the crack of the cavity's opening, just like a kiss; it was somewhat red and swollen after being stabbed at again and again, but it had also loosened quite a bit. It was no longer just a vestigial, scar-like thing.

"I, I..." The Beta's gaze was blurry; he hugged the Alpha's neck tight, seemingly wanting to say something, but what ultimately came out of his mouth was only a long moan as his blushing body trembled violently...

The Alpha turned on the vibration, and the huge head began rubbing and swaying right against that swollen entrance. Pain and pleasure exploded simultaneously in the Beta's mind; his mouth fell open, eyes nearly rolling back into his head, his pale, thin legs kicking as if he were convulsing.

Slick flowed out in waves under the massager's high-speed vibration, making his hole wet and slippery; even his buttocks grew sticky-wet from the fluids, and felt amazing to touch. Guan Shanjin didn't hesitate to give them a few good pinches. Wu Xingzi cried aloud, twisting his ass; it was hard to tell if he was trying to get away or asking for more. The snowy white flesh of his rear was covered in red marks.

"I'm going to start the next step, darling. Can you feel that little place in your belly opening up?" Guan Shanjin pecked the Beta's plump lips, gazing deeply into eyes so wet they appeared to be melting. "I'm going to take that little toy you saw earlier and poke it inside. Remember to take deep breaths."

"Mnn..." The Beta had been kissed so hard he couldn't respond. All he could do was shoot his Alpha an accusatory glare, one so soft it looked more like a coquettish pout. The Alpha was so absolutely enamored with this little look that he hugged him tighter, leaned his head against the gland on the man's neck, and started gnawing at the spot again and again. Whenever his hot tongue swept over the sensitive patch of skin, the body in his arms would tremble; how could one man be this cute?

The slit at the opening of the womb had loosened up, revealing a small opening just slightly larger than the womb massaging tool which protruded from the head of the toy. Though the fuzzy tip of this object was somewhat thick, it didn't meet much resistance when pushed in along with all that slick, and managed to enter completely after only a few thrusts. The Beta, already trembling and moaning as if he were sobbing from the pleasure of his gland getting licked and bitten, didn't show any sign of pain.

His womb had already completed the initial stage of development; all that was needed now was some proper stimulation, and soon enough he would be able to take the Alpha's entire length, allowing them to finally experience a knotted orgasm.

It was only when the womb massager began to spin that the Beta realized how naive he'd been.

The fine, fluffy hairs may not have looked like much, but once they were inside his sensitive womb, the pleasure wrought by those hairs tickling the soft, thick walls of flesh was infinitely magnified. It felt as if countless tentacles were in there rubbing and teasing against every last inch of muscle they could reach. The Beta cried out incessantly, entirely unable to resist the intense pleasure spreading out from his belly. He twisted around so much that the Alpha could barely hold onto him; he was as dripping wet as a big white fish.

"Aaahh—" The Beta suddenly let out a scream. His womb was burning from the stroking, an indescribable sort of heat gushing out like a fountain. He buried his fingers in the coiled muscle of the Alpha's shoulders, scratching bloody marks into his skin. His slender waist rose high into the air, trembling uncontrollably. His legs were tensed and quivering. Even his pale pink toes were curling from overstimulation.

The next instant, a gout of juices gushed from the slit of his womb, pouring out even around the thick massager stuffed into it, and soaking the Alpha's hands and belly.

Guan Shanjin's gaze grew even darker. He could barely suppress the desire filling his body; he pursed his beautifully shaped lips with the effort of enduring it, his eyes turning bloodshot. Sweat beaded on his forehead and neck, carrying the cloying scent of pheromones. Each drop that fell onto the Beta's body was like a bullet shattering his sense of self, reducing him to nothing but the Alpha's bitch. He continuously climaxed in the all-encompassing cloud of pheromones, slick gushing out endlessly.

His womb's conditioning was now complete. The Alpha retracted the massaging tool with trembling fingertips, then slowly pulled the massager out from that spasming hole, bringing a piece of tender flesh out with it. This flesh was such a soft and brilliant red that he couldn't stop himself from lowering his head for a lick. The Beta screamed and another wave of juices gushed out, pouring into Guan Shanjin's mouth. The mixed scents of grass and osmanthus were so sweet as to make a man's blood boil. The Alpha's partner had finally worn down what little remained of his rationality.

Once the Alpha's long, thick, scalding hot length replaced the massager inside the Beta's sodden little hole, the two men gasped in tandem, both lost in desire. The old man in particular was still trapped in wave after wave of climaxes thanks to his partner's pheromones; he continuously twisted his body, and Guan Shanjin's cock slipped out several times from his endlessly spasming chrysanthemum.

Before this it had never been wet enough, but now it was far *too* wet. Pheromone-laced juices spurted out wildly from the narrow, tightly squeezing tunnel of flesh. Again and again, the Alpha only managed to get the head of his cock in before it slipped out, and the mounting frustration made his feelings grow ever more violent; he angrily roared, gripping the Beta's writhing waist hard enough to leave noticeable fingerprints on his snow-white skin. The Beta was truly unable to break free. His plump behind swayed from side to side, continuously pushing upwards in pleasure.

Guan Shanjin now used his long and powerful legs to hold down his partner's wildly kicking ones, finally locking the person beneath him like a sacrifice tied to the altar. Wu Xingzi tilted his head pitifully to reveal the numerous bite marks overlapping over the bleeding gland on the side of his neck, giving himself up to be dealt with as his handler desired.

This was an astonishing sort of beauty, a fragility which elicited the desire to ruthlessly abuse; that extremely ordinary face was beyond ugly with tearstains and sweat, yet the Alpha couldn't help but kiss him over and over again.

That fearsome cock finally entered the Beta's body in its entirety. The massager, with its simulated blood vessels and protruding veins, was nothing compared to the heft and heat of the real thing; the old man opened his mouth as if to scream, but all he let out was a hoarse and breathless gasp as he felt the Alpha's girth expand its territory within him. It rubbed hard against every inch of sensitive flesh, emitting obscene noises as it mixed together with the wet slick.

A stinging wave of numbness shot straight to the Beta's brain, and he lifted hazy eyes to murmur pleadingly, "I can't...my stomach is so sore..." But that cock, made thicker and longer from soaking in his juices, gave a violent twitch at the sound of his moan and immediately expanded another size. The pulsing of the veins which covered it caused the Beta to burst into tears with a shriek. "Too much! A-Jin! It's too much!"

"Darling, how could it be too much?" The Alpha caught the tip of his tongue and gave it a suck, coaxing him with the most tender affection. "I haven't gone all the way in yet. Here, touch your little belly, give it a feel."

Tremblingly placing his hand on his belly as directed, it felt as if he could make out the shape of the Alpha inside him; just like Guan Shanjin had said, it really didn't seem to be all that deep yet...

The two exchanged passionate kisses, their lips and tongues making smacking noises as they entwined together. The Beta's whole body softened with pleasure under the kissing, and the spasms from his climaxes calmed by quite a bit too, finally freeing the penis inside him from the death grip which had prevented it from pushing in any deeper.

Seeing his chance, the Alpha lifted the Beta's buttocks up high, then fucked into him with all his weight behind him, brushing past the prostate as he thrust all the way into the still-open entrance of the womb in one swift movement.

"Aaahh—!" Although he'd just gone through training, getting so vertically penetrated down to a place no man had touched before was still far too stimulating for him. The Beta tried to push Guan Shanjin away, but naturally failed to so much as shake him.

The Alpha's penis was much harder and hotter than any toy; in an instant it had poked its head halfway into the womb, which help-lessly wrapped its soft inner walls around it in an attempt to show goodwill. However, Guan Shanjin repaid this attempt by roughly rubbing and pushing it open, each thrust slamming against soft and sensitive flesh. The twitching of Wu Xingzi's womb was helpless to stop that Alpha cock from fucking deeper and deeper inside.

"You're totally soaked, darling." The Alpha felt so good in this moment that his breathing was erratic, his scalp felt numb, and white light flashed before his eyes. He'd never had such thorough, delightful sex before, and he wanted more than anything to be eternally connected to the trembling Beta beneath him, never to separate again.

"Aaahh—I'm going to diiiee—slow down please, I'm begging you! Urk—" The Beta was hiccupping with tears. He hadn't realized that his attempts to push his partner away had already changed to invitation. The pleasure of being completely dominated was so joyous it was as if he and the Alpha were no longer distinguishable from one another; no one was capable of resisting the pleasure of being drawn in by their partner's pheromones.

"You're not going to die. I'm going to knot you and pump all of my cum into your womb. I'm going to make sure you'll be dripping with it wherever you walk tomorrow, so everyone around will know that you're mine, and I belong only to you!"

Following this declaration, the Alpha fucked him faster and faster, ruthlessly penetrating the Beta's womb. The glans repeatedly slammed against its soft inner walls, as if he was about to completely run him through with his cock.

The Beta by now had already fallen into another wave of endless climaxes. His entire body was flushed pink, his pale and slender legs twitching and kicking wildly on Guan Shanjin's shoulders. He himself had no idea what he was moaning; all he knew was that he had to do what he could to keep up with the Alpha's speed, and he tried desperately to keep his body relaxed as he waited for that final knotted climax and the semen that would soon fill him...

The two men's gasping breaths intertwined with each other, their sweat mingling; their pheromones intimately blended together until there was no distinction between the two. The smell of desire was so powerful that it spilled out of the room, and the two guards who had been standing outside were forced to retreat from the door. They had to go over six hundred feet away to escape the cloying scent. By the time they got that far, their faces were both flushed, they were panting slightly, and their cocks were half-hard, tenting their pants.

Meanwhile, the Alpha penetrated the Beta with such force it was as if he were going to fuck him to death on the bed. The umbrella-shaped head of his cock was fastened so tightly to the womb's little entrance that it was difficult to pull back out, so he simply continued to fuck into it with a mix of deep and shallow thrusts; several waves of orgasmic juices spilled onto the glans as the two of them entangled even more closely in their joy, refusing to separate any inch of their skin which could possibly press together as they rubbed their bodies against each other.

The Beta, fucked nearly to the point of unconsciousness, had used up what little remained of his strength. His delicate penis trembled and shot out a thin, watery stream of semen, leaving a fishy-smelling mess on both his stomach and the Alpha's lower abdomen and adding new stains to the already ruined sheets.

His womb spasmed as well, clamping down on the Alpha's cock. Guan Shanjin exhaled harshly once, twice, before finally giving a few deep, heavy thrusts, hard enough to make that soft flesh lose its elasticity and gently suck at his girth instead. His knot swelled with blood, and he shot his load deep into the Beta's newly developed womb.

The savage force with which it pumped into him made the Beta's eyes roll back into his head, his body endlessly convulsing. His stomach was full with hot liquid, but the knot was still pressing against his prostate as well. The two-fold pleasure made the old man's vision fill with bursts of colorful light, before finally turning to pitch-black as he fainted clean away.

The Alpha flopped down in contentment, having finally filled his partner with cum. It would still be a while before his knot retracted. For now, he could look forward to the Beta carrying their child in his stomach—it was fine if it didn't happen, though, as he could just come a few more times until it did. Once the Beta was carrying the child they'd been hoping for all this time, he'd go get a vasectomy, and then he'd no longer have to worry about sharing his partner's attention with any more children than that.

As soon as he officially took the position of marshal, he'd go to the Imperial Academy of Sciences to withdraw his partner application.

That'd piss off all those old coots, and that inveterate villain of an emperor, too!

If you were to ask what was currently the hottest gossip in the empire, it would probably be about the man who'd taken office a few days ago as the youngest marshal in history—the next head of the Guan family, the most powerful Alpha in the empire, Guan Shanjin. To be more specific, it was about Guan Shanjin's marriage.

It was common knowledge that the Guan family was the most independent family in the empire. They showed absolute loyalty to the emperor, never getting involved in any factional struggles of succession. The Third Legion had not once changed hands in a hundred years. It had been steady as a rock since the day it was established, and had earned outstanding military achievements as well, making it the most valiant and powerful army in the empire.

There was no doubt that an Alpha capable of leading this army was going to be extremely powerful. To top it off, Guan Shanjin was the perfect culmination of his family bloodline, and the highest level of Alpha as well. As a result, he'd been unable to find a partner with a high compatibility score ever since first reaching sexual maturity. This worried the emperor tremendously—Guan Shanjin had already reached his prime, after all, and it would be a great pity if he couldn't take advantage of the ideal time to continue his bloodline.

But to everyone's surprise, on the second day after Guan Shanjin took up the position of marshal and gained full control of the Third Legion, he withdrew his partner application from the National Academy of Sciences and publicly announced that he'd married a male Beta.

It was unthinkable that the highest level Alpha would not establish a mating mark with an Omega and choose to instead marry a

Beta male with extremely poor fertility. Even if they'd been publicly announced as a 100 percent pheromone match, no one had high hopes for this pair.

Marshal Guan Shanjin would regret this sooner or later. That ugly old newlywed partner—that's right, the marshal's Beta mate was actually a whole eleven years older than him—would soon become an abandoned wife.

Those families with outstanding Omega boys or girls were all competing with each other in secret, while those who coveted the Guan family's power were raring to use the Beta's infertility as an opportunity, a weak point they could attack in order to shake the Guan family's influence.

Everyone was busily planning away...only for those plans to fall apart a month later when Guan Shanjin announced on the interstellar web that his Beta partner was pregnant.

The highest level Alpha's fertility was truly amazing, if he could even get an old clam to produce pearls.

And now, this old clam of a Beta was currently weeping pitifully as he sat astride his husband's legs. He was already three months pregnant, and his stomach was noticeably bulging. The bulge looked a little *too* big in comparison to his otherwise slim figure, but, after all, the weight of two babies was truly far from small.

His pants had been tugged down to hang off his right ankle, baring his pale, slender legs; his underwear, meanwhile, had been torn apart, leaving only the elastic band around his waist. From the big hole ripped in the crotch, his fair-skinned, tender cock pointed straight up at his belly, its head dripping wetly. Farther down, you could vaguely see his bright red perineum, swollen from the previous night's play, and with two or three bite marks still on it. Moving our view to the back, his round, perky buttocks were red and swollen with a good many overlapping handprints, as well as fingerprints which were starting to bruise. The flirtatious hole between his buttocks winked as he twisted his body impatiently, looking like an insatiable little mouth begging to be fed.

That actually wasn't far from the truth: He was in fact currently begging his husband to fuck him, but between how self-conscious he was and the fact they were in the marshal's office, where could he find the courage to beg for sex out loud? All he could do was pitifully rub his dripping hole against Guan Shanjin's crotch, soaking the fabric in the process and leaving many even darker marks on his already dark-colored imperial military uniform pants.

"Xiao-Jin, Xiao-Jin..." He bonelessly hugged the man's neck, pressing against his ear as he begged, "Touch me, touch me, pretty please?"

The pregnancy had made the old Beta's sex drive exponentially stronger. Whether it was the effect of hormones or pheromones, his ass had been constantly wet for the last two weeks, with so much lasciviously sweet-smelling slick dripping out from his chrysanthemum that a mere few hours was enough for it to stream down his pant legs and make it look like he'd pissed himself.

He hadn't noticed at all on the first day, and made a big fool of himself when he got up after drinking tea with his mother-in-law in the living room. Fortunately she was a gentle person with previous experience, and she comforted her son-in-law after making a call to summon home her son; the couple then went to their room, shut the door, and had a good, long, satisfying fuck. During this, Guan Shanjin even penetrated the womb, causing the Beta to convulse all over for fear that he'd lose the children.

But Guan Shanjin's children were clearly not your ordinary fragile little lives: They staunchly endured their father's brutal fucking without even any blood in the aftermath.

From that day on, the Beta's sex drive only kept on increasing, until he was finally able to keep up with his Alpha's daily needs and was no longer so easily fucked unconscious.

Today, he'd come to deliver lunch for his husband. The Third Legion had all three of the secondary sexes, and their balanced ratio was a benchmark for the rest of the empire. There were even Omega squad leaders, and none of the Alphas in those squads could be seen disobeying orders; after all, this was a world where people spoke with strength, and if an Alpha couldn't beat an Omega, how could they have the face to continue exposing their own shortcomings?

The old Beta was, therefore, able to easily walk around the Third Legion without the worry of any Alphas deliberately emitting pheromones to as a display of dominance. It also meant that when he pushed open the door to the marshal's office and found himself confronting the smell of an Alpha in rut, all the old Beta could do was let his knees buckle as his needy hole squirted out juices.

Guan Shanjin had started showing signs of rut two days ago. But he'd been busy with the war against the Insectoids recently, and his old enemies in the Alliance had been making frequent moves in secret; over the course of all the war councils he'd been required to participate in, he'd long forgotten about taking inhibitors to delay his rut.

Although his slutty Beta's pregnancy had finally made him capable of handling his daily sexual needs, the needs of an Alpha in rut were far from the usual; to put it simply, at a time like this they could even fuck a pregnant Omega to the point of miscarriage. Guan Shanjin certainly wouldn't dare to relax his vigilance on this front. It was true, yes, that no matter how much he overdid it in the bedroom lately, penetrating the Beta's womb who knows how many times, his children had been strong enough that there hadn't even been any blood. But that didn't mean they could make it through his rut just as easily.

Unfortunately, when the Beta showed up in his office, all his reason went to the dogs as he stared at him with a red-eyed gaze. His Beta's belly had an obvious bulge, and his ass had grown a size larger from the pregnancy hormones; it swayed back and forth as he walked, making it hard to resist ripping his pants off and mounting him then and there.

He collapsed as soon as he smelled the scent of rut, his fragrant sexual juices spilling all over the floor. His eyes narrowed as he gazed at his Alpha with reddened face and panting breath.

Shit! This old Beta is beyond slutty!

He motioned to him with a hand, but the Beta couldn't even stand. He had to crawl slowly towards him on all fours, leaving a wet trail behind him. When mixed together with Guan Shanjin's scent, it was comparable to a powerful aphrodisiac.

"Xiao-Jin..." The Beta crawled up to his husband's legs and rubbed his cheek ingratiatingly against those sturdy thighs, his tongue even poking out slightly from his mouth.

"Sit up here." It was said an Alpha in rut lacked any humanity. This didn't just encompass their extraordinary sexual ability, though; it also referred to their tendency to display absolute dominance, with that part of them once controlled by their faculties of reason fully released. Of course, Guan Shanjin was already relatively rough in the bedroom to begin with, but now...

The Beta whined as he clung to his legs in an attempt to pull himself up, but the smell of the Alpha's rut was devastatingly strong. That on top of his pregnancy was making his limbs so weak that he couldn't get up no matter how hard he tried. In the end it was the Alpha who couldn't wait any longer. He pulled him up to press him down on his thighs in one swift motion, tugging his pants off with such force that he tore his underwear.

"Do you want your husband to fuck you?" Guan Shanjin asked as he sucked on the earlobe of the marshal's wife. The Beta had started wriggling the moment he sat on his legs, rubbing that obscene chrysanthemum insistently against the crotch of his pants. If it hadn't been for the high quality of his military uniform, his huge dick might have torn right through the fabric with how hard it was.

"Xiao-Jin...Xiao-Jin..." The old Beta was dying of thirst. It was as if the mouth of a spring were located inside his ass, endlessly gurgling out more fluid; he felt simultaneously itchy and empty, eager to be penetrated by that fat cock as soon as possible.

"What did your husband teach you?" The Alpha smilingly kissed his cheek, licked down it to his slender neck, then tore open the Beta's shirt so that he could pinch his nipples, which had become increasingly swollen in recent days. These two little things had once been a pale, soft color, but lately they'd become dark crimson, as debauched as fully ripe fruits, and felt soft and elastic in his mouth. Guan Shanjin was absolutely fascinated with them.

The Beta's nipples had become much more sensitive since he'd gotten pregnant, too, and he cried out ceaselessly, pushing out his chest. "Husband, husband," he begged in a high-pitched voice, "give your wife's nipples a suck..."

"You old slut," Guan Shanjin teased him with a smile. His desire for dominance satisfied, he took one of the Beta's nipples into his mouth and started sucking.

"Aaah, it hurts, be a little gentler." Though the Beta was begging for mercy, he kept arching his chest as high as he could to make it easier for the Alpha to suck on it.

That nipple quickly became more swollen than before. Even the areola turned red from his ministrations, looking like a cherry shivering upon the snow-white expanse of his slender chest. The Alpha wasn't just sucking, either; he pushed and poked at the nipple, rolling it around on the tip of his tongue, and waiting until the Beta couldn't take any more before sucking hard again.

The Alpha wasn't sure if it was due to the pregnancy or simply a product of his imagination, but he could swear the taste of milk was trickling out from the tiny openings in those nipples. He'd asked both his mother and the doctor before though, and was told that while Betas were capable of giving milk, it wouldn't happen until at least the second trimester of pregnancy. They were only at the three-month mark, so it was highly unlikely to be happening now.

"H...Husband, suck the other side..." This suckling had left the Beta beyond comfortable, but unfortunately only one of his nipples was being cared for, leaving the other one feeling unusually empty.

His wriggling waist rubbed against the huge cock that was straining so hard it was about to break through his husband's pants. He hugged Guan Shanjin's head against his chest as he kept arching it forward and pleading.

The Alpha readily switched to sucking on the other nipple, and soon enough both sides were enlarged and swollen from his teasing, glistening lewdly with moisture. The Beta's ass was so soaking wet it was ready to be fucked into at Guan Shanjin's leisure; by now a small puddle of slick had collected on the ground.

"Husband, fuck me...fuck me..." The Beta unzipped his Alpha's pants with shaking fingers, and that thick, scalding hot cock hit against his perineum with an audible slap. He let out a sharp moan and eagerly tried to stuff the cock into his hole; at this angle, however, all he could manage was making it brush past his entrance.

The old Beta cried with frustration. "Husband, hurry and enter me," he begged tearfully, softly.

The Alpha gripped his waist with one hand and gripped his own huge rod with the other, thrusting it in with one quick, loud pop which hit straight to the womb entrance at the end. The Beta threw back his head in a scream at this sudden assault, his narrow waist spasming as semen shot out from his little cock at the front.

"Aaahh it feels so good! Husband, move a little..." Finally receiving the dicking he'd so desired, the Beta's waist twisted back and forth as his slutty hole kept hungrily stroking that massive cock, bringing all the most sensitive parts of his inner passage to meet it as it thrust in and out of him. Even though he'd come just moments ago, his insides still sucked tightly around the fat cock inside him; the Beta's eyes were rolling back into his head, yet he was still infinitely eager for more.

There was no way the Alpha could endure such a slutty look, especially not in the middle of his rut. He grabbed the Beta's waist without another thought and began to viciously fuck his ass. The marshal's wife trembled and cried at the ferocity of it, his entire body spasming as he dug his fingers into his husband's shoulders. His slender white thighs tensed where they hung limply on either side of his thighs; even those ten cute little toes curled.

Their movements dragged more and more slick from his hole, gushing like a never-ending fountain and making a huge mess beneath them. The Beta arched his neck and moaned intermittently with the force of his Alpha's full-force fucking; if this office hadn't had exceptional soundproofing, he likely wouldn't have had the face to ever deliver meals to his husband again.

The Alpha's goose egg-sized glans hit several times against the outside of the womb, making his Beta cry out in a mix of pain and pleasure. It was only in this moment that he regained some semblance of sanity, pushing off from his husband's shoulders in an attempt to gain some distance. A rutting Alpha was incomparable to anything he usually dealt with; he genuinely feared Guan Shanjin would fuck right into his womb and cause a miscarriage.

After some back and forth, the Alpha started to feel that his dominance was being challenged. A tyrannical urge swelled up within him as he made up his mind to penetrate the womb and give it a good, thorough fucking, not leaving a single inch of tender flesh unblemished. That place belonged to him, after all—to think these two little creatures who'd only just grown full human forms would have the audacity to challenge his ownership of it!

The Beta began struggling in terror as he realized the Alpha's intentions, but it was no use: An Alpha in rut had higher stats in every respect than in his normal state. He gripped the Beta's slender waist with one hand and started to thrust in hard, his swollen balls slapping against his wife's ass, and pressed him down hard in concert with his thrusts.

"Don't do this, Xiao-Jin—*aaah!*" The Beta suddenly tensed, his eyes rolling back and tongue lolling out of his head. He almost forgot to breathe. His entire body twitched and spasmed uncontrollably...

The Alpha had entered his womb.

That tight womb sucked the Alpha's length comfortably, and he contentedly held the Beta's waist fast as he thrust in again, wanting nothing more than to stuff even his balls inside.

The Beta failed to recover even after convulsing for a while, and he let out a wail of despair as he covered his stomach with his hands. He was being fucked so hard by the sturdy man beneath him that he was on the verge of collapse, swaying back and forth so much that he was almost about to fall from Guan Shanjin's thighs; the only thing preventing his fall was the thick cock that currently penetrated him so deeply that he felt like he was being skewered like meat on a stick.

Although this position let him sink in deeply, the Alpha couldn't move freely like this. After tossing his slutty Beta up and down with a few hundred more thrusts, he swept everything off the table with one hand before—not bothering to pull out his dick—he set the other man down on the wide table and continued to fuck him relentlessly.

In the moment he adjusted their positions, Guan Shanjin's cock had slid out until all that remained was its enormous head. This made the Beta think he was going to pull out entirely, and despite his crying, his ass wrapped itself around him, the swollen hole biting that umbrella-shaped tip like a greedy little mouth, its soft, tender flesh sucking tirelessly at it. The Alpha's eyes reddened at his partner's lascivious reactions; if it weren't for the fact he still remembered that the Beta was physically weak, and had two children in his belly as well, he'd certainly have fucked him to death—literally.

Taking a deep breath, Guan Shanjin grit his teeth before switching to viciously biting his lover's lips instead, his long, thick tongue plunging into that warm mouth as he kissed Wu Xingzi until he was drooling. He only pulled back a bit when the Beta was near to fainting from lack of oxygen, and he narrowed his eyes happily as he licked away the silver thread of saliva which connected them.

The Beta had only just managed to catch his breath when Guan Shanjin grabbed his waist and thrust his huge cock once again into the bottom of the womb in one smooth movement.

"Aaahh—" The Beta cried out tearfully. With his hand on his stomach, he was no longer able to discern whether what he was feeling was the Alpha's cock or his own pregnant belly. All he knew was that, in tandem with the loud slapping noises of the Alpha's fucking, it would be swollen one moment and even more swollen the next, that goose egg-sized glans seeming to poke against his palm through the skin of his stomach.

"Xiao-Jin...be gentle... The babies can't take it..."

All you could say was that the Beta's brain had broken from being fucked so hard. Veins popped out on that thick, long cock, which had grown even more frighteningly thick and long from soaking in his slutty juices. It rubbed and pulled against the tender flesh of his inner passage, each thrust moving with maximum force, the head pulling out to his entrance before slamming back in again. The womb had lost the ability to close itself, its tiny mouth sucking ingratiatingly as waves of pleasure pushed the old Beta repeatedly over the threshold. His consciousness had become as thick and sticky as a pot of boiling congee and he was him incapable of thinking anything at all; all he managed was to blurt out the word "babies."

This time he'd absolutely crossed the Alpha's bottom line.

"You're still thinking of the babies?" The Alpha suddenly stopped moving, his cock pressed deep into the lower part of the womb. It was fortunate that the two little guys were especially tenacious— even after going through a full round of fucking, they continued to huddle agreeably in a corner of the womb, without a hint of blood. Their Alpha father, however, was right in the middle of his rut, and lacked any humanity at all. "You're actually resisting me for these two microbes? Hm? How about I fuck you into a miscarriage?"

In this moment his voice was as full of passion as a siren's song, yet the words he spoke made the Beta, who still had yet to recover from his climax, begin to tremble in fear.

"Xiao, Xiao-Jin... Nnaaah!" Before he could stop him, the man grabbed him and started fucking again. This time he really was fucking into him with everything he had, the head of his cock slamming past Wu Xingzi's prostate every time without fail, then stabbing hard against the entrance of his womb before pushing hard against its bottom and ravaging away. It only took a few dozen thrusts before the Beta's whole body was twitching all over, his face awash with tears, mouth open as he threw back his pale and slender neck. He could barely even breathe.

After more than ten minutes of this back and forth, the Beta's passage had practically lost the ability to even wriggle, reducing it to little more than a fleshy condom to be played with at Guan Shanjin's leisure. No matter how the Alpha fucked him, salty-sweet slick would gush out with each outward movement; the cocklet at his front had been soft for some time, too spent to ejaculate anymore, and the pitiful opening of its urethra made the tender pink flesh swell out slightly as it rubbed against the Alpha's hard-packed abs.

After another few dozen minutes of fucking, the Beta's face was flushed a bright red, his whole body seeming to radiate the decadently broken beauty of a person who'd been fucked to absolute ruin. His eyes were completely unfocused as he stared blankly at Guan Shanjin's lust-shrouded, ever more handsome face. Occasionally, he would twitch. The hand which had been covering his belly had at some point fallen limply to the table, no longer able to lift so much as a single finger.

The Alpha was panting heavily, his pheromones growing increasingly stronger to the point that the detector in the hallway started letting out an ear-piercing buzz; the whole floor had been cleared and sealed off half an hour ago, for fear that the overly dense pheromones might trigger the heat or rut of other Alphas and Omegas in the area.

"Xiao-Jin...Xiao-Jin..." The Beta called out to his Alpha in a murmur. His body tensed, stiffening for a moment before suddenly starting to convulse. But with Guan Shanjin keeping him pressed tight beneath him, there wasn't a sliver of a chance of escape.

The Beta's mouth was open wide, the tip of his tongue sticking out, only for the Alpha to catch it between his teeth and drag it into his own mouth to nibble and suck on. Meanwhile, the huge cock below was buried deep within his womb, filling it with wave after wave of semen, while its knot expanded to catch right against where his prostate was. The pressure of it drew him to another climax.

The multiple orgasms layered atop each other completely surpassed the Beta's limits of endurance; he couldn't even pass out due to the overstimulation. Instead, he found he could feel more clearly than ever how the Alpha possessed him, fucking even each individual cell within his body.

By the time the Alpha was finished coming, the Beta's stomach had swollen so much he looked six months pregnant; he felt like he could hear the semen sloshing in his belly with every breath he took.

With the first stage of rut having passed more or less safely, Guan Shanjin regained some semblance of lucidity. Once the knot deflated, he carefully pulled out his cock. A mixture of semen and slick flowed out, dripping into a little puddle on the floor. There was still no sign of any blood; the children had staunchly weathered the whole ordeal.

Guan Shanjin couldn't help but chuckle as he took his partner's hand to rub that swollen belly together. "It seems our children aren't so simple..."

"Mn..." The Beta didn't understand a word he'd said, his consciousness having yet to return.

The Alpha found himself filled with feelings of both regret and love as he looked down at the old Beta he'd nearly broken. He quickly injected himself with an inhibitor during this space before the second wave of rut could begin. While it wouldn't be as effective as if he'd used it before his rut, it would at least go some way to suppressing his violent Alpha urges.

He really ought to find the time to go get that vasectomy one of these days—otherwise the Beta might accidentally get pregnant again, and he couldn't bear the thought of that.

Leaning down to kiss the Beta's closed eyelids, he kissed a line from the soft curve of his face down to his belly, leaving scattered red marks the whole way.

"You two need to come out quickly and stop torturing your dad," he complained to Wu Xingzi's belly. The two children, who'd been called microbes just moments ago, had no choice but to swallow the hurt.

REPAYING FAVORS IS PLEDGING ONESELF IN MARRIAGE (BEASTMAN AU)

HOW HAD THINGS turned out this way? For the life of him, Wu Xingzi still couldn't figure it out.

He'd been knocked down onto the bed by a huge white tiger. There was no way the narrow bed could handle a full-grown tiger's weight when it was already teetering on the verge of collapse to begin with. The creaking sound made him shake with terror for fear that it would fall apart beneath him. The white tiger would definitely be fine, but he himself probably wouldn't be; never mind the splinters, if a tiger landed on him in the same way a wild goose might fall on the sand, he wasn't certain he'd make it out alive.

But...how had all of this happened?

The story began five days ago, when Wu Xingzi had gone to the mountain to pick wild vegetables, only to find a man in the ravine. This man was dressed all in blood-stained white, with a full head of white hair; even his skin was as pale as white jade. Even in these dire straits, his blood-spattered face was still so breathtakingly beautiful that Wu Xingzi found himself stunned by the sight.

And so, following the worldview that one should save the dying and heal the wounded—and also out of a feeling of appreciative admiration for beauty—Wu Xingzi went to great pains to carry the man home on his back, even boiling some water to wash the dirt off his body for him.

Just as he'd thought, the man looked even more attractive once he was cleaned up.

In the days following, Wu Xingzi took diligent care of the stranger. He invited a doctor to come treat him, but even the doctor couldn't explain why this man wouldn't wake up from his slumber. Not that Wu Xingzi was in any sort of hurry, though; as long as the man was still alive, he'd just keep taking care of him and feeding him medicine, and one of these days he might just wake up...

But this unknown future turned out to be far beyond what anyone would normally expect...

The white tiger licked Wu Xingzi with its broad, rough tongue, and the scratching of it made his whole body tingle. He'd be crying right now if he'd been able to produce any tears.

Was the tiger getting a taste of its prey before it ate him?

Never in his wildest dreams could he ever have imagined that the man he'd brought home would turn out to be a white tiger spirit!

After licking his face, the tiger moved on to his thin neck. It had already torn off all of Wu Xingzi's clothes when it first pounced on him, so he was completely naked; though the tiger's fur looked smooth and soft, it felt somewhat rough when it brushed against his skin. It tickled him all over, but he was too frightened to struggle or squirm in any way.

Once it was done licking his neck, the big tiger narrowed its eyes and snorted twice in what appeared to be an extremely meaningful way, finally scaring Wu Xingzi enough that he really did begin to cry.

"G-Great Immortal Tiger... W-would it be okay to ask, if you really plan to eat my insignificant self, could you please make it a quick death? Maybe as thanks for my taking care of you the past five days?"

The white tiger responded with a low growl, and Wu Xingzi saw what appeared to be a look of displeasure on its (also incredibly attractive) tiger face.

Looks like that's a no, then... Wu Xingzi consoled himself with the thought that all events had their reasons, telling himself he just needed to endure until it was over.

And so he closed his eyes, trembling like a quail, as he quietly waited for the white tiger to bring its jaws down upon him.

Rather than the sharp teeth he'd been expecting, however, what came down upon him was that broad, thick, rough tiger tongue. It licked its way inch by inch from Wu Xingzi's slender shoulders down to his thin chest, where it brushed over a dainty little nipple.

"Ooh!" Wu Xingzi shuddered at the somewhat painful tingling sensation, but that pain also carried with it an unfamiliar feeling which made his body go limp, and he couldn't help moaning aloud.

The white tiger stopped its licking as if triggered by a fuse, but before Wu Xingzi could breathe a sigh of relief, its tongue came back down again to lick incessantly at his nipple.

"Wait, s-stop..." Wu Xingzi's entire body turned boneless under its ministrations. He felt as if there were a fire burning inside him, and he cried out as he tried to push the tiger's head away, only for the big brute to bare its sharp white fangs right at him. A terrified Wu Xingzi retracted his hands and switched to pitifully pleading. "Great Immortal Tiger...Great Immortal Tiger, could you stop licking, please? I'm begging you..."

He'd never realized his nipples were such a dangerous area. It wasn't long before they were red and swollen from being licked by the tiger's rough tongue; even worse, they tickled so much that he couldn't stop trembling, and his breathing began to turn heavy.

The tiger's tongue was extremely dexterous, sometimes licking straight across with its flat surface, sometimes using the tongue tip to press an erect nipple into the flesh of his chest, sometimes brushing over the narrow tip of the nipple, and finally even wrapping around both the areola and the breast together to give them a suck.

By the end it had left Wu Xingzi in a daze, his thin arms laying limply on the tiger's head as he moaned.

When those nipples were swollen to the size of red beans the tiger seemed to have licked its fill; its tongue began to make its way towards Wu Xingzi's soft abdomen, teasing the sensitive flesh there, brushing across that cute depression in his belly, and finally hovering over that pink and tender little stem below.

The soft, pink, fleshy stem was a delicate thing, dainty in both thickness and length. It looked almost as if it had never been used before, yet it was now standing tall, nectar dripping from its tip. The white tiger leaned in to sniff it and, very much pleased by its sweetly fishy smell, impatiently moved to lick it.

The glans was always one of a man's most sensitive areas, and the tiger's barbed tongue was licking with quite a lot of force as well, those short fleshy barbs directly scratching the tender flesh inside his urethra. Wu Xingzi shrank back with a scream, but the tiger placed a paw on his waist before he could try to escape, and he immediately lost the ability to move.

"Great Immortal Tiger, Great Immortal Tiger..." Wu Xingzi begged for mercy with panting breaths, but the white tiger acted as if it hadn't heard a word of it. That salty-sweet nectar which flowed onto its tongue and was swallowed into its belly was a delicacy it had never tasted before, and it was unable to stop itself in its eagerness to make the tiny thing before it produce even more delicious nectar.

The broad tongue licked Wu Xingzi's penis from tip to base, then up again towards the precum-oozing head. After a few rounds of this, Wu Xingzi was finally brought to tears from the pleasure, his glans gushing with juices. The tiger cleanly licked up every last drop, leaving his dick coated in the tiger's saliva and looking even more tender and delicious than before.

Wu Xingzi felt like the licking was also devouring his mind bit by bit, leaving nothing in its wake. He was hot and boneless all over, as if millions of tiny insects were biting their way through his flesh. Shuddering from the itching, he let out an endless string of broken moans.

The tiger, truly addicted to this man's delicious flavor, keenly noticed that below the pair of cute balls lay the mouth of another spring which could satisfy it even more. Following its intuition, it moved downwards, first rolling those two little balls on the tip of its tongue, their soft texture feeling better than the most tender animal meat.

The white tiger tilted its head, toying with those little balls in different ways, even taking them into its mouth and scratching them with its sharp teeth. That painfully numb, numbingly soft, softly itchy sensation left Wu Xingzi's entire face a mess of tears. Pressed beneath the tiger's paw, he shuddered and shook so hard he was nearly spasming.

Wu Xingzi was half-dead by the time the tiger was done playing with his little balls, already on the verge of spending himself in climax. But it was here that Great Immortal Tiger pulled away, leaving him in a troubling state. The heat in Wu Xingzi's body was mixed with an indescribably numb limpness which seemed to burn away at his last sliver of clarity, and he said, "Lick me again... Please, Great Immortal...lick me..."

A hint of a smile appeared in the white tiger's eyes, and it lifted up Wu Xingzi's lower body, getting his slender legs to sit atop its back and completely exposing the little pink flower hidden between the plump hills of his buttocks. The tiger's tongue gave his ass a haphazard lick before sweeping towards his tightly puckered hole without any hesitation.

That fleshy chrysanthemum was small and delicate, its wrinkles tight and such a tender pink it seemed as if it might drip water; in fact, it really *was* wet with his own cum and the tiger's saliva, making it look even softer and smoother than normal.

The fleshy barbs on the tiger's tongue made it like a small brush, sweeping across his asshole over and over again. The bashful little flower twitched and trembled as if trying to hide from this onslaught, looking so cute as it did that the massive tiger was even more unwilling to stop, and started licking it with greater enthusiasm than before.

Wu Xingzi was gasping and trembling all over, his stiffened dick on the verge of ejaculation yet constantly kept just short of going over the edge. He swayed his slender waist in an attempt to at least get some friction from rubbing it against the tiger's fur, but the paw on his waist was far too heavy to let him move; all he could do was wriggle in place. The sight of those jiggling buttocks was enough to make the tiger dizzy, and before he noticed, its hideous cock had popped out from beneath its fur, standing ramrod straight and covered in clearly delineated spines. He was honestly terrified to imagine what it would be like to get fucked by such a thing.

The tiger's long, thick tongue licked those snow-white, perky, extra-plump buttocks until they were sparkling with moisture.

His little asshole was licked until it was soft and moist, its tiny mouth opening and closing ever-so-slightly in a way which was beyond seductive; it was even dripping with fragrant slick. The tiger assiduously lapped it up so as not to miss a single drop, then smacked its lips, craving more.

The skinny human before it tasted far too delicious, his slick not only pleasing to the tongue but also stoking the fire in the great tiger's lower belly, filling it with the increasing desire to swallow him in a single bite.

But the chrysanthemum before it was far too small; it knew very well that its prick was far from ordinary, so much so that even females of its own species couldn't always handle it, let alone such a delicate human. With that thin, narrow waist and squishy little stomach, it could probably penetrate right to the deepest part of him with a single thrust, thrusting his belly upwards with the movement!

The big tiger's golden-eyed gaze deepened as this thought flashed through its mind, and after a couple of snorts, it curled its thick tongue into a tube and probed it into his asshole's tiny open mouth.

The licking left Wu Xingzi feeling ticklish all over, his mind a fuzzy blank, mouth open yet unable to make a sound.

The tiger's tongue was far too dexterous for that little flesh chrysanthemum to withstand, and it took just a few licks for it to open up, powerless to stop the brush-like tongue from having its way with its insides. Wu Xingzi's sensitive, soft flesh felt weak and numb, and he found himself stopped in time at the moment before climax; the pleasure was so much that his entire body hurt, every inch of him too sensitive to touch. But the tiger's tongue was a long one, still licking its way into his hole. When its fleshy barbs brushed across a slightly protruding area inside him, the old man let out a

tear-filled cry, his passage clenching down on the tiger's tongue and preventing it from moving further.

"Don't lick there... It's too ticklish..." His frail, fair-skinned body flushed a bright pink, and he couldn't help trying to push the tiger's paw off his waist, but it wouldn't budge an inch. There was no way the tiger would do as he desired, of course; instead it started licking his twitching, tender flesh with even more force than before, its barbed tongue focusing its efforts on the spot which had so affected him.

The old man at this point was drowning in so much pleasure that he was entirely disoriented, and crying so hard his voice was hoarse. He wriggled his buttocks in an attempt to get away, but that tiger tongue kept on licking there without pulling away at all, continuing its ministrations until he broke down with a wail, his tiny dick spurting out a stream of transparent liquid before releasing its male spunk. Salty-sweet slick welled up from the depths of his asshole as well, and the tiger lapped up every drop of it, licking again and again in hopes of more. Wu Xingzi naturally reacted to this by moaning as he came repeatedly, before finally his eyes rolled back into his head and he fainted, still convulsing.

The massive tiger was also satisfied after filling its belly with sexual fluids. It pulled its tongue out of the softened anus, flipped the human over, and positioned him so that his buttocks were raised high in the air, baring his soaking wet lower body to the world. That tender pink chrysanthemum was swollen from all the licking, and had turned a lewd shade of red; it was no longer able to close all the way, twitching intermittently, its tiny mouth wide open.

The tiger liked this view no matter how it looked at it. It bent down over Wu Xingzi's body, the pointed head of its prick pressing against his slightly protruding asshole. The tiger's cock was covered in fleshy spines, leaving only a tiny nipple-like point at the tip; it looked like a syringe which could perfectly penetrate into a female's uterus, increasing the chance of conception.

Considering it was looking at a man, though, there was no question of pregnancy at all. The tiger couldn't help thinking that was a pity, as it did somewhat want to see this quail-like old man's squishy little belly swell with its cubs...

It lowered its body, but had trouble stretching out on the little bed when it was so much larger than a human being. It needed to spend some time adjusting its position before finally pushing the head of its cock into that tiny chrysanthemum.

It went in slowly at first, and the unconscious old man let out a keening moan. The multiple orgasms had left him feeling extremely sensitive all over, making the brushing of the tiger's fur against his skin beyond unbearable. Though he was yet to wake, his cute little dick was already hard again, swaying pitifully back and forth with the tiger's movements.

The glans may have been relatively narrow, but as far as Wu Xingzi's asshole was concerned, it was still nearly too big to swallow—never mind the thick, spiny stem that was still to come.

The big tiger pressed the trembling old quail beneath its body, panting hard as it pushed its cock in inch by excruciating inch; before long, it hit an area of soft flesh—probably the part its tongue had fucked swollen moments earlier—and took this opportunity to press up against it and fuck it several times. The intense pleasure this brought about was enough to bring Wu Xingzi back to consciousness with a sob, and he tearfully cried for mercy.

"Great Immortal Tiger...please spare me, don't thrust there..."

If it wasn't allowed to thrust there, naturally that meant it should thrust even more fiercely than before. Besides, it had yet to get even half of its tiger prick in, so how could it show mercy at a time like this?

Wu Xingzi could feel the weight of the tiger's prick acutely inside his passage, as well as that hard glans with its syringe-like bump at the tip. The thick stem was covered in fleshy spines, causing a mix of prickling numbness and bone-melting pleasure as it was thrust into him; it wasn't until it pulled out that he finally realized he was in big trouble.

Although these fleshy spines were soft, when that tiger prick pulled out, the spines following it were pulled into individual barbs which rubbed against his soft flesh as they passed, feeling practically as if they were biting him. Wu Xingzi screamed until his voice grew hoarse. His insides were burning, yet within that pain was also a sore, numbing, ticklish sensation, and he had no idea what to do about it; another wave of slick gushed out, his inner walls twisting around the fearsome tiger cock in their spasming.

"N-no... Spare me, Great Immortal Tiger, spare me..." His soft flesh sucked ingratiatingly as he cried, making the big tiger's scalp go numb with pleasure. It made a low growl and thrust its cock back in once more, smashing it ruthlessly against that swollen protrusion within.

"*Aaaahh*—" Wu Xingzi tearfully let out a lewd cry, unable to discern whether he was feeling pain or pleasure. His dick swung with their movements, but there was nothing left for him to ejaculate. Unable to escape the big tiger's rutting, he lay pitifully on the bed, his eyes dazed.

Despite this, his inner passage quickly adapted to being ploughed like this. The thick, hideous tiger cock went deeper with every thrust, when suddenly it poked against a small opening deep within Wu Xingzi's intestines, causing the old quail to convulse again, screaming as he sank into madness.

While it didn't know what this spot was, the big tiger was certain was that if it pierced through this little opening, both it and the old quail would gain even more pleasure. With that thought in mind, it pulled out a little bit, gathered the strength in its waist, and began to fuck into that spot with brutal enthusiasm.

"You can't... You can't..." Wu Xingzi cried and tried to struggle; he knew what the Great Immortal Tiger was planning to do, and was filled with both terror and expectation at the thought.

"*Uwaah—*" All of a sudden, that syringe-like tip seemed to find the right spot. The once-impregnable little opening was finally pushed open, and the tiger's spined prick slid right in, causing a large bulge to swell out on Wu Xingzi's thin belly.

His belly so scalding hot it was as if a fire were burning within, the old quail whimpered and cried as he reached to touch it with a trembling hand. He could practically feel how prickly that tiger dick's spines were through the thin layer of skin; it was throbbing slightly as well, and as he touched it, it slid a little farther in under his hand, almost seeming to press against his stomach.

Wu Xingzi was crying pitifully, yet the massive tiger was so comfortable it was purring. Its golden eyes narrowed as it took a moment to savor the squeezing and sucking of the flesh wrapped around it, in the process also allowing the human beneath it to catch his breath.

What followed after was a fucking with the violence of a thunderstorm.

Wu Xingzi's narrow asshole had already been entirely fucked open by this point, making obscenely wet noises with each vigorous thrust. Every individual spine on the tiger's penis was sticking up, hooking on that sweet spot every time they pulled out. Again and again the small circle of tender flesh turned outwards only to get forcefully fucked back in again immediately after; the tiger's pointed cockhead pushed open the entrance of his rectum in the process, thrusting even farther inwards. After more and more of these thrusts, both his asshole and rectal opening were rubbed red and swollen, spurting out sexual fluids to soak the tiger's fur and clenching down on the tiger's increasingly fast and furious thrusting.

The huge tiger growled with pleasure; this human's tight passage had a perfect level of elasticity, and it was so soft and wet. The body under the beast was shuddering from sensitivity, so breathless that the man could only whimper quietly. All this only served to exacerbate the tiger's sadistic desires, and it started recklessly thrusting away even harder than before.

"Uwaahh... Y-you're going to break me... Spare me, Great Immortal Tiger... Spare me..."

Wu Xingzi's face was soaked with tears, and he trembled as he gripped the sheets beneath him, drool dripping from the corners of his mouth. He was an absolute mess, physically and mentally. He'd never been the most intelligent to begin with, but now he was lost and dazed, his brain like burnt congee.

The tiger's immense head nuzzled against his nape, its broad tongue licking nipples so swollen they were the size of red beans. The dazed old quail wailed as he thrust his nipples into the tiger's mouth, compliantly twisting his narrow waist back and forth; this licentiously conflicting behavior made the tiger all the more eager to fuck him to pieces.

"No, uwaah... I can't take any more..." A boiling hot tide was rising within his stomach; it felt as if something were about to explode outwards. Frightened, Wu Xingzi unconsciously pressed a hand against his belly in hopes of stopping this heat from overflowing; but he was stuffed so full with the tiger's prick that not only did pressing on it fail to stop that sensation, it made those feline spines press even deeper into his lascivious body.

He stiffened all over for a moment. Then his body began to jerk so violently that he nearly threw the enormous tiger off from on top of him. A huffing sound somewhere between crying and yelling spilled out of his throat, and his thighs kicked back a few times before falling into a violent trembling, his entire person seeming to fall apart. His inner walls contracted so tightly that it put the tiger's prick in pain, and red-hot tiger seed was shot directly into the depths of the old quail's intestines. The heat of it had him spasming for a moment, and then collapsing bonelessly on the bed.

Though the man appeared to have fainted, his narrow passage was still sucking away, clamping down on the tiger's cock—which was still as hard as ever despite having just come and showed no signs of softening at all. The spines on that cock seemed to be showing off their power, as their rubbing brought the unconscious old quail to climax again. With him ejaculating in the front and spurting out liquids from the back, there were wet spots all over the place, filling the house with the obscene scent of sex.

The still unsatisfied tiger naturally wouldn't let the man beneath it go so easily and—without regard for whether or not the old fellow could handle it—began yet another round of fierce fucking. The unconscious man's sweet-voiced moans changed to half-awake wails. His little pink dick came again and again, swelling a magnificent red, before finally the half-hard cock's slit opened to send drops of leftover semen flying out along with the tiger's vigorous thrusts. The salty-sweet smell excited the big tiger into a more frenzied state than ever, and it ruthlessly moved its hips to thrust itself ever deeper, wanting nothing more than to skewer the old quail on its cock.

This unending pleasure left the old man half-conscious as he lay prone on the bed, ass raised in the air. His eyes were open but completely unfocused, staring blankly at the house's only window, his plump lips hanging slack and somewhat crooked from how they were pressed against the bed as he drooled into the bedding.

The big tiger licked Wu Xingzi's slender neck and back and his narrow shoulders as it fucked him, before finally shoving its barbed tongue into his open mouth and licking over every last inch of that satiny space, lovingly playing with his tender pink tongue. It continued this kiss until Wu Xingzi began spasming on the bed from lack of oxygen, but even then it still refused to release him; its hips thrust more violently than before, slamming against the human's buttocks until even his perineum had turned red and swollen from the onslaught.

Suddenly, the tiger's penis swelled even further, its spines stiffening until they nearly embedded themselves in the tender flesh of Wu Xingzi's intestines. The hard, pointed head swelled as well, its nipple-shaped tip filling with blood until it stood as erect as a needle. Wu Xingzi's mouth was so full of tiger tongue that he couldn't have cried out even if he wanted to; only his thin, trembling waist showed a vague hint of the fear he felt towards what was about to happen.

After a few more thrusts, the tiger suddenly thrust deep inside, and a stream of scalding hot liquid shot into the depths of Wu Xingzi's stomach with even more force than before.

The tiger's cum this time was much thicker and more plentiful, making the old quail's eyes roll and sending his body twitching as the stuff pumped endlessly into him until his belly had swollen to the size of a third-month pregnancy. Tiger semen was much thicker than that of humans, blocking up Wu Xingzi's insides like a comfortably warm hot water bottle and making him feel bloated with it;

when the tiger at last pulled out, barely any of it dripped out. It was all safe inside his stomach.

For a moment his swollen, red asshole couldn't even close up from being fucked so hard. A small amount of transparent sexual fluids dripping out from the tender crimson flesh. His swollen red cocklet twitched one last time before spurting out a trickle of leftover urine, making even more of a mess of the scene than before.

The tiger gazed upon this beautiful scene of destruction with its sparkling golden eyes. It had been thinking of using its tongue to clean the old man up, but its mind was much clearer now that it had ejaculated twice—it had no choice but to disappointedly abandon the idea out of concern that the human before it wouldn't be able to handle all that licking.

It raised its head with a contented snort, then curled its body up. The sound of sinew and bones moving out of place echoed within the still lust-warm little house, and before long the massive tiger had disappeared without a trace, replaced by a completely naked young man with lightly tanned skin and a slender, graceful figure packed with tightly coiled muscle. At first his eyes still retained the tiger's golden color, but after a few blinks they became a deep, calm black, limpid and smoky and filled with passion and charm. With his sword-sharp eyebrows, straight nose, and moist red lips, he looked like a work of fine art.

But his heavy cock also looked much more savage like this.

He leaned down to place a kiss on Wu Xingzi's neck, roughly wiped him down, then dug out a clean set of sheets to replace the soiled ones. Then he heated up a big tub of water and carried him in for a bath.

Wu Xingzi was beyond exhausted. Having just lost his virginity to an enormous tiger of all things, he was now entirely unable to wake.

He obediently leaned into the man's embrace, his body still trembling pitifully.

The man lovingly patted his back, rubbed his muscles for him, and quietly whispered into his ear. "Don't worry, I'll be very good to you from now on."

An uninvited guest had recently come to the house.

That day, Wu Xingzi had just come back from picking wild herbs on the mountain. He'd even caught a pair of small rabbits and was feeling quite pleased with himself over it. He couldn't help feeling sorry for the big tiger at home—it hadn't had meat in quite a while, and yet it always accompanied him in eating vegetables without a word of complaint.

Honestly, as a tiger yao, the white tiger didn't actually need to rely on a frail human to take care of him. But Wu Xingzi was worried that his injuries hadn't fully healed yet, and that if he returned to the mountain unprepared he might run into the one who'd injured him again, so he refused to let the white tiger casually leave the house.

The white tiger had no objections to this. He wanted Wu Xingzi to be happy, and so the most he'd do was wait until Wu Xingzi went out to work on his field, or went up the mountain to hunt and gather firewood, then resume his original form and prowl up the mountain to hunt as well, protecting the old quail's safety while he was at it.

The two little rabbits were a little skinny, but their liveliness more than made up for it, ready to leap up and escape at any time despite having been caught by their ears. Wu Xingzi had been living off the land for many years, however, and was certainly no pushover. He easily braided a rope out of weeds, tied the little rabbits up nice and tight, then cheerfully hurried home.

However, the moment he opened the door, he was shocked speechless by the scene he saw before him.

The house was a small one, with only a table, two chairs, and a bed, plus another door on the left which led to the kitchen. Wu Xingzi looked on helplessly as two figures entwined upon the same bed which he and the white tiger had been cuddling on just yesterday: One was the tall, strong back of the white tiger, while the other was pressed beneath him, revealing only a pair of pale, slender, beautiful long legs and as a head of satin-black hair. Even if he could see nothing else, he could easily imagine what an absolutely captivating beauty this must be.

The two rabbits fell to the ground with a *plop*, and Wu Xingzi frantically fled from the house, slamming the door behind him and leaning against it as he panted continuously for breath.

What had he just seen? The white tiger was on his bed...committing sexual relations with another man? As soon as this thought flashed through his mind, Wu Xingzi's chest began to hurt, and he pressed his hands tightly against it, his eyes burning; to his own surprise, he was at the brink of tears.

Just then, the door was pulled open, causing him to lose his balance and fall backwards into a familiarly sturdy embrace. The portrait-like vision of the white tiger's sharp brows, tall nose, and passionately warm eyes also entered his vision...upside-down.

Wu Xingzi blinked, unconsciously putting on an ingratiating smile, but couldn't look the man in the eye.

"Did I scare you?" The white tiger dexterously turned Wu Xingzi around, wrapping him in his arms, then rubbed the tip of his nose against his slender neck a few times before taking in a deep breath, almost as if the man in his arms were a meaty bone. A red-cheeked Wu Xingzi tried to push him away, only to suddenly catch a glimpse

of the beauty currently walking towards them; before he could even understand his own actions, he'd wrapped his arms around the white tiger's neck instead.

"Jin-er." When the beauty spoke, it was like the warbling song of an oriole. Just the sound of it sent a comforting thrum through Wu Xingzi's bones. Yet this man also had a reserved bearing; his white clothes made him look like a willow tree swaying softly in the wind, so pure and otherworldly that no one would dare profane his presence. There wasn't the slightest trace of that magnificent beauty who'd been pressed down into the bed just moments before.

"Laoshi." The white tiger turned his head to answer without bothering to release Wu Xingzi from his tight embrace, and looked as calm as ever as he made the introductions. "Xingzi, this is Mr. Lu, the elder of the white fox clan, and my teacher."

So he's a fox spirit? Wu Xingzi immediately forgot his earlier dejection, turning instead to gaze with wide-eyed fascination at the beauty. He had to admit, fox spirits really were different! That figure, those looks, that sophistication, that charm so alluring it seemed to seep from the man's very bones... Wu Xingzi's face reddened and he started acting shy, only for his eyes to be immediately covered by the white tiger's large hand.

"Ai." Wu Xingzi was a little disappointed. Of all the creatures he could have met, none was as well-known as a fox spirit; now that he'd finally seen one, how could he possibly be satisfied with just a single look?

"So you're the one who rescued Jin-er?" The fox spirit's voice was far from friendly, even seeming somewhat cold, but it still managed to retain that same spine-tingling allure. Wu Xingzi turned red from his neck up to his ears, and he vigorously and repeatedly nodded his head, then shook it instead.

"I didn't really do anything, just brought him home, is all," he said bashfully. Afterwards he'd been inexplicably devoured, but the two of them were now living together quite happily, so he couldn't quite say who'd rescued who anymore.

"Home?" The fox spirit clearly disapproved of this answer. "Jin-er is the lord of the Fulong mountain range. Can this little shrine of yours truly provide for such a great immortal?"

Hm? Little shrine? Great immortal? Wu Xingzi stared blankly for a few seconds, following which a blush bloomed on his cheeks, his entire body turning red as a boiled lobster. He opened his mouth to speak, but after a few failed attempts could only lower his head in silence instead. This little shrine of his really had provided countless times for this great immortal white tiger! But there was no way he could say that out loud!

The white tiger realized what he was thinking and couldn't resist lowering his head to kiss the old quail until he breathlessly collapsed in his arms.

"Jin-er, if you've recovered from your injuries, you should return with me." The fox spirit was nettled by the scene before him and his voice grew colder than before; even someone as slow-witted as Wu Xingzi couldn't help shrinking his shoulders, lowering his head, and rubbing his nose awkwardly.

"Many thanks for the concern, Laoshi," the white tiger replied without any discernible emotion. "This student will naturally return when the time is right; there is no need for Laoshi to trouble himself over the matter." It was only now that he decided to remove his hand from Wu Xingzi's eyes. He asked with a smile, "You caught two rabbits today, would you like me to cook them for you?"

"Ai, those are for you..." Wu Xingzi hurriedly looked over at the rabbits, only to find them cowering against the ground as if having already accepted their fate; when he then turned his gaze back to the white tiger, it was with a look of admiration.

"In that case, you and I can have one each." The white tiger liked him more with every glimpse. He truly wanted nothing more in this moment than to devour the person in his arms, licking and biting him over and over—but he couldn't bear to frighten him. He settled for tightening his hold instead, and the rabbits flew into his grasp with a single wave of the hand. "Would you like spicy? Or sweet?"

"A little sweet is good." Wu Xingzi happily played with the rabbits' little claws, then suddenly thought of something and turned his gaze to the fox spirit. "Oh right! What about Mr. Lu? He's a guest, so why don't I share my rabbit with him?"

"No need," Mr. Lu said with a cold humph. A dazzling light flashed around his body, and in the blink of an eye the beauty had transformed into a slender white fox with smooth, shiny fur, which arrogantly left the house.

At first they both assumed that Mr. Lu had gone back to Mount Fulong. As the two of them were getting ready to sleep that night, the white tiger changed to his original form and used his thick, rough tongue to lick Wu Xingzi all over. It was just as his tongue began to play with the tiny chrysanthemum between his buttocks, however, that the fox spirit returned to squat silently at the head of the bed; just as Wu Xingzi was about to climax, shouting with ecstasy, he found himself meeting the fox's gaze.

Wu Xingzi stared blankly for a moment before screaming in fright, his stiff, dripping little cock instantly wilting as he scrambled to hide himself under the covers. No amount of coaxing from the white tiger could get him to come out again.

A few days passed in this way, and the white tiger was beside himself with irritation. When in human form a bestial golden light would shine in his dark eyes, pinning Wu Xingzi with a hot gaze that burned the old quail's skin red. That night Wu Xingzi made up an excuse and left the house before he'd even finished dinner.

"I hope Laoshi won't try to follow us." Knowing he couldn't let this opportunity slip by, the white tiger shot the fox spirit a warning glare before running out after Wu Xingzi.

Though the fox spirit who'd been left behind was brimming with resentment, the white tiger had already said his piece, and he didn't dare disobey the command. Instead he stayed put and hatefully left multiple deep claw marks on the table.

Wu Xingzi was only human, and getting up there in years besides; though he knew the mountain very well, he couldn't outrun a man whose original form was a white tiger. He'd only just reached the cover of the woods when the man pounced on him from behind, and he felt a sudden pain in the back of his neck—he'd been bitten out of habit.

You couldn't blame the white tiger spirit for this behavior. Being a tiger, he'd been hunting since he was young, and the first thing you did after pouncing on your prey was to bite the back of its neck. All that considered though, his teeth in his human form weren't as good as those of his original, and they only left a somewhat-deep bite mark on the old quail's thin white neck. It swelled in a frightening yet incredibly intimate way.

Wu Xingzi trembled, barely able to breathe as he was pulled into the white tiger's embrace. A rough, spiny tongue licked a path from his cheek down his neck, soon pulling his clothes open to reveal a slender collarbone and the barest glimpse of two pink nipples. These in turn quickly hardened under the tongue's ministrations, transforming immediately into moist little red beans which trembled falteringly in the open air.

"Ai... B-be gentle..." Wu Xingzi had no intention of rejecting him. He'd actually been just as pent-up these past few days; if it hadn't been for that fox spirit—and his own thin face—it was likely that he'd already have had quite a few rolls in the hay with the white tiger by now.

The white tiger ignored his words. He'd always been more beast than man. Now that he could finally eat his beloved quail again, how could he possibly hold back?

He sucked a red bean-sized nipple into his mouth with gusto, using his rough, dexterous tongue to poke and play with it. It was like a sticky rice dumpling, springy and delicious; as the round little thing gradually grew bigger and harder within his mouth, he couldn't help turning his teeth to it, pulling it a few times before giving it hard suck. He didn't spare the areola or the flesh of that flat chest either, gnawing on them as well.

"*Aaahh*—" Wu Xingzi was left feeling sore and swollen from this suckling. Even if the white tiger did his best to control his strength when he bit him, those sharp teeth still poked into the delicate flesh of his chest. It wasn't hard enough to draw blood, but it still elicited a slightly painful tingling sensation, pleasure overtaking his brain like a flood and instantly making him so dizzy that he could no longer tell what was going on.

It wasn't until those pink nipples had been bitten to the size of soybeans that the white tiger reluctantly moved his mouth away. He continued licking his way downwards, making sure to cover every last inch of Wu Xingzi's skin as he did so, leaving the man beneath him twitching, his tiny cock even spurting out its thick white milk. The tiger lapped it up so meticulously he didn't even spare even the leftover semen in the tip, his tongue poking open the slit and burrowing in to scrape it all out. The tiny spines on his tongue's surface scratched against the unimaginably tender walls of that place, and Wu Xingzi let out a high-pitched scream as he twisted his waist in an attempt to escape. But he was held down with only one hand, leaving him with no other option but to let the white tiger do as he wished.

Now, though, the white tiger became addicted to licking him, insistently playing with that slit until it was swollen and forced to ejaculate again. The little cocklet then limply shrank onto his lower abdomen, looking as if it wouldn't be able to recover for quite a long while. Only then did the satisfied tiger turn his tongue to licking Wu Xingzi clean instead.

Even if he was currently in human form, his natural behavior was still that of a tiger.

He infatuatedly licked the old quail from head to toe, the sound of the old thing's whimpering moans making his huge cock so hard that pungent masculine-smelling juices wouldn't stop flowing from the crack at its tip. He rubbed it against Wu Xingzi's thigh until the soft flesh there had been rubbed raw, and was covered with his scent.

"How about I lick it for you, my darling? It won't hurt if I lick it loose first." No matter how many times they fucked, Wu Zingzi's asshole was still as tightly puckered and bashful as ever. Every time he'd fuck it until its gaping little entrance was oozing lewd juices and creamy-white semen, yet the next day it would be good as new again, like a virgin flower that had never known sex.

Wu Xingzi's first instinct was to reject him, but his body had already been brought to multiple orgasms by this point, and his lust, once woken, could not be so easily brought to heel. Unable to so much as utter the word "no," he could only whimper some more as he buried his face in his hands like a coward.

But with the white tiger's powerfully keen eyesight, how could he possibly miss the flirtatiously lascivious and misty gaze with which Wu Xingzi was peeking at him through his fingers? This was more enthralling than any aphrodisiac, setting the big tiger's heart so ablaze with excitement that he nearly changed back to his original form to give the old quail a good loving with his thick tiger prick.

However, right now they were outside, and it would be bad news if he were to catch someone's attention in his tiger form. He just barely managed to hold back the urge.

He squeezed between Wu Xingzi's legs and knelt down, pulling up one of his thin legs and rubbing those plump, perky buttocks with both hands before lifting them up; the view between his legs was a bewitching sight. Out of concern that this position might hurt the back of Wu Xingzi's head, though, the white tiger made sure to take off his shirt, ball it up, and stuff it behind him as a pillow.

He stared down at the scene before him with a deep gaze; he had yet to even really touch him, yet that gaze alone was almost physically scalding, and Wu Xingzi grew hot all over as it wandered over every sensitive part of his body. His asshole twitched uncontrollably, drooling brightly glittering love juices.

"D-don't look...please don't look..." he gasped, trying to close his legs, far more embarrassed by this than if his lover had been directly touching him. But how could the white tiger let him succeed? No matter how he tried to close his legs, it would only serve to press the tiger's head closer to his lower body.

With one last heavy breath, the white tiger stopped dawdling and leaned down to lick Wu Xingzi's taint, the tip of his nose pressing against the tiny balls dangling above it as the tip of his spined tongue meticulously licked its way back and forth across that lewd yet tender spot.

Wu Xingzi let out a shrill scream. The perineum was an extremely sensitive place for any man, let alone someone with such a naturally submissive body as him; it wasn't long at all before he found himself tingling so unbearably that it was as if small insects were biting their way down his bloodstream.

But the white tiger couldn't be satisfied with licking alone. Soon he opened his mouth and devoured Wu Xingzi's whole taint, partway between kissing and biting at the tender flesh, until the man beneath him was twitching all over and begging him to stop. That little cock falteringly stood to half-mast again despite having already come twice, yet he still refused to let go.

"A-Hu, A-Hu..."[7] Wu Xingzi wriggled his narrow waist in discomfort. It was difficult to discern whether he was trying to avoid or embrace his lover's ministrations, but he was always embarrassed at the start; once he got into it he'd become a lot more open. His straddling legs quietly rubbed against the back of the white tiger's shoulders, arousing him even more, until the man's huge cock was bouncing wetly against his muscular abdomen.

His lips slid down from the perineum to the exposed asshole below, which was opened to the size of a child's fingertip. The lascivious fluids which flowed from it had a salty-sweet smell which made the white tiger forget himself with lust, his mind consumed by the need to fuck the old quail into the ground. He wouldn't share a single piece of meat with anyone else; he'd savor each bite, then swallow him into his stomach.

The tip of his tongue made its way to the tightly puckered chrysanthemum and licked each individual petal, the juices leaving a sweet taste on his tongue. The white tiger massaged his lover's buttocks, patiently licking that chrysanthemum until the opening

---

7   "Hu" means tiger.

was wide as a finger, then rolled his tongue into a cylinder and poked it into the hole.

"*Aaah*—" Wu Xingzi's waist trembled, his fingers pulling up weeds as they clawed at the ground, covering his fingertips with the sour taste of green grass. "Lick me," he murmured thoughtlessly, his face painted with lust. "A-Hu, lick me more..."

Deference was no substitute for obedience. The white tiger smiled faintly, then unfurled his tongue within Wu Xingzi's asshole and pressed hard into the soft passage.

"*Uwaaah*—" The sharp pleasure made Wu Xingzi throw his head back with a lewd moan, his legs suddenly tensing, even his smooth, round toes curling.

The white tiger's movements were very well-practiced. Salty-sweet slick spread across his tongue as it swept over every inch of that passage. Seemingly unable to withstand any more of his licking, the fleshy walls soon began to spasm, clamping down on the tiger tongue wreaking havoc within. But the tiny spines on the surface of his tongue forced those twitching walls into constant retreat. Their incessant squirming not only failed to fend off this invasion but allowed him to lick even deeper.

The white tiger's tongue was quite a long one; though it wasn't as thick or spiny as his tiger prick, it made up for it with dexterity. His tongue's surface was covered in seemingly soft barbs...but the spines on a tiger's tongue would normally be capable of stripping the meat right off its victim's bones, and if he hadn't already cultivated into a spirit capable of transforming certain parts of his body, his tongue would have been just as deadly.

Instead, though, these fierce spines had become a tool for pleasure. When they scratched over the flesh of that passage, it couldn't stop itself from tightening, clenching down hard on the broad tongue within it. Occasionally, when it was licked too hard, it would even clamp down hard enough that the tiger found it difficult to move his tongue.

The white tiger's eyes narrowed with pleasure, licking, sucking, and swallowing down all of the juices which flowed from within Wu Xingzi's asshole. There was a hint of sweetness mixed with the otherwise salty taste of the slick, akin to the highest quality wine.

At first the flesh of the old quail's hole was still capable of resistance, but as the licking continued, after it drove him to orgasm twice more, the rough tiger tongue was able to do as it pleased. It licked its way deeper, inch by inch, until finally it found its way to the entrance of his rectal passage. There was a tiny bend in the path there; the white tiger knew very well how much pleasure the person beneath him would be drowning in once he penetrated that spot. He knew how he'd cry and wail as he melted into a puddle of lust, how that thin belly would swell with the shape of his huge cock, slick pouring out like a broken dam. It was a shame his tongue was unable to reach quite that far—at best all he could do with his tongue was brush against the already red and swollen entrance.

"Spare me..." This teasing was too much for Wu Xingzi. He was shaking all over, his gaze unfocused. His entire body was a soft and tender red. Drool slipped out from the corner of his mouth.

He knew he was stuck with this white tiger for life. The thought was particularly strong in this moment, when his ass tightened once more around that thick, long tiger tongue, hands on his stomach as he spasmed his way into yet another orgasm.

The white tiger seemed to have finally satisfied himself with licking. He carefully pulled out his tongue, sweeping the slick-soaked appendage back into his mouth to savor as he swallowed the fluids into his stomach. Then he moved on to lapping up the semen on the old quail's belly as well, a look of intoxication on his face at the delicious taste of it.

Wu Xingzi was practically half-dead at this point.

He was just a mortal man, after all, and he wasn't exactly in the best of health; there was no way he could possibly compete with the astounding physical strength and lust of a spiritual creature like the white tiger. Right now he was still twitching uncontrollably, bathed in the afterglow of the previous climax; his eyes were too dazed to make out what sort of expression the white tiger currently had on his face.

The big tiger absolutely loved the way his lover looked in this moment, and he stopped tormenting him to wrap the old quail's slender white legs around his waist instead. His burning hot tiger prick ground a couple times against the outside of that still-gaping little asshole, the way it squirmed against his egg-sized glans feeling as if a tiny mouth had given it a bashful suck in a way that expressed both eagerness and reluctance at the same time.

He let out a low grunt, and pushed his huge cock in to the hilt in one swift movement.

"*Aaah*—" The fat shaft wasn't as unique as the tiger's original form—it was more or less the same as that of a normal human man. But the glans was somewhat narrower, like the head of a spear, and it split open the soft inner walls as it passed through to viciously stab against the entrance of that deep-set rectal passage. The fleshy stalk behind it was thicker, and had spines on it as well, stretching the intestinal passage open and preventing even a drop of that stomachful of slick from dripping out of his hole. All Wu Xingzi could feel of those fleshy spines was them rubbing faintly against his sensitive spots as it went in, but the instant it pulled out again, he fell to pieces in the blink of an eye.

"A-Hu, naaah...A-Hu..." He flailed, face red with tears as the spines on that tiger prick scraped backwards along the flesh of his passage. He couldn't clearly describe the sensation, but he felt as if his very soul were going to get fucked out of his body. Tears caught in his nose, and he began simultaneously coughing while begging for mercy, his thin waist writhing uselessly under the tiger's vise-like grip.

The feeling was so vivid and powerful that Wu Xingzi was soon left unable to vocalize anything but a moan. Pink tongue poking partway out of his mouth, he tilted back his slender neck, baring his lightly bobbing Adam's apple; the sight made the white tiger's eyes burn with desire, and he lowered his head to catch the little knot for a nibble.

After a whirlwind of violent thrusts, he grabbed the old quail's buttocks and thrust his massive dick deep inside, its somewhat pointed head hitting the bend behind that rectal entrance, allowing its fleshy spines to ruthlessly ravage the chestnut-sized gland which resided there. Wu Xingzi's body tensed, abruptly twitching a few times, his eyes rolling back until all that could be seen were the whites.

That tight, virgin hole had been fully fucked open by this point. Even the wrinkles had been smoothed out; it bulged outwards slightly like an insatiably greedy little mouth.

The man kept biting his throat, fucking him harder and harder as he did so. The old quail let out a broken scream, twisting his waist in an attempt to catch his breath. But all that did was further excite the white tiger spirit's bestial instincts; he gripped his waist with one hand, cupped his buttocks with the other, and pressed him violently against his crotch.

Wu Xingzi's tiny cock was fucked back into hardness, thin trickles of clear liquid dripping from its tip as it slapped again and again against his soft belly. His little testicles—already emptied of cum—

shrank into a pitiful lump, swaying amid the white tiger's rough pubic hair as the man thrust hard and fast into him.

"A-Hu...you're going to kill me..." The old quail had been fucked into a state of delirium, loose hair splayed around him as he wailed, even his toes curling in from his spasming.

That tiger prick hit again and again against the entrance of that bend within him. The fragile spot was unable to withstand the onslaught for long, and in one sudden instant it was finally fucked open, the firm glans thrusting directly into an even deeper part of his body and making the thin surface of Wu Xingzi's belly bulge outwards.

"*Aaaahh—*" Wu Xingzi screamed like a debauched madman, his emptied-out cocklet trembling a few times before pouring out a stream of piss.

The white tiger's gaze was fixed unwaveringly on the mortal beneath him, his pupils changing to vertical slits, the dark irises gradually paling into a glittering gold. He'd left a good many bite marks all over the old quail's neck, and now moved on to licking the petite nipples on his chest until that insubstantial area was a ruined mess as well, and the tiny nipples swelled to the size of red beans.

"A-Hu...A-Hu..." Wu Xingzi couldn't keep up with the white tiger spirit's pace to begin with, but right now he felt like a single small boat set adrift at sea, floating along at the whims of the wind and waves. Pleasure pushed him again and again towards climax, yet refused to let him catch his breath, layering over itself in an endlessly building wave until his entire body was twitching and his gaze lacked any focus, lacking even the strength to struggle.

The white tiger spirit had reached his breaking point too; he was panting through gritted teeth, and felt as if the only thing which could satisfy him in this moment would be to fuck the old quail so hard he'd penetrate right through his belly.

The sound of their fucking, mixed with the white tiger's heavy panting and the lewd cries of the man beneath him, lingered like an obscene melody around the pair's ears.

"Darling... How about bearing a cub for me, hm?"

"Oohhh—" The old quail couldn't understand a word the white tiger was saying. He was shivering all over, pink tongue sticking partly out of his mouth, his eyes rolled slightly upwards; there was no way he could make out anything at all at a time like this!

"I'll take that silence for a yes, then..." The white tiger kissed him with a low chuckle, then gave the tip of his tongue a suck. After a few more rough thrusts, he finally, suddenly, pierced into the deepest part, bulging testicles slamming hard against Wu Xingzi's buttocks as bursts of thick semen shot into the asshole-turned-cocksleeve. The gouts of thick cum were enough to swell the old quail's stomach until he looked pregnant.

The tiger contentedly pulled the passed-out mortal into a deep kiss and—in order not to waste any semen—toppled them both over in the shade of the trees without pulling out. He stayed there motionless for a good while.

Though the old quail was a mortal, and a man at that, lacking that part which could bear offspring, none of that mattered to the white tiger spirit. He was a spiritual creature, after all, and a spirit's breeding methods were different from those of any natural lifeform; he had plenty of ways around this issue.

"I'll bring you back to Mount Fulong with me..." The white tiger spirit licked the tearstains on Wu Xingzi's face, then buried his head in the crook of his neck, humming contentedly.

Legend had it that beneath the Fulong mountain range lay a dragon who broke the laws of Heaven, giving the mountain its name of "subdued dragon." At first this dragon was merely suppressed at the foot of the mountain, and was allowed to return once more to the heavenly court once five hundred years had passed. However, this dragon was an especially arrogant one. He was a direct descendant of the ancestral dragon, and by the time existence had settled from its primordial chaos, there were already none left in the world who could stand against him. He was domineering and aggressive, wayward and reckless; he refused to show the slightest respect for the Heavenly Emperor or his laws and caused a multitude of disasters, inciting an endless string of complaints from immortals and humans alike.

As far as the gods were concerned, this dragon was merely causing messes for them to clean up in a busy panic, but to the ordinary people of the mortal realm, these were far from minor issues which could be so simply and easily brushed aside.

The dragon clan's role in Heaven was to be responsible for the rain. There were strict rules regarding when, where, and how much rain should fall, as well as whether an area would be subject to good weather or disastrous floods or droughts. These events could only be set into motion according to written instructions from Heaven; after all, they impacted not only the survival of the mortal men of earth, but an infinite number of destinies and karmic cycles as well.

Despite that, this primordial dragon was quite neglectful of his duties. Though the area under his jurisdiction wasn't large by any means, it was the most densely populated and prosperous, and even an inch less rain than what was required could lead to a catastrophe. Yet he still refused to take his position seriously. When he was in a good mood he would send down the exact amount of rain according to the mandates, but when his mood was a bad one he would slack off.

Luckily the difference was never a great one and the amount of rain deviating by two days at most, and so the Heavenly court could only turn a blind eye to his behavior...

"Ai, that won't do." At this point of the story, Wu Xingzi couldn't hold back any longer, and he interrupted the big tiger's low and gentle voice. He covered his stomach with his hands, a troubled look on his face. "Tell me, if the child hears a story like this, is it possible they might try to follow the primordial dragon's example in the future?"

It was all well and good for a child to be lively, and there was no problem if a child enjoyed causing mischief, but being *so* dismissive about people's lives would be straying a little too far to be acceptable. After all, the tiger had previously said that children like theirs—mixed-race children between human and yao—historically tended either to be unparalleled geniuses capable of cultivating into yao immortals, or stubborn, unruly tyrants.

But white tiger yao Guan Shanjin wasn't particularly worried about how unruly his own child might become. Just look at how soft and glutinous the old quail in his arms was, unable to say a single harsh word no matter how angry he got. When he first brought him back to his cave dwelling on Mount Fulong, a few of the less obedient yao under his rule—after seeing all the tricks they'd pulled while he was missing uprooted in the blink of an eye—then turned their attention to Wu Xingzi. They wanted to use this seemingly powerless human to threaten the white tiger yao into abdicating his position as yao king of Mount Fulong, hopefully with the added result of his leaving the mountain altogether.

Regrettably, the great white tiger's subordinates discovered them before they could put their plan in motion, deftly tying up these miscreants and handing them over to the white tiger for punishment.

These yao, realizing how grim their future looked, quickly abandoned the idea of begging for mercy. They instead pointed their fingers at the man currently sitting on the white tiger's lap in such a lovey-dovey manner and loudly cursed him out, saying that this human would bring disaster to them all. Just look at what their once wise yao king had done: Not only had he abandoned all the hundreds of yao who lived on Mount Fulong and left them to their fates for several months, the moment he returned he'd even tied up these old loyalists and prepared to put them to death! They insisted they had no regrets about dying, of course, but they feared that the yao king, deceived by this creature of ill portent, would put all the many yao of Mount Fulong in danger of complete annihilation.

There were many loyal yao chieftains present at the yao king's trial of these villains; upon hearing these clearly logical accusations, quite a few of them couldn't help turning suspicious gazes upon the human whom their king had raised to be so fair and soft-skinned. Some of the more straightforward ones even stared directly at Wu Xingzi's belly—and everyone present was well aware of the meaning of *that*.

Indeed, all the yao knew about their king's strange behavior. The big white tiger used to be as cold and stern as a sharp, unsheathed blade. Mount Fulong also had a local god of the land watching over it, but he never dared show himself within Mount Fulong's territory. Instead he pretended he didn't exist, and only looked after the human territories nearby.

It wasn't as if there were no evil spirits from other areas who ever came by to provoke them, of course but the great white tiger always swatted them all away with the same ease as killing ants.

In the opinion of the many yao of Mount Fulong, their king was a cold-blooded, unfeeling yaoguai—but what need did yaoguai have for feelings? Most of them chose to surrender to the white tiger because they worshiped his strength, and he'd taken good care of the mountain over the long time they'd lived here together. Even gods and buddhas kept their distance from the blade that was the white tiger, so naturally everyone's loyalty grew to become sincere.

Of course, there were still some yao around who overestimated their own strength, thinking they could usurp the great white tiger's position. Just look at these foolish yao right here: They were probably going to be killed so thoroughly that their very souls were crushed to smithereens.

Yet after he'd returned with a human yao queen he'd brought from the outside world, the white tiger had changed entirely. With this human he was as gentle as a warm spring, his face wreathed in smiles; aside from this human, anything else which appeared in front of him could be shoved away and ignored. The words "passionately devoted" were practically created just to describe the big white tiger—that is, specifically to describe his behavior towards the yao queen. Not to anyone else.

And look, this yao queen was a man to boot! For a yaoguai to impregnate a human man, they first had to expend one hundred years' worth of their own power to create a gestational sac within the man's abdomen, then use countless of spiritual plants and precious natural materials to refine a nourishment pill, which the mother would have to eat every day to nourish the fetus until the day he gave birth. The amount of medicinal ingredients required to refine just one batch of these nourishment pills was enough to send a low-ranking family of yao nobles into bankruptcy, and the yao queen would need to eat at least three batches of them before he gave birth.

This expenditure was practically abhorrent in its extravagance. The way the man who had once been their cold and wise yao king now wallowed in such decadence before the queen truly beggared belief!

If this had been a human emperor, it was possible a good many old, loyal ministers would have bashed themselves against the pillars of the imperial hall, using their deaths as a form of remonstration towards their ruler.

Even if they were to consider this the yao king's own family affair... After all, he'd been a yao for thousands of years, had traveled unhindered across the known world and beyond, and had accumulated a fortune beyond the imagining of any ordinary yao. If he was happy using his own private treasury to nourish his partner for childbirth then none of them had the guts to point fingers over it. But this child was going to be one of mixed blood between yao and human, and that was where the problem lay.

Human-yao hybrids were a rare breed, but most of them did indeed tend to incite calamity; after all, such children ran counter to the laws of nature, so it was inevitable that Heaven would take some sort of action in response. A small and blessed few, whose parents were blessed with profound good fortune, would become the most highly favored children in yao society; they were extremely gifted both in yao power and mental ability, and could often find their way to Daoist enlightenment and immortality. But this was, again, a rarity. The great majority were violent and cruel, and ultimately corrupted into demons.

They all looked at the sticky-soft yao queen. There was no sign of the golden thread of fortune anywhere on this yao queen's body; he looked so average as to be entirely forgettable. Even now, with him currently nestled in the yao king's arms, they struggled to remember what he looked like; even now, when he'd just been insulted, under the intense scrutiny of all the yao present, he still seemed as timid as a quail. He didn't even show any intention of loudly berating the traitors for speaking nonsense... A yao queen like this was...

The yao exchanged glances as the same thought arose in all of their minds: If the yao queen really did give birth to an evil demon lord, it would definitely be the yao king's fault. After all, no matter how malicious a quail might be, it was still just a quail, nothing more.

Wu Xingzi was feeling somewhat apprehensive under the stares of all these yao, and naturally wasn't happy about having been so vocally condemned, but he was gentle by nature, and wasn't the type to argue. Besides, these people who were condemning him had very little time left to vent their anger, so he didn't take any of it to heart.

But while he may not have minded, the great white tiger was quite unhappy. He himself couldn't bear to say so much as a stern word to the old quail, having treated him like precious porcelain since they first met; he loved him so dearly that it was beyond his ability to express in words. But these traitors were quite the bold ones. Did they think losing their heads would just leave them with a big scar and nothing more?

So it was that the incensed yao king had the old quail escorted back to their cave to rest, then personally used the most tortuous methods to crush these old yao traitors' cores one by one before finally taking their lives. This was also a display of his stance: If you wanted to attack him then go on and try, he wouldn't mind it. But if you wanted to do something to his old quail, then what awaited you was the absolute destruction of your very soul!

Of course, Wu Xingzi had no idea they'd been dealt with in this manner. All he knew was that from then on, the yao all treated him with courtesy and respect, and even a little cautiousness.

Sadly, he was unable to figure out the reason for this before the white tiger's efforts paid off. Wu Xingzi had been taking nourishment pills and indulging in sex every day, the big white tiger using the excuse of having children to fuck him on every inch of land on every part of Mount Fulong. He even teased him by saying, "This mountain will surely be exploding in greenery next spring! And it's all thanks to my slutty darling watering them."

Ai! Do you know how embarrassing that is to hear?! Wu Xingzi was as angry as he was ashamed, and he hammered his fists against the white tiger's chest a few times in reproach. But this action hurt as much as a kitten scratching an itch, and all it did was rile up the big tiger, who flipped over to press him against the ground again and fucked him for another few hours.

It was only to be expected that he'd become pregnant.

The old quail became even softer and more fair-skinned now that he was with child, growing three sizes fatter than he was before. His waist—once so slender that you could feel his bones—became rounder as well, feeling so soft and tender to the touch that the big white tiger desperately wanted to swallow him whole. The child in his belly appeared to be very well-behaved, as aside from the first two months at the very start, Wu Xingzi didn't feel any nausea or soreness whatsoever. He was hungrier than ever, enjoying everything he put in his mouth; his appetite had been incredible to begin with, but now it was impossible to find a moment he wasn't eating something. The big white tiger was happy to provide. Their cave was always filled with all kinds of treats and snacks, whether sweet or salty, strong-flavored or light. If he wanted a main course then all he needed to do was wait a quarter of an hour for it to be served. He was eating for two now, after all, and carrying a yaoguai's mixed-blood child was even more physically demanding for a human than a normal pregnancy. The big white tiger wasn't worried that Wu Xingzi might clean out Mount Fulong of all available food; he'd be more worried if Wu Xingzi *didn't* eat.

By the six-month mark, Wu Xingzi's belly was noticeably swollen, looking as round as the full moon. The skin of his stomach was stretched somewhat thin due to the baby, with a few blue veins crawling across it; occasionally you could even catch sight of the baby's little fists or footprints as it rolled around inside him.

Wu Xingzi had become a total lazybones at this point. His big belly made it difficult to move, and he was constantly hungry. He'd previously made it a point to go outside every day for a short walk, just to look at the scenery and stretch his muscles, but these past few days he'd stayed holed up in their cave estate taking care of the growing fetus; all he did each day was sleep, eat, and talk to the baby. The big white tiger, fearing he might get lonely, also stayed constantly by his side, telling stories to amuse Wu Xingzi and their child while he was there.

Just take today, for example, where Wu Xingzi got curious about the origins of Mount Fulong's name, and so the great white tiger told him.

Seeing the old quail worrying over the possibility that their child might learn bad habits before it had even left the womb, the white tiger kissed his cheek and asked, "Well, then, how about I tell a different story instead?"

"A different story?" Wu Xingzi pressed his cheek against the big white tiger's chest and nuzzled it, letting out a small yawn. It wasn't that he actually wanted to sleep so much as that he always felt especially relaxed when by the tiger's side, and his stomach didn't feel as uncomfortably heavy as usual.

He didn't realize it, but this was because the child in his belly needed the nourishment of yao energy due to its half-yao heritage— after all, how could a human like him provide yao energy? It was only natural that he'd think his child felt inordinately heavy. But the great white tiger knew how to provide yao energy as nourishment for this child; it was for this reason that he stubbornly trapped the old quail in his arms every day. After all, nourishment pills ensured that the mother wouldn't be sucked dry of nutrients by the half-yao in his stomach, but did nothing to placate the baby—who had in fact already gained consciousness.

"What else would you like to hear?" The great white tiger swayed the person in his arms, picking up a sesame ball to feed him.

He'd specially sent subordinates running to an old stall in the capital to buy these sesame balls, and the yaoguai of Mount Fulong had taken the entire batch the second they left the pot. It went without saying that these sesame balls were especially tasty—their skins fragrant and crispy, the inside sticky-soft and chewy, with an exquisitely smooth red bean paste filling at their center. Each one was as delicious as the next, perfect for tossing in your mouth in one bite, and they wouldn't make you nauseous no matter how many you ate. The big white tiger quite liked them as well.

Wu Xingzi's eyes narrowed in pleasure as he chewed on the sesame ball. After some thought, he replied, "You've never told me about yourself before. I'd like to hear that."

The big white tiger suddenly stiffened. He sighed. "I never thought you'd still end up asking this question in the end."

"What's wrong? You don't have to talk about it, if it makes you unhappy." Wu Xingzi felt a twinge in his heart at the sight of the big white tiger's downcast expression, and couldn't help blaming himself for it. It was said that yaoguai were born from nature, lacking parents, so wouldn't his question be striking the big tiger right where it hurt? *Ai, Wu Xingzi, you idiot.*

"It's not that it makes me unhappy, it's just that I suddenly remembered...I forgot to tell my parents about you." The big white tiger scratched his cheek, noticed the human in his arms gazing at him with a blank look on his face, and couldn't resist lowering his head to give him a few rough kisses. It wasn't until the other man's tongue was stinging and his lips were embarrassingly swollen that the contented white tiger finally withdrew. He used his spined tongue to lick the side of the old quail's neck until his moaning partner collapsed bonelessly in his arms, panting for breath.

While the saying that demons were born from nature wasn't wrong, it was only true for that first batch of yaoguai who had appeared in the very beginning; by the time the big white tiger had been born, all the yaoguai in the world had parents. And having lived with humans for so long, they'd picked up quite a few human habits as well, with many yaoguai having grown accustomed to dividing their forces by family, the way humans did. Not only did this make it easier for them to take territory by strength of numbers, it also meant that older generations of yao could help prevent their juniors from going astray on the path of cultivation.

So it was that the yao gradually came to have positions of royalty and nobility just like those of the mortal realm—though in their case the yao world had a yao king for each spiritual mountain rather than any sort of unifying empire.

For example, Mount Fulong was one of the most famous of those spiritual mountains in possession of a vein of yao energy. This area had once been swarming with yao, with none submitting to any others; neither were there any great yao powerful enough to subdue the other yaoguai and take the Mount Fulong area under their rule.

It was important to note that Heaven wasn't pleased with this situation either. As long as there was unrest in the spiritual mountain's yao vein, it would affect humanity—there would be less peace in the human realm, too, which in turn would naturally affect the offerings Heaven received. This cycle wasn't good for anyone involved, and so, if a yaoguai took over a spiritual mountain and proclaimed himself king, as long as he could manage the area well enough, Heaven was willing to assist him.

The great white tiger wasn't from this area; his birthplace was a spiritual mountain outside of the capital. The spiritual energy there was so thick that it was actually able to condense into water, forming a constant fog over the mountain forests, and there was also a spiritual vein beneath the ground. This mountain had given rise to quite a few yao noble families.

Guan Shanjin was the eldest son of one of the three greatest families on that mountain.

"So your family are all white tigers?" Wu Xingzi's eyes widened in astonishment. He'd only ever met one white tiger in his life; tigers were usually orange with black stripes, and weren't anywhere near as attractive as this celestial-looking white tiger.

"They aren't, I take after my mother. White tigers are rare, after all; most are orange with black stripes." Guan Shanjin proudly puffed out his chest. He used to dislike his white fur, but after meeting the old quail he'd grown to be quite proud of it. If he hadn't been all white, after all, someone as timid as the old quail might not have had the guts to rescue him.

"On that note, why did you come out here to Mount Fulong, instead of staying back in your hometown?"

The big white tiger was naturally quite happy to see how engrossed the old quail was in his story, and so he continued his tale.

There was no particularly shocking or touching or intriguing reason why the big white tiger hadn't remained on that spiritual mountain near the capital. The simple fact of the matter was this: He had a first cousin once removed who'd taken his entire family on a tour of the country before finally settling down on Mount Fulong. On a whim, this cousin joined in the battle to occupy the mountain as king, only to get himself killed as a result, leaving all the members of his family surrounded by danger on all sides and unable to leave even if they wanted to.

The most powerful yao on Mount Fulong at the time had been a foreign lion. It was said that this lion was some sort of blood relation to the mount of Manjushri Bodhisattva, and so had particularly powerful yao energy as a result; he had already subdued about seventy or eighty percent of Mount Fulong's yaoguai.

This lion had his eye on the cousin's youngest daughter, and used every method he could think of to forcefully take her home as his queen. But the heavens finally showed fair judgment; though the tigers could not escape, they did manage to get someone to deliver a message to the main family, asking them to come and rescue them.

When this letter for help was delivered to Guan Shanjin's father, he clapped his tiger paws together and said to his son, "You go! The saying goes that a man's ambitions are to go west, so it would be a pity for you to stay here in our den without getting to stretch your wings. Go make our Mount Qingling tiger clan proud! If you can take the position of yao king of Mount Fulong, then all the better."

What else could the great white tiger do? He wasn't fond of spending his days idly to begin with; seeing as his father had given the word, he simply gathered some like-minded companions and charged into Mount Fulong, firstly to rescue his clansmen, and secondly to establish some territory for himself.

There was no need to elaborate on how the battle raged so fiercely that Mount Fulong quaked for three days and nights, or how they caused such a ruckus that the gods themselves sent down heavenly soldiers to find out what was going on. To sum it up, that lion was indeed powerful, but lacking in luck, whereas the white tiger—though still somewhat inexperienced—had fortune at his side. The results went without saying: That kingdom which the lion had put so much time and effort into conquering was taken at much less cost by a white tiger who'd only just reached adulthood. So it was that Mount Fulong, mired in turmoil for hundreds of years, finally had a yao king to rule it.

From that day onward, the white tiger had also never again returned to his old home, and so in a moment's carelessness he'd accidentally forgotten he even had parents.

"Is that really a thing you can forget?" Wu Xingzi was dumbfounded by the idea. After a moment, he then worriedly rubbed his stomach and asked, "Then, is it possible that our child might forget me in the future too?" Just the thought of it made him sad, his eyes inadvertently reddening. The white tiger felt a pang in his chest at this sight, and quickly pulled him into his arms to console him.

"Don't overthink it, that won't happen. If this bastard even dares to forget you, I'll teach the little brat a lesson for you." Despite his own words, the big white tiger didn't particularly want the old quail to start ignoring him in favor of worrying over the child. In the future, once this child was old enough, he'd follow the same pattern his own father had: He'd chase them off so he'd be free of a nuisance.

"Don't, it's unavoidable for a child to make mistakes; at times like these we should gently explain to them what they did wrong, not chase after them with a broom. My father used to say that if you beat a child too often, they won't necessarily learn their lesson, but they'll definitely learn how to deceive their superiors and subordinates alike. That's why he'd occasionally punish me with memorizing books, but most of the time he'd gently reason things out for me to hear."

It was a rare thing for Wu Xingzi to speak up about his parents, too. The white tiger was filled with interest at these words. He and

Wu Xingzi had been together for a good while now, but this was the first time he'd ever heard him talk about his parents.

"That's right, you've never told me about your parents either, only that they left when you were sixteen."

"Ai..." Wu Xingzi rubbed his roly-poly tummy, thinking for a moment. "My parents were killed by bandits. I still remember my father had taken his hand-written calligraphy that day, and my mother had some jerky and wild herbs and things which she'd cured herself, so they could sell them in town for a little money; it was almost the new year, and we needed money to purchase and prepare everything for the new year celebration. Mother liked white sugar sponge cakes, but she'd only ever buy a few to eat on the new year; and Father loved Mother more than anything, so he always made sure she could have some."

When his parents later ran into bandits, unfortunately losing their lives, Wu Xingzi was forced to struggle to suppress his grief as he buried them. After that he continued living his days alone in that little mountain cottage. It was a little lonely, yes, but he couldn't bear to leave the house his father had built with his own hands; if it weren't for the great white tiger and their child, he'd still be wanting to go back there even now.

The white tiger was filled with distress upon hearing this story, and would have charged right out to exact revenge for Wu Xingzi if the old quail hadn't told him that the bandits had later been eliminated by local authorities.

In this manner the days passed one after the next, with the old quail's belly growing continuously larger. After a checkup, the yao doctor was also able to finally confirm that the yao queen's belly didn't have just one baby in it, but a pair of them.

The old doctor stroked his long beard as he consoled the yao king—the news of two children had made him so nervous that the fur on his tail had puffed out explosively. "Don't worry, my king, the yao queen's body has been taken care of very well, and the richness of your yao energy has also nourished the children in his belly, so it won't cause any harm to the queen's health. But..."

"Didn't you just say it won't harm his health? Where did this 'but' come from?" Now even the fur on the white tiger's back was standing on end. He'd changed back to his original form for once because Wu Xingzi had said it was a long time since he'd petted his fur and he wanted to see it again; he hadn't expected to end up showing such a pitifully foolish appearance as a result.

"Calm down, my king, and let me finish what I was going to say." The old doctor was a mild-tempered deer yao who wasn't the slightest bit impressed by the big white tiger's aggressive demeanor. He said in a perfectly leisurely voice, "When all is said and done, the yao queen is ultimately still a man, and lacks the birth canal required to give birth. As such, during delivery I will need to cut open the queen's belly to take the children out..."

"You want to kill him?" The white tiger let out a violent roar and viciously pounced on the old doctor, knocking him down; the doctor, forced to reveal his true form, blinked innocently up at the dismayed and furious yao king with his round deer eyes.

"A-Hu, let go of Doctor Deer, just let him finish talking!" Wu Xingzi hurriedly supported his belly as he got up off the soft couch to stop the great white tiger, for fear that he might actually kill the doctor.

At the sight of him walking over with his huge round belly in his hands, swaying, the white tiger hurriedly changed to human form and stepped forward to support the old quail, worrying that he might lose his balance and hurt himself in the fall. "Running around instead of taking proper care of yourself when your belly is this big, are you trying to kill me from worry?"

He'd passed the buck with the neatest efficiency. Wu Xingzi's eyes widened, and for once he glared at the big white tiger in wordless censure. If he hadn't lost his temper and attacked the doctor, Wu Xingzi wouldn't have had to rush over with hands on his stomach to stop him in the first place.

The big white tiger knew he was in the wrong, and let out a couple of awkward, wry laughs. Then he turned his head to Doctor Deer. "Why're you puttering and panting so much when you talk?" he said rudely. "If you have something to say then get it out already!"

The man was practically impervious to reason.

Doctor Deer inwardly heaved a sigh, keeping to his original form. "It is inevitable that you would be anxious, my king. I naturally wouldn't dare to cut open the yao queen's belly so easily—the queen is a human, after all, and lacks the physical sturdiness of yaoguai like us, so I would risk injuring him if I truly cut into his body." At this point, the doctor keenly noticed the yao king about to lose his temper and attack him again, and hurried to speak faster. "Therefore! I have given it some thought, and there is a peacock yao on Mount Qingling, peacocks being part of the phoenix bloodline, so if I could obtain a single tailfeather from the peacock king, I would be able to ensure that the yao queen can recover as normal after the cutting of his stomach!"

This was easy enough to say, but a difficult task in reality.

Qingling Mountain did in fact have a flock of peacocks, and they were on quite friendly terms with the tiger clan, so normally it wouldn't have been difficult to ask for a single tailfeather. Unfortunately however, the peacock king had been losing feathers rather severely as of late due to his old age, and as a result had grown to greatly treasure his resplendent feathers; if anyone dared so much as mention the idea of plucking them, they'd surely be pecked to death by the peacock king's razor-sharp beak.

And naturally a fallen feather wouldn't do for something like this, where it was needed for prolonging life and healing wounds; it had to be one that had been plucked out by force, leaving a trace of life energy still attached to it.

Guan Shanjin wasn't afraid of the peacock king's sharp beak, but if plucking a feather hurt the relations between their two clans, the loss would outweigh the gain.

"Is there no other way?" the great white tiger asked with a frown. He'd sent an invitation letter to his parents not long ago, which also introduced his wife and sons. His parents were naturally so overjoyed that it was possible they'd be willing to hold down the peacock king and pluck his feathers out in his place. But this was ultimately still a last resort; if two high-ranking noble yao families started butting heads, nobody would come out of it a winner.

"None." The doctor's answer came without the slightest hesitation, leaving the white tiger to sink into deep contemplation.

"Forget it, it's alright even if we can't get it. I trust that Doctor Deer can sew my belly back up without risking my life, and I don't mind if my health won't be as good as before in the future." Wu Xingzi patted the white tiger's shoulder in a consoling manner, then gently wiped away the creases in his brow, his face wreathed in a beatifically content smile. "What matters most is our children; there's just another month or so before they're born! What do you think they'll look like?"

"It'll be best if they have your pudgy nose." The white tiger laughed, pinching the old quail's plump nose.

Wu Xingzi actually hoped the children would both be as attractive as Guan Shanjin—even better if they could also transform into white tigers.

With Wu Xingzi soon to give birth, Guan Shanjin thought long and hard over the matter before ultimately deciding that he was going to get the peacock king's tail feather, no matter what it took. He couldn't bear to let Wu Xingzi suffer any pain, but childbirth was bound to be painful in and of itself. As such, he should at least allow him to recover properly, so that he could avoid any sort of serious long-term illness. A human's lifespan was already short enough as it was; there was no way he could let it be shortened by another few years.

But the peacock king was a tough egg, and had phoenix blood as well; even someone as powerful as a tiger yao had no way of fighting him head-on. This required some long and careful planning... Or he could simply act on impulse.

The great white tiger found a day to run back to his old home on Qingling Mountain, and told his parents everything about Wu Xingzi's situation. The three of them calculated that Wu Xingzi would have his cubs in three to five days at most, which meant—they definitely weren't making any long-term plans! Screw the consequences, what they were going to do was let Guan Shanjin tear out the peacock king's tail feather, make a run for it, and let his parents take care of the rest. This was definitely the most reliable solution.

As for earning enmity or whatever, forget about that; Guan Shanjin was now the king of Mount Fulong, they could just have the whole family move over together if it came down to it.

Now that they'd agreed on the plan, it was time to take action!

Fortunately, Guan Shanjin's childhood friend and most capable assistant, Man Yue, overheard the tiger yao trio's hot-headed discussion. He lived on Mount Fulong with Guan Shanjin, and of course he knew very well that Wu Xingzi was about to give birth; these past few days he'd been carefully keeping an eye on his master in case he did something impulsive, and here he'd caught him doing exactly that!

The great white tiger Guan Shanjin had always been a wise and calm master, yet he became such an obvious fool around Wu Xingzi that it was unbearable to watch.

"Isn't the peacock king losing tailfeathers every day?" Man Yue blocked the door, raising his voice to ask his question to the three tiger yao who were about to lose all control of reason.

"That's right, he loses seven or eight a day, which is why he so treasures the ones he has left." Madam Guan put her hands on her hips, a displeased yet puzzled look on her face as she glared at the little white rabbit in front of the door. "Man Yue, have you gained weight again?"

Man Yue pretended he hadn't heard the question. If he'd gained weight it was all Guan Shanjin's fault for making him worry and overwork himself every day; Mount Fulong had practically been thrown entirely under his management this past year.

"In other words," Man Yue said, "if we secretly pull a tailfeather while the peacock king is sleeping, there's no way he'll find out, right?"

"You mean..." Man Yue's words finally woke Guan Shanjin from his anxiety-addled haze, his tiger eyes lighting up with a golden glow so hot it was like the blazing sun in June. "We should get the peacock king drunk, then take that opportunity to pluck one of his tailfeathers?"

"Right, that's exactly what I mean, there's absolutely no need to use force on the peacock king." Seeing that his master had regained his sanity, Man Yue wiped the sweat from his forehead and breathed a sigh of relief.

"Hm... This could work! That old peacock king is particularly fond of his drinks, and will want to have a taste of any unique wines he sees. Man Yue, do you have any alcohol that could catch the old peacock's interest?" Madam Guan's eyes lit up as well. The peacock king had been her neighbor for a thousand years, and she knew him very well; she immediately thought of a plan.

So it was that, with good wine and a good plan, the peacock king lost one of his precious tailfeathers without ever suspecting a thing.

And three days later, right on schedule, Wu Xingzi's stomach began to hurt: It seemed he was about to give birth.

Doctor Deer brought his young assistant and a wetnurse along to help Wu Xingzi with the delivery, blocking everyone else outside of the cave.

Normally humans and yao alike would be screaming in pain during childbirth, but Wu Xingzi's screams were far from loud—they were thin and weak, so quiet you barely knew he'd cried out at all, a fact which had the yao outside practically besides themselves with worry. Soon-to-be father Guan Shanjin was the worst of them all; pacing back and forth in circles without managing to calm himself, he then started repeatedly punching a towering old tree, breaking it in half in just a few blows. This still wasn't enough to fully vent his anxiety, and so he got the idea to go find some trouble-making monsters to fight—a decision which was fortunately stopped by Man Yue.

And so all the yao continued to stew in anxiety as they waited and waited. After waiting for two and a half shichen, a baby's wailing cry sounded from within the cave, and the wetnurse happily ran out to announce the good news: "Congratulations, my king! The yao queen has given birth to two male tigers, both with white fur!"

Who cares what kind of fur they have! Guan Shanjin hurriedly asked, "Can I go in to see him?"

As soon as the wetnurse nodded, the great white tiger abandoned all the other yao to run on inside. The cave dwelling was filled with all sorts of not-particularly-pleasant smells, and a pale-faced Wu Xingzi was lying on the bed, not showing a single sign of injury aside from some blood on the hem of his robes. Guan Shanjin finally breathed a sigh of relief, and pulled him into his arms to nuzzle him with everything he had.

As for the two little white tigers crying with everything they had without earning even a single glance from their own father, it was their grandparents who finally picked them up and consoled them instead.

The two tiger cubs were both incredibly cute; due to their half-yao heritage, they weren't entirely tiger-shaped, only showing fluffy, snow-white ears and tails. Their features mostly took after Guan Shanjin—beautiful, delicate, charming, yet sharp—but the cub which had come out second had a nose like Wu Xingzi's, round and pudgy, not droopy but still extremely cute, so that anyone who saw it would want to give it a pinch.

As for whether they'd ascend as immortals or fall as demons in the future—in this moment, who really cared?

AFTERWORD

I HOPE EVERYONE had a lovely time with this story.

Thank you for picking up this book and reading until the end. I'm Blackegg, AKA the mother of this book, eh heh.

I'm slightly nervous and afraid right now. This was my very first published BL novel. I hope you enjoyed reading it, and that it was a lovely experience. I hope you don't think there's something wrong with me.

I actually don't know how to write an afterword. Should I be more playful or more serious? I've always been too lazy to write an afterword for any of my self-published works before. I'm deeply regretting not collecting points for the necessary skills now. So if you think this afterword seems particularly lost and doesn't have a real ending, that's normal. Because right now, that's the kind of disoriented, mistake-prone state I'm in.

But! Don't worry! I just wanted to get across how grateful I am that you finished this book. I'd be very happy if you liked it!

You've Got Mail: The Perils of Pigeon Post was my first work after my four-to-five-year-long break. Before that, all my works were self-published. I used to come out with a new one at every CWT, until four or five years ago. In those five years I only wrote extras for stories I'd already written, and I hadn't really seriously written any chaptered works.

At the time, I was stuck in a terrible writer's block. I had no ideas, and felt like a lifeless fish. I thought I might really have to give up being a writer.

One day, I was chatting with a friend, and we somehow brought up the topic of dating apps. Unfortunately, I have always been single, and perhaps might continue to be single, since I have given all my life...to 2D men, heh heh. Anyway, back on topic, back to the idle conversation between me and my friend. Basically, my friend suddenly said, "Why don't you write a story where two characters fall in love because of a dick pic! You don't need plot, you just need porn. Wouldn't that be nice?"

So I thought, *Why not! Haven't I wanted to write porn without much plot for a long time? What an excellent idea!*

At the same time, I was suddenly struck by the muses, and decided to set the story in ancient times. Even our ancestors need dick pics.

Yes, I originally only wanted to write porn. Like the kind where they just strip without saying anything. But...perhaps because I hadn't written anything in a long time, now that I had a topic, I carefully laid down an outline, and many goals. And so the PWP of my dreams remained just that: a dream, crying at my feet.

As for Guan Shanjin and Wu Xingzi, it really took a lot of emotional energy to write them, even more than I expected. Guan Shanjin was the type of character I'd written before, but Wu Xingzi, from personality to appearance, was very different from any of my past works. He was a character 100 percent out of my comfort zone.

I used to worry that he would be too stereotypical. After all, it was too easy to make a gentle, shy, older man into a stereotype. But luckily Xingzi turned out exactly how I wanted him to. He's a guy who has his own ideas. Somehow, slowly, he became a friend that existed in my life. He's very gentle but also very stubborn; self-conscious and anxious, yet still strong. He has wisdom nurtured by his environment and experience, yet still longs for happiness. He's very realistic, but still romantic.

So he's the one Guan Shanjin fell in love with, and he's the one that became the center of *You've Got Mail*, making me pick up the pen once again to improve. As his mother, I can't help giving him all of my attention, but I also didn't want to limit his growth. As a result, during the latter half of the serialization, I started to slow down. I couldn't just write whatever I wanted; I had to consider if this really was something Xingzi would do. Would he be happy? Which of his experiences resulted in his current self? Naturally, the page count grew longer and longer.

I added a lot of things to the physical book, because Xingzi and Guan Shanjin's story isn't over yet. They'll spend every day together under the sun, extraordinary days and ordinary ones alike, watching over each other until they grow old.

Actually, the main side characters all have their own stories too, like Yan Wenxin and Lu Zezhi. In the story, you might've hated them or they might've made you feel uncomfortable, but their lives haven't ended yet either. I really wanted to share it with you guys, and before I realized it I'd written more and more. I hope everyone is satisfied with those extras.

I'd just said I didn't know how to write an afterword, but now I've written so much... Thank you for reading up until now. If you have any thoughts, feel free to message me or find me on Plurk.

And lastly, *You've Got Mail* may be over, but this world hasn't ended. Hei-er and Rancui have their own story, and I'm working hard to write it. I hope it will bring something new to all of you.

I have updates on Plurk and ptt. If you're interested, you can go take a look~

I hope I can meet all of you again soon.

Blackegg

Fall 2018

You've Got Mail: The Perils of Pigeon Post
FIN

Character & Name Guide

Characters

WU XINGZI 吴幸子: A lonely, gay middle-aged man who recently gained a new lease on life when he discovered the Peng Society.

GUAN SHANJIN 关山尽: The renowned and formidable young general of the Southern Garrison.

PEOPLE IN THE CAPITAL CITY

MAN YUE 满月: Guan Shanjin's vice general and childhood friend.

HEI-ER 黑儿: One of Guan Shanjin's bodyguards.

MINT 薄荷 AND OSMANTHUS 桂花: Sisters who work as maids for Wu Xingzi.

LU ZEZHI 鲁泽之: Guan Shanjin's teacher and his unrequited first love.

RANCUI 染翠: Manager of the Goose City branch of the Peng Society.

PING YIFAN 平一凡: An apparently unremarkable young man who runs a business in the capital.

YAN WENXIN 颜文心: Wu Xingzi's first love, who took advantage of him and abandoned him. Has since become a high-ranking official.

HUAIXIU 怀秀: Yan Wenxin's adopted son and his right hand.

BAI SHAOCHANG 白绍常: A member of the Peng Society, renowned for his musical talent.

PEOPLE IN QINGCHENG COUNTY

ANSHENG 安生: Wu Xingzi's crush, who introduced him to the Peng Society.

AUNTIE LIU 柳大娘: Old Liu's wife, a gossip who is fiercely protective of Wu Xingzi.

CONSTABLE ZHANG 张捕头: Wu Xingzi's colleague in the magistrate's office, and Ansheng's life partner.

AUNTIE LI 李大婶: A gossipy woman who doesn't think much of Wu Xingzi.

Name Guide

Diminutives, Nicknames, and Name Tags:

A-: Friendly diminutive. Always a prefix. Usually for monosyllabic names, or one syllable out of a two-syllable name.

DOUBLING: Doubling a syllable of a person's name can be a nickname, e.g., "Mangmang"; it has childish or cutesy connotations.

DA-: A prefix meaning big/older

XIAO-: A diminutive meaning "little." Always a prefix.

-ER: An affectionate diminutive added to names, literally "son" or "child." Always a suffix. Can sometimes be a fixed part of a person's name, rather than just an affectionate suffix.

Family:

DI/DIDI: Younger brother or a younger male friend.

GE/GEGE/DAGE: Older brother or an older male friend.

JIE/JIEJIE: Older sister or an older female friend.

YIFU: Adoptive father or godfather.

Other:

GONGZI: Young man from an affluent/scholarly household.